STEALING THE LIGHT

BOOK 1

LEGEND OF THE DRAGON LORD

PETER WACHT

Stealing the Light
By Peter Wacht

Book 1 of Legend of the Dragon Lord

This book is a work of fiction. Names, characters, places, and incidents are the product of the author's imagination or are used fictitiously. Any resemblance to actual events, locales, or persons, living or dead, is coincidental.

Cover design by Ebooklaunch.com

Published in the United States by Kestrel Media Group LLC.

ISBN: 978-1-950236-57-2

eBook ISBN: 978-1-950236-58-9

Library of Congress Control Number: 2025901347

❀ Created with Vellum

ALSO BY PETER WACHT

THE REALMS OF THE TALENT AND THE CURSE

LEGEND OF THE DRAGON LORD

A Painful Truth (short story)*

Stealing the Light

Sacrificing the Queen (Forthcoming 2025)

Roar of the Broken Bear (Forthcoming 2025)

Rise of the Dragon Lord (Forthcoming 2026)

THE TALES OF CALEDONIA

(Complete 7-Book Series)

Blood on the White Sand (short story)*

The Diamond Thief (short story)*

The Protector

The Protector's Quest

The Protector's Vengeance

The Protector's Sacrifice

The Protector's Reckoning

The Protector's Resolve

The Protector's Victory

THE TALES OF THE TERRITORIES

(Complete 8-Book Series)

Stalking the Blood Ruby (short story)*

A Fate Worse Than Death (short story)*

Death on the Burnt Ocean

Monsters in the Mist

The Dance of the Daggers

Bloody Hunt for Freedom

A Spark of Rebellion

Shadows Made Real

Shadow's Reach

Storm in the Darkness

THE SYLVAN CHRONICLES

(Complete 9-Book Series)

The Legend of the Kestrel

The Call of the Sylvana

The Raptor of the Highlands

The Makings of a Warrior

The Lord of the Highlands

The Lost Kestrel Found

The Claiming of the Highlands

The Fight Against the Dark

The Defender of the Light

THE RISE OF THE SYLVAN WARRIORS

*Through the Knife's Edge (short story)**

THE FALLEN KNIGHT SERIES

*The Death of the Dragon (short story)**

The Dragon Awakens

Duel With a Dragon (Forthcoming 2025)

Beware the Dragon (Forthcoming 2025)

The Dragon Returns (Forthcoming 2025)

* Free stories can be downloaded from my author website at PeterWachtBooks.com. My books are also available on Amazon and other online retailers.

YOUR FREE STORY IS WAITING...

This eBook is a prelude to the events in my epic fantasy series *The Tales of Caledonia* and is free to readers who receive my newsletter.

Join Peter's newsletter and get your FREE short story.
PeterWachtBooks.com

1

WORRISOME DISCOVERY

"This can't be right." Mikel frowned as he stared at the flakes of white that had hardened into ice and left several crusty shapes in their wake.

Lost in his own thoughts, he had almost missed them, never expecting to see footprints twice the size of a man's so far away from the jagged peaks that rose to the east.

The prints had the same number of toes as a human but the pointed indentations dug several inches down into the packed snow. They resembled claws more than feet. Those talons could rip open a man's gut with a single swipe.

"Not a good sign," he grumbled to himself. "Why would they come down from their caves?"

Mikel snorted, shaking his head, realizing that he was talking to himself again. It was a habit of his when he spent too much time by himself, which was a fairly regular occurrence these days thanks to his frequent trips into this frigidly cold often monochromatic landscape.

"No reason to ask," he murmured softly, answering his own question. "There's only one reason why a clan would come down from the mountains."

Adjusting the small pack that hung over his shoulder, he ignored the short sword scabbarded across his back, his hand instead drifting down to his hip. He took some comfort from the two-foot-long mace strapped there. Lightweight despite the hammer head on one end, a nasty curled spike on the other -- good for stabbing or slicing throats -- gave an experienced practitioner of the weapon a variety of options for defending himself ... or killing what required killing.

He knew that for a fact, having needed to do both more times than he cared to remember. Nightmares from several of those encounters ensured that he didn't sleep for very long or very well during the cold winter nights.

Those troublesome memories had no place in the here and now, however. Better to stay in the present. Better to live with his own nightmares rather than become a victim of one of the nightmares that had decided to hunt well beyond their mountain territory.

He stood atop a small bluff hidden by snow and ice, a barely visible trail snaking its way down the side to the Great Barrow. For the next few leagues, looking to the west and deeper into the Frozen Waste, he saw nothing else except for large, rectangular, snow-covered dunes that were a hundred yards wide and three times as long. Burial mounds Cadmus had explained, some containing the remains of creatures long dead and best forgotten.

There were broad paths between the mounds. Even so, when he entered the frosty ground set aside for the dead, he always stayed close to the side of a barrow and kept a wary eye.

Mikel was well aware of what to look for to avoid the death-traps hidden along those paths. Sinkholes dotted the space between the mounds, covered only by a thin crust of snow and ice.

If you didn't die from the fall, you'd die in the pit if you didn't have the proper equipment for climbing out.

He did. Nevertheless, he had no desire to risk becoming trapped in a sinkhole, even if only for a few minutes.

Not when he was more worried about what was haunting the Great Barrow.

The tracks he identified, although wiped away to a large extent by the blustery wind, led in the direction he needed to go.

He shook his head in aggravation. More at himself than anything else.

Teodor had been right. His friend had argued against making the trip on his own, believing that Mikel should wait until he could join him.

It would only have been a delay of a few days. And there was other business he could have conducted on the Crux during that time.

That didn't matter, however. Despite his friend's wise counsel, he couldn't wait. Not with what he needed to do.

Mikel had made a promise.

And he always kept his promises.

No matter what those promises might cost him.

The trust placed in him was too important.

It was hard earned ... and much too easily lost.

Mikel stayed where he was for a few minutes more. Wanting to get a better lay of the land. Seeking to identify anything out of the ordinary.

He didn't see anything from his perch that gave him any cause for concern. That meant very little, however. With the creature that made that imprint, he knew that he had virtually no chance of catching a glimpse of the monster before it buried a claw in him.

He needed to listen to have any chance of avoiding being caught by surprise, having little desire to be added to the cookpot.

He did that now.

Closing his eyes so that his vision didn't betray his hearing, he stood there for several minutes more. Not in a rush. Knowing exactly what he was listening for. And, thankfully, not hearing the rustle, sigh, or brief exhalation, that faint whisper or slight crunch, that meant his death approached.

Yet.

Because he had no doubt that it would only be a matter of time before he did.

Opening his eyes again, he studied the landscape of white that spread out before him. For as far as he could see, there was nothing but snow and ice. From where he stood, beyond the burial mounds that were closest to him, the environment appeared to be flat, the color and wind-swept nature of the ground hiding the rugged landscape, allowing it all to blend together.

A trick of the mind and the light.

A range of highlands extended toward the horizon to the west. In between, besides the barrows, there were a host of perils in addition to sinkholes and monsters with razor-sharp claws that viewed human flesh as a delicacy.

That thought stuck in his mind, Mikel reached down and rubbed his right leg. It was bothering him. That much-too-common ache that pulsed with greater intensity as he hiked down out of the mountains, his knee feeling as if it were filled with shards of broken glass.

An old injury. An aggravating injury. But not a debilitating one, and there was little else that he could do except deal with it.

Besides, there was a value to the pain.

It served as a reminder of what could happen if he lost focus in the Frozen Waste for just a heartbeat.

Maybe he would get lucky.

Maybe the monsters had moved on, not finding any worthwhile game here.

Yes, and maybe a street rat like himself could live just below the Royal Ring on the Crux. A ridiculous notion.

He hiked a few hundred yards farther down the trail. All the while he kept a sharp ear. Just as much keeping a sharp eye out for any movement, even though he believed that if he did see something it would probably be too late.

He stopped again when he reached the bottom of the trail, standing in shadow, the first of the burial mounds greeting him.

Studying the churned-up snow at his feet, he rubbed absently at his leg and knee, seeking to reduce the pain to a more manageable level.

He realized then that his hope that the monsters already had moved off was no more than that. Just as he believed it would be.

He identified the tracks of several different beasts, their claws punching deeply into the packed snow.

Intermixed was another distinctive print that he hadn't expected to see here. Almost lost in the crush. A boot. A good bit smaller than his own.

Those tracks wound their way along the edge of the barrows. The larger tracks followed.

Other than himself, what fool would take the risk of coming here on their own?

Everyone in the kingdoms to the south and east knew to stay clear of the Frozen Waste without the invitation of those who ruled this hard, unforgiving land.

And Mikel knew of only one human who currently had that invitation.

Even the bandits who roamed the mountains at his back stuck to the heights on the western side for the most part, having learned the hard way that the inhabitants of the Frozen Waste would be more than happy to make an example of them.

What to do about his unexpected discovery?

Mikel's own business called to him. His finding might serve

as an opportunity to avoid confronting these monstrous hunters himself.

Should he continue on his way and take a different path that led away from what would likely prove to be a bloody and gory mess?

Or should he follow the tracks and get a better sense of how many of these monsters had come down from the mountains?

Quite the dilemma.

He knew what he wanted to do.

But he rarely did what he wanted to do.

Usually he did what he thought he needed to do.

Even though that inevitably got him into trouble and made his life more difficult than he wanted it to be.

2

AN APPETIZER

Drin pushed herself up from where she crouched in the snow. Wary now. Scanning around her. Seeking any hint of movement. Any sound.

There was blood at her feet.

A lot of it with a few pieces of tufted fur and long slices of flesh dotted with red that were already frozen still clinging to what was left of the skeleton.

When she picked one strand up between her gloves, it was so thin, so delicate, the flesh snapped in two when she applied barely any pressure thanks to the frigid cold.

"What could have done this?"

The carcass was that of a reindeer. She was sure of it despite the missing head. The few hoofprints she spotted in the snow confirmed it for her.

"Not a polar bear," she mused. She swept her gaze once again around the sullied snow. There were no tracks suggesting one of the largest predators in the Frozen Waste was roaming close by. "So what then?"

Drin swiped her hair out of her eyes, realizing she was doing it again. Talking to herself. A habit her father said she needed to break before she assumed her rightful place in the Kingdom.

Thankfully, with her father in excellent health, she had little cause to worry about that happening anytime soon.

Still, he was right. Talking to herself wasn't a good look when she was in line for the throne of the Crux. The First Families were always looking for any hint of weakness. But she could work on that later.

Right now she needed to make a decision.

Should she head back the way she had come or continue on the route she had selected?

"It's a long way to go," she murmured to herself, Drin referring to the many hours and hard travel through the snow demanded of her to reach her current location.

The trail she sought that would take her back to the mountains and then home was less than an hour away from where she stood. It would save half the day. But it would lead her in the direction taken by whatever had killed the reindeer.

She decided on expediency in the place of caution. Drin took a few steps along the trail of blood that led away from the kill ground before she stopped abruptly.

She had been listening to nothing more than the whistle of the wind as it gusted through the spaces between the barrows.

Until just then.

A rustle that was different from any other noise she had heard since making her way down the trail to the maze of massive mounds teased her senses. It sounded like a snake sliding through the snow.

Without making a move, Drin searched around her, seeking any hint that might give away the cause of the noise that had set a bell of concern pounding in the back of her head. She saw nothing but white and heard ... nothing except for the wind playing across the icy tundra.

Her search was made all the more difficult because she lost

the sun when she left the trail, the shadows lengthening along the paths between the burial mounds. The wind grew louder in her ears.

She reconsidered her decision to come down here, ignoring her father's warnings and slipping away from her responsibilities for a few days. Slip away from the person who she believed was asking more from her than she was ready or willing to give.

Drin shook her head. "Think before you do," she murmured to herself. Advice her father offered her more times than she could recall. Irritating because of its frequency. Now, useful.

The blood led off between the barrows.

That was the fastest route out.

What to do?

She needed to decide. Quickly.

This was her first time in the Frozen Waste. Admittedly, she was barely across the eastern border of the great white expanse, which began at the mountains towering behind her. Still, it was an entirely different world compared to the one she was used to. And her few hours of exploration excited her in a way that nothing else had in quite some time.

It was beautiful.

Just as she had been led to believe.

Perilous as well.

Just as the blood at her feet demonstrated.

After listening to all the stories while she was growing up, the desire to visit this strange land became an irresistible urge. In large part because she felt the need to do something that wasn't what she was supposed to do.

For as long as she could remember, she always did what she was supposed to do.

She didn't view that as a weakness.

She believed it a good thing that she took her responsibilities seriously.

Nevertheless, with all that was pushing down on her shoulders, at least for once in her life, she needed to feel ... free.

Drin really couldn't explain it in any other way.

She wasn't running away from her responsibilities. She knew what was required of her, and she accepted the burden. Gladly, in fact, understanding that the power and privilege her family enjoyed came as well with an accountability that she couldn't ignore. That she wouldn't ignore.

When she returned.

She just needed to slip away from Innsbruck for a few days and gain a brief respite from the constant pressures of her position.

She shouldn't be here. She acknowledged that now.

The Frozen Waste was forbidden unless you were invited to cross the border by the Giants of the Rime. And from what her uncle had said, the keepers of this frigid wasteland had not issued an invitation for decades. Perhaps even a century. No one could really recall the last time the Frost Lord allowed a visitor into his domain.

Which made her all the more curious about how weapons, glass, and several other unique items were sold in Innsbruck. Items that were clearly of Giant making.

Though Drin had broken the bonds that formed the boundaries of her life if only for a few days, she hadn't broken the treaty between Innsbruck and the Giants of the Rime. She was just on the edge of the glacial, barren landscape. The border between the Frozen Waste and the Kingdom of the Crux was never really decided. Neither Realm put in the time and energy necessary to hammer out a resolution to the argument that had lasted since ... well, she really didn't know when.

Besides, her disobedience already had been rewarded. She would need to deal with the Giants eventually. Best that she got a sense of their world before she did so.

Much of what she had seen after trekking along the edge of

the Frozen Waste for only a few hours astounded her. Her lessons on what to expect not doing the captivating environment justice.

The massive barrows were only a part of it. Glaciers reached for the sky. Frozen rivers with ice thirty feet thick were so clear that she could still see the water rushing below even though she couldn't hear the surge. Crevices were hollowed out from the base of icy tors by the wind that polished the snow until it was blindingly bright when struck by the sun. Arches of strange and mesmerizing designs connected the tors to create what looked like natural aqueducts. Dozens of pingos, huge mounds of solid ice, dotted the barren landscape seemingly without rhyme or reason.

She had not anticipated half of what she had seen. She had anticipated the cold and believed she was ready for it. Learning much to her detriment that she wasn't. The frosty temperature and even more frigid wind chilled her to the bone despite being bundled up in a thick, fur-lined jacket and leggings along with a hat that failed to cut the bite of the wind.

Even so, she was glad that she had taken her uncle's advice, surprising though it had been. Particularly since he was even more wedded to his duty than she was.

Having made her decision, Drin took a step down the bloody path. But no more than a step.

She didn't see anything around her. Nevertheless, she sensed that she wasn't alone.

How close her stalkers were, she couldn't say. But she was certain there were more than one.

"Think before you do," Drin repeated to herself.

Another whisper of movement to her front. Then one more at her back.

Her hunters had set the snare, and she had walked right into it.

She took a few steps to the right. There was another path

there between the barrows that would lead her back toward the trail that she had taken down from the crag. The longer way home. Perhaps the only way home now.

Another dreaded whisper. This time from the west.

A shiver ran through her that wasn't caused by the cold.

Her hunters were herding her.

Either they wanted her to move in the only direction open to her or they hadn't closed the trap fast enough.

It was time to make another choice.

She heard the whisper again. Like a silk cloth being pulled across the ice.

Drin looked back over her shoulder. Her hunters were no more than twenty feet away based on the noise. Where could they be? She saw nothing more than the frosted side of a barrow.

No more time for thinking. There was only time for doing.

Hearing two more whispers of movement coming from both her front and back and only packed snow greeting her eyes, she selected the sole option open to her. She could only hope that there wasn't a fourth hunter waiting for her just up ahead.

She dashed off, pumping her legs as fast as she could, her boots crunching into the hardened snow as she ran between the short sides of two barrows.

The wind had returned. The blustery gale that she was running into slowed her down. Forcing her back toward her pursuers.

She pushed even harder, hearing the movement at her back. She didn't need to look over her shoulder to know that her hunters were right behind her and closing the gap between them, the terrifying whisper of their movements replaced by a heavy crunch.

The end of the path coming up on her quickly, a deep howl that sounded much like a wolf's ripped between the barrows.

It faded quickly.

Sinkhole.

It had to be.

She probably ran right over it without disturbing the trap. But her hunters were bigger than she was, and they were heavier. That realization and the fact that they could stay with her despite the punch of the wind narrowed down what could be chasing her, none of what came to mind what she wanted to think about.

Drin picked up her pace as best as she could. The wind slacking. Allowing her to move with greater speed down the path. Unfortunately permitting her hunters to do the same.

She was less concerned about how many hunters remained. Now more concerned with finding a better spot to defend herself.

Although she had no doubt that she stood little chance of escaping, what she saw to her front gave her a very brief moment of hope.

Racing out from between the barrows, she found herself on a small plain, her hope dying quickly. A large bluff on the far side ensured that she had nowhere else to go.

Still, right in the center of the plain a fantastical ice sculpture rose several hundred feet into the sky. Her uncle had told her about these marvelous creations.

They were crafted by the strange and powerful lightning strikes that often came with the blizzards that swept over this barren land. The energy blasted into the snow, throwing it into the air, the charge creating a design that froze in seconds because of the frigid temperature. What remained molded over time by the sun, cold, and wind.

Drin didn't stop to admire what waited before her. Instead, she sprinted right toward it, aiming for a spot where several of the razor-sharp branches carved of ice would offer her some protection.

She wasn't where she wanted to be, but it was the best that she could do.

She knew that she had to fight. There was no way to avoid it. At least here she could limit the number of hunters who could come at her at one time.

Skidding to a stop when she was between the razor-sharp branches, she spun back around, pulling the short sword strapped to her back in a smooth motion and ready to defend herself against whatever it was that hunted her.

Her heart froze when she identified the monsters that approached.

They peeled out of the white background as they drew closer.

Their confident steps confirmed that they didn't feel the need to rush. Certain that they could kill her whenever they desired.

MIKEL COULDN'T UNDERSTAND why the woman was out here in the frigid wild on her own.

In a forbidden land.

Clearly having little real sense regarding the many dangers to be found in the Frozen Waste ... until some of those dangers found her.

Still, he was impressed.

The woman knew how to fight.

Short sword in hand, how she gripped the blade suggested that she had quite a bit of training.

That wasn't how she was defending herself, however.

Not yet.

Not until she had no other choice.

Instead she employed a unique skill rare in this part of the world.

Spikes of energy as well as other lethal creations made from the Talent shot from her palm. Keeping her attackers at bay for now, the position she selected ensured that she only had to worry about an assault from one direction.

A skilled fighter and a Magus.

Intelligent. Creative. Quick thinking. Headstrong as well to enter the Frozen Waste on her own without fully understanding the perils waiting for her, which suggested as well a worrisome obstinance.

A dangerous mix in his experience.

Mikel had to give the woman credit, though. She was doing well considering the challenge set before her.

She was facing off against Northern Trolls.

A fist all told, and there were more coming her way, drawn by the howls and barks of their brethren.

Mikel had fought Northern Trolls a few times before. He had never enjoyed the experience. And in each instance he had been grateful that he walked away.

Determined beasts. Cunning as well. And hungry. Always hungry.

The creatures were covered in a short but thick coat of white fur. It kept them warm in the below freezing temperatures of their homeland.

It also allowed them to blend in almost perfectly with their snow-covered environment. Quite an accomplishment since a Northern Troll was twice the size of a tall man in both height and breadth and exceedingly strong, muscles growing upon muscles.

Even their eyes were white. As were the tusks that curled up from their bottom jaw and the razor-sharp teeth that resembled fangs that were visible when they opened their short snouts to roar.

Each of the Trolls carried either a very large battle axe with a blade sharper than steel or a mace, both crafted from an ice that was harder than stone and found only in their mountain territory.

And, as the Trolls danced around her, seeking a way past her defenses, the Magus was learning that these gigantic creatures were terribly fast. Likely as well that they were strong enough to bear the brunt of her attack, knocking away with their oversized weapons the energy she sent their way.

Watching the engagement, Mikel also had to give the Northern Trolls some credit because they displayed a disconcerting cleverness. Rather than standing against the Magus' magical strikes, they used their speed to their advantage, evading her attacks more often than not. Ensuring that she did little more than tire herself out as they waited for more of their clan to arrive.

Based on how her expression had changed in just the last minute, it seemed that she had reached the same conclusion as he had.

Yet despite her difficulties and that blood-chilling realization, she demonstrated a tenacity that Mikel could only admire.

The Magus looked to be young. Maybe a few years younger than he was. And she clearly had not done her research before entering the Waste, because she had yet to figure out the best way to deal with Northern Trolls.

More than unfortunate for her. Likely a death sentence.

Once again, Mikel had a decision to make.

He could go about his business and leave the Magus to her fate. Some might even say a fate she deserved for so foolishly entering a forbidden land without the appropriate resources.

Or he could intervene.

Against a fist of Trolls.

With more of the beasts coming this way.

If this was strictly a business matter, weighing the advantages and disadvantages, the decision was quite easy. Besides, he needed to get moving. He had somewhere to be.

But this wasn't just a business decision now.

There was more at stake here than money to be made or a favor to be earned.

Mikel uttered several choice curses as all the relevant variables ran through his mind and he calculated the odds of the several paths open to him as he lay atop a barrow only a few feet from the crest.

With barely a thought, relying on his instinct, he flipped himself over.

Just in time.

The massive mace crafted from ice smashed down right in the spot where he had been lying only a moment before, punching deep into the crusted snow and leaving a large hole rather than crushing his chest. The Troll who had snuck up on him from behind hissed in anger as he pulled his weapon free.

When the Troll lifted the mace above his head to continue his attack, Mikel was nowhere to be seen, having scrambled back behind the creature.

"Come on, ugly. Time for you to go to the other side."

The Troll spun around upon hearing Mikel's words. However, instead of rushing at him, the Troll held his ground. Grunting and huffing. Brandishing his weapon.

Mikel frowned. Not the usual behavior from a ravenous ...

He ducked and rolled, the huge axe crafted of ice sweeping through the space where his head had been just a second before, the blade taking a few locks of his hair rather than a large portion of his scalp.

He had just been thinking about the Northern Troll's cleverness, and his own attempt at cleverness had almost cost him his life.

And perhaps it still would, because now he stood against two of the giant monsters, the second approaching just as quietly as the first.

He turned sideways to his opponents. They seemed more

than willing to take a few seconds to study him. Not too concerned despite his discovering them before they could kill him.

He kept one eye on the Trolls while he searched the landscape at his back with a quick glance over each shoulder. Mikel hoped that there weren't any more of the creatures lying buried in the snow, waiting to take him from behind when the combat began.

He didn't think there were. All he saw were the tracks made by the two who had crept up on him and the perfectly smooth snow atop the barrow courtesy of the always blowing wind. There were no lumps to suggest he needed to worry about a third Troll joining the party.

That was a good thing.

Not so good was the movement to his front.

Mikel took a step back and pivoted, allowing the Troll to pass by him.

The beast missed with his axe again, the power of his swing pulling the creature off balance.

Mikel was more than happy to make use of that mistake. Trailing a leg behind him, he caught the Troll's back foot, which sent the creature sprawling when that errant back foot hit his other foot.

All the Troll was going to eat that afternoon was a face full of snow, Mikel attacking before the Troll could push himself up.

Jumping onto the Troll's back with his knee and pushing the beast's tusks back into the icy crust, Mikel brought the sharp blade of his mace down, piercing the back of the Troll's neck. He could have used the hammer on the other end of his weapon, but Northern Trolls had notoriously hard heads. If he didn't crush the creature's skull in a single blow, then he likely was a dead man, a result that he wanted to avoid.

The Troll flopped a few times like a fish out of water, then lay still.

Mikel pushed himself up from the creature's broad back and turned to face the other Troll. The creature hadn't moved, surprised by what he had just witnessed. Never anticipating such a result.

Wanting to take advantage of the Troll's indecision, Mikel sprinted across the top of the barrow, mace held above his shoulder as if he was planning to swing down toward the creature's hip.

Mikel's movement jolted the Troll into action. The creature raised his mace, prepared to catch the blow.

But it never came.

Instead, Mikel ducked and rolled past. In the same motion he sliced with his weapon's blade across the back of the Troll's legs.

Cut across both hamstrings, one severed completely, the other partially, the Troll dropped to his knees, bellowing in anger and pain.

The Troll was fast.

Mikel was faster, and he did much as he had to the first Troll. Slamming into the creature's back with his knees, he forced the beast's maw into the snow while also punching his blade through the back of the Troll's neck.

Two kills in two minutes. Probably less.

A good fight.

Nevertheless, Mikel wasn't happy.

Grumbling to himself, he pushed off the rapidly cooling corpse and turned away from the dead Trolls, the heat from the bodies drifting up into the frigid air. At this temperature, in just a few minutes they would be no more than icicles.

It seemed like his decision had been made for him.

Taking a quick look from the top of the burial mound to

gauge what was happening below, he scrambled back from the lip. None of the Trolls were aware that he was above them.

Pulling free his snowshoes that were clipped to the back of his pack, he fitted them to his boots and locked them into place. He then pulled out two thin, fire-hardened boards that he fitted over the webbing on the underside of each snowshoe.

Knowing what would happen if he took a moment to think about what he was about to do, Mikel sprinted toward the lip of the barrow, mace in hand.

"You were a fool," Drin grumbled to herself as she carried on a constant commentary on her decision to enter the Frozen Waste. "Putting yourself at risk on a whim. Just because you ..."

She didn't get a chance to finish berating herself, twisting to her right side and blasting a series of short, sharp bursts of magical spikes toward the beasts inching toward her from that direction.

Against other opponents, she already would have won this combat. Few had the strength and ability to stand against a Magus.

But she was battling against Northern Trolls. And much to her consternation, they knew how to fight a Magus.

A fact that she wished she had known before she began her ill-fated journey. Because if she had known, she probably would have stayed in Innsbruck.

She had gained very little in her many attacks against the beasts other than a few superficial wounds that failed to slow down the dangerously swift giants. Learning quickly that the best that she could hope for was to buy a few more minutes to search for some avenue of escape as she struggled to keep the Trolls away from her.

Drin shook her head to clear it. There was no point in castigating herself now or reminding herself of the many mistakes she had made, in particular with respect to this clash.

She needed to focus on staying alive, and that meant ensuring the Trolls kept to her front. If one got on her flank, she was done for.

That was becoming a more difficult task as the cunning creatures patiently brought a more intense pressure to bear upon her.

She had picked a good place from which to defend herself. Three sides protected.

But she had trapped herself as well.

With the jagged spikes that guarded her, she had nowhere to go other than through the beasts who, based on the drool dripping down their tusks, viewed her as that night's meal.

What really got her goat was that her use of the Talent didn't bother her hunters in the least. The creatures not only demonstrated an admirable skill in defending against her attacks, but also feinted toward her regularly. Keeping her on her toes. Inching toward her. Tightening the noose. Soon to be in a position to strike a fatal blow.

It wouldn't be long before one of the beasts came in close and forced her to use her short sword. When that happened, the other Trolls would rush her and the fight would be over.

Both Talent and steel of little use.

And she had no doubt that moment was approaching swiftly. Several more Trolls had joined the hunt, drawn by the sounds of the combat and the calls of their brethren.

Savvy creatures indeed. The Trolls were allowing her to tire herself out.

At the same time, they made sure she had little chance of getting away from them. They were more than happy to bide their time, looking for just the right opportunity, clearly unconcerned that they hunted a Magus as they sought to push her into that single mistake that would lead to her death.

Drin was angry.

At herself for taking this risk.

For not realizing what strategy these Trolls were employing before it was too late to break free.

Even more so for not really understanding the threat these creatures presented before she entered the Frozen Waste.

Big. Fast. Dangerous. Clever.

Clearly displaying attributes she had not learned about during her training.

A lethal mix as she feared she was about to discover.

An instant later what she dreaded most occurred.

She made a mistake.

One of the Trolls on her left side had climbed the mesmerizing ice sculpture, ignoring the sharpness of the frosty limb that cut into his claws, more concerned with coming at her from the flank.

She defended herself with the Talent, targeting the branch rather than the Troll.

The blast of energy shattered the ice, sending the beast flying backward, his body riddled with bloody shards.

She wasn't done. Sensing the movement on her other side, when she swept back around to manage the Trolls pushing in on her right who sought to take advantage of the distraction provided by their badly wounded brethren, her foot slipped in the snow, taking her down to one knee.

Recognizing her peril, she could do nothing more than rely on her instincts, raising her sword to defend against the battle axe already sweeping toward her head.

Drin knew without a doubt that her efforts wouldn't be enough.

The Troll was too fast and too strong.

The beast's axe would shatter her blade then split her in two.

Right before the icy blade bit into her flesh and bone, a blur slid by her, slamming into her attacker with a bone-crunching smack.

The collision left her rescuer just a few feet away from her while the Troll tumbled through the snow, coming to a stop when the beast slammed against the sculpture, a long shard of ice sticking out of his chest. The great weight of the Troll snapped off the branch, the creature sagging to the snow, only able to manage a soft gurgle as he died slowly, the icy lance having skewered his lungs.

Drin had less than a second to take in her unanticipated though much-appreciated champion.

He was big, almost hulking. Even so, he moved with a surprising nimbleness. Kicking off his snowshoes, he placed his back to hers.

"I'll take the right flank," he said.

She didn't have the chance to argue, the Trolls on her side pushing toward her once again. The shock of seeing their brethren impaled was wearing off quickly.

To hold them, Drin fired several bursts of energy at her attackers, forcing them back. A few even growled in pain, unable to avoid the searing heat she blasted in their direction.

Those few seconds she earned allowed her to observe the newcomer assisting her in this fight. Despite his size, he was deceptively fast. Efficient as well. Economical and graceful in his movements and his decisions. Almost as if he'd come up against Northern Trolls before.

Forgoing the short sword scabbarded across his back, he feinted toward a Troll to his right who was trying to sneak around them.

The Troll took a deft half-step back. A natural reaction, but also one that cost him as a slice of ice from the jagged branches behind him pierced his back.

Mikel left his adversary gasping out bubbly blood as the Troll dropped to his knee, struggling to breathe. Continuing his motion, Mikel spun around swiftly while bringing himself close to the snow-covered ground.

With all the strength that he could bring to bear, Mikel slammed his mace into the second Troll's knee, grinning devilishly when he heard the bone shatter followed just a breath later by a roar of agony.

Before the wounded Troll hit the ground, he was dead.

Mikel swiped with the other side of his weapon, his already bloodied blade slashing across the falling creature's throat.

One opponent eliminated, Mikel turned toward the beast with the bloody back.

The wounded Troll bellowed in rage. Ignoring the pain and the blood gushing down his back and between his fangs, the beast swung with his axe.

Mikel dodged out of the way. When the blade of ice swept past him, he kicked out with his boot, connecting with the beast's knee and bending it backward at a severe angle.

The Troll bellowed in anger again, though this time not only because of the pain of his second injury, but also because his wild swing threw him too far to the right, sending him stumbling into the icy branches on that side.

Mikel finished the Troll with a swift kick to his lower back, ensuring that the beast was fixed in place, caught on the frosty spikes that stuck out from his back in four different places, three of them fatal wounds all on their own.

Pivoting toward the Magus, Mikel ready for the next combat, the Trolls appeared to have lost interest in the fun of the hunt after losing so many of their brethren. They wanted only the kill now, and they were preparing to rush their quarry come what may.

"Target the ground in front of the Trolls!" he shouted.

Drin didn't hesitate even as she cursed herself for a fool. Sheathing her sword, she did as ordered, sending blazing bolts of energy blasting into the crust just twenty feet in front of her.

Right where the Trolls stood.

They were fast. They were strong. But they stood little chance against the power she exercised.

Particularly since the environment worked with her, the eruption of white blocking the sun.

When the gusts of wind buffeted away the snow and ice swirling in the air, 'several sinkholes were revealed that just needed a little nudge before giving way, taking three of the Trolls a hundred or more feet belowground.

She doubted that trio would be escaping their prison, assuming they survived the fall. Three more of the Trolls wouldn't be rising again either, their smoking and charred bodies confirming that fact.

That left only three of the beasts standing against her.

Feeling more confident after her first taste of success and with an ally covering her back, Drin decided on a different approach. Remembering what happened to the Troll who dared to climb the branches of ice, she made use of the sculpture that had offered her some much-desired protection. Using the Talent, she broke apart several of the branches above her then with a flick of her wrist sent the razor-sharp shards streaking toward the surviving Trolls.

Two died in seconds. They were able to defend against a few of the icy lances though not all. The third escaped harm except for a slice across his side only because his companions bore the brunt of the attack for him.

Realizing that he was alone, wounded, and stood little chance against the Magus and the human who wielded his mace as if it was a part of his hand, the last Northern Troll turned and fled as swiftly as he could.

With the wound he had sustained, it wasn't as fast as he wanted. His gait more a staggering stumble than a sprint.

Mikel reacted with barely a thought, refusing to allow the beast to lead more of his brethren after them. Pulling a slim dagger from his belt, tip of the blade between thumb and fore-finger, he flung the blade end over end through the air, the steel coming to rest in the back of the Troll's neck in much the same place where Mikel had dispatched several other Trolls at the beginning of the fight.

Nodding with satisfaction when the Troll crumpled in the snow, he kept his mace in hand as he walked across the battlefield. He checked each body to make sure they were dead. Then he examined the sinkholes with the same thoroughness to confirm that they had nothing to worry about from the beasts who fell through the ground. Heading toward the Troll farthest away from them, Mikel pulled free his dagger, wiped the blade clean on the dead beast's fur before sheathing it, and walked back completely at his ease, almost as if a clash against the most feared monsters of the mountains was just a normal day for him.

Stopping in front of Drin, Mikel gave the Magus an appreciative nod. For someone half his size, she certainly packed a punch. Sharp eyes matched her sharp features, and the lines around her mouth suggested that she liked to smile, although not now. Anger her primary emotion.

"This isn't a full clan," Mikel said, not put off by the Magus' close study of him. "I took down the last one so that he couldn't bring the rest this way. But I likely only bought you an hour. Best that you get moving now."

Drin heard what her unexpected ally said. She chose to ignore him. There was some aspect to the man that caught her eye, though she didn't know what exactly. And that bothered her. Usually she could read people with just a glance.

He was big. Not only tall, but also broad. Though it didn't look like he had an ounce of fat on him.

He wasn't particularly good looking. His nose had been broken several times and was permanently crooked. His short beard failed to hide the several scars that crisscrossed his cheeks and neck with a deeper one across his brow.

Yet his smile put her at ease despite his cold eyes. Colder than the gust of wind that blasted into her and turned the sweat covering her body to ice.

He wore clothes quite different from hers. A thin jacket unlike the bulky one that was doing very little to keep her warm. Thin pants as well, not lined with fur. Gloves. A knit cap.

All a mesh of grey, black, white, and blue that allowed him to blend into the environment almost as well as if not better than the Northern Trolls did.

Where did he get clothes like that?

And why was he there in the first place?

No one had permission from the Giants of the Rime to enter their homeland.

"Who are you?" she asked.

"You did hear what I said, right? You have an hour at most. You need to get moving."

"I did." Her voice took on a harder edge. "I ask again. Who are you?"

"No thank you?" He offered her a raised eyebrow. "I don't know that you would have made your way out of this mess without my assistance."

"I had everything well in hand," she replied, though her voice lacked the conviction to support her statement.

"Of course you did." His sarcasm dripped from his voice like molasses.

"Nevertheless, my thanks." She nodded as if she had completed a slightly unpleasant task and now it was time to move on to the next one. "Now answer me. Who are you?"

Mikel smiled in amusement. Just like every other Magus he had met. And he had met more than he cared to. They were single-minded to a fault and dangerously hard-headed. "No one of consequence."

"Are you always this difficult?" Drin demanded. He had aided her. Saved her life most likely, though she refused to admit that to him. Still, her natural curiosity was getting the better of her manners. That didn't bother her, however, because she was not used to being treated this way.

"Usually, yes," Mikel replied without a hint of embarrassment. "Now you need to get out of here. The snow is moving through the glass."

"The snow? Isn't it supposed to be ..."

"I was just taking literary license is all," Mikel explained, finding it harder to keep the smile on his face as the young woman poked and prodded. "You need to get moving, Magus. The Northern Trolls aren't done with you."

That last comment seemed to break her train of thought. "Why would they be down from the mountains?"

"Hunting," Mikel replied with a shrug, as if it was the most obvious of explanations.

"For what?"

"You."

"Me?" How could they know who she was? Why would they care?

Then it came to her. Who she was didn't matter to them.

"They're hungry. You crossed their path instead of the reindeer or polar bear they were seeking. Easy prey they probably thought. Though you'd be no more than an appetizer for them."

"I don't know how to take a comment like that," Drin replied, almost laughing because she wanted to avoid thinking about what would have happened if her rescuer had not arrived when he did.

"However you like. Nevertheless, I suggest you take my advice. Head out of the Waste. Quickly. If you get into the lower peaks and one of the forts along the trail before dark, you should be fine."

Mikel turned then. Picking up his snowshoes, he strapped them to his pack and strode toward the trail that would take him deeper into the Barrows.

"Pleasure to meet you, Magus," he called over his shoulder, giving her a wave without looking at her. "Now you know the Giants of the Rime are only one of the threats to be wary of in the Frozen Waste."

In just seconds, he was gone. Fading into the snow and ice. Moving just as quietly as a Northern Troll.

Drin took a breath, the moisture she released frosting. She had been holding it until he disappeared. More than just curious about him now.

Who was he?

Why was he there?

Perhaps most important, why did he risk his life for hers?

3

EISA

Once past the Barrows what looked like a straight shot across the frozen expanse toward the mountains far to the west was anything but. From a distance, the land appeared flat and smooth, completely unmarked, the blustery wind scouring the white earth.

It wasn't.

A series of knolls and hollows scarred the landscape. Icy caverns and frozen waterfalls, rivers flowing dozens of feet below perfectly clear ice, crevices and gorges crafted by time, water, and the wind, all were crusted by a thick frosty white.

Beautiful.

Captivating.

Dangerous.

Unless you were familiar with the several hidden trails that led through the bitter wild.

And Mikel was familiar with them all.

He was following one right then between two high cliffs that kept the gusts of frigid air to a soft growl rather than a lusty bay.

Only a few hours had passed since he found the tracks of

the Northern Trolls that led him to the Magus and the brief though bloody clash. Now he had found something else just as curious, which was why he had chosen this trail after exiting the Barrows rather than taking the one that would have gotten him to his destination several hours faster.

Thankfully it was not Trolls this time.

Whatever imprints there might have been were crushed into the snow, the surface of the path smoothed down. Probably because of a sled being dragged through the crust behind the intruders.

That could mean only one thing.

Poachers.

Not very common these days. Not after the examples the Giants of the Rime had made of the last few groups of bandits from the Splintered Empire who dared to invade their territory.

Once again Mikel had a decision to make.

Continue on his way and ensure that he wasn't late?

Or take another chance and determine why a group of poachers risked the Frozen Waste?

It was an easy decision to make, his curiosity getting the better of him.

Just as it usually did.

After all, he didn't like unanswered questions.

MIKEL PUSHED himself up from where he was kneeling in the snow.

He had been following the same smooth track for more than a league. Here, though, for the first time he saw a few faint indentations that were barely visible in the icy crust that covered the rocky ground. A good number of boots moving off the trail and into the high ground were on each side.

He was getting close.

Only a few questions remained. The most prominent?

How many?

What was their game?

"You going to come out or are you going to continue stalking me?" An eyebrow raised, Mikel directed his expectant gaze toward the cliff to his left.

"When did you know?" a deep, disembodied voice replied.

"Two miles back," Mikel replied. "You've been with me since the Dagger's Claw." The landmark was properly named in his opinion.

A deep chuckle emanated from the base of the ice-covered crag as a figure half again as tall as a man peeled himself out of the stone and ice. The Giant of the Rime had whitish blue skin. White hair. Bright blue eyes. And he wore the same thin, warm clothes that Mikel wore. A perfect match to the cold colors of the Frozen Waste.

"Why am I not surprised?"

"Good to see you, Cadmus." Mikel offered his hand, which was quickly engulfed by the Giant's meaty paw. "It has been too long."

"That it has, my friend," replied the ruler of the Giants of the Rime.

"And what of me, Steelheart?" Another Giant followed in Cadmus' wake, this one a head shorter than he was. She looked much like her father except for her long hair, which was braided down her back in an eye-catching pattern.

"Good to see you as well, Julia," Mikel replied, unable to hold back his smile, Julia's too infectious, as he offered Cadmus' daughter a nod of respect.

"I would think that you would be more interested in seeing me than seeing my father." Julia's smile shifted then, one lip curling, becoming more provocative.

"Too true," Mikel replied. "I simply didn't want to insult the Frost Lord."

"I am still not happy," Julia groused, although her bright blue eyes displayed her good humor. She stepped forward and gave him a hug that crushed the air from his lungs. "I have yet to escape your notice."

Mikel nodded. Julia wasn't pleased that he had seen through her efforts to hide from him. "You can never escape my notice, Julia. You know that."

The wink he gave her made Julia's smile quite a bit larger, even bringing a hint of red to her pale cheeks.

"I take it that you didn't come this way just to flirt with my daughter," Cadmus rumbled, not feeling the need to allow the teasing to continue.

"No, I didn't, Cadmus."

The Giant nodded. "The poachers." A growl emanated from deep within his throat. "Several of my hunters watch them now."

A shriek erupted from less than a quarter mile away. It contained pain, anguish, and more than just a hint of desperation.

Mikel turned toward Cadmus. "Shall we join the hunt?"

MIKEL'S EXPRESSION darkened as he advanced into the hollow. He was disgusted by the sight that greeted him.

The poachers knew their work. Ten of them had wrangled the animal into the natural trap, poking at her with long spears. Not to harm her, but rather to distract her so that she couldn't focus her attack on any one of them. More importantly, so that she never had a chance to make her escape. The stone pressing in on her back and along both sides prevented that.

Because of their success, another ten men had just finished the dangerous and hard task of chaining the young ice dragon and muzzling her. The final step would be dragging her into the cage fixed atop the sled and locking her up. Then they could worry about getting the ice dragon out of her natural habitat and to whomever had funded this expedition.

The poachers' grins and good humor hinted at their pleasure. They were looking at a big payday since ice dragons were so rare. If the buyer wasn't a lord seeking to add to his collection of exotic beasts then he was a merchant who believed that there was more money to be made from the animal's hide, bones, and organs, many superstitions holding that the various body parts of an ice dragon were essential to a variety of miraculous cures.

The dragon was less than ten feet from her nose to the tip of her tail. Just a youngling. She was still exceedingly dangerous, however.

If she survived this experience, she would grow to three times her current size. Perhaps even four. Her bluish white scales helped her to blend into the Frozen Waste. And she was not without the means to protect herself with the use of her sharp claws and whiplike tail, though she could do little with them now.

As she got older, she would learn to breathe an icy mist that was just as powerful as a fiery blast and perhaps even spit ice crystals that would feel much like being pierced by spears, only the strongest steel able to stand against such an onslaught. But those abilities were beyond her at this age. It would be a few months more if not a full year before she could do all that.

"That's quite the risk you're taking."

Mikel's words froze the poachers. They stood as if they had been caught in one of the blizzards that swept across the Frozen Waste with scarcely any warning.

The largest of the men who were seeking to drag the ice dragon into the cage -- all of them staying well away from her front claws, which they had failed to tie as they had her back claws -- stepped away from his work and approached Mikel.

"Who might you be friend?"

The poacher rested his hands on his belt, close to the short sword and several long daggers sheathed there.

"No one of consequence," Mikel replied with an easy smile, amused by his second use of that same phrase in just the last few hours.

"No one of consequence," the poacher repeated as he eyed Mikel closely. Then he snorted. "If you're out here like we are, then you're likely one of us."

Mikel laughed softly at that. "I admit to having a variety of business interests, several of them less than legitimate just as yours is. However, I conduct my business according to certain standards. I do not steal animals from their natural habitat."

"So you're better than us, or at least you believe that you are," the poacher grumbled, a spark of anger appearing in the back of his eyes. "I don't like being insulted."

"No one likes to be insulted," Mikel replied, "and I didn't say that. I'm simply more discerning in how I apply my talents as I really don't care to harm such beautiful animals like the one behind you."

The ice dragon had gone silent just like the poachers had when they stopped trying to haul her into the cage, Mikel interrupting their work. She hissed now. The best that she could do with the muzzle keeping her jaws closed. But she made no other move. Apparently just as curious about Mikel as her tormentors were.

"We all need to make a living," the poacher explained. "We all need to put food on the table."

Mikel nodded. He wasn't in a position to disagree with that. "We do. Nevertheless, there are better ways to put food on the table than this. Why don't you cut the dragon free? I'm sure we can come to an arrangement that allows you to feed your families without having to harm the young one."

The poacher stared at Mikel for several seconds, trying to

make sense of what was going on. The hulking fellow wasn't making a threat. At least not overtly. Not yet. But was he ...

"Are you offering me and my crew a job if we release the dragon?"

Mikel smiled, glad that the poacher figured it out. Worried for a moment that he wouldn't. "I am. Not many men are brave enough, or desperate enough, to enter the Frozen Waste without the permission of the Giants of the Rime. I could use men like that for certain work that is required from time to time."

The poacher stared even longer at Mikel after that pronouncement, then he looked back over his shoulder. His men all were looking at him, all with the same confused expression as he wore. None of them knew what to make of the intruder.

When he turned back toward Mikel, the poacher's confusion only increased. This interloper had no business being here. Yet there he stood only a dozen feet away calm as could be. A score of his men, all experienced fighters, staring right at him. And it didn't bother him at all. The man's preternatural calm was impressive, and it made the poacher uneasy.

He pushed his concerns to the side, seeking to bolster his wavering confidence with the fact that this irritant was here all by his lonesome. That realization confirmed how he was going to handle the man who had decided to interrupt their work.

"What's your name friend?"

"I have many names," Mikel replied.

The poacher smiled, though not in a good way. "I'll take just one ..."

"Because you like to know the names of the men you're about to kill," Mikel finished for him.

The poacher laughed softly at that. "I do, you're right."

"Like I said, I have several." Mikel didn't reply right away, deciding to drag the conversation out a little longer. He had never expected this poacher and his men to accept his offer. Mikel just wanted to give his friends a little more time to get into place.

"Then give me one," the poacher urged.

"Just one?" Mikel asked.

"Just one."

Mikel shrugged, going through the exercise of deciding. "The Fox."

"The Fox?" the poacher repeated. Why did that sound familiar? Yet for the life of him, he couldn't recall why.

Mikel nodded. "The Fox. Just one of many as I said. The Knife. The Broken Bear. I could provide more, but I don't want to confuse you any more than I already have."

"Boss ..." one of the other poachers said, stepping up next to the leader of the increasingly nervous gang. He was worried. Kory obviously didn't recall just who the Fox was. But he did. That knowledge made him turn slightly green. The acid in his stomach roiling.

Kory brushed off his man. "A strange name."

"Just one of several strange names."

"Boss ..."

"Not now, Razza." Kory pushed his man back a few feet with a hand to his chest, not wanting to be interrupted. "You entered the Frozen Waste on your own."

"I did," Mikel admitted.

"Not so clever for a fox. And you decided to challenge me and my men."

"Right again." Mikel shrugged. "Although I didn't challenge you so much as suggest that you might want to pursue a new line of work."

"Because if we don't you'll kill us all and free the dragon?"

"Something like that," Mikel confirmed. His tone became more menacing, matching his expression.

Kory barked out a laugh to hide his discomfort at the confidence the one called the Fox radiated. "You've got a lot of nerve."

"Or maybe it's cunning, like a fox."

Kory barked out another laugh, this one longer and louder, seeking to mask his jittery nerves. Something wasn't quite right with this fellow who had the courage to challenge twenty armed and very dangerous men. "You're quite amusing, I'll give you that."

"That's kind of you to say," Mikel replied, inclining his head slightly. He judged that he had earned his friends the few extra minutes they needed. It was time to move on to the main event. "Although I need to disagree with you about one key factor."

"What would that be?" Kory asked. Suddenly feeling as if the roles between them had been reversed. As if this Fox actually was the one in charge of this encounter.

"Not all of your assumptions were correct, and that's going to cost you."

"What do you mean?"

"I did enter the Frozen Waste alone. I did decide to challenge you and your men. But I didn't come *here* alone."

A handful of large shapes pulled free from the sides of the surrounding crevices. A few also jumped down from the heights above, landing with a soft crunch in the crusty snow.

All of them were difficult to see unless Kory kept his eyes locked on their movement and didn't let go.

He took a step back when he realized who had joined the confrontation, his nervousness swiftly becoming fear.

Giants of the Rime.

And they were carrying large scythes made of a shimmering blue steel that flashed with the brightness of the ice struck by the sun.

Death in their eyes.

~

"ARE you sure you want to do this?"

"No," Mikel replied very softly, hoping not to spook the target of his attention.

"Then why are you doing it?" Cadmus asked, his usually deep rumble now just the soft murmur of a brook.

"Someone has to. It's the right thing to do."

"And you always have to do the right thing?" Julia asked, already knowing the answer to her question. She stood next to her father, watching as Mikel took a few more tentative steps closer to the ice dragon.

Still muzzled. Still chained to the outside of the cage. And still dangerous, her front claws free to rip Mikel apart if she didn't like the look of him.

"Not always," Mikel replied very, very quietly. He stopped, slowly reaching out a hand as he studied the ice dragon. Her flinty blue eyes stared right back at him. She had made no move to attack him. Instead, she waited there patiently. Growling, though Mikel hoped less in warning and more as her way of telling him to speed up his efforts to free her. "But now, yes. Because you are all cowards."

"Cowards?" Cadmus grumped. He looked around the hollow, the score of bloody and broken corpses littering the white landscape now stained with red suggesting otherwise. "If anyone else but the Steelheart said that, he'd already be dead."

"I appreciate your forbearance," Mikel acknowledged, although he was scarcely paying attention to the Frost Lord. He took a few more slow steps closer to the ice dragon. The animal pushed herself up as best as she could from where she sat on her haunches during the clash, obviously interested in getting involved in the fight, but unable to do so because of her bonds. "But you're still a coward."

Mikel waited now, hand extended. He wasn't going any further. It was up to the ice dragon now.

"We're not cowards, Steelheart," Julia explained. "We're just not suicidal like you are. We take calculated risks. Not foolish ones."

"Fair enough," Mikel replied in an almost silent whisper, his eyes locked onto those of the ice dragon. Hoping that the animal read the truth in his eyes.

Lifting herself higher, the dragon's shoulders were even with his own. Then, slowly, hesitantly, her snout glided forward, nostrils catching his scent. She sniffed at his hand like a dog deciding whether he was a friend. In this instance, however, he was certain that she was simply deciding whether to kill him rather than allow him to help her.

"Easy girl," Mikel murmured ever so quietly. The dragon drawing ever closer, her snout was now only inches from his face as she continued to sniff.

Mikel stayed perfectly still. Not wanting to startle her. Understanding that his fate now rested in the claws of the animal.

"You are braver than I thought, Steelheart," Julia said, watching intently as Mikel stood toe to toe with the ice dragon. "Although foolishly so."

"I've been called worse than a fool," Mikel replied. He gave a start when the ice dragon pulled back with a snort, her examination complete.

He took a deep breath, struggling to quiet his racing heart, all the while never taking his eyes away from those of the ice dragon. When he detected a slight nod, he stepped up next to her.

Mikel started with the muzzle first. Then he worked his way down to the noose around her neck, releasing the dragon from the chain connecting her to the cage. Lastly, he released the ties around her hind legs.

The entire time, the ice dragon stared into his eyes. Not watching what he was doing. Rather it seemed to Mikel as if she was ... learning him. Seeing him for who he truly was.

A strange thought, but one that he couldn't escape.

With the dragon finally free, her breath cool on his face, instead of stepping back as any sane man would, Mikel stepped forward. Reaching out, he stroked the scales on her neck, enjoying the rough feel on his skin. Even scratching along her jaw and by her ear, his touch earning him a rumble of pleasure from the dragon.

"Thank you, Eisa," Mikel said a few seconds later when he stepped back, not wanting to push his luck. "The honor was mine."

Eisa.

Mikel didn't know why he named the ice dragon. And that of all names. In the language of the Caledonii, Eisa translated to fire. He could see that quality in the ice dragon. A contradiction in one sense. In another, an inner truth.

"Be free, Eisa. Know that I will think of you frequently."

Eisa stared intently at Mikel a few heartbeats more. Then with a nod and a loud shriek, she launched herself into the sky.

She was lost to sight after just a few flaps of her wings. Her scales, which allowed her to blend so well into the landscape of the Frozen Waste, did the same when she was in flight, in large part thanks to the glittery blue scales protecting her belly.

Mikel searched for her even when he could no longer see her.

Strange, he thought, as his eyes tracked from left to right.

She was invisible to him from where he stood, yet he believed that he knew exactly where she was in the sky.

"You named her?"

"I did," Mikel confirmed. He couldn't tell from Julia's expression whether the Giant was amused, worried, or both.

"Why?"

Mikel shrugged, not really having a good answer. "It just seemed like the right thing to do."

"And as we know, you do the right thing ... even when you shouldn't," Cadmus chuckled.

"One of my many failings," Mikel agreed with a sigh and a self-deprecating smile.

"Why did you help her?" Julia wondered out loud. "You put yourself at risk for a wild animal. One that could rip your head from your shoulders without a second thought."

"She needed help," Mikel replied, tiring of Julia asking the same questions. "I gave it."

Julia shook her head. "You just can't help yourself."

"What do you mean?"

"Your soft heart will be the death of you one day."

"Soft heart?" Mikel challenged. "I feel like I should be insulted with a charge like that."

"I'm just speaking the truth, Steelheart."

"Keep your opinion to yourself, Julia," Mikel requested, though his tone wasn't as hard as it could be. "If that gets out it could ruin my reputation in the Splintered Empire."

"The dragon didn't sense a soft heart," Cadmus clarified, his eyes holding the knowledge of a Giant who had ruled his kind for several hundred years. "The dragon, Eisa I believe you named her, recognized another lost soul."

Mikel didn't reply right away, staring at his friend and thinking about what Cadmus shared. He had little desire to pursue the path Cadmus had set before him. Knowing where it would take him ... and fearing it.

"Will she be all right on her own?" Mikel asked, seeking to change the subject.

"She won't be alone," Cadmus answered with a calm certainty. "She will find the other ice dragons living here in the Frozen Waste."

"Do I need to worry about more poachers making another play for her?"

"No, we will post another warning near the border," Julia said. In fact, the Giants already were preparing for that, beginning the grisly process of cutting heads from necks. "I doubt we will see any more poachers for quite some time. Have no fear of that."

Cadmus nodded, agreeing with his daughter, then he reached out with one massive hand, clasping Mikel's shoulder warmly. "Join me at my fire, Steelheart. You are here because we have some business to discuss, and there are several new and unanticipated matters that we must add to the list."

4

MAKING A PLAY

"You are missing out on an opportunity, my King. Think of what we could achieve if we were working together."

"You're simply looking to cut down on the import taxes you pay to bring your goods into Innsbruck." Charles Dengannon leaned against his throne. He sat on it only when required, finding the seat distinctly uncomfortable. Literally and metaphorically. "How does helping you help me, Lucius? How does a reduction in the taxes you pay help the citizens of the Crux?"

"It allows me to use the taxes saved to increase my holdings in several different trades here," the Lord of House Hanover replied while offering his best smile. He was young and handsome, wearing his long blonde hair in the latest fashion by allowing it to trail well beyond his shoulders. "Spices. Silks and other fine fabrics. Other luxury items. To succeed in business, my family must continue to diversify. And we must be able to compete."

"And again, Lucius, how does that help me?" Charles wasn't taken in by Hanover's play. In the parlance of the First Families, diversify usually meant an attempt to monopolize. Fewer competitors led to greater profits. Something that all the great Houses of the Splintered Empire sought in the never-ending struggle for wealth and power.

Lucius smiled even more broadly, realizing that his first attempt to convince the man standing atop the dais had fallen flat. His white teeth flashed in the lamplight that kept the throne room as bright as noon even at midnight, ensuring that no matter the hour a kaleidoscope of flashing colors played across the floor thanks to the stained glass that ran along both sides of the long chamber.

"I would not make such a request unless it benefited you, my King." Lucius found the effort to maintain his smile tiresome. The need to control his temper even more irksome.

His was one of the richest of all the First Families in the Splintered Empire, if not the richest. That was an argument in which only a select few of the Lords and Ladies residing on the Ninth Ring of the Crux could partake. An ongoing argument that had recently been replaced by another. How to remove the current King from his seat.

Lucius had no doubt that Dengannon understood what the Hanovers truly desired. Dengannon would understand as well that a little flexibility on both their parts could lead to a compromise that would be palatable ... at least for a time.

But the relic who sat on the throne was turning a deaf ear to Lucius' proposals, proving once again that Dengannon was more an obstacle than a help. And the Hanovers had but one tried and true method for dealing with such obstacles.

"Explain," the King ordered.

"What you lose in terms of the import taxes will be more than made up on the additional taxes you will receive as my businesses grow within the city." Lucius' smile somehow broadened further even as his blue eyes became smaller. Darker. He refused to come across as obsequious. Hanovers only negotiated from a position of strength. "And you will gain the good will of me and my family. A promising arrangement, don't you think? Especially with the many challenges that you face."

"For you, Lucius, yes, a promising arrangement." Charles pushed off his throne and unwrapped his crossed arms, not missing the veiled threat Hanover offered him. Because he was well aware from which quarter came many of the challenges he faced. "But there are a lot of ifs in what you propose and not a lot of guarantees."

"Meaning?"

"Meaning there are other merchants in Innsbruck who run similar businesses as yours. There is no guarantee that you could succeed with the entities you seek to unleash. Many of these merchants are well entrenched in the city. It would be quite difficult for you to compete with them regardless of the assistance you request."

"I believe that I can, Charles." Lucius' smile faded, replaced by a hard gaze that seemed incongruous with the young man's reputation for an easy-going nature and the supposed desire for fun rather than conflict.

"And I believe you want me to lower the import taxes so that you can undercut your competitors and corner those markets, essentially driving any other merchants in those spaces out of business. In fact, that's the only way you can compete in those markets. Is it not?" Charles didn't miss the change in Lucius. He understood that reputations could be created and crafted meticulously, not just earned, and then lost with a single decision whether that reputation was real or simply a construct.

"And there's a problem with that?" Lucius asked, not understanding why Charles was hesitating. Not understanding why he would so foolishly place himself in opposition to House Hanover when there was more than just money at stake.

Charles smiled thinly. "And is this the same arrangement you have with Malor Dragoran? Has he allowed you to corner the market there so that you can expand your holdings in the Kingdom of the Tor beyond Grassdorf?"

Lucius didn't reply right away, not certain what to say. His gaze, already tight, became razor fine. Shrewder. He realized that he wasn't in a position to deny the charge and that it would only weaken his position if he did so. So he chose not to answer the question at all. "I did not know that you were so well informed, Charles."

The King of the Crux studied Lucius for quite some time before replying. He allowed few to call him by his first name while he stood upon the dais. He could correct his frequently overreaching visitor, but what was the point? He would allow the familiarity, because that was a card he could play in the future.

Hanover was young. He was impetuous. He believed that because of his wealth he could do whatever he chose to do in this world. And he had yet to learn that money was only one form of power and often not the best one for certain situations.

Charles nodded knowingly, deciding to poke a bit and see what kind of response he earned. "And I take it that because you didn't answer my question Malor is proving to be difficult as well."

Lucius pursed his lips, frowning as he realized that he had underestimated Charles Dengannon. He promised himself that it wouldn't happen again.

"Malor is proving to be more difficult than I anticipated. That I won't deny. In fact, he is proving to be ... inflexible. His demands are ones that I prefer not to accept."

Charles nodded again, this time with a cunning smile. That was an understatement.

Malor Dragoran was power-hungry, ruthless, and certainly not a partner to take on without ensuring you protect your back from the knife that the man inevitably would try to bury there. Therefore, Charles could understand

Hanover's hesitation. But that's all he believed it was. Hesitation. If getting into bed with the King of the Tor was a necessary step to achieve whatever larger scheme he had in play, Hanover would. Kicking and screaming perhaps, but still he would.

"You tire of having to deal with Malor Dragoran, so you seek to improve your position in my Kingdom first. Thereby giving you what you perceive as leverage against the King of the Tor."

Lucius smiled, although at the same time his insides churned. He had believed that he could play the King of the Crux like a maestro played a violin. Apparently not. And that annoyed him greatly.

He was disappointed in himself. However, learning now that Dengannon was more skilled in the game they played would help him in the future. The King of the Crux's political astuteness confirmed the path Hanover would need to take to ensure his and his family's future.

"I was interested in obtaining your help, yes," Lucius admitted. "Just as I have been saying. Think of what we could accomplish if we work even more closely together than we are already."

Charles shook his head, snorting out a soft laugh. He really shouldn't have been surprised. Ever since Hanover declared his interest in his daughter, the young lord had been pushing for privileges that Charles was reluctant to give. Having no doubt exactly where those privileges would lead. And just how much they would truly cost.

He understood as well that Hanover was seeking these favors just as all the other First Families did. The competition between those serving on the King's Council intense ... and occasionally lethal.

Hanover just happened to have more chips to play than did his competitors. It was one of the unique results and requirements of maneuvering from a place of power and privilege within the Splintered Empire.

Two Kingdoms now straddled the land from the mountains bordering the Frozen Waste to the Silent Sea to the east where one emperor had once reigned, the Realm torn apart by civil war when Marcus Aurelian died and his two sons quickly followed him to the grave.

The unrest that followed devolved into a war between seven different generals. All with armies. All with wealthy backers. All greedy for the throne.

After more than ten years of conflict, a truce was reached when only two generals still breathed. Neither of them desiring to continue with the conflict that had devastated the former empire. Both satisfied with what they had taken for themselves.

To the northwest, the Kingdom of the Crux was centered around Innsbruck. To the southeast, Graz served as the capital of the Kingdom of the Tor.

There was no fixed border between the two Kingdoms, although Charles Dengannon believed that his domain running to the east ended in the exact center of the Splintered Bridge that spanned the Trench.

Malor Dragoran disagreed, believing that he was the one best positioned to assume the place of Marcus Aurelian. However, the King of the Tor did not have the resources to press his claim to the west. He was unable to cross the Splintered Bridge with his army and unwilling to brave the deadly perils of the Trench.

Yet though there was a clear split of the Splintered Empire politically and geographically, the First Families, almost all of them descendants of the generals who fought for the throne during the War of Chaos, had interests and holdings in both Kingdoms. Thus, they engaged in a constant negotiation to maintain their power in the face of two competing monarchs as well as the many schemes and strategies that were always in play as the Families vied for greater power and wealth, usually at the expense of the other First Families.

Thus, ruling either Kingdom required a deft touch. Maneuvering around or through various machinations to ensure that none of the First Families were ever in a position to make a play for the throne.

Of course in recent years, as his daughter reached her majority, that task became more difficult for Charles. Because his daughter had become another chip to be played. The most valuable of them all, in fact. Whoever hooked her guaranteed that they would join her on the throne of the Crux at some point in the future. And, if it was Hanover, the sooner the better in his opinion.

"I tire of Malor Dragoran just as you do, Lucius. He has no desire to work with me just as I have no desire to work with him. He has demonstrated many times over the years that he does not understand the concept of compromise. And even when he offers his word, he breaks it just as quickly."

"Quite right, Charles." Lucius nodded. "On that we agree."

"Then let's stop wasting time and go right to the heart of the matter. Why would I want to help you? You want my throne. Why would I make it easier for you to obtain it?"

Charles offered his statement as a simple fact, ensuring there was no hint of animus attached. Because he had no doubt that every First Family wanted his throne. That was the hard reality of governing in Innsbruck. The need to maintain a balance among always changing competing interests, much as if he were trying to keep his feet on a log spinning atop the water.

"I do," Lucius replied, not backing away from his desire and not apologizing for the admission either. "And I'll have it when the time is right. You know it just as well as I do. Of all the First Families, House Hanover stands above them all."

Charles' gaze narrowed, now understanding the real reason

Hanover had requested this audience. His desire to expand his family's business interests in the capital was only a part of it. He sought to expand his power in other ways as well. "Celindria."

"Celindria," Lucius confirmed. "There is no one who can offer her, and you, what I and my family can. Of all her suitors, she knows me best. She likes me, perhaps even loves me, our spending so much time together when we were growing up preparing us both for this moment. You know as well that she finds me the most desirable option."

"How could she not?"

Lucius missed the King of the Crux's sarcasm. Charles knew his daughter's mind.

She wasn't interested in Lucius, seeing him for exactly who he was. A man who would use anyone to gain what he desired, and then toss them away when they were no longer necessary.

"And where is the lovely Celindria? I have not seen her for several days. Out on another of her adventures?"

Charles wanted to say that Hanover's guess was as good as his. He didn't, however. He didn't want the preening lord to discover that Charles didn't really know where his daughter was. "She is with her uncle."

"The Splintered Bridge?"

Charles nodded. Lucius wouldn't doubt it since Malor once again had begun to exert pressure at the one place that connected the two Kingdoms. An increasingly frequent occurrence that required a great deal of the Battle Lord's attention.

"And other places," Charles replied cryptically. His only daughter and heir to the throne had an annoying and dangerous habit of skipping out of the Citadel without his knowledge on a much-too-frequent basis. A habit that he had never been able to break her of, every effort he engaged in to do just that making his daughter dig her heels in all the more. Disobeying him whenever she chose and slipping away from the soldiers tasked with guarding her with a confounding ease.

Celindria argued that her frequent excursions into Innsbruck and the surrounding countryside were necessary. To clear her head. So that she could learn what was really going on in the Kingdom of the Crux.

She might even be telling him the truth. And she could be right.

Nevertheless, Charles believed as well that she spent so much time out of the Citadel so that she wouldn't have to deal with Lucius Hanover and her flock of other suitors, all of them unfortunately though not unsurprisingly cut from the same cloth. If anyone was to claim his daughter it would have to be someone who ...

"She will be back soon?"

Hanover's question led the King off the path he had been following. "I'm sure she will be," Charles confirmed. And he was certain that when Celindria returned, she would have little interest in spending time with the young Hanover. They had been good friends while growing up. That was true. But something had happened between them that soured the relationship for Celindria. Something that she had never shared with him.

"You and I both know that I am the best match for your daughter, Charles."

"So you've been telling me for several months now, Lucius."

"With Malor causing problems again and the hint of unrest here in Innsbruck, perhaps it would be best to speed things along." Lucius shrugged, suggesting that he was willing to make the sacrifice required of him. In the best interest of the Crux, of course. "Best to surrender to the inevitable, don't you think? It will make life easier for everyone. We can then ensure that Innsbruck is quiet and peaceful, placing us in a much stronger position with respect to our friend to the east."

Charles didn't reply right away, not feeling the need to reveal that he knew the truth. The unrest spoken of was coming from factions within the city loyal to Hanover's family.

"I will take your suggestion into consideration, Lucius." There wasn't a hint of emotion in Charles' voice, though his eyes revealed quite clearly what he thought of Hanover's proposal. Did the upstart think him a fool? That he would actually invite the fox into the henhouse?

"That would be good of you, Charles. Just don't wait too long. You know how quickly events can change. Sometimes for the better. Sadly, often for the worst."

Charles refused to acknowledge Hanover's veiled threat even as his anger burst to life within him, his eyes flashing. "If we're done here, Lucius, I have other matters to attend to this afternoon."

Charles walked toward the door set in the wall behind the throne before a few soft words from Lucius foiled his escape. "Just one last matter. One of the reasons I sought concessions from you is because I am having a hard time negotiating with my competitors."

"Competition is critical to a well-running economy, Lucius," Charles offered in a neutral tone. "You should know that as a result of your political aspirations."

Lucius ignored the barb, refusing to be put off. "That may be, but it seems that my competition is being aided in a way that I had never anticipated and that I can only describe as unfair. It is why I came to ask for your help."

"Is that so?" Charles had no idea in what direction the conversation was about to go.

"It is," Lucius confirmed with a nod. "I was hoping that you could tell me what you know about the King of the Underworld. My agents have been unable to dig up anything useful. I'm told that he operates both here and in Graz. From all accounts, if my sources are to be believed, it seems that he exerts from the shadows the power of the last Emperor. And that power is hindering my plans to improve the fortunes of the Crux."

Charles' immediate thought was to suggest that perhaps Hanover should develop better sources, but he understood that insulting his most obvious competitor for the throne wouldn't prove helpful to his desire to end this conversation ... or to his daughter's future.

"A myth, Lucius. No more," Charles replied. "That's likely why your sources have been so unsuccessful."

"Really? From what I understand, he has quite a business empire. Taverns. Brothels. Pickpockets. Other criminal activity. Assorted other businesses. Most illegal, some not. So many interests, in fact, that he could rival you for the throne if he chose to."

"If this mythical King of the Underworld is as successful as you say, why would he bother? Taking my throne would only serve to increase his problems."

"A fair question, Charles," Lucius nodded, his eyes shifting. Becoming more discerning. More devious. A clear threat in the very back. "Are you protecting this King of the Underworld, Charles? Does he serve a purpose for you?"

"I do not make it a habit of protecting those engaged in criminal activities," Charles growled, offended by Lucius' claim. "Be careful, Hanover. If you'd like to spend a few nights in a cell so that you can better understand the real power I wield, I can make that happen. In fact, after your unfounded insinuation I'd very much enjoy making that happen."

Lucius smiled, just a brief quirk of his lips, before his sly expression returned, having learned all that he wanted to know from Charles' response. "No need. My apologies, Charles. Although I am still curious about this King of the Underworld."

"Why would you be? As I said, he's a myth. No more."

"Perhaps," Lucius admitted. "Then again, several of the stories I have heard are quite specific. And if you hear enough of these stories, you start hearing much the same thing."

"In all rumors there is a nugget of truth, Lucius. But in this matter, I have no doubt that the nugget is quite small indeed."

Lucius ignored Charles' attempt to shut down the conversation. "Did you know that many of these stories say that the King of the Underworld is a Caledonii?"

"Those stories say as well that he is a giant among men. That he can defeat ten soldiers in a single combat without breaking a sweat and using nothing more than a spoon. That he can make the waters of the Crux flow as he commands. I have heard those and many more stories, Lucius. Just as you have. And I give little credence to any of them. Nor should you. *What if* matters little when set against *what is*."

"A wise approach, Charles. Still, I must ask. What if this mythical King of the Underworld exists? And what if he really is Caledonii?"

"I prefer not to waste my time on rumors, Hanover. And as I just said, neither should you."

"I'd like to know your position, Charles," Lucius pressed. "If the King of the Underworld is real, and if he is Caledonii, as I understand it, Caledonii have no rights in Innsbruck or anywhere else within the Splintered Empire. They are outcasts, one and all, because of what they can do and what they have done."

Charles sighed then grunted softly with displeasure. "I can only assume that you are interested in seeking out this mythical King of the Underworld."

"The thought had crossed my mind."

Charles' frown deepened. He had no love for Caledonii, a people who were one of the original twelve tribes that settled in the Realms. But he had no desire to stir up a hornet's nest either, well aware of the unique skills Caledonii could employ that few others could.

That concern guiding his thinking, he adopted and employed a policy of coexistence. So long as any Caledonii in his Kingdom left his people alone and didn't bring any undue attention to themselves, he left them alone.

His tolerance driven by his sense of realism. His Kingdom was built upon commerce. Most merchants and traders would work with anyone who could put a steady stream of coins into their coffers, even if they were Caledonii.

Although it was unlikely that there were many in the Kingdom of the Crux to begin with. The Caledonii usually stayed in the Dragon's Spine, having no desire to deal with the persecution that was common in almost all of the other Realms.

Charles' frown deepened into a scowl, his cheeks coloring with the first specks of his building anger. "I would strongly recommend against seeking out Caledonii who might be living within Innsbruck with the goal of seizing their property."

"But they have no legal rights, Charles. I would be doing you a service since you have so many other matters that require your attention." Lucius offered Charles a cunning grin, choosing that moment to reveal that not all of his sources were useless. "Such as locating your itinerant daughter."

The spots on Charles' cheeks deepened, not missing what Hanover was telling him with respect to Celindria. "Perhaps the Caledonii don't, but they're not fools." He chose to ignore Hanover's latest veiled threat just as he did the previous ones. "Those Caledonii in the Kingdom of the Crux with business interests have protected those interests through legal means ... and through other means as well. Best not to shake the beehive if you can't kill the queen. And with respect to the Caledonii, you can't kill the queen."

"I'll keep that in mind, Charles. Thank you for the warning. Although be aware that when I rule here -- and I will when your daughter and I are married, it's just a question of when -- my policies will differ from yours in some respects. I will not tolerate those who do not deserve to be tolerated."

With that, Lucius offered the King of the Crux the barest nod of respect before turning on his heel and marching out of the throne room.

Charles watched him go. The young man truly was a treacherous jackass. Unfortunately, he was a very powerful and politically astute jackass.

In consequence, he couldn't ignore what he had learned from Lucius Hanover. The man who wanted his daughter's hand so that he could take the throne for himself.

Charles was concerned about the questions Hanover had asked and the implications of each one. But there was one question playing through his mind that dominated his thoughts. A question with no good answers.

What could he do to protect his daughter from Hanover that wouldn't put his family's hold on the throne under threat?

5

A NEW COURSE

"I didn't think you'd waste your time on a visit."

Mikel smiled. "Before I finalize a deal, I like to look my prospective partners in the eye."

"Prospective?" Agger frowned. He was a tall man. Thin. Thanks to his facial features and his long, wispy mustache, he resembled a rat walking on two spindly legs. "We did the deal weeks ago. Goran signed off. I bring my cargo into Innsbruck through your smuggling routes and distribute from here. That was the deal. I require nothing else from you."

"And as you saw, my smuggling routes are of the highest quality," Mikel replied. "However, you have not yet convinced me that you are a high-quality business partner." His eyes sharpened. His tone more demanding. "And I only do business with partners of the highest quality."

Agger's frown deepened into a grimace. "I don't understand. We have a deal. I pay you for a service. Beyond that service ... there's nothing for us to discuss. I run my business as I see fit."

"We do have a deal, Agger." Mikel nodded toward Teodor. The giant of a man stood a few feet to Mikel's right, holding up the signed contract. "But it's a provisional deal, just as the contract Goran signed says. I have the right to end our relation-ship at any time if you don't meet my required standards of business."

"Required standards of business? I thought that was all a bunch of gobbledygook, so I didn't pay much attention to it."

"Gobbledygook to you, maybe. For me, that's the most important language in all of my contracts. Like I said, I only want to do business with people who are willing and able to meet my standards. I have a reputation to protect, because without my reputation I don't have a business." Mikel's voice turned as cold as the wind that blasted across the Frozen Waste. "I'm sure you understand."

Agger's grimace deepened into a scowl, his face seeming to drop several inches from the effort. Then he nodded reluc-tantly, understanding the limitations of his position. "As you can see, all is in order. All is going as it should. You get my goods here and I pay you. There's nothing else for you to worry about beyond that."

Agger waved his hand at all the activity at his back. Crates were being opened, products being placed in smaller canvas satchels. Those satchels getting stacked to the side to be checked before distribution began.

Mikel spun around slowly, taking it all in. "That remains to be seen."

When Mikel agreed to this arrangement, the contract he signed had been with Goran. A merchant with an impeccable reputation who offered merchandise that was in demand and of the highest caliber, already having buyers lined up throughout Innsbruck.

However, since that deal was put in place, Goran had passed away under mysterious circumstances. Agger, his brother-in-law, stepped into the void. And from what he saw now, Agger had made some changes to the business model that bothered Mikel a great deal.

He also had heard some rumors about Agger and his business methods that had pushed Mikel and Teddy to dig deeper. That's why they had decided to conduct the inspection themselves rather than having one of Mikel's associates take care of it.

In addition to giving Goran access to his smuggling operation, Mikel had leased him a new warehouse deep beneath Innsbruck. The capital of the Kingdom of the Crux sat atop a massive dormant volcano that extended three miles from end to end and rose right where four powerful rivers – the cleverly named Western, Eastern, Southern, and Northern – met.

The Crux from which the Kingdom had earned its name.

Because of the limited space on the island, construction was up rather than out. As the population increased within the capital, so did the levels, the city building higher and higher upon itself.

Where you lived was determined by your wealth and your power. King Dengannon resided in the Citadel, which looked down upon all else. The First Families resided right below the Royal Ring. And so it went until you were at river's edge. Nine Rings in all.

Of course, where you lived in Innsbruck not only denoted your success, but it also could determine your likelihood of survival. Quite literally, in fact.

Because at certain times of the year and with the stronger storms, the four rivers crested their banks, flooding the city. The highest a flood had ever reached was the Third Ring where some of the less prominent merchants and tradespeople lived. More than ten thousand had died during that disaster, all of them living in the First and Second Rings.

Because of the very rough water that resulted from four major waterways coming together in the same place, the only relatively safe option for getting across from the shore involved the gondolas that rivaled the dragons of old in size. Those were linked to their docks on both sides of the confluence by massive chains and hooks, pulled across so as not to be placed at the mercy of the maelstrom. The smaller gondolas, owned by the rich and powerful, were airborne and not dependent on the often unpredictable whims of the tempestuous rivers.

Owing to the obvious restrictions of the environment, most would assume that smuggling items in and out of the city would prove to be a difficult task.

And it was.

Except for Mikel.

Because in addition to knowing every inch of Innsbruck built atop the now sleeping volcano, he knew every inch of the small city located beneath the surface. A city that he had helped to construct. Half as many people lived beneath Innsbruck as lived above, a web of tunnels, bridges, and rope ladders connecting homes and businesses that were carved out of the caverns that pockmarked the massive crag.

And, perhaps most important, anticipating the floods to come, Mikel had constructed aqueducts, drains, gates, and other mechanisms proposed by some of the finest engineers in the Kingdom of the Crux and beyond that worked together to drain excess water quickly. As a result of his efforts, in the last flood, just two months' past, though the height of the rivers reached the Second Ring of the City Above, the City Below faced nary a challenge from the inundation. Life continued as usual for those forced to make a life for themselves below.

"What say you?" Agger asked, at the same time nodding to no one in particular. Several rather large men, although none who compared in height and breadth to Teodor, emerged out of the shadows to stand close to their employer and give his words some added weight. "Shall we continue doing business together? I have the goods as you can see. You have the smuggling routes. We should both net a tidy profit. And isn't that all that matters? Profit?"

Mikel didn't respond, continuing to take in everything that was going on in the warehouse. Agger was correct. The spices and fabrics from the east that Agger was bringing into the city would fetch a good sum. And he had put his operation in place in only a few days, which said something for his efficiency. Nevertheless, Mikel didn't like all that he saw.

The workers his primary concern.

When Mikel met with Goran, all of his workers were experienced. All of them were older. All of them were family.

Agger had changed that aspect of the business model as soon as he assumed control.

He caught the eye of a young girl. He guessed that she was fourteen. Maybe fifteen.

The bruises on her wrists and arms suggested that she had been abused recently. Beaten. Perhaps tied up or chained during the night. Forced to work by the many toughs standing around the warehouse and doing nothing more than picking their noses.

Mikel's gaze tightened when a tingle sparked across his skin much like goosebumps. A familiar feeling. Though one he experienced rarely on the Crux.

He studied the girl more closely. She was frightened. Of the men around her. Even more so that he might reveal her secret.

He smiled, trying to reassure her. Then he gave her a nod and a wink.

He understood now. The men standing around the warehouse didn't do the work. They made sure the children did the work. Whips on their belts helped to communicate their expectations.

Why would the girl who continued to stare at him still be here? She didn't have to be.

Then he understood.

No more than a few seconds passed, and in just that brief amount of time, three of the guards approached one of the children, displeased by something the boy failed to do or perhaps wasn't doing quickly enough.

As soon as the guards moved in the boy's direction, the girl pulled her eyes from Mikel's, fixing her gaze on each tough. What would likely have been a beating became nothing more than a verbal warning.

Impressive.

The girl demonstrated a unique and powerful skill. Crudely applied yet quite effective. He could only imagine what she would be able to do with the proper training.

"This isn't right, Teddy," Mikel murmured just under his breath.

"Mikel, I understand you're angry. So am I. But now?" Teodor shifted his gaze around the warehouse. At the same time, he placed his ledger in the knapsack strapped across his chest and then his hands went to his belt, the cudgels strapped to the back within easy reach. "They have a distinct advantage in numbers."

"We've faced worse odds," Mikel replied. His eyes were locked onto those of the girl's for a heartbeat more. Then he nodded again, hoping that she understood what he had in mind.

"Yes, but here we'd be relying more on luck. You know how I feel about that."

Mikel snorted softly. "That I do. You prefer calculations and percentages that tell you exactly how something is going to play out."

"I do indeed. And for good reason."

"But as I keep telling you ..."

"I know, I know," Teodor grumbled in his very deep voice. "Numbers and facts can take you only so far. You need to go with your instincts as well."

"Exactly, my friend. And though the odds are poor, I have a wildcard."

"What would that be?"

Mikel's grin broadened. "I have the best bareknuckle boxer at my side and a little surprise for Agger and his men if there proves to be a need."

"That may be," Teddy began. "But you know how ..."

"You're the Giant, Teddy," Mikel cut in, the flintiness of his tone suggesting that the discussion was over. "You have a reputation to uphold. Just like I do."

"Yes, we do. All I'm saying is that we're outnumbered ten to one. We can come back with a few crews and finish this the right way."

"We could," Mikel agreed.

"But you don't want to."

"You know I have little patience for what Agger and his boys are doing. And if it's just the two of us ..."

"It makes even more of a statement," Teddy sighed, understanding that Mikel already had decided on their course of action.

Teddy couldn't say that he disagreed with it, but he couldn't say that he liked it either.

He had worked with Mikel for quite a long time, often serving as his friend's conscience and counselor when required. Just as always, he had felt the need to be the voice of reason.

Sometimes Mikel listened. Sometimes he didn't.

And now that Teddy had fulfilled that task, though it had proven to be a fruitless effort he could focus on what he and Mikel needed to do. "Let's get to it. Children shouldn't be treated in this way."

"My thoughts exactly, my friend." Mikel turned toward Agger. "Our business partnership is null and void. You don't meet the required standards."

"I'm sorry, what did you say?" The rat-faced fellow turned away from his men. Confused as to why they didn't give the boy who had dirtied several folds of silk a few smacks to remind him that such laziness wouldn't be tolerated.

"Our partnership is null and void. I don't allow child labor."

Agger's eyes widened in shock, then his face slowly turned red. "We had a deal! When Goran died that deal remained intact. His arrangement transferred to me."

"It did, you're right," Mikel agreed amiably, although there wasn't a hint of humor or good will in his dark eyes. "However, if you read the agreement before you killed your brother-in-law, you would know that I have the right to cancel our contract at any time. You and your men will leave the warehouse and then Innsbruck. The children will stay here with me. Am I being clear? You have ten minutes to gather any personal items and get off the Crux. I don't want to see you tarnishing my city again."

"Ten minutes? That's not enough time to take a proper crap!"

Mikel didn't reply right away, slightly disturbed by the image Agger gave him. "Ten minutes for you and your men to leave the city? That won't be a problem. I'll actually assist you in that regard. And, again based on the contract, your goods are forfeit for your breach as are your workers. You can check the language with the Giant if you like."

Agger stared at the man who stood several heads taller than any of his toughs. The bookkeeper's expression hinted that he would much rather wrap his hands around Agger's neck than pull out the contract from the satchel across his chest. Not wanting to take the risk, Agger decided to stay right where he was.

"My goods? My workers?" Agger couldn't quite believe what he was hearing. "What in bloody hell are you talking about?"

"The contract, Agger. If you have any questions, you can speak to the Giant." Mikel nodded toward Teddy, his friend's countenance darkening swiftly, his eyes sparking with menace.

Teddy didn't like to fight. But when he was in the proper frame of mind, as he was now, he was a sight to behold. "He has all the paperwork."

"By what right do you claim my goods and my workers?" Agger's shriek led to a deep silence in the warehouse. Every eye, guard and child, turned toward the simmering confrontation.

"I might conduct much of my business outside the boundaries of the law," Mikel explained, "but I do uphold certain standards that I will not allow to be broken. Forced labor, particularly of children, violates those standards."

"Standards? What in blazes are you talking about? Business is business. All that matters is the profit. And I remind you that you'll be earning a good sum by working with me. More than you would have earned if Goran was still alive."

"Killing your brother-in-law to seize the business? That doesn't bother me. But forcing children to work for you to cut down on your costs? That I won't permit." Mikel stepped forward then. Only a few feet away from Agger now, his right hand drifted down toward the mace strapped to his belt. "Ever. Children deserve better than that."

Agger didn't know how to reply at first. He hadn't really read the contract. Just skimmed it, his brother-in-law the one who had made the deal. But that was of little concern to him now.

His primary worry was losing his stock and his workers. That would put him out of business for good. Then he snorted. Finally understanding. So this was the way of it.

"You want to take my business. That's why you're doing this." Agger nodded sagely. "I won't allow it."

"I'm doing this because I hate people who take advantage of children." Mikel's voice was colder than the blustery wind that originated in the Frozen Waste and often swept down from the mountains and across the Crux. "That's why I won't allow it. I'm taking your goods so that I can use the revenue earned to feed, clothe, and educate these children now that they're free from you."

Agger was too stunned to talk, which was a bit of a shock to him and his men, because he never lacked for words. "You're going to do what?"

"We're done here, Agger. Leave. Now. You and your men. Ten minutes. Go back the way you came. I'll make sure you get off the Crux."

"You want me to leave my livelihood here for you to ..." Agger still couldn't quite comprehend what was happening. It all seemed implausible. And this bastard thought that he was going to just roll over like a dog desperate for a belly rub?

Agger's expression turned shrewd. "You and your accountant believe that you can handle me and my men? Just the two of you?"

Mikel offered Agger a smile filled with a palpable menace. "If you decide that a fight is necessary, then yes, I have no doubt that the Giant and I can manage you and your men."

He stepped in even closer to Agger so that they were no more than a hand apart now. "Choose wisely. Because my offer of free passage lasts for just one minute more."

Agger's shrewd gaze became predatory. "What do you think would happen if I dethroned the King of the Underworld? Do I become the new King?"

"You'll never find out, Agger. Leave now or you die."

Agger glared at Mikel. His fury palpable. He tried to hide it by nodding and taking a step back. "Keep the goods. Keep the kids. We're done here."

Agger turned away from Mikel, motioning toward his men. "Let's go boys."

Mikel didn't move. Knowing what was coming next. He had glimpsed the decision in the back of Agger's eyes.

When Agger twisted back toward him and lunged with the dagger he pulled from his sleeve, Mikel was ready.

Agger's eyes widened in shock and then pain when he missed with his lunge, Mikel allowing the man to slide by him. Although not without smacking him on the back of his head with his mace, crushing Agger's skull with a single blow.

Their boss' quick death froze eight of the ten men who had been advancing toward Mikel. The two foolish enough to attack after such a display never saw what hit them.

Teddy struck blindingly fast with each of his cudgels. The pair of toughs joined Agger on the warehouse floor, their misshapen skulls leaking blood, brain, and pieces of bone.

The men slow to act took a few steps backward when Teddy strode forward, a bloody cudgel in each hand.

"The rat's dead, boys," Teddy said in a lethally quiet voice, "and two of your overeager mates as well. The offer of safe passage off the Crux still stands. Choose now and choose wisely."

Several of the guards shifted uncomfortably, after what they had just witnessed not certain that attacking the King of the Underworld and his accountant was the best course to take. Although they were certain that with Agger's death they wouldn't be getting paid.

"Thank you," one of the men said. Seeking to take advantage of the offer while it still stood, he turned away and trotted quickly for the warehouse's main doors. As soon as he started moving, his compatriots followed, clearly believing that a fight wasn't worth it when there was no reward on the other end.

"Free passage, Teddy?" Mikel growled, not happy with the arrangement his friend had made. "They hurt children. They don't deserve their freedom."

"They don't, you're right. But I don't want to do anything that will put any of these little ones at risk." He feared that if a broader combat broke out, a few might get caught in the middle.

Mikel breathed deeply, letting some of his anger go. Teddy

was right. There were eighteen all told. Taking care of them wouldn't be a problem. But putting them in the middle of a larger fight wasn't a good idea. "Fair enough. I assume you have something in mind."

With all of the men out of the warehouse, the children staring at Mikel and Teddy and not knowing what to make of them or what had just happened, Teddy strapped his cudgels back to his belt after wiping the blood on the shirt of one of the toughs lying at his feet. "I do. We'll take the kids to Leona. She can get them squared away for a few nights before we put together more permanent arrangements."

Mikel nodded his approval. "And Agger's men?"

"You promised them safe passage off the Crux. They'll have it."

"And after that?"

"They enslave children. Once they're off the Crux, they're fair game."

Mikel patted Teddy on the shoulder. "Good man. Whatever crews you set to the task, double their hazard pay. Once they're done, I want an example made to ensure that everyone in the City Below understands that children are off limits. Yes?"

Teddy nodded, not put off by the anticipated violence. Actually looking forward to it. "I have just the crews in mind."

"Excellent. Thank you, Teddy."

"My pleasure."

"What else is on your mind?" Mikel asked. "I can see the wheels turning."

"Nothing, it's just that even after all this time together, you surprise me."

"How so?"

"We met because you're a thief. A smuggler." Teddy shrugged. "Yet you feel this innate need to do what's right. Always. Without fail."

"I don't always do what's right, Teddy. You know that better than anyone."

"True," his friend admitted. "But that doesn't stop you from trying."

Mikel frowned, not having the desire or the energy to engage in a conversation like this one just now since there were other matters he still needed to deal with. Besides, he tried to avoid introspection if he could. He wanted to keep certain memories buried. "Like you said, Teddy, I'm a thief and a smuggler. What I do, I do because it's good for business."

"Just because you say it, Mikel, doesn't make it so."

"Actually, it does, Teddy. What the King of the Underworld says, so will it be." Mikel was impressed with himself. He was actually able to speak the words without breaking out into a laugh.

"Spare me," Teddy snorted. "How we've been friends for this long I don't really understand."

Mikel grinned. "We have the same weakness, Teddy."

"What would that be?"

"We have this incessant need to do what's right even when it costs us."

"WHAT'S YOUR NAME?" Mikel walked up to the girl who had caught his attention. Teddy was already herding the younger children together and preparing to take them to Leona.

She didn't reply at first. Instead, she examined Mikel with a look that suggested that she was savvy well beyond her years. "Did you have to kill him?"

Her question surprised him. "Did my killing Agger bother you?"

"No," she replied. "He was why I was here along with the other children."

"How did he acquire you?"

"Runaways some," the girl shrugged, "and a few were sold by their families to make ends meet."

Mikel sighed heavily. Hearing that last angered him immensely. Thanks to their commercial success and centuries of making their fortunes off the backs of those less fortunate than them, the King and the First Families as well as the upper crust of society in the Kingdom of the Crux had access to an almost unimaginable wealth. Yet they offered little in the way of charity, seeking to maintain their riches and the influence that went along with it while demonstrating little concern for those in need.

"I'll take care of them," Mikel promised, "and make sure they get what I promised. Food, a place to stay, an education. Opportunities that they wouldn't have gotten otherwise if they can't or don't want to go back to their families."

"So did you have to kill him?" she asked again, refusing to be put off.

Mikel once again took the time to study the girl. Young woman, he corrected. Likely closer to fifteen than fourteen. Maybe even sixteen. She had the look of someone who had seen more of the world in her few years than she should have. And not by choice.

"I did have to kill him. He came at me with a blade. When that happens, best not to take any chances. Best to finish it quickly."

"Did you enjoy killing him?"

"No," Mikel replied without any hesitation. "I don't enjoy killing. Even someone like Agger who deserved it. Unfortunately, it's necessary from time to time."

"Agreed," the girl said.

"And your family? Would you like me to take you back to them?"

"No," she replied immediately.

Mikel nodded. "Gone or ..."

"Both," she replied.

For the first time he saw a crack in her composure. Tiny to be sure, but still there. Revealing that although she had been forced into adulthood sooner than she deserved, she was still a young girl in many respects cursed to see the darker parts of the world that the children living in the top Rings of Innsbruck never had to even think about. In that way, he could certainly relate to her.

"What's your name, little miss?"

She didn't say anything. Instead, she stared at him even harder.

She didn't trust him. He understood. She had little cause to do so. "Well, if you don't want to tell me, that's fine. But I'll need to call you something. So how about ... Peanut."

"Why Peanut?" she asked, her frown confirming her displeasure at the appellation he selected.

Mikel shrugged. "When I was your age there was a girl I knew who was called Peanut. She was nice. She was a friend."

"Did she like peanuts?"

"Hated them," Mikel replied with a broad smile and a wink.

The girl nodded at that, considering. "You're a strange man."

Mikel nodded. "Yes, I probably am."

She smiled. The first time she had. Mikel hoped that she would smile more in the days to come. It would help her break free from what he was certain were some very bad nightmares.

"You're not going to sell us?"

Mikel shook his head, trying to put her at ease. Clearly, she didn't believe what he told Agger. And why should she? There was no trust between them. Not yet. "Sell you? I buy and sell goods. I don't buy or sell people. And if I find people who do ..."

"You kill them." She seemed pleased by that. The black and white of it all.

"I do."

"And the men working for Agger? They did this to me and many of the others." She held up her wrists, her sleeves falling down and revealing several more nasty bruises.

Mikel's eyes flashed. His anger plain. "They enslaved children." He didn't think that anything else needed to be said.

The girl nodded. Obviously in agreement. Obviously unconcerned by the upcoming bloodletting. "What's your name?"

"Mikel," he replied.

"Not the King of the Underworld?"

"Just Mikel." He chuckled. "Not the King of the Underworld. That's just one of many titles I've picked up over the years."

She nodded. "I'm Natalya." Her eyes hardened.

Mikel tried not to smile too broadly. She certainly had fire. He liked that about her. "Natalya, a pleasure to meet you."

"Nat."

"I'm sorry?"

"Nat," she repeated. "I prefer Nat when speaking with my friends."

Mikel offered her a slight bow of his head, acknowledging the trust that she was placing in him. "Nat. It's a pleasure."

"Ready to go?" Teddy said.

The other children followed behind him, each one with a small treat in hand if they weren't already chewing on the candy. The Giant had a sweet tooth. Usually, he didn't share his food. When it came to children, however, he revealed a soft spot.

"Yes, but first allow me to introduce you to Natalya."

"Nat," the girl corrected.

Teddy leaned down, smothering her small hand with his large paw. "A pleasure to make your acquaintance, Nat. My name is Teddy."

"Not Giant?"

Teddy laughed heartily at that. "Not when I'm with friends."

Nat smiled again, beginning to feel more comfortable. "Teddy doesn't seem like the right name for you."

"Why do you say that?"

"Someone as big as you should have a scarier name."

Teddy appeared to think about that for a time. "Perhaps you're right. Maybe you could give that some thought. Offer a few options."

"I'll think about it. You really do need a different name. Teddy is a name for a scholar or schoolteacher."

"Yes, I'll give you that. But there's something I can do that most scholars and schoolteachers can't."

"What's that?"

"Crush your skull with my hand like a melon." He reached out a big paw and placed it gently atop her head, earning a laugh from Nat.

"Actually Teddy is a former scholar and teacher," Mikel explained, smiling. Pleased that the very serious young lady was laughing. "He's trained in mathematics and accounting."

"Yes, you don't want to cheat Mikel," Teddy said. "If you do, you'll have to deal with me."

"I'll keep that in mind."

"Nat, what would you like me to do for you?" Mikel asked.

"What do you mean?"

"You're older than the other children here by several years. I know what you've been doing for them. That you could have gotten away if you wanted to."

"I hoped that you hadn't noticed." A bolt of fear flashed across her face.

Mikel nodded. Understanding her concern. Seeking to put her at ease. "I did. At your age, what you need is different from what the other children need."

"In terms of ..."

"Finding a new home. A school. Someone who might be able to help you with your unique ability."

"You're trying to get rid of me already?" she asked, unable to keep the hint of fear from her voice.

"No," he said quickly, not wanting to upset her. "I just want you to understand that you can do what you want. If you don't know what you want, that's fine. We can talk about it and decide when you're ready. I know several families in the city who can give you a good home as you start thinking about what you might want to do next."

She thought about what Mikel was offering, although not for long. "The only thing I want right now is to stay with you."

"You want to stay with me?" Mikel failed to keep his surprise from his voice.

"Yes," she replied with an unerring confidence. "You can use someone like me to help keep an eye on you."

Mikel didn't respond, instead turning toward Teddy. His friend shrugged, the glimmer in his eye revealing his amusement.

"She's right, you know," Teddy rumbled. "You do need looking after."

6

DRUDE INTRODUCTION

"Will you do it?"

Charles Dengannon stood on the balcony of his private apartment atop the Citadel. He enjoyed an excellent view of the Crux and the four rivers surrounding the island. Or he would have, if not for the darkness and the fog that had drifted in and limited visibility to less than a hundred feet.

Still, he could hear the roar created by the powerful torrents coming together. Churning. Swirling. Competing. The rush of the water over the rocks hidden just beneath the surface added to the cacophony.

"Why me?" A tall shadow with a soft voice stood next to the King of the Crux. Hooded. Protected from any watching eyes. Though he doubted that there were any to worry about. He had made sure. And he knew how to move around the Citadel without being discovered just as he did the city, both above and below. "There must be others in a better position to aid you."

"There are others," Charles agreed.

"But you don't trust them."

"I don't really trust you either," Charles admitted. "However, based on our previous engagements, I have no cause not to trust you. The others ... I have cause not to trust."

The shadow remained quiet for a time. Thinking. Considering the risk the King was asking him to take. "I'm expendable."

Dengannon didn't back away from that truth. "You are." Charles turned toward the shadow, giving him a smile and a nod. "But you knew that before you agreed to meet with me."

A soft laugh drifted out from beneath the shadow's cowl. "You ask a great deal, King Dengannon. If I agree to your request, I put more than just myself at risk. I have responsibilities that I must meet. People who depend on me."

"I do ask much from you, you're right. But I have no choice. I wouldn't ask if I didn't believe it was necessary. For all of us."

A long silence followed, the weight of the King's words adding to the heaviness of the fog.

The shadow turned to go. "I will see what I can do. But I can make no promises."

"As you consider my request, please keep in mind one key variable," the King requested.

The shadow stopped, sighing. Fully expecting that this would come. "What would that be?"

"This isn't just business as we normally discuss. There is more to this than that. This is my daughter. This is the future of the Kingdom of the Crux."

"I understand, King Dengannon. I will keep that in mind. No promises, however. Not yet."

"That's all I can ask. Thank you."

There was no reply, the shadow already gone from the balcony.

The King was certain that his visitor would have little trouble exiting the Citadel, his guards unaware that he had ever been there.

He was certain as well that his visitor would do as he asked.

Their partnership was not based on friendship. It was based on need. And they both still needed something from the other.

Charles sighed. He wished that it hadn't come to this. Yet it had.

He had no other options to speak of. Not after his last conversation with his daughter. She had left only a few hours before. Angry. Furious, actually. Disappointed. Resigned. Feeling trapped.

He understood. But they both had roles to play. A result of the privilege they enjoyed and the power they exercised.

He didn't like exerting such pressure on her.

Especially not after his meeting with Lucius Hanover earlier in the day.

The pompous jackass was much too full of himself. Much too sure of his own success.

Even so, the jackass was right. Lucius was powerful. He had resources that few of the other First Families could put to use. Resources that even Charles couldn't call upon.

Worse, the popinjay had little in the way of morals, which meant that he would do whatever was required to get what he wanted. No matter the consequences. Because Lucius didn't believe that consequences applied to him.

And Charles knew what Lucius Hanover wanted. What he craved.

Staring out into the darkness, listening to the crash of the water against the island, he hoped that the strategy he had just put in play would offer the protection that his daughter required.

He didn't like the deal he just made. But what he liked didn't matter. What mattered was what he and his daughter needed. What the Kingdom needed.

Although he hadn't told the shadow everything, what he did share was the truth.

Now, he could only hope that the shadow and sometime partner would do as he asked.

Because his daughter's life depended on it, as did the future of the Kingdom.

Charles spun away from the railing. A sound incongruous with the roar of the four rivers pulling him away from his thoughts.

His hand went to his side, blood trickling through his fingers.

He continued to move, sliding along the banister. Ignoring the pain that set his gut on fire.

He ducked, hearing a screech that sounded like steel sliding across steel, the sparks appearing on the rail confirming it. In the same motion, he rolled to his left then stumbled back into the light of his suite, the sizzling wound along his ribs slowing him down.

He felt the wetness that drenched his shirt, his blood dripping down his leg. The pain that accompanied his wound a fiery char. It felt as if his skin was burning and flaking away.

He was about to yell for the guards stationed just beyond his doors. He kept quiet instead. Not wanting to waste his breath.

A large pool of blood was expanding beneath the door, covering the tile of the entryway.

A flash of black appeared at the corner of his vision. Before he could turn, another sharp pain flared, this time along his other side.

Charles pulled a dagger from the sheath on his hip, slashing to his front. His effort gained him some additional space and the few seconds he needed to retreat, putting a couch between him and his attacker.

His eyes bulged when he recognized what stood before him. He couldn't quite believe what he was seeing.

A mist hovered just above the thick carpet, and it had an unsettlingly distinct shape.

A woman.

Beautiful in her features.

Deadly in her intent.

A woman there but not really there.

Both substance and mist.

He had heard of these malevolent spirits, yet he had never thought Druden were real. Believing that they were no more than a tall tale meant to scare children when it was time for bed.

Clearly, they were much more than just that.

He searched his memory, seeking some way to not only defend himself, but also to destroy the creature that hovered before him.

What little he recalled offered him nothing of value.

Druden were creatures released from the Spirit World and chained with the Curse. Forced to perform whatever acts their master required, they took the shape of their master while under their control.

Knowing that, the hard truth struck him like a punch to the jaw. The only way to destroy the Drude was to kill the woman he thought long dead. The woman who controlled this Drude. The woman who was a Dark Magus.

Because only then could he break the woman's hold on the spirit ripped from its realm.

A wispy arm shot out, a claw forming in the place of the woman's hand in a heartbeat.

He knocked it away with his dagger, although his strike had little impact, doing nothing more than pushing the claw past him rather than into his gut.

The Drude drifting just on the other side of the couch smiled then. Amused. Less than impressed. Growing impatient as well.

Charles growled in dismay. The Dark Magus could be anywhere in the city. With his guards dead, he stood little chance against this creature.

That being said, he refused to give in. He would fight until he couldn't fight anymore.

Rather than waiting for the Drude's next attack, Charles advanced as best as he could. Ignoring the pain that wracked his body, he placed one foot on the seat of the couch then jumped and lunged for the Drude with his dagger.

A searing agony erupted from his chest.

An agony so intense that it blinded him for several seconds.

When he came back to himself and could see once again, the film of black clearing from his eyes, he looked down.

He tried to gasp, but he couldn't. Unable to draw any air into his lungs.

He was eye to eye with the Drude. His feet not touching the ground. Suspended by the creature's bloody claws, which punched through his chest and out his back.

"Always so brave," the Drude hissed.

The voice sent a shiver through Charles even as he hung there. He knew that voice.

"But still the fool," the Drude continued. "You should have accepted the terms I offered you, Charles. You would have gained so much more than you ever possibly could have imagined."

"And lost more … than … I … was … willing … to … give." He was barely able to speak the words, the pain becoming unbearable, the lack of air making him gasp.

The Drude snorted. "Your archaic principles have only led to your own death. You can't stop me now. I will take her."

"You … will … not … have … her."

Having taken his last breath, the light leaving his eyes, Charles realized that his only hope now rested with an outcast.

A man who preferred to work where the light rarely shined.

A shadow.

7

JUST CAN'T HELP HIMSELF

"I can't believe he would make such a demand," Drin growled.

She was talking to herself again. She didn't care. She would talk to herself as much as she wanted to whenever she wanted to.

She needed some way to release the tension building up within her after her latest conversation with her father. Deciding to slip out of the Citadel and wander the city usually was the best way to do that. Yet she was still struggling with his nudges that sounded more like ultimatums.

Her father kept pushing her. Despite her request that he give her time to think.

She understood the necessity of what they were discussing. Still, that didn't make it any more palatable even though she couldn't deny that the pressure that she was feeling likely was nothing compared to what he was experiencing.

What her father suggested was a way to solidify their position for the next generation, which was becoming more tenuous by the day thanks to the Hanovers and some of the other First Families who sensed an opportunity. A crack they were anxious to exploit.

"There has to be another way," Drin whispered. "I just need to find it." What her father proposed to her held little appeal. Yet what choice did he have? He needed to think not just about her but also about their position on the Crux.

Growling again, she kept her head down and the hood of her cloak up as she prowled the streets. She doubted that she had much to worry about. With the heavy fog, it would be difficult to recognize her from more than a few feet away. Still, a hard habit to break.

Her father had been more insistent this time. Almost demanding. That meant the balance had shifted. That something had happened.

But what?

She had asked during their argument. He refused to say, however. He just kept repeating in different ways that with privilege and power came responsibility and with that the need to make decisions neither of them wanted to make.

From her perspective not very helpful. As she was learning, however, right on the mark unfortunately.

Because her father refused to tell her all that was going on, she decided to do a little digging on her own. Another reason she decided to leave the Citadel, wanting to get a feel for the city.

Determine its temperature.

Escape the pressure he was placing on her.

The pressure resulted in large part from the First Families seeking to expand their hold on the Kingdom at the expense of the Crown's power.

Closing her eyes and taking a deep breath, she attempted to shift her focus. "Concentrate on the present," she urged herself. "Think about how it fits with the past and how it could with the future." Words to live by offered by her mother before she died.

When she opened her eyes, she studied all that was going on around her. And just as much what wasn't.

Even at this late hour, the streets usually were bustling. The markets still open. The taverns full.

But not on this night.

On this night, it seemed as if the fog had suffocated Innsbruck, and she could sense the unease in the few people who shared the streets with her.

They moved hesitantly, often looking over their shoulders, feeling uncomfortable in the grasping grey. As if they weren't alone. Some presence lurking just beyond their perception.

She believed that they had good cause to do so. Because she felt it as well.

The prickle along her spine made her feel as if she were being hunted.

Like she was back on the Frozen Waste before the Northern Trolls decided to make a meal of her.

That thought made her entire body shiver. She had not enjoyed that feeling of being chased among the barrows. And she certainly didn't enjoy what she was experiencing now.

Although she doubted that she had anything to fear from Northern Trolls this evening.

So what was it that made her feel so ill at ease? That appeared to be putting everyone who braved the fog on edge?

She didn't know. Worse, she didn't know how to find the answer. That failure bothered her more than it should.

Her sense of discomfort increasing as the fog thickened around her, she decided to head back toward the Citadel, the main gates just a quarter mile off as the crow flies but two Rings above her.

Drin had only gone fifty yards back the way she had come when she stopped abruptly. Despite the denseness of the grey, she could tell that she was alone on the street.

That by itself shouldn't have worried her. She was in one of the more prosperous neighborhoods now. Lesser lords and ladies lived here, as did some of the most profitable merchants, so she had little to fear from the ne'er-do-wells who called her city home.

Nevertheless, the feeling that all wasn't quite right had become much more insistent.

She spun around slowly in the fog, trying to catch even the briefest hint of movement.

Nothing.

Just the slowly swirling grey punctuated by the lamplights closest to her, even those little more than dim glows.

That stood to reason as the murk thickened with every passing second.

And with it a menace that radiated from within the grey.

A menace that was drawing closer to her.

Desperate to identify the source of her unease, Drin grasped the Talent and extended her senses into the fog.

What she discovered put her on her toes, hand drifting toward the dagger on her belt.

Stay or fight?

"Go," she whispered to herself. There were too many.

She was off in an instant, sprinting down the middle of the street toward the main gate two Rings above her.

"How did it go?" Teddy walked next to Mikel through the smothering fog. His friend had emerged from an alley on the back side of the Citadel, and now they were making their way down from the Royal Ring.

"Not how I anticipated."

"Is that good or bad?"

"I haven't decided," Mikel replied, his voice carrying a hint of concern.

"Wonderful." Teddy knew what that response meant. They had known each other for quite a long time, and he deciphered his friend's moods better than he knew his own. Mikel was troubled, which never boded well. "So definitely bad."

"I didn't say that," Mikel murmured absently, lost in thought. He ran the conversation through his mind one more time. What was not said just as important as what was said. A truth that Kaduna taught him. Taking the context into account, he could only assume that events were moving faster than he expected.

"You didn't have to," Teddy replied. Before he could say more, he reached out and grasped Mikel's arm, pulling him under a dark awning and up against the wall of the goldsmith's shop at their back. He whispered, "They're not ours?"

Mikel shook his head. "No."

Just then a cowled woman drifted swiftly through the fog and up the street, seeking the Ring above.

She was wary. Clearly, she had a sense that all wasn't right. And for good reason. Her movements were being tracked from the alleys and the balconies that lined the broad boulevard, which was why Teddy had guided them off the road.

Teddy placed a large hand on Mikel's shoulder. Squeezing. Holding him in place. He could tell what Mikel was thinking.

"Don't do this again," Teddy warned.

"Do what?"

"Go off plan."

"If I didn't go off plan when we met, you'd be dead," Mikel countered in a soft voice that couldn't be heard beyond where they hid in the gloom.

"And for that I'm grateful," Teddy conceded. "Just don't do it now." The sense of menace within the fog had grown much more powerful. It made Teddy think that a doom was about to descend and crush them into the cobblestones, and he was far from the superstitious man his father had been.

Mikel gave Teddy a look, catching his friend's eyes. The giant shook his head, sighing softly. He should have assumed as much. Trying to keep his friend from getting involved was wasted effort. There was only one way that this scene was going to play out.

"I don't have a choice," Mikel sighed, nodding over his shoulder and up toward the Citadel that towered above him. "There's a new plan. Not of our choosing."

Teddy sighed even more heavily. He should have assumed as much. "It's her?"

"Looks like."

Teddy shook his head in resignation. "All right. What do you want to do?"

Mikel briefly outlined what he had in mind.

"They have the numbers," Teddy said. "You really think that's going to work?"

"Probably not," Mikel replied with a grin.

"Fair enough," Teddy grumbled. "At least we both agree on that. Now let's get to it."

"THERE'S no point in trying to run, missy," a raspy voice called from the fog. "There's no place for you to go."

Drin turned, cursing herself for a fool. She could just make out a dim shape about twenty feet in front of her. And he was right.

She was trapped. And it was her own doing.

Thinking that she could lose herself in the fog, she had stepped into a small garden just off the main boulevard.

Somehow, her hunters had stayed with her, the murk not impeding their search in any way.

"You know who I am," Drin said in a commanding tone. She noticed quite a few more shadows standing in the grey. Not moving. Just watching her. "Step aside or face the consequences."

"We do know who you are, that's true," the voice called again. "That's why we're here." The dim shape stepped a few feet closer, still no more than a faint figure in the gloom. "Where is it?"

"Where is what?" Drin replied, thoroughly confused.

She took a few steps backward. She didn't know how many sellswords pursued her through the grey, but she believed that they were the least of her concerns.

She had glimpsed a figure not too far behind her hunters. Hidden beneath a black cowl. Radiating a sense of evil that chilled her to the bone.

"Don't play dumb with me, missy. We'll get what we want, one way or another. And once we have it, we'll deal with you."

The sellsword stalked toward her, finally revealing himself. He was compact, his arms corded muscle. A battle axe in one hand. And his eyes. Drin couldn't look away. They were the meanest eyes that she had ever seen.

Reacting instinctively, she reached for the Talent and sent a bolt of energy streaking right at him.

The blast shattered the cobblestones at the sellsword's feet, sending a spray of rock into the air. Stunning him. Shards of stone pierced his flesh. His men scrambled backward, almost all of them turning away.

By the time they spun back around, Drin was in among them. A dagger in each hand, she attacked with a calm resolve.

She had no idea who these men were or what they wanted.

But she did know that the next few seconds were absolutely essential to her not only staying free, but also staying alive.

Kill a few and the rest might waver.

Then she might have a chance to go after whatever it was that commanded these mercenaries and hovered just above the ground, staring at her with pitch-black eyes that glowed in the grey.

"YOU SURE WE need to get involved?" Teddy asked. "She's putting on a good show."

"She is," Mikel agreed even as he ignored his friend's question. "Come on."

"What about whatever's behind her?" Teddy asked. "I don't like the look of whatever it is. Is it even alive? Even human?"

"We'll worry about whatever it is when we reach that point," Mikel once again not really responding to his friend's questions. And not wanting to take a closer look at the figure that concerned Teddy, because then he might rethink what he was about to do. Just like his friend, he didn't like the look of that malevolent presence. Rather than focus on that, however, he stepped silently through the fog, getting closer to the clash, playing out in his head how he wanted the next few seconds to go. "She needs our help. We can't wait."

"Isn't once in a day enough?" Teddy asked.

Not because Teddy wasn't interested in getting involved. He was. He didn't like bullies. Hated them with a passion, in fact. And that's what he saw now. A bunch of sellswords trying to bully a young woman.

So he welcomed the feel of his cudgels' leather grips in his hands. He was looking forward to this even though it seemed like the dark, cowled shape at the back of the fight was floating above the ground. Definitely not human, although he was willing to wait as long as possible to cure his curiosity.

"There's more to it than just the fact that she needs help now."

Teddy frowned then nodded, understanding coming to him. "And you want to go against that?" He nodded toward the source of their disquiet that had yet to move so much as an inch.

"Not really," Mikel admitted, his mace now in one hand, long dagger in the other.

"But you will if necessary."

"Only if necessary," he promised.

"You can sense the evil coming from it just as well as I can. Are you certain this is going to work?"

Mikel smiled. His friend was always nervous right before a fight, which he found ironic. Since most people ran from Teddy if they saw him coming with those cudgels of his in his hands. Of course with the fog that currently was an impossibility. The sellswords wouldn't see the Giant until he knocked a few of them from the fight. "Of course not, but you know the saying."

"What saying? You have many. More than I can keep track of."

"To dare is to do," Mikel offered.

"That's not too far away from to dare is to die."

"Funny," Mikel chuckled, understanding that with that touch of humor his friend was ready. "Let's go."

DRIN SPUN TO THE SIDE, then crouched. Avoiding the baton that swept past her and was supposed to disable her rather than kill her, she pushed herself back up and jabbed.

The sellsword grunted in surprise as her dagger slid between his lower ribs.

She didn't have time to admire her handiwork. Another tough was coming at her from behind.

Sensing the baton already streaking down toward the back of her head, she ducked and lashed out with her right foot.

Drin didn't catch the man's knee like she intended. She found a more delicate target instead that worked just as well.

"Serves you right," she grumbled to herself.

The sellsword collapsed to the cobblestones, gasping for air as he grasped his aching groin.

Her initial instinct was to finish the tough who was mimicking a guppy out of water. One less threat to worry about.

She didn't follow through, however. Adopting a more cautious approach, she stepped back to gain a few more feet on her attackers upon glimpsing several more faint shadows entering the small garden that had become her battleground.

She had hoped that if she dispatched a few of her hunters, she could make a break for it. Lose herself in the swirling grey. But it wasn't to be.

She already had removed three from the clash. One permanently.

Yet she was no better off now than she was when the fight began. For every sellsword eliminated, another appeared.

"You need to do better," she mumbled just beneath her breath.

Then she saw her chance. The leader was drifting toward her from her left. Perhaps she could put him under her blade and gain some leverage on his men.

The instant before she could implement her new plan, she jumped backward. Her feet slipping on the cobblestones because of her sudden movement, she ended up sprawled on the ground.

She was grateful for her clumsiness.

A streak of sizzling black energy shot through the space where she had been standing just a heartbeat before.

Whatever hovered by the main road had decided to join the fight. Probably guessing at what she had in mind and not wanting to give her an opportunity to get clear.

After that she didn't have any more time to think.

She scrambled backward like a crab, then rolled before coming back to her feet. Another streak of black missed her by no more than a hair, slamming into the cobblestones and leaving a wide scorch mark in its wake.

Drin had a split-second to study her new attacker as the sellswords pulled back toward the garden entrance to avoid being struck themselves.

From where she stood, there wasn't much that she could make out besides a cowled figure that seemed to be just a darker part of the fog.

No more than a shadow.

Although the power the figure exercised was unmistakable.

The Curse.

That could mean only one thing.

A Dark Magus or perhaps even something worse … if there was something worse.

That realization terrified her.

How could she ever expect to defeat a Dark Magus along with all these sellswords?

"This is getting a little ridiculous," she murmured, watching as the toughs drifted back toward her in a wide semicircle, the Dark Magus apparently having decided to leave the dirty work to them.

Drin steeled herself. She resolved to make them pay in blood for their efforts.

Reaching for the Talent, she sent a streak of energy sizzling through the grey toward where she had last seen the Dark Magus, the fog hiding and revealing the combatants on a whim.

"Take her quickly!" the leader of the gang shouted.

Drin's eyes widened when she realized the danger she faced. Toughs rushed at her from multiple directions. He wanted to get her under wraps before she could use her unique skill against him and his men.

She could remove a few from the fight as they drew closer, more with the Talent than the blade, but not all. The leader's strategy was going to work.

Promising herself that she wouldn't go easily, she watched in astonishment as two large shadows burst out of the fog, charging at the sellswords to her right and joining the fight. That touch of luck allowed her to focus on the men closing on her from her left.

TEDDY TOOK a particular pleasure from the sound that echoed in his ear, knowing exactly what it meant.

Another adversary knocked from the fight. Quite literally, in fact. His bell rung or his skull crushed. Either possibility really didn't matter.

He didn't rest on his success, however. Displaying a remarkable agility for a giant of a man, he leapt over the steel slashing for his hip then closed with the sellsword nearest to him in just a heartbeat.

Teddy took the sellsword out of the fight with three swift blows. First to his gut. Then to his jaw when the man bent down reflexively after the first strike. A final smack across the back of the man's head finished him.

He turned to face one more adversary who was rushing toward him out of the gloom on his right side. Teddy cursed up a storm when he missed with his cudgel, though he took a great deal of pleasure when he saw the delight in the man's beady eyes shift instantly to fright.

The sellsword initially thought that he had a free run at him. When he realized that he didn't, Teddy's other cudgel screaming toward him, the tough tried to halt his progress in time. His abrupt stop led to a slip to the cobblestones. Landing hard on his ass saving the sellsword's life.

The man scrambled away on all fours. Teddy, having no desire to chase after him, took the brief break he had earned to glimpse Mikel at work.

Bodies surrounded his friend, and Teddy doubted that any would be returning to their feet soon if at all.

Hearing a heavy breath just off to his right, he turned swiftly. With one powerful swing he broke the sellsword's jaw. He caught his attacker perfectly with his cudgel. His range of motion greater than what the man could bring to bear even with his sword.

The sellsword flew backward, lying still and silent when the back of his head smacked against the cobblestones.

Teddy grunted in satisfaction. Having cleared his part of the battlefield, he rushed toward Mikel, who now faced off against the last three sellswords.

Teddy was on the man to Mikel's far left in a flash, forcing the attacker away from his friend and never giving him the chance to recover after taking him by surprise.

This time it took only two blows to end the fight. A bone-crunching thwack to the sellsword's knee followed by an uppercut to his jaw that left the man broken and bleeding in the street.

Mikel took full advantage of the opportunity Teddy gave him. Shocked by the speed of the giant who rushed into the fight, the momentary distraction proved to be the downfall of one of the other sellswords.

Mikel caught the man to his far side just beneath his jaw with the blade that extended from the back end of his mace. Then he placed his full attention on the leader of the gang, who also had been too slow to react when Teddy inserted himself into the clash.

"Who in blazes are you?" he demanded. "This is no business of yours."

"Just a concerned citizen," Mikel replied, giving the leader a roguish grin.

"A concerned ..."

The sellsword never had a chance to complete his thought, Mikel already on him.

The mean-eyed thug knocked away the dagger Mikel thrust at his ribs. However, he wasn't fast enough to deal with the mace that Mikel smacked into the side of his head an instant later.

The sellsword crumpled to the street, his scalp a bloody mess as his eyes glazed over.

"Nice work," Teddy said, coming to stand next to his friend.

Mikel nodded. "Bloody work."

"Yes, very final on your part."

"It seemed like the appropriate course to take."

"Definitely necessary," Teddy grunted. "Should we ..." He nodded toward the young woman who stood only ten yards away.

"No, let's wait," Mikel said. "I don't want to get in her way."

Drin's rescuers removed the threat presented by the sellswords with a remarkable efficiency. The greater peril remained, however.

A shard of pitch-black energy streaked through the fog. Coming right at her.

This time she stood against the attack, refusing to dart out of the way. Crafting a shield of blindingly bright energy that she affixed to her forearm, she bore the brunt of the strike. The Curse shattered against her barrier much like the sound of a chandelier crashing to the floor, the thousands of pieces of energy that clouded in front of her fading into the gloom.

Shield still in place, Drin squared up to the shadowy presence that drifted closer. No more than fifteen yards separated them now.

She took a step back, eyes widening when she finally got a good look at the figure she opposed.

She wasn't fighting against a Dark Magus.

At least not in the flesh.

It was a Drude.

She braced herself, blocking another bolt of tainted energy. And then another. Followed by a third.

Each strike more powerful than the last. Forcing her to take several steps back each time.

At first, she couldn't believe the strength that was being brought to bear against her. But she should have.

Only the strongest of Dark Magii would have the capacity to enslave a creature from the Spirit World.

Drin tried to fight back, blasting several streaks of blazing energy toward the Drude.

Her shots were wild, however. The monster never gave her a clear target, gliding this way and that faster than she could track with her eyes.

She gasped when she heard the hiss and felt the grip on the edge of her shield.

The Drude had closed the distance between them in a single breath. Right in front of her, just inches away, the monster resembled a woman.

More concerning, one of the Drude's hands was pushing down on her shield while the other reached over the top. And that hand was shifting swiftly as it reached toward her, the fingers elongating into a razor-sharp claw.

Drin tried to pull back from the Drude.

To put some space between them.

She couldn't.

The monster was too strong.

The only way to break free was to release her hold on the Talent and allow her shield to disappear, and she feared doing that would only make the Drude's goal that much easier to achieve.

Desperate to avoid the claw reaching for her, she tried to raise her dagger.

She couldn't.

She was using that hand to prevent the shield from dropping too far.

She was stuck.

Her dagger was caught between her and her shield.

And she couldn't use the Talent to defend herself.

She couldn't do anything except watch as the claw extended toward her throat.

A loud hiss jolted Drin from her trance, watching in amazement as a steel hammer thwacked into the Drude's claw with a bone-crunching thwack.

Surprised by the attack, the Drude drifted backward, releasing its hold on Drin's magical shield.

Mikel claimed the space that opened up between the creature and the young woman, ensuring that the creature would need to go through him to get at its quarry.

He lifted his mace in front of his face, swiping away the claw that sought to take his eyes. Then he slashed with a backhanded blow, hoping to catch the monster across the gut.

No such luck, the creature slid away from him.

He refused to allow the monster to escape unharmed. Dancing forward, he sliced and slashed. At least three times he cut into the creature's misty black garb.

Yet it had no effect whatsoever.

When he stepped back and looked into the monster's pureblack eyes, the rest of its features cloudy rather than clear, he realized what he truly was up against. It was then that he felt a brief tinge of regret at placing himself in such a precarious position.

Kaduna had been meticulous in her instruction, ensuring

that he was well acquainted with all the creatures touched by the Curse.

Steel had no lasting effect on a Drude.

Not even the Talent offered much help if you weren't as strong as the Dark Magus who freed the creature from the Spirit World.

And he feared that he was about the pay the price for involving himself in this doomed combat as he watched sparks of black spinning around one of the monster's claws.

The Drude was fast.

Faster than Mikel.

The lethal shard of the Curse the monster blasted toward him punched him right in the center of his chest.

And did nothing at all.

Mikel took a deep breath, then smiled and sighed with relief.

A strange gift from his people. The only gift, in fact, that he was willing to accept from them.

Pleased that he was still among the living, Mikel's flinty eyes fixed onto those of the Drude.

He advanced toward the creature from the Spirit World with a calm and certain purpose. He might not be able to destroy the monster, but he could frustrate its efforts to take the young woman.

Realizing that as well, rather than holding its ground, the Drude retreated into the fog with an angry hiss. Reluctant to offer its prey a reprieve yet having no choice but to obey its master.

Fading away in just a breath.

Gone.

The Dark Magus controlling the Drude decided that the risk of continuing the combat wasn't worth it.

"How could you have survived that?" Drin demanded. She

stepped around Mikel, squaring up to him, wanting to get a good look at one of her rescuers.

The swirling fog stymied her efforts. Even though he was no more than a few feet away, his features remained hazy. All she could tell was that he had a rough appearance.

She wasn't surprised by her failure. Even the bodies scattered around the small courtyard couldn't be seen unless the grey decided to reveal them.

"Poor aim," Mikel shrugged. "Lucky I guess."

"I saw the Curse *hit* you." Drin refused to be put off. "You should be dead!"

"I should be, you're right," Mikel replied in an amused tone that became a bit harder when he realized the young woman intended to continue to press him. "But clearly I'm not. So the Drude missed."

"The Drude was less than ten feet away from you," Drin protested. "There is no way that monster missed."

Mikel shrugged, a movement that Drin had trouble picking out in the dense grey. "Everything looks a little bit off in a soup this thick. Like I said, I was lucky."

Drin was about to argue some more, but something her rescuer said stopped her. "You know what a Drude is?"

Mikel almost let loose a string of curses at his slip. She was right to wonder even more about him now. Druden weren't common knowledge. No more than myths to most. "My tutor was very thorough. She made sure that I had a very broad and eclectic education."

"That may be, but Druden are not ..."

Mikel stopped her. "We don't know if there is anyone else hunting you. Perhaps we should think about getting out of here instead of all the questions."

Drin's first instinct was to object. She wanted an answer. Her natural obstinacy threatened to take hold. She didn't give in to that desire, however, because what the man standing before her said made too much sense. She nodded.

"You know where to meet me?" Mikel asked Teddy.

Drin's other rescuer was no more than a dim shadow in the swirling grey. Much to her irritation, Drin hadn't gotten a good look at him either. She didn't even see the large figure nod, but she knew that he already was gone.

"Is there somewhere I can take you where you'll be safe?" Mikel asked. "Back to your home?" He didn't want to reveal to her that he knew who she was. "If not, I have a few places where I can keep you for a time."

"I don't think so," Drin replied. "I'm not interested."

Mikel was confused, not understanding what she was implying. Then he snorted softly, amused.

"You think quite highly of yourself."

"I'm sorry, what did you ..."

"You're not my type, so have no fear of that."

"Not your type?" Drin was shocked. She had never been told that before. Every other man she had come into contact with had wanted something from her.

"You're a Magus," Mikel said, interrupting her. "I prefer to stay away from Magii."

"Afraid of us?" she challenged, giving him a raised eyebrow.

"No, not afraid of you," he replied, appreciating her spirit. "I just prefer not to take risks if I can avoid them."

"Really? You and your friend challenged how many sell-swords? Six? Eight? Maybe more?"

"That may be, but we could handle them as you saw. We wouldn't have involved ourselves otherwise."

"And then you decide to step in front of a Drude using the Curse?"

"In all fairness, I didn't know it was a Drude until I was already engaged," Mikel explained. "If I had known that, I might have left you to that monster." He shrugged. "Besides, it missed."

"You have an answer for everything, don't you?"

A silence fell between them. As it dragged out, Drin felt the need to fill the quiet. Mikel beat her to it, sensing her growing discomfort.

"Most of the time, yes. Now do you want to go home with me or is there somewhere I can drop you safely?" Mikel hoped to get a rise out of her with his statement. It worked.

"I know where I'm going," Drin growled.

She started to walk up the street toward the higher Rings. Mikel followed her, trotting to catch up despite his leg protesting, the combat aggravating his old injuries.

"I told you I know where I'm going."

"You did," Mikel agreed. "I just want to get you there safely. That's all. Then you'll be done with me. I promise."

She stopped and stared at him, although that proved almost impossible because the fog somehow was getting worse.

"Fine, come on," she snapped, realizing that she wasn't going to get rid of him easily.

Drin started off again, almost to the point where the boulevard curled up to the next Ring. Mikel hustled to catch up to her. She was setting a hard pace. His bad leg confirming it.

She was angry. With him? With the attack? With the Drude? He didn't know. So he left her to her silence.

As they completed the next Ring and curled up toward the highest, he thought that she might take him right to the gates of the Citadel. Instead, she stopped a hundred yards below what was rightfully named the Royal Ring.

He smiled. He had to give her credit. She didn't think that he knew who she was, and she wanted to keep it that way. Smart. Cautious.

Of course, if she was smart, she wouldn't have been wandering through the Frozen Waste or the streets of Innsbruck on her own. But he doubted that she would appreciate his raising that point with her at exactly that moment.

Drin turned toward him. At her back was a doorway to an apothecary that only she could open with the Talent. It was one of several ways she got in and out of the Citadel without anyone noticing. The hidden tunnel in the basement of the shop led beneath the wall to a location not too far from her suite in the fortress.

"Thank you." Drin offered her gratitude grudgingly. She didn't like it when she needed assistance. Especially assistance that she had not asked for. Nevertheless, she couldn't ignore the contribution and sacrifice the man who walked her home made on her behalf.

Without him and his friend …

Against the sellswords and a Drude …

She didn't want to think about what could have happened.

So she wouldn't.

Not until later.

Now she needed to get to her father as quickly as possible. She had escaped the frying pan, but she still needed to avoid the fire.

"You're welcome." Mikel started to go, although he wouldn't go far. Not until he was certain that she was safe inside the shop.

"I didn't ask for your help," she called after him.

Mikel stopped. He couldn't see her in the fog. Though he could sense her. One of his unique skills.

For just an instant, he remembered his younger days in Innsbruck and what he used to do when a fog like this rolled in. He had faced certain challenges then as well, though never a Drude. "I know."

"I didn't need your help."

"Of course not," he agreed. He didn't see the point in arguing with her.

"Just so we're clear."

"Crystal. Before we never see each other again, just one thought?"

"Can I say no thank you?" Drin countered.

"No," Mikel replied, his tone suggesting that he was smiling. "We all can use a little help from time to time. Don't be afraid to accept it when it's offered freely." He started to walk farther down the slope. "Though of course only if the help is necessary. Otherwise, it just gets in the way."

"You do realize what you just said, right?" Drin called after him. She smiled even though she didn't want to. "An argument against your own argument."

"I did, you're right. But I have no doubt that you'll take my meaning."

Drin frowned. For just a heartbeat, she caught a glimpse of his back. He was limping slightly.

She wanted to call him back to make sure that he was all right, but he was already gone. Swallowed up by the fog.

She stared after him for several minutes before she unlocked the door with the Talent and walked into the apothecary. For some reason she didn't quite understand, he seemed familiar. He made her think of her experience at the edge of the Frozen Waste.

Could this be the same person who helped her then?

She snorted at the ridiculous thought.

More than just a bit farfetched.

She poked her head out the door, believing that he was still close by. "You're not going to tell me your name?"

Silence greeted her question for a time.

"No. Have a good night, my lady."

8

MUCH TOO CURIOUS

Mikel's few hours of sleep had been troubled. His dreams were dominated by the Drude and the questions connected to that monster.

Because of that, he was happy to be up and about despite the early hour. The sun, only a few hours old, burned away the fog that had settled over the Crux the evening before.

As he walked into The Fox's Lair, one of the many taverns he owned in Innsbruck, just as he always did he tapped with his fingers the wooden sign above him. The fox head carved into the placard seeming to grin mischievously as he passed beneath.

He was hoping for a quiet morning. He realized after entering the common room that was going to be unlikely.

"Where have you been?" Teddy asked, although he didn't pick up his head. Instead, he continued to point at the papers in front of Nat. Mikel's foundling bent over the books opened before her, scribbling away.

"I had some unexpected business that needed tending."

"Do we need to talk about it?" Teddy moved his finger across the page, identifying an error. He didn't tell her what mistake she had made, requiring Nat to identify it herself. She grumbled as she crossed out what she had written and started over.

"Later," Mikel said.

"You can talk about your business in front of me. With Teddy teaching me your books, I already have a good sense of what you two do and how you do it."

Mikel offered her a fox's grin. He didn't offer any of the details she wanted. "I know. But I want you to finish your lessons first. We can talk when you're done."

"When we're done," Nat repeated, not lifting her head as she focused on the puzzle she needed to solve, her tone turning his statement into a bond that couldn't be broken.

Mikel snorted, acknowledging the contract. He had learned quite a lot about Nat in the few weeks that she had been living with him. Quite a few of her characteristics stood out. Perhaps most evident? No matter what he tried, he couldn't put her off. She was worse than a dog with a bone.

"Carry the two there," Teddy instructed, watching carefully as she did her work. "Then you'll need to average that out for the remaining months of the year."

She growled. "Right, I remember. It's a balance sheet. So the expenses and the revenue have to balance."

"There you go," Teddy agreed.

"I'm going to leave you to it." Mikel walked past the bar. "I need to check on some of our stock in the warehouse."

Mikel smiled as he stepped through the kitchen and out the back door. Nat impressed him more and more.

She was quick. Sharp. She didn't miss a thing.

And that's what worried him as well.

Because he saw a lot of himself in her.

He stopped abruptly, only halfway down the back alley, the warehouse just ahead at the end of the walled path.

He wasn't alone.

That same sense of peril that plagued him the night before while caught in the fog struck him again. The unease was gaining strength with every step he took toward the warehouse.

He pulled the mace from the scabbard across his lower back. More out of habit than any real belief that the weapon would be of use to him.

He knew what waited for him.

Seconds later, the cause for his wariness materialized out of the shadows up ahead.

The same cowled figure that sought to kill the young woman who had left the safety of the Royal Ring.

The Drude.

Why the creature felt the need to make a play for him now, he had not a clue.

Unless the monster sought revenge for Mikel's role in preventing the woman's murder. He doubted such an emotion would drive a creature from the Spirit World. Although it could drive the Dark Magus who had brought the creature into the Natural World.

That realization striking him like a blow to the jaw, his first thought was to escape. He could sprint back into the tavern and lock the door.

Mikel discarded that idea immediately. He doubted a wooden door, no matter how stout, would offer much of a defense against a Drude. Moreover, he had no desire to put Teddy and Nat at risk.

Not wanting to go back, and not wanting to stand still, he was about to advance toward the Drude when a cloud of black erupted from the monster's palms.

When the Curse struck him, Mikel was caught in the middle of a whirlwind. The corrupted power swirled around him. Poking at him. Prodding. Seeking some way to consume him.

Yet doing absolutely nothing at all to him.

The attack was an annoyance. No more than that.

Through the blustery black, Mikel gained a brief glimpse of his adversary.

The Drude was stunned that he remained on his feet. It wasn't long before the monster, who looked vaguely like a woman, though the resemblance was hazy at best, released its hold on the Curse.

Mikel smiled viciously, pleased by his initial success.

Even though both his parents were Magii, he couldn't use the Talent, so he was at a disadvantage in some respects.

All of his people were Magii, in fact.

Except for him.

Perhaps that's why Kaduna had raised him instead of his parents.

They were ashamed of him. Embarrassed.

He never asked.

Kaduna never said.

And she never judged him.

His parents clearly did.

Mikel had never understood why he could not make use of the Talent.

It was unheard of.

All Caledonii could use the Talent to a greater or lesser degree.

It had been that way since the Caledonii came to be.

All Caledonii except for him.

That failing had hurt when he was younger. Worse than a blade in the gut.

Now ...

He didn't understand why he had a natural immunity to

both the Talent and the Curse. Kaduna had never been able to explain it.

But now his failure as a child worked to his advantage.

Because unlike last night, there was no fog that would allow the Drude to fade away.

Mikel charged the creature from the Spirit World, swinging with his mace.

The Drude raised a forearm, absorbing the blow then responding with a quick swipe of its claw.

Mikel danced backward, though only so long as to set himself so that he could lunge, long dagger in his other hand.

The Drude hissed. Not so much in pain as in surprise. The steel sliced right into the shadowy black where its ribs should have been.

Mikel didn't know if he wounded the Drude. He didn't know if he could wound a Drude if he couldn't use the Talent or a Talent-infused weapon.

He didn't care.

He just knew that the Drude was off balance. Not quite certain what to make of the man who was supposed to be that morning's victim.

And he wanted to use the monster's unease for as long as he could.

That goal top of mind, Mikel maintained a steady attack. Mace and dagger no more than steel blurs as he sliced and slashed, swung and cut.

Maintaining the Drude's full attention.

More than holding his own.

Dictating the combat.

Mikel should have been pleased with himself.

But he wasn't.

Rather, he was frustrated.

Because despite his success, which he judged primarily as

still being alive, he couldn't vanquish the monster from the Spirit World.

And that failure irritated him in a way that little else had in quite some time.

Worse, after last night's battle with the sellswords and this same Drude, Mikel's leg was aching. He anticipated the pain, but he still wasn't happy about it. Assuming he survived this combat, it meant that he was in for a very long, excruciating day.

Mikel darted to the side, knocking away the Drude's swipe with his hammer and continuing his movement so that he could slash for the creature's throat with his dagger.

The Drude glided backward in an instant. Mikel following. Refusing to allow the monster to break away. Seeking a way past the creature's defenses with mace and dagger.

There had to be something that he could do to best the Drude.

But what?

Every Caledonii was born with the spark of the Talent.

Where his spark should have been, there was an emptiness. A hole. As if what should have resided there had been stolen from him. And he had no idea how to fix it.

In fact, after all this time, he didn't believe that he could.

Still, there had to be something that he could do against his adversary. Otherwise, his attempt to destroy the Drude was doomed ... as was he.

As he spun and wove, ducked and dashed, slashing and slicing at the Drude with a controlled abandon, Mikel explored the hole within himself. Striving for some solution. Seeking some answer. Desperate for some way to send the Drude back to the Spirit World.

Mikel pivoted to the side, the Drude's claw slipping by him. Missing him by less than a knuckle.

Much to his embarrassment, he realized that he was

allowing his hopes and desires to get in the way of what he needed to do.

He needed to focus on the reality that was trying to gore him.

He couldn't do anything against a Drude other than aggravate the creature.

Delay it. No more than that.

Allowing his mind to wander had almost cost him.

Badly.

Still, what he would give, if just once, to send …

A bolt of the Talent shot right over his shoulder, sizzling past his ear and blasting right through the Drude's midsection.

The monster froze, an expression of shock fixed on its face. Looking down, the creature couldn't quite believe what it saw. A massive hole in its chest. Bits of shadow flaking away from its body like cinders from a burning log.

In just seconds it was done.

The Drude dissolved into a swirling cloud of black ash that faded into nothingness, the creature returning to the Spirit World, its link to its Dark Magus broken.

Mikel breathed a little easier when he turned and looked back over his shoulder, remaining wary, nonetheless.

A tall woman stood there. Long dark hair flowing in the breeze, she was beautiful in a cold way. Yet there was also a familiarity to her that he didn't understand and found more than just a little unsettling.

Not because she was a Magus.

That wasn't what was making him nervous.

It was as if he knew her. Or he should know her. Yet for the life of him, he couldn't figure out why.

"Thank you." He offered her a nod of gratitude.

The Magus nodded in return. "It was my pleasure. Although I must admit I did not expect to face a Drude so early in the morning. Especially in an alley such as this one."

"Neither did I," Mikel replied. "And how is it that you found yourself in this alley so early in the morning? My alley, in fact." Because of the height of the walls, the only way in was through the back of the tavern.

"Your friends said you were out here."

Mikel nodded to hide his distrust. He took a few seconds to study the woman, an aura of confidence and power radiating from her. It was best to be cautious around Magii. Although around this one, who seemed to think that dealing with a monster from the Spirit World was just another part of the day ... caution might do him little good. "And you are?"

"Assindra," the Magus replied.

Mikel frowned ever so slightly. He knew all the Magii in Innsbruck and the surrounding countryside. He didn't know her. "My thanks, Assindra. And you are here ..."

"Because of you," she replied.

Her smile was warm, while at the same time her eyes remained frosty. Yes, definitely a woman and a Magus who required a great deal of caution on his part.

Particularly because how she replied sent a jolt of concern through him. "Really?"

She laughed. "Have no fear, Mikel. If I wanted to kill you as the Drude intended, you would already be dead."

"Good to know." Although he didn't find the Magus' admission the least bit comforting.

"May I have a few minutes of your time? I have some business that I would like to discuss with you."

"It wasn't easy to find you," Assindra said as she followed Mikel into the kitchen of The Fox's Lair. "No one wanted to talk. In truth, I had to visit three of your other establishments before coming upon you here, and that was by chance."

Mikel nodded. Not surprised. Though he was pleased. It meant that the people working for him were doing as they should. Keeping his trust, just as he trusted in them. "I prefer not to be found unless I want to be found."

"That I can understand," Assindra murmured as they walked through the swinging doors and into the common room. "Very wise as well."

"Everything all right?" Teddy was looking up from the books. He had one hand below the table. Not liking the look or feel of the woman.

Mikel shook his head, the movement barely perceptible. There would be no need for his friend to use one of his cudgels. And even if there was they'd be of little use. "Couldn't be better." The sarcasm wasn't very thick, but it was still there, and Teddy didn't miss it.

"Who's this?" Nat asked. Her tone challenging.

She also had a hand beneath the table. Mikel assumed that she was grasping one of the daggers he had gifted her soon after she had taken the apartment across from his on the top floor.

Nat didn't like her either. Then again, Mikel had learned quickly that Nat approached any new situation or person with caution and suspicion, which was certainly justified considering what she had suffered through before finding a place with him.

"My rescuer."

"Rescuer?" Teddy asked with a raised eyebrow.

Mikel nodded. "A shady friend from last night made an appearance in the alley just now. My new friend took care of it for me."

Teddy nodded. "So she's ..."

"Yes, I'm a Magus. You may call me Assindra."

"Is that your real name?" Nat frowned at the woman, clearly not happy.

Because the woman was a Magus or just because of how she presented herself, a haughtiness plastered across her features and her stance that could not be chiseled away by even the best sculptor, Mikel didn't know. But he intended to find out once this encounter was over.

Assindra stared hard at Nat, her gaze questioning. Then she smiled, sensing the spark within her. Even better, the girl didn't flinch or back down. "It is. For now." She studied Nat a bit more closely, nodding to herself in a mysterious way all the while.

"I leave you alone for only a few minutes and you can't stay out of trouble," Teddy grumbled. He wanted to pull Assindra's gaze away from Nat. Nervous. The Magus was examining their ward with too much intensity. Assindra's expression was predatory to start. Then becoming shrewder when she noticed Teddy observing her.

"Trouble seems to find me, Teddy. You know that better than anyone."

Assindra didn't miss the nuance in his words. "Is there somewhere quiet where we can talk? I prefer to keep my business my own."

Mikel nodded, glad for the opportunity to lead Assindra away from Nat. Not so much because of what the Magus might do to her, but rather because of Nat. He had never seen her like this. So fixated on the Magus. As if she were preparing for a contest of skill and will. "I'll be back in a few minutes."

He directed Assindra to his office behind the bar.

Nat reached out a hand as he passed by her, gripping his arm strongly and pulling him down so that she could whisper in his ear. "Be careful around the Magus. Something doesn't feel right about her."

Mikel nodded. "I know. Don't worry."

"I will worry."

Mikel smiled appreciatively as he continued into his office, patting Nat on the shoulder. It was funny how protective his foundling had become of him and how quickly.

"You didn't help me out of the goodness of your heart." Mikel stepped around Assindra after he closed the door to his office. She was already sitting in one of the chairs facing his desk.

"No," Assindra replied, "of course not. I need you to do something for me. And you wouldn't be able to do it for me if you were dead."

"I assumed as much." Mikel sat down behind his desk, unaffected by her bluntness.

Assindra twisted her lips into a smile as the seconds passed. She hadn't expected him to wait patiently. She thought he would want to get right to it. "You're not going to ask?"

"I'm afraid to ask."

"You should be," she confirmed, nodding to herself as she examined him.

Seeing more than just the image that he presented to the world.

Seeing an individual driven to be the best.

To take risks that others wouldn't.

She wondered why.

Then she crushed the thought.

Why didn't matter. All that mattered was that he was willing to take risks that others would shy away from, because that's what she needed from him now. Perhaps just as important, he wasn't wilting under her hard gaze. That impressed her.

"You're not afraid of me. Why is that?"

"Because you want something from me," Mikel answered quietly. His eyes were keen. Taking in everything about her. Understanding that he would need to make a decision and then live with the consequences.

Assindra nodded, then leaned forward. She liked the man sitting before her. And she liked very few people.

He was a realist. He understood already that any partnership between them lasted only so long as it continued to prove useful to them both. As soon as that changed, the partnership would conclude. Although what her prospective partner might not have concluded yet is that she would determine when their partnership came to an end.

"There's something about you, Mikel Stahlherz, that I find quite interesting."

Mikel forced himself not to react. Few people knew his last name. That's how he liked it. For Assindra to have acquired that information meant that she had done quite a bit of digging before approaching him. And she wanted him to know that. "I'm afraid to ask what it was that grabbed your attention," he responded cagily.

"In this case, you want to."

His expression sharpened. Recognizing that she was trying to play him, he didn't say anything. Instead he waited. Watching as her smile slipped the longer the silence dragged on between them.

"You're not going to ask?" The Magus didn't bother to hide her disappointment.

Mikel smiled, but he didn't say anything. A bit childish, perhaps. Still, he preferred to keep his guest off balance if he could.

"I should have assumed such stubbornness."

Mikel shrugged. "It's proven its utility over the years. More often than I can recall, it's kept me alive."

"I can understand why, King of the Underworld."

Once again, Mikel forced himself not to react. He didn't want to reveal his rising concern. He was less than pleased that this Magus knew more about him than she should. Then again, she was a Magus. So he shouldn't have been surprised. In his experience, Magii had a skill for ferreting out information that others wanted to remain buried.

Still, he wouldn't give her what she wanted. She would need to work for it.

"I am here for a simple reason, and one that could and should prove quite profitable for you." Assindra leaned forward, giving him a devilish smile. "I need you to steal an item that was stolen from me."

He had assumed the conversation would head in this direction as soon as she referenced his unofficial title. In Innsbruck, Mikel exercised as much power as any of the First Families, perhaps even more than the king, though he did so from the shadows.

"Why should I trust you?"

"You'd be smart not to. But you owe me. Without me, the Drude would have killed you."

Mikel didn't reply, realizing that he was caught in a trap of his own making. He could tell that she was dangerous, the fact that she was a Magus only a part of that.

But he did owe her.

Worse, he was more than just a little curious.

And that was never a good thing.

Because his curiosity rarely took him down the safest road.

TERRIBLE LOSS

"You can't blame yourself for what happened to your father."

"I should have been here." Drin wiped away her tears, all the while knowing that more would come.

She stood in the foyer. She had taken one look at his body. That was all she could manage. Although she couldn't look away from the large pool of dark blood that stained the tiles in the entryway, a chilling reminder of the guards who were murdered before her father met his end.

"It wouldn't have mattered."

"It would have mattered, Uncle Henri." She shook her head in frustration, struggling to keep her grief from consuming her. "If I had been here, I might have been able to save him."

"You don't know what killed him," Henri Dengannon said softly. Angry at the loss of his brother. Wishing with all his heart that his niece didn't need to deal with this terrible loss ... and all that would follow.

"I don't, you're right, but that doesn't matter."

"Celindria, please understand that I have seen many horrible things in my life, much of it because of the position that I hold." He stepped in close to her, making sure he caught her red-rimmed eyes. "I have never seen anything like what happened to my brother. Anything. Whatever killed him wasn't human."

"That's not making me feel better, Uncle."

"It's not meant to," Henri replied. "Just because you're a Magus doesn't mean you can defeat all challengers. Whatever killed your father ..."

He didn't feel the need to complete his thought. The wound that had killed his brother Charles was obvious. It was what was done to his body afterward that had sickened his daughter and filled Henri's heart with fury and dread.

"It's because I'm a Magus that I'm the only one who could have stood against whatever it was that killed him."

Henri reached down, his hand gripping his niece's shoulder, offering her what little strength he had left. He never had children of his own. His service as Battle Lord of the Crux demanded too much from him. So he viewed his niece as the daughter he never had.

"I appreciate your courage, Celindria. In that you have never lacked. Still, there is a hard truth you must hear."

"That if I was here with my father, I would be lying next to him right now, my limbs torn from my torso." She stated it matter of factly. Dispassionately. Blocking away as best as she could the pain and loss surging through her.

"I'm sorry, but yes," Henri said barely above a whisper. "Exactly that."

Drin nodded sadly, then she shook her head in frustration. "How can you be so calm right now? After what happened to father?"

"I am calm right now because I have to be," Henri replied solemnly. "Not because I want to be."

Drin took in the lesson, though reluctantly. Her uncle was right. She could blame herself later. When the time was right she could release the remorse and anger that flowed within her with the strength of the four rivers that merged at the Crux and raged against the seawall surrounding the island.

Now was not that time.

Drin had gotten in late after last night's adventure. When she appeared in her rooms after stepping through the hidden passageway behind her bed, she was shocked to find her uncle and a full company of soldiers waiting for her.

Her father was dead. And after escaping her own assassination attempt, she could only assume that the Drude that came for her had visited her father first. The only distinction in their encounters being the fact that she survived because of her unnamed benefactor while her father's guards were unable to protect him.

She felt guilty about that. About not being here to defend her father against what claimed his life. About how she had left things between them when she stormed off after their last conversation just after dinner the night before.

Guilty and responsible, the weight of her father's murder resting squarely on her shoulders.

And perhaps it was right that it did so.

Before the urge to expel the contents of her stomach got the better of her, she had studied her father's terribly disfigured torso. The claw marks in his chest didn't confirm what killed him.

Several creatures could have caused such a horrific wound.

She was certain it was the Drude because the pieces of her father's body were a greyish blue. Desiccated. His skin almost brittle to the touch. Splotches of black marred the surface, making her think of frostbite. As if his remains had been frozen shortly after he died.

That suggested to her that before he went to the other side the Drude drained her father of his spirit.

The Drude was the key.

The Drude obeyed a Dark Magus.

A Dark Magus wanted her father dead.

Wanted her dead.

Why?

That was the easy question to answer.

The hard question?

Who was the Dark Magus?

She didn't know how to find out the answer to that query. But she knew where she wanted to start.

With the man who had rescued her.

The man who had some familiarity with a Drude.

A man who could withstand a Drude's attack with nary a mark on him.

"You know what needs to be done?"

Drin nodded. "Yes, though I'm not looking forward to it."

"Nor should you, but you have no choice."

"I haven't had a choice since I was a girl."

"Now is not the time to sulk, young lady," Henri said sharply. "There is more at stake here than just your happiness."

Drin's eyes widened. Her uncle rarely spoke so harshly to her. Only doing so when he believed it was necessary.

She nodded, recognizing what she had been doing. Disappointed in herself.

She needed to think of the Kingdom first.

She needed to demonstrate that she could rule. That there was little need to begin the Search. What the First Families would do if they didn't have confidence in the heir to the throne of the Crux, initiating a process that allowed various other claimants to seek the throne. A process that had not been employed for centuries. Since the first Dengannon assumed the throne, in truth.

There were never any guarantees once a Search began, other than the fact that the claimant who lost the confidence of the First Families – in this case, her – never lived very long once a new claimant won the throne.

Drin might not be able to avoid a Search. There was already a great deal of unease in the Kingdom, not all of it because of Malor Dragoran marshaling so many of his troops on the eastern side of the Splintered Bridge.

She would do what she needed to do to secure the Kingdom, no matter how distasteful that might be.

Then she could think about herself.

Then she could think about her father.

Drin promised herself that his murder would not go unavenged.

She promised herself as well that she would find the man who aided her the night before. The man who might be able to give her the answers that no one else could.

10

A REAL FIND

"This was a really bad idea," Mikel murmured ever so quietly to himself.

He needed to stop giving his curiosity such free reign. Then again, he did owe the Magus his life.

"You're just rationalizing," Mikel reminded himself, struggling to clear his mind. What he was about to attempt required his full concentration. "Get what needs to be gotten, then get gone."

That had been Kaduna's advice the first time he had taken a job. He had been just on the other side of ten.

Kaduna hadn't approved of his decision, though she understood. He had little choice, and he was just trying to do what was right. He was trying to do for her what she had done for him.

They were impoverished. Almost to the point of living on the streets of Innsbruck. About to be evicted from their small apartment. But he had an opportunity.

Several of the gangs that roamed the city were circling Mikel. He chose the one that wouldn't require that he sell himself to make some money.

His mother, as Mikel thought of Kaduna, could no longer make the charms and medicines that had saved countless lives in the lower Rings and the City Below and had given them a poor though comfortable life. Reaching for the Talent placed too much of a strain on her weakened body, the decay buried deep within her and spreading with each passing day. The irony being that she couldn't heal what ailed her. No one could.

That's what happened when touched by the Curse.

Just a tiny touch, admittedly, when she had taken Mikel with her. Helping him escape a certain death, at the same time ensuring her own death. Because once touched by the Curse, no matter how strong the Magus, there was only one possible result.

That tiny touch grew slowly. Ever so slowly. Kaduna fought it all the while. Until she couldn't fight it anymore, the Curse consuming her from the inside out.

Only then did Kaduna give her approval. Because she realized that upon her death Mikel needed some way to survive in the city atop the Crux that didn't demand from him more than he should be willing and able to give.

This wasn't what she wanted for him. Yet what she wanted didn't matter.

Mikel remembered the look on Kaduna's face when he returned, the job going off without a hitch. His take enough to ensure they ate for the next month. Devastatingly ironic, since Kaduna only had days to live.

She had been happy for him. Sad as well. Telling him that once he stepped onto the road that beckoned to him, and he had gotten a taste of the potential reward – believing that he would thrive on the risk and danger as well, it would prove difficult if not impossible to step off.

Mikel pushed that memory back into the recesses of his mind where it belonged.

He missed Kaduna, thinking of her often, even after all the

years since she had passed. She had been his guiding star. She still was, in fact. Her voice, just as it had been only a moment before, continuing to play through his mind. Of course, he doubted that she would agree with all the decisions that he had made.

Such as accepting the task of stealing an item wanted by a Magus whom he doubted could be trusted once she had said item in her possession.

But that was a worry for later.

Now he needed to focus on his most immediate challenge.

Finding the artifact in a fortress swarming with hundreds of very edgy soldiers.

Sneaking into the Citadel was risky enough. Doing it just a day after the murder of King Charles Dengannon might be described as suicidal.

Mikel had argued as much with Assindra. She had told him not to worry. The soldiers would be distracted. They would be looking for other threats. They would be focused on protecting the Princess, who was now the Queen Heir.

Besides, she needed the artifact. As soon as he could acquire it. There was no time to delay. Whatever else was happening was of no relevance. And as she had noted, more times than he cared to remember in fact, he owed her.

"I need to start making better choices," he murmured to himself as he stepped out of the hidden passageway and emerged from behind an ancient, musty tapestry that hung from the ceiling to the floor.

Mikel had known where the young woman he had helped save from the Drude was going when she stopped in front of the apothecary shop. There were several such entrances into the Citadel hidden about Innsbruck.

She likely knew a few of them.

He knew them all.

The one he used brought him to one of the smaller halls on

the main floor that was rarely used and close to the kitchens on the back side of the fortress. Set aside to feed the entourages of visiting dignitaries, at the moment there were none. Though that would change when news of the king's death spread.

He wiped away some of the dust and the few cobwebs that had accumulated on his shoulders. He had taken great care to clean the uniform he acquired and wanted to keep it that way to maintain the ruse.

What better scheme to avoid the notice of the many soldiers rushing about the Citadel than to be dressed like a soldier himself? In this case, a Sergeant.

He selected the rank purposefully. A soldier of a higher rank wouldn't notice him, and a soldier of a lower rank wouldn't want to be noticed by him.

For all intents and purposes, he was invisible.

A necessary choice in garb for what he needed to do. Also, the primary reason he left Teddy behind.

His giant of a friend would draw too much attention to them.

Teddy understood Mikel's reasoning, although he hadn't been happy about it. Nor had Nat, who had spied on their conversation after the Magus left.

He would have taken her to task when she revealed herself if not for her genuine concern for him. In just a short time a strong connection had formed between them. A connection that neither of them wanted to lose.

Though Mikel usually preferred to work with Teddy on a job like this one, in this instance he was glad that his friend couldn't join him. He was the one in the bind. He didn't want to rope Teddy into it. There was too much at risk as it was.

But there was another reason for wanting to manage this task on his own.

The job felt wrong.

It had the instant Assindra gave it to him.

It felt even more wrong now that he stood in the Citadel.

Usually, when a vague sense of unease struck him on a job, he would step back. Reevaluate. Make sure that he wasn't missing something important. That there weren't any hidden perils lurking.

Yet some aspect of this job in particular made him even more curious than he already was. It was almost as if he was supposed to be here. That he was getting pulled in a direction not of his choosing. And rather than resist as he normally would, he wanted to see where the urge would take him.

Regardless, there was nothing for it.

"Get what needs to be gotten, then get gone," he murmured again, repeating the mantra that always brought a smile to his face because it brought a picture of Kaduna to mind.

Pulling out the small stone that the Magus said would function as a divining rod, Mikel turned to his left. He followed the pull of the rock he carried in his hand into a long corridor, striding through the Citadel like he owned the fortress.

"THERE IS an easy solution to your problems, Celindria."

"My father died the day before yesterday, Lucius." Her eyes were red. Not just from grief. Anger as well. She didn't want to deal with him. Not when images of her father's torn-apart body kept flashing in front of her. Not when her uncle's words kept playing through her mind. "You want to talk about this now?"

"You don't have much choice," he replied in a calm voice. "I'm just trying to help you."

"More like trying to help yourself." Though she didn't speak the words. Putting it all into a glare.

He offered her a brief shrug that she assumed was meant to serve as his condolences. Although she doubted that he cared about her loss in any other way than how it benefited him.

With the throne vacant, he had an opportunity now that he clearly wanted to exploit.

Lucius sat across from her on a terrace that gave them an excellent view of the Crux where the Northern and Western Rivers met against the crust of the dormant volcano.

Drin kept the several additional biting responses that came to mind because of his callousness to herself. No matter how much she might not like it, her uninvited guest was correct. She didn't have much choice. Just as her uncle had told her.

There already were rumblings among the First Families, and those rumblings were only going to get louder once her father was buried the day after tomorrow. Especially since the Coronation would take place only a few days after that.

Whether it would be her Coronation or someone else's …

That was yet to be determined. Rumors and schemes were flying among the First Families.

And of all the First Families, the Hanovers were in the best position to call for a Search. Therefore, she had no doubt that the cause for all the rumbling among the powerbrokers living just below the Royal Ring started with the man sitting across from her, his beard and the tips of his mustache oiled to sharp points.

No matter how distasteful she might find it, duty demanded that she find a way to avoid a Search. As her uncle had explained, and she could not argue, her Kingdom before her personal interests. Always.

She understood that sentiment.

She had been raised to believe it.

To live it.

To understand the necessity of such an approach as she made her way through her world.

Nevertheless, the thought of what likely was going to be required of her now …

Drin closed her eyes, seeking a calm that refused to come.

Nevertheless, she did as duty demanded. "The Dengannons have ruled the Kingdom of the Crux for almost four centuries, Lucius. We have a great many allies among the First Families."

Lucius nodded in a patronizing manner, offering her a sickly sweet smile as he drank the last of his wine. Feeling no need to rush. Viewing the future that he imagined as inevitable.

They had engaged in a private lunch, what was really a chance for them to test the waters, even though Celindria chose not to look at their encounter in that way. Rather, she viewed it as a combat. One without steel, yet just as dangerous. And just as crucial to her future and that of her family.

"You do," he admitted. "That's quite true, and deservedly so. But you don't have allies among all the First Families, unfortunately. You know it just as well as I do."

Drin's eyes narrowed, hearing what Lucius really was telling her. "Is that a threat?" She smiled when she said it, then laughed softly. Enjoying his brief scowl.

"Far from it, Celindria." He leaned toward her, reaching across the table. She allowed him to grasp her hand, not having any good excuse to withdraw it before he grabbed hold. "We have known each other since we were children, Celindria."

She didn't respond right away, a sick feeling taking up residence in the pit of her stomach. She had known that eventually their conversation would take them in this direction. "We have."

"And in that time we have grown to become good friends, have we not?"

His tone contained a thick film of scum that made Drin cringe on the inside, though she was proud of herself for controlling her reaction. "Friends, yes."

"Perhaps even more than friends." Lucius squeezed her hand then reached with his other hand, lightly stroking her forearm. Just as he had done only a few years before when first his touch had excited her.

"I don't know about ..." She desperately wanted to pull her hand free. She resisted the impulse, however, understanding that she needed to play the game. She didn't have any other option.

Lucius leaned in even closer. She smelled the garlic on his breath, making her nose wrinkle. "Come now, Celindria. You can't have forgotten the time that we spent together. The fun we had."

"I don't see how that's ..."

"You face a great many challenges, Celindria," Lucius continued, ignoring her. "The loss of your father must be acknowledged, and he must be mourned." Lucius' expression turned sad, although the emotion never reached his eyes, which contained what they always did. A self-serving cunning and pragmatism. "Just not now."

"If not now, when?"

Drin cursed herself for a fool, realizing the mistake she made. The door that she had kicked open for him.

"When questions about the Succession have been put to rest." Lucius smiled, although it wasn't a warm smile. It more resembled a Northern Troll who had tricked an unsuspecting victim into his cookpot. "And I can help you with that."

"You can?"

There was a great deal more that Drin could have said. That she wanted to say.

She didn't. Because her uncle was right no matter how much she didn't want him to be.

"I can." His eyes flashed with a promise. More for him than for her, of course. "I can make sure that all the questions regarding your Succession are answered as they should be. I can make sure that there is no Search."

Drin hated playing this role. She couldn't avoid it, though. So as she was expected to do, she infused a hint of hope into her voice. "Truly? You can?" All the while certain that the primary threat to her ascension to the throne came from the preening peacock sitting across from her.

"I can."

"You propose an alliance." Drin had no doubt that he would take the bait, hoping as well that he understood what she was offering him and what she wasn't. The sick feeling in her stomach began to churn like the waters around the Crux when he didn't chomp at it immediately.

"An alliance of sorts," Lucius replied. He gripped her hand with both of his, his eyes latching onto hers and burning with a previously hidden desire. Though Drin doubted that desire was as much for her as for what she represented. What he could take from her personally likely just a bonus. "I propose a proposal."

A numbing coldness settled within Drin. It was as if she were looking at the world through someone else's eyes. Watching as she engaged with Lucius Hanover.

She had known that it would come to this. That he would ignore her subtlety. Yet still ...

She wanted to scream at the top of her lungs. Instead, she forced herself to smile as best as she could and do what she must. "I believe that we can set aside a time to discuss your proposal."

"Wonderful!" Lucius exclaimed. "I knew that you would see things just as I do." He had not yet let go of her hand. Instead, he leaned in even closer to her. Too close for her tastes. "There is only one question that remains."

"And what would that be?"

"Our compatibility."

Drin frowned. "Our compatibility?" She didn't quite understand. Until she did. His comment dredging up that horrible night from several years before. Lucius making the most of Drin's innocence. "But we were just talking about ..."

"Our compatibility in a more personal sense," Lucius said,

his eyes sharpening, making her realize exactly what the Lord of House Hanover truly was. A predator. "Much ... much ... more personal."

"Lucius, I don't know that now is the best time for this conversation. My father ..."

Maintaining his grip on Drin's arm, Lucius pushed himself up from his seat then knelt down next to her.

Drin tried to push her chair back. She didn't like how he was crowding her. Almost on top of her. But she couldn't. She was stuck against the railing.

Lucius' right hand let go of her forearm and drifted down to her knee.

She gasped.

He interpreted her response as an invitation to continue.

First, squeezing in a much-too-familiar way. Then, he began to rub softly. His hand slowly moving higher up her thigh.

"Your father is gone, Celindria, you're right," Lucius murmured in a soft voice, almost in her ear, "and you should mourn him." He leaned in closer, which didn't seem possible. "But right now, you don't have the luxury or the time to mourn. There is only one decision you can make right now. A decision that is absolutely essential to ensuring the health and well-being of the Kingdom of the Crux."

His hand was well up on her thigh now. Squeezing more insistently. She froze for just an instant, unsure of what to do. His touch not just making her feel ill. Also making her angry.

He sought to take advantage of her in this way now?

She understood quite well what was at stake. She understood as well what her responsibilities were.

Nevertheless, there was only so far that she could be pushed. Only so far that she was willing to go.

In that moment, Lucius' predatory eyes made her feel like nothing more than another of his conquests.

She had no desire to meet her responsibilities.

She only desired to lash out.

She wanted nothing more than to remind Lucius Hanover who she was and the power that she could call upon.

She didn't care about the consequences as her temper began to boil.

~

"WHY DO I KEEP DOING THIS?" Mikel grumbled under his breath, having no intention of giving himself the answer he didn't want to hear. Shaking his head in annoyance. At himself. Because of what he was considering.

He was on a job. He needed to keep going. Yet he couldn't seem to make himself do it.

The Queen Heir was just past the doorway he was leaning against. The Lord of House Hanover with her. That same lord apparently seeking to force himself upon the Queen Heir during her time of grief.

He didn't like that. In fact, it made his blood boil.

He might be a thief.

He might be many things, in fact.

But he lived according to certain standards and rules imprinted upon him by Kaduna.

Standards and rules that chafed at times.

Standards and rules that if he ignored would make his life quite a bit easier and simpler.

But he couldn't ignore them.

He would be true to himself.

He would be true to what Kaduna taught him.

He wouldn't ignore them, just as he didn't ignore the Queen Heir when she needed help with the Drude.

Even though the stone in his hand wanted him to continue down the corridor.

He knew where the stone was leading him. There was a

secret passageway just up ahead that would take him several levels below and into the many basements of the Citadel.

His job would have to wait, however, if only for a few minutes.

"Tell me. Do you know the difference between a fool and a lord?" Mikel placed himself in the doorway that led out onto the terrace.

A shocked silence descended.

Lucius Hanover glared at him in anger, not expecting to be interrupted.

Celindria Dengannon offered him grateful eyes that flashed when she realized who he was. She hadn't been able to see him clearly in the fog. Nevertheless, his voice was quite distinctive and one that she would never forget.

"I can't say that I do," Drin replied, more than willing to play along. Hoping that her rescuer was offering her a chance to get out of this situation without having to take the more severe approach that, though quite appealed to her, would only make her life more difficult in the days ahead and put her future rule in peril even more than it already was.

"A fool knows that he is a fool," Mikel explained, his focus entirely on the lord kneeling next to Drin, his hand still on her thigh. He didn't like that at all, fighting the urge to pull his dagger. "And the true fool does not mind that knowledge."

"And the lord?" Drin prompted.

"The lord refuses to acknowledge that he is a fool, and because of that he is the bigger fool of the two."

Drin chuckled softly at that, understanding at whom her rescuer directed his barb. Lucius understood as well, his face turning red with rage as he rose quickly, stepping around the table and squaring up to Mikel.

"You dare to involve yourself in our business, Sergeant?" Lucius demanded. "Do you not know who I am?"

Mikel frowned, offering Hanover a confused expression.

Enjoying how his reaction only turned his adversary's face that much redder. "I can't say that I do." He shrugged his shoulders apologetically. "Am I supposed to?"

"If nothing else, you should know your betters," Lucius hissed.

"That I do," Mikel replied. "Although I doubt that I will find one in you."

Drin snorted softly, fighting to control her laughter. Needing some way to release the tension that had been building up within her. That enraged Lucius all the more, yet there was only one target upon which he could unleash it.

"Of all the insolent ..." Lucius caught himself. He wanted nothing more than to smack this Sergeant across the face. He kept that desire in check, however. He could commit such an action without penalty. And he was tempted. But there was a unique coldness in the soldier's eyes that stopped him and made his words catch in his throat, needing to clear it several times before he could say what he wanted to say. "I am Lucius Hanover. I rule in Grassdorf, and I have a great many business interests here on the Crux as well as the Tor. I, Sergeant, am quite obviously your better."

Lucius expected some kind of recognition from the Sergeant upon his pronouncement. Some kind of deference. He didn't receive it.

Instead, Mikel gave him a quizzical look. "Did you say that your name is Luscious Hanover?"

"What?" Lucius couldn't quite believe this half-wit would risk making fun of him. Everyone knew the power and wealth of House Hanover. "No, you witless cretin! Lucius."

Drin was laughing softly now, enjoying how easily her rescuer had flustered her suitor. Even more pleased that Lucius' hand was no longer on her leg.

"If you say so," Mikel shrugged. "It sounded like Luscious. That's why I needed to ask."

Lucius stepped in close to Mikel. Invading his space. Their noses no more than a few inches apart. Attempting to force Mikel backward and thereby exert an animalistic dominance over him.

It didn't work.

Mikel didn't move.

Only his smile changed. Becoming a smirk. An insult.

"Why are you here, Sergeant?" Lucius demanded. "I would think that you would have more important business to attend to rather than interfering in the matters of your *betters*." He bit off the last word, seeking to emphasize his point.

"We're going down this road again?" Mikel asked, completely at his ease, having dealt in the past with a lot worse than a lord whose britches were a bit too big for him.

"I asked you a question, Sergeant!" Lucius could barely keep his rage in check.

"You did," Mikel replied.

He didn't offer any more than that. Instead, he locked eyes with Lucius and then stepped toward him. Swiftly. He understood the purpose of the game that Hanover had started. If that's what he wanted to play at, he was more than happy to oblige.

Lucius stumbled back a few feet, caught off balance because of Mikel's sudden movement. Never expecting the Sergeant to advance toward him.

Hanover's hand dropped down to the dagger on his belt. He didn't reach for it, however. Those frigid eyes locking onto him once again.

There was something about this Sergeant that unnerved Lucius, though he was loath to admit it to himself. The man stood there seemingly unconcerned that he was challenging the greatest House in all the Crux.

"Why are you here, Sergeant?" Drin asked. She was intrigued by the confrontation between the two men, strangely relishing it in fact, but she feared what would happen if it continued for much longer.

"The Battle Lord sent me, Queen Heir," Mikel replied, standing straighter, offering her title in a very loud voice. Making clear as well that he answered to her and not to Lucius Hanover. "He requests your presence in your office."

"Did he say why, Sergeant?"

Mikel shook his head. "Only that it was important, Queen Heir. And that he needed to speak with you immediately."

Drin rose elegantly from her seat and strode past Lucius, coming to a stop next to Mikel. "I'm sorry, Lucius, but we will need to continue this conversation another time. Duty calls."

Lucius did not reply right away. Instead, he took several deep breaths, though none of them helped to calm him. His face was still red with rage, his hand on the hilt of his dagger.

He was jolted from his bloody musings when the Sergeant placed a hand on the hilt of the short sword strapped to his belt. A surge of warning raced through Lucius. Those cold eyes still locked onto him.

"Tomorrow, then," Lucius growled as he walked out into the hallway. "And be wary, Sergeant. You have poked the bear."

"Have I?" Mikel asked, his voice carrying a hint of amusement that shifted swiftly to a cold certainty. "I usually only poke a bear if I mean to kill it."

That comment stopped Lucius for an instant, although he didn't turn back around. It was too late now, he realized. The moment was gone. He would need to lick his wounds until the right chance was presented to him. Because he would have his revenge against this disrespectful upstart.

When Lucius started walking away again, Mikel let him go. He had gained what he wanted, so there was no cause to keep pushing. Besides, fun though it may be to twist into a knot the knickers of one of the leaders of a First Family, he needed to get back to work.

He was about to head into the hallway when a strong grip on his arm held him in place.

"I know you."

This time, Celindria Dengannon took her time studying her rescuer. He was big, that much was obvious. And he wasn't handsome, although he did have a face that her mother would have said had real character. She had never been able to figure out if that comment was a compliment.

Yet just as before the feature that drew most of her attention was the man's eyes. The frigid cold that was always in the back even when he smiled, just as he was doing now, sparking a feeling within her that she didn't quite understand.

"A pleasure to see you again, Queen Heir." He stepped back from her quickly, her hand falling away from him. He moved closer to the doorway, seeking to make his escape. Not wanting to get drawn into a long conversation with her. Worried that Lucius Hanover might send a few soldiers this way if he sensed that something was off about him other than his insolence. "I apologize, but I must get back to work."

"Thank you ..." she said, expecting him to offer his name.

He didn't. Mikel nodded. "It was nothing, Queen Heir. I hope you can enjoy the rest of your evening." He took several more steps away from her. Reaching the doorway. The corridor beckoning to him.

"You aided me in the fog."

"I did," Mikel confirmed with a nod, seeing no reason to lie. To do so would insult her, and he had no desire to do that.

"Yet you didn't tell me who you were then."

"I didn't." Mikel offered her no more than that.

Drin's smile became a frown. The feeling he caused within her remained. A feeling she did not want to explore even though she enjoyed how it played through her. Yet there was some feature to her rescuer that didn't make sense. "You're a Sergeant in the army?"

"For the moment, yes," he replied. "Only for as long as I need to be actually."

With that last comment, he disappeared, striding down the hallway.

Drin was too stunned to do anything at first. He was a Sergeant, but he wasn't? And no one had ever treated her this way. With so much familiarity and so little deference. She didn't know what to make of it.

"Wait," she called after him. "Where are you going? I haven't dismissed you."

"I have some business to attend to," Mikel replied, his voice drifting back down the hallway.

"In the Citadel?" she asked. She was beginning to realize that her rescuer wasn't all that he seemed to be.

"Yes," Mikel replied, poking his head back through the doorway. "Have no fear. I'm not here to do anything you need to worry about. Have a good evening, Queen Heir. And stay clear of Luscious if you can. He's sour on the inside."

Mikel disappeared again.

For a few seconds, all Drin could do was stare at where he had been standing. Then she jolted herself into motion, rushing through the doorway. Searching the corridor in the direction he had gone.

How could he ...

"Guards!" she called as she strode in the direction the Sergeant had taken. "There is an intruder in the Citadel."

11

OUT OF THE DARKNESS

Mikel stood silently, patiently, in the lowest basement of the Citadel.

It would have been pitch black if not for the ensorcelled stone that had led him here, the rock glowing with greater intensity with each step he took. It allowed him to see down the length of the musty corridor, massive cobwebs blocking his way. A sense of abandonment filled the narrow space.

He would have preferred the darkness, in fact he was used to working in the darkness, but there was no way around it. He had no control over the stone. And he couldn't get what needed to be gotten without it.

He pushed his apprehension to the side.

He was alone. That's what mattered.

With all the dust and disrepair, there was no sign that another person had been down here in ... he didn't know how long.

So Mikel focused on what waited before him.

Ten storerooms in all. Five along each side. The doors carved from a thick oak difficult to come by in the north, none of those doors appearing to have been opened in years. Probably decades.

The large metal locks on all of them showed clear signs of rust. Several most likely sealed shut by the decay.

Before he allowed the stone to pull him where it wanted him to go, what he guessed would be the far end of the hallway based on where the stone had led him, he closed his eyes and did nothing more than breathe.

He tried to get a sense for the space around him, believing that any dangers he would need to face already would be down here with him.

He doubted that he had anything to fear from the soldiers sweeping through the Citadel far above him thanks to Celindria Dengannon's cry right after he stepped into the hidden passageway and closed the door behind him.

They wouldn't make their way down here for quite some time ... if they ever did.

Mikel had been on jobs like this before. Straightforward. Lacking surprises or any real threats.

Then why did he feel so ill at ease?

Why did he feel like he was walking into a nest of scorpions?

"Get what needs to be gotten, then get gone," he reminded himself.

Kaduna's words playing through his mind, her smile calming him, he allowed the stone to pull him to the storeroom at the very end of the corridor on the left.

The stone was glowing with even greater intensity than it was before. Pulsing. A sign that he was in the right place.

Anxious as well. The intensity suggested that the magic in the stone wanted him to keep moving and stay on task. To not delay any longer. Not with the piece so close.

He didn't rush, however, taking the time to study the door. Needing to decide on what approach would allow him to get past the hardened wood most easily. Having learned all that could happen if he was anything but cautious.

Upon examining the mechanism, he decided that he might be able to work the lock despite the rust. Best to start with that as it would take the least amount of time if he could manage it.

He reached beneath the sleeve on his right forearm and pulled free the fine tools he had sheathed there.

It was a simple lock, just old. Slim piece of metal in hand, he knelt down, about to begin.

He held off instead.

That feeling of discomfort was getting stronger.

He looked back down the hallway that was illuminated by the rock he had placed on the floor.

He didn't see anything.

He didn't hear anything.

He just sensed ... he didn't know what.

He feared that ...

Mikel frowned.

All was quiet.

All was well.

Yet some sense hidden deep within him warned him to be wary. Had something moved back the way he had come? Still hidden within the gloom.

Drawing closer.

Watching.

Waiting.

Was it a figment of his imagination?

Or more than that?

And if so, what?

There was nothing to see other than shadows where the stone's illumination began to fail.

A stronger hint of warning flowed through him.

Just because he couldn't see it, just because he couldn't hear it, didn't mean it wasn't there.

So he waited.

Allowing the minutes to pass.

Wanting to make sure.

Ignoring the increasingly insistent pulse of the stone.

Ready.

Patient.

Yet nothing happened.

His frown deepened, still not convinced, that hint of warning tingling with greater vigor, Mikel set to his task.

Focused, but remaining vigilant.

There was only one way out. Back the way he had come. If something was waiting for him, he might as well have the artifact in hand when the confrontation occurred.

Still, he kept one ear open as he worked, massaging the tools into the crusted lock and gently worrying the rusted mechanism.

In the end, despite the rust, it only took him a few minutes to unlock the door. It took longer for him to pull it open, the wood swelling over the years and fitting even more tightly against the frame.

After a few minutes of straining, the door swung open noisily on squeaky hinges.

Rather than stepping into the storeroom, the light of the stone now directed into the chamber, once again Mikel waited.

He didn't care for surprises on a job, whether coming from the storeroom or at his back.

The movement that he thought he had sensed just minutes before still bothered him.

He looked back down the hallway. Seeking anything that might suggest a threat hid from him.

Nothing at all.

Growling, a mix of anger and unease, he picked up the stone and stepped into the storeroom.

He was greeted by shelves, cubbies, and cabinets set into

the walls on each side that held almost every weapon imaginable.

It was exactly what he was told to expect.

No surprises so far. Just the way he liked it.

Then why was the sense of doom that had been plaguing him for the last few minutes pushing down on him with even greater weight now? Why did he feel like he was standing at the gallows with the noose about to be slipped around his neck?

Mikel shook his head, trying to clear the chilling sensation so that he could focus on what he needed to do.

His efforts not working, he decided that speed now was the key. He strode into the storeroom, one hand on the hilt of his mace, the other holding the stone, the magical tracker leading him all the way to the back.

Swords. Spears. Cutlasses. Sabres. Daggers. Bows. Halberds. Whips. Suits of armor, chain and mail. Shields of all sorts. Some weapons of war that Mikel had never seen before. None that had been used since the door had last been opened.

He should have expected as much.

He stopped at the very back of the storage space.

The stone in his hand had grown warm. Almost hot. It was pulsing in rhythm with his heartbeat, the blinding light pointing toward his left. Illuminating a shelf that was level with his chest.

That was strange.

There was nothing there.

It was the only empty space in the entire chamber.

Then why was the rock so insistent that he come to this exact point?

Mikel was about to take a step farther to his left where a dozen or more swords lay in a pile. Instead he gasped in pain. The rock flashed with a scalding heat. Threatening to burn his hand.

Mikel shifted his focus back to the empty shelf, the heat of the rock dissipating in an instant. His guide was now just warm, though pulsing just as swiftly as before. Its beam of light only shining on that empty shelf.

More than strange.

It reminded him of when he was younger. A friend had dared him to play one of the games of chance set up on a street corner in a seedier neighborhood of Innsbruck.

There had been a large box with three holes, all large enough for a hand.

Insert his hand and see if he picked right. If he did, he doubled his money when he extracted the carved piece of wood. If he didn't, he died, the very angry snow adders curled up inside not wanting to be disturbed.

He had never played the game, preferring to control the odds whenever he could. But it didn't seem like he could now.

The magical rock having gotten him this far, he did the one thing that he didn't want to do.

Mikel placed his hand on the empty shelf ... and discovered that it really wasn't empty.

His eyes widened in disbelief when the image of the empty shelf shimmered as his hand disappeared. It felt like he was pushing through jelly.

Some kind of magical ward he realized.

Was this why Assindra maneuvered him into this task? His immunity to the Talent and the Curse protecting him from any magical wards?

He wouldn't put it past her.

Perhaps more important, there wasn't a snow adder waiting for him on the shelf. Instead, his fingers wrapped around the hilt of a sword.

He picked up the weapon and pulled his arm back, the image shifting as he did so, never revealing the shelf, the magical weave returning to its original construction when he was done.

This had to be the artifact he was searching for.

The light from the stone shone brilliantly, almost as if it were congratulating him.

But why this artifact?

Why was it so important to the Magus?

It certainly didn't look like much.

It was just a scimitar. Three feet in length. And it looked old. Perhaps even from the time of the Ancients.

There wasn't much in the way of adornment. It was just a serviceable weapon. No more than that.

He twisted and turned the blade, examining it from every direction.

There, etched into the steel on both sides of the blade. Most wouldn't understand the writing. Mikel did, however. Kaduna made him master the Old Tongue. He had never understood why, Kaduna simply explaining that it would benefit him in the future. Once again, she was right.

"When the darkness surrounds, the Light will prevail."

Mikel was sure of the translation as he read it to himself. Thanking Kaduna once again for the knowledge she shared. But what did it mean?

Another mystery for him to solve, though that would have to wait.

He whipped the scimitar through the air, the steel's passage sounding almost like the crack of a whip.

That brought a smile to his face. And he liked the feel of the weapon in his hand. It was perfectly balanced. Almost like it was made for him.

What he found most impressive was that even after however many years the scimitar had lain on the shelf – decades, centuries -- the blade still held a keen edge.

Although that didn't surprise him, not after he recognized the quality of the craftsmanship.

He had seen pieces like this before. Only a few smiths in all the Realms could craft a weapon such as this one. All of them located to the west in the Frozen Waste.

The Giants of the Rime.

That conclusion only piqued Mikel's curiosity.

Why would a weapon of this quality be left in a storeroom?

It seemed that Mikel wasn't done with his questions.

Perhaps Cadmus would be able to offer him some knowledge regarding the blade.

Although discovering the maker of the blade answered one of his queries.

Creatures touched by the Curse couldn't touch weapons crafted by the Giants of the Rime because the blacksmiths of the Frozen Waste shaped their weapons through a unique process that involved fusing light and the Talent into the steel.

A weapon such as the one he held now would have been crafted at the request of the Order of the Magii.

Having but one purpose.

To be used against those tainted by the Curse.

Why was it then that Assindra wanted him to steal the blade?

Why not her?

She had the means and the power to locate it. To claim it as she desired.

The realization struck him like a bolt of lightning.

It all seemed too convenient.

Too neatly wrapped.

He was being played. Assindra was the one who created the debt in the first place. To get him here. So that he could get for her what she couldn't get herself.

Because she wasn't just a Magus.

Understanding now the peril he truly faced, he would need to choose his next steps carefully. And he realized as well that Assindra wouldn't just let him go. No, he would need to deal with her if he could, not liking the idea of a Dark

Magus waiting to stab him in the back the first chance she got.

His thoughts already turning toward what few options he might have for extricating himself from what was looking more and more like an untenable situation, Mikel slashed through the air with the scimitar a few more times.

He had held a great many swords over the years, several Giant made. This one felt different, and he didn't know why.

He couldn't escape the sensation that the scimitar was more than just a weapon.

Mikel growled again, beginning to lose patience with himself. He needed to get moving.

A shiver of warning ran down his spine.

He should have assumed as much.

He had delayed for too long. His natural curiosity almost getting the better of him.

Sensing the presence that had joined him in the room, and disappointed that he had been right, Mikel turned slowly, scimitar held out to his front.

The Drude.

He could see the resemblance now, the creature summoned from the Spirit World taking on the appearance of its master.

Assindra had used him to gain the blade. Now she meant to get rid of him so that she could do what she would with the magic-infused steel.

He had assumed from the very beginning that she would try to play him. Although he had to admit that he hadn't anticipated that she would do it in this way.

And instead of being angry or afraid, he was eager.

There was unfinished business between them.

He welcomed the clash to come because there was a certainty to it.

There was only one question that required an answer.

Could he kill a Drude?

There was only one way to find out.

Mikel was about to step forward when the light provided by the rock winked out.

"Blasted Magus," he growled.

Even with complete darkness draping itself around him, Mikel sensed the Drude moving slowly past the shelves and toward him. The sense of menace emanating from the monster intensified.

He assumed that he wasn't going to like the answer to his question.

Knowing with absolute certainty that he stood little chance if he couldn't even see his adversary.

Then much to his shock the blade of the scimitar blazed to life, a bright white light illuminating the chamber and revealing the Drude just a few feet in front of him.

Mikel didn't think. Instead, he allowed his training and instincts to guide him.

He feinted a lunge, then twisted his hand, sweeping the steel in a wide backhanded arc across his body.

He grinned devilishly when the fiery blade cut through the wispy strands of black that made up the Drude.

The creature hissed in shock as it glided backward. The essence Mikel cut from the monster faded into what resembled cinders and vanished entirely before they struck the ground. The summoning from the Spirit World clearly diminished.

Mikel's grin disappeared an instant later, replaced by an expression of wonder.

How it happened, he didn't know. He didn't care either.

An explosion of energy – clean, pure, cleansing – surged through him.

The Giant-crafted blade was no longer just a tool. It was a part of him. Just as he was a part of the blade.

Two consciousnesses now one. Linked. Whole.

More than just a meeting of the minds. A joining of heart

and soul as well. The blazing blade a physical manifestation of his will.

He had heard of this happening long, long ago, but he had never come across a Giant, even Cadmus, who could tell him why it happened or what it was like when it did. He knew only that it was possible, though incredibly rare. A gift. A burden as well. Though he chose to ignore that last part.

Mikel relished the sensations that raced through him. Gaining an awareness that he had never experienced before. A power that he ...

Mikel's expression shifted once again.

This time to a relief that almost brought tears to his eyes.

The Talent.

The scimitar contained a reservoir of the Talent – or what Mikel took to be the Talent -- and the artifact was gifting it to him. Allowing him to make use of it.

Unlike all the other Caledonii in the Realms, he had never enjoyed this sensation before.

He had never touched the Talent, this key part of his heritage denied to him.

But no longer.

His eyes narrowed, filled with purpose.

Mikel had never used the Talent before, but he had watched Kaduna work with it, and he had learned a great deal from her.

Accepting the gift granted to him, he sent more of the power into the steel, reveling in that natural magic all around him that up until that moment he could never sense or touch. Blazing as bright as the summer sun, the blade burned away the last of the shadows in the storeroom and highlighted the Drude so that the creature couldn't slip back into the darkness.

Hissing again, the Drude glided toward him, the creature's movement so fast that it was little more than a blur.

Mikel was ready.

The Drude shrieked in pain, sliding backward just as fast as it had advanced, the claw that reached for Mikel severed when it made contact with the blade, dropping toward the floor, flaking away, the ash disappearing as if swept away by the wind, returning to its land of creation.

Mikel refused to allow the assassin to escape, wanting just as much to send Assindra a warning as he wanted to kill the Drude.

He attacked with a ferocity that he could barely restrain. Slicing at the edges of the shadowy creature, cutting away bits of misty black that drifted toward the floor and faded before they hit the stone, each time Mikel struck true the Drude hissing both in pain and fear.

Acknowledging its dire circumstances, the Drude fled for the safety of the corridor beyond the storeroom, seeking to escape into the gloom beyond. Knowing based on past experience that to attack the Bearer of the Blade with the Curse was a waste of time and effort.

Mikel had been waiting for his adversary to make such a play.

As soon as the Drude turned to flee, Mikel grasped the hilt of the scimitar with both hands. Bringing the weapon back over his head, he threw it.

The scimitar spun through the air, resembling a blazing ball of light before it slammed into the wall just beyond the doorway and pierced the stone.

The Drude stood right in front of the swaying steel.

Frozen in place.

A long, neat slice in its back allowing Mikel to see through the creature from the Spirit World.

A burning stench filled the chamber, the charring edges of the wound flashing then racing out in all directions. Devouring the misty black. Consuming the Drude and destroying the Curse.

Mikel grunted in satisfaction, pleased that his tactic worked.

He strode toward the gleaming steel.

He still had a great many questions. But at least he had gained one answer.

He could kill a Drude, and he took a great deal of pleasure from that.

Yet, there was still more to be done.

His business with the Dark Magus not yet complete.

12

TESTY EXCHANGE

When Mikel accepted the job Assindra gave him, they had not agreed on a day and time to complete the exchange. He had assumed that she would know when the job was done and then she would pay him another visit.

Certain in that knowledge, he avoided his usual haunts once he left the Citadel. Working his way quietly and surreptitiously through the City Above, he took his time to ensure that no one was tracking him as he meandered down from the Royal Ring to water's edge and then into the City Below. He snuck through passages that were closely guarded by his fighters and steered clear of the thousands of people who had taken refuge and made new lives for themselves in the caverns and tunnels that pockmarked the island.

When he reached the lowest inhabited level within the Crux, he kept going. Taking secret paths that only he knew about that led deep beneath the dormant volcano. He didn't stop until he reached a ragged chamber, stalactites reaching down from the craggy ceiling.

There he waited, several hundred feet below the rivers that swirled around the island, a rent in the wall on the far side revealing a sluggish stream of lava that flowed down the rock and slid past slowly through a network of channels that resembled a broken spiderweb. Confirming what few suspected and what even fewer didn't want to believe.

The volcano that was the Crux indeed was dormant; however, it was not dead.

When would it wake again?

Just another worry Mikel had no good answer for.

He kept nothing down here, not trusting the lava. He just liked the serenity of the cavern ... and the knowledge that no one would find him here unless he meant for them to find him.

Rather than studying the scimitar whose very essence had taken up residence in the back of his mind, the comfortable weight sheathed across his back, he thought instead of the Dark Magus who had used him.

There was a familiarity to the woman that awakened emotions within him that he didn't understand and that he thought he had suppressed years before. What troubled him even more, however, was that he couldn't figure out why those emotions chose to breach the walls he had built up since his youth now. Why did she touch nerves that he thought long dead?

He had never done business with her before directly. He was certain of that. If he had, he would have remembered. And in all his time in the two Kingdoms that formed the Splintered Empire, he had not run across her. Not strange in and of itself. Still ...

Cursing in frustration, needing a distraction since his mind was spinning wildly, Mikel pulled the blade free from its scabbard. The steel flashed brilliantly when it caught the light of the lanterns hanging from the spikes he had driven into the craggy wall not long after he discovered the chamber.

He examined the weapon once more.

Taking his time.

Running a finger carefully along every inch of the keen blade.

Truly masterful work.

A blade that never required sharpening and without a speck of rust on it set in an unadorned hilt.

He wondered why, knowing that there had to be a reason. A blade like this usually would have a more extravagant grip.

Mikel studied one more time the Old Tongue inscribed on both sides of the blade. Done by a sure and skilled hand.

The words had been playing through his mind ever since he read them the first time.

"When the darkness surrounds the Light will prevail."

He really needed to set aside a few days to return to the Frozen Waste and speak with Cadmus, believing he was one of the few who could answer his many questions. Assuming, of course, he survived the next few minutes.

"Quite a scheme," Mikel said as he turned toward the cavern's entrance. Having no doubt that she would come. Just not knowing when. "The Drude was a nice touch. Insurance of a sort."

"Drude? What are you talking about?" Her words may have sounded true in her ears, but not in Mikel's.

"Don't bother denying it." His voice was as hard as the stone of the cavern. "You tried to play me."

Assindra stepped into the dim light, offering Mikel a cunning smile. "I did what you would have done to me."

"You're wrong there, Magus. I conduct my business honorably, even when the business itself isn't honorable."

"Does that help you justify your actions?" Assindra mused. "Assuage your conscience? Make you feel better about what you do?"

"No, I don't require justification for what I do," Mikel replied calmly. "I'm well aware of my failings."

"If only more could say the same."

"It's how I choose to live," he shrugged. "Clearly, you follow a different code."

"I follow a simple code, Mikel."

"I'm afraid to ask."

Assindra smiled. She enjoyed speaking with this young man. A pity she would need to kill him. She couldn't afford any loose ends. "Nothing matters more than gaining what must be gained."

"By any means necessary?" Mikel challenged.

"Indeed. There is always a price for our actions. Better that others pay it."

"A harsh perspective," he frowned. "Selfish as well."

"But a necessary one in my line of work."

Mikel nodded. "Yes, and just what is it that a Dark Magus does other than create misery for others?"

Assindra pursed her lips, unused to being spoken to in such a direct manner. Her surprise faded swiftly.

She should have expected this from him after she observed his performance against the Drude and discovered that he exited the Citadel while her Drude did not, her servant sent back to the Spirit World.

Rather than responding as she usually would, she restrained herself. Taking a closer look at the man who had achieved a task that she couldn't on her own.

She had a great deal of power at her beck and call, yet despite that she had no way to pierce the illusion that protected the artifact. Attempting to do so would have revealed what she was doing to those whom she wished to remain anonymous, as well as guaranteeing a very painful and potentially deadly backlash since she had been touched by the Curse.

But now, a thief had done her work for her. Who better to acquire an ancient magical object attuned to the Curse than the one who couldn't be harmed by the Curse?

"You believe that I am a Dark Magus," Assindra replied,

nodding in understanding. "That is an archaic label. One applied by those lacking any real understanding of the power available in the Natural World to those willing to demonstrate the strength and the courage to take it. I am simply a Magus who chooses to use whatever power may help me achieve my goals."

"A poor justification if I've ever heard one." Mikel chuckled softly while he shook his head in disappointment. "And you're worried about my business practices?"

"Not a justification," Assindra challenged. "Simply the truth."

"The truth as you perceive it, you mean."

Assindra's smile deepened. "The truth as *I* perceive it *is* the truth."

"Because of the power you wield?"

"Exactly so," Assindra confirmed. "Because of the power I wield, I create the truth."

"Quite an arrogant perspective," Mikel mused. "Truth is often based on perspective, I won't deny it. Yet it seems like even with all the power at your command, crafting the truth can prove to be a difficult thing since there are so many perspectives in the world."

"A fair point," Assindra agreed, "and one I cannot argue now." Although this conversation with her thief appealed to her, time was short. Obtaining the blade was just one part of a larger strategy that already was in play. "May I see it?"

Mikel smiled, then held out the blade. However, rather than offering it to her, he maintained his grip on the hilt, tip pointed toward her.

She took her time studying the weapon. At first glance, it didn't look like much. But when examining the sword with the power that was solely at her disposal, the weapon was truly remarkable. A tool that would allow her to accomplish things that her enemies could not even begin to imagine.

"You won't give it to me?"

Mikel shook his head. "No, not willingly."

Assindra's smile deepened, becoming more of a sneer. She had assumed that it would come to this. "The Drude was necessary. I had no cause to trust you. Now I see that I can."

Mikel heard the lie and chose to ignore it. "It's not because of the Drude."

"Then why? You don't believe that I'll allow you to leave here once you give me the blade?"

"I know you won't," Mikel replied with a calm that was almost startling. "Because I know what you truly are. I know why you needed me to steal the blade. I know that you can't afford to keep me alive."

Assindra clucked her tongue. "You're too smart for your own good."

"I've been accused of a great deal worse than that."

Assindra laughed softly. She truly was enjoying their conversation. A real pity that she had to eliminate him. "Do you mean to kill me with the sword and then walk free? I promise you that won't happen. You can't stand against me. To even try is a fool's errand."

"To be honest, though I should kill you, the urge to do that isn't very strong right now."

"And why is that?" Assindra asked, intrigued.

"I wish I could tell you," Mikel replied. In truth, he didn't want to tell her that he felt an affinity for the Dark Magus that frightened him.

Eyes narrowing, Assindra studied Mikel, almost as if she were trying to delve into his mind and pull out what he was thinking. Seeing something within him that she didn't quite understand yet called to her, nonetheless. "Serve me, King of the Underworld. You will walk free if you accept, and I promise that you will prosper in a way that you could never before have imagined."

"A tempting offer."

"Then accept. Do not test my patience. For I will not offer again."

"No," Mikel replied instantly, understanding just how dangerous her proposal was.

"Why not?" she demanded.

"Because I already have all that I want."

"You have all that you want?" Assindra couldn't quite wrap her mind around the concept. "I didn't take you for a fool until now."

"A pity that I care so little for your opinion."

"One last chance." Assindra's tone was hard now. Demanding. An expectation of subservience contained within it. The result of her frustration with the thief. "Serve me."

"Never."

"So be it," she replied.

Assindra acted swiftly, sending a ropy black mist shooting from each palm. The Curse streaked across the space separating them, seeking to wrap itself around the blade and pull it free from his hand.

But it couldn't.

Every time the Curse touched the ancient steel that glowed a soft pure white it burned away. Flaking. Fading. Vanishing. Just as had happened to the Drude.

Mikel wasn't surprised, not after what he had witnessed. And he couldn't say that he wasn't enjoying himself, particularly because of the shock and anger that now marred Assindra's usually very calm and haughty visage.

"What did do you?" she hissed.

"Nothing." He shrugged. "The sword did it."

That revelation stopped Assindra cold. Her look of surprise quickly transformed into one of horror. "You linked to the blade. How could you have done that? You don't have the Talent within you."

Mikel frowned. He hadn't done anything. Whatever happened, the blade did it. Or rather the Talent contained within the blade had done it. "It wasn't a conscious decision so much as an agreement between two parties with similar interests. Besides, it was a simple choice. I trust the blade more than I trust you."

"Do you not comprehend what you've done?" Assindra cried, her raised voice echoing off the walls of the chamber. "What this means?"

"You mean other than frustrate you?" he replied with a smug grin.

"You brainless bas ..." Before she completed her thought, a blast of the Talent shot from her palm.

The energy sped right toward Mikel, the heat on a par with the magma running across the floor just to his side.

There was no time to move. No place to go. So he stood there. Stock still. Terrified. Hopeful. What choice did he have?

When the Talent struck, it glanced off him. Leaving him whole. Alive. His shit-eating grin broadened and his confidence grew.

Growling in anger, Assindra tried again. This time sending a blast of the Curse streaking toward him.

Mikel didn't bother to move. And why would he?

The tainted energy struck him full in the chest.

He should have been dead.

A shriveled corpse, smoking and charred.

Yet her attack had no effect upon him whatsoever.

"Better the pain of death than the pain of failure," Assindra muttered.

Mikel's smug grin driving her toward rage, the Dark Magus prepared to intensify her efforts. Calling upon more of the Curse, several spheres of fiery black danced atop her palms.

Mikel took a few steps back. Not because of what she was

doing. He didn't fear her next attack. Rather because of what she had just said.

"You're Caledonii."

He had not heard that phrase uttered since he was a child. Kaduna had used it a great many times while they lived in the mountains of the Spine. Even more while they made their escape from the tribe that was supposed to be his family but instead viewed him as something less. A failure as soon as he emerged from his mother's womb.

"How could you know that?" Assindra hissed, the spheres of black poised on her fingertips. She had done a great deal to ensure that truth remained hidden. Even with his resources, there was no way the King of the Underworld could have discovered it.

"Because I know you," Mikel replied, his eyes widening as the realization struck him harder than the Dark Magus' attacks with the Talent and then the Curse.

Not quite understanding what he was saying yet feeling a strange tremor of fear running down her spine, Assindra demanded an answer. "Who am I to you?"

Mikel didn't answer. Shaken. His thoughts spinning wildly as he tried to comprehend what he believed was the truth. Even though he didn't want it to be the truth.

He took several more steps backward. He had selected this cavern as their meeting place for several reasons. One of those being that there were several exits at his back that he could choose from that someone who had never been here before could easily become lost in.

He realized then that confronting Assindra like this wasn't a good idea. Particularly with his mind now a mess, an old hurt he thought long buried mixing with new knowledge that threatened his ability to make good decisions.

"Someone I no longer have any desire to deal with," he said so softly that he assumed only he could hear his words.

"You will hold, King of the Underworld! Our business is not yet done."

Assindra flung the black spheres of energy dancing atop her palms. Though not at Mikel. Understanding that her efforts would have no effect upon him. Instead, guessing at his intention, she sent the corrupt power slamming into the wall at his back.

Mikel ducked, less to get away from the Curse than to avoid the shattered and splintered stones that exploded behind him, the cavern shaking and swaying dangerously from the power of the strike.

Coughing out the grit, he covered his mouth with a shirt-sleeve and waited for the cloud of dust and debris to clear, standing once again when he could take a deep breath. Cursing in frustration. There was only one way to exit the chamber now.

Through the Dark Magus.

"As I said, our business is not done," Assindra purred with a deadly menace. "And I do not need the Talent or the Curse to kill you." She pulled a blade seemingly out of thin air, the long dagger a dull black that flashed with an evil glow.

Mikel took a few steps away from her, then realized that he had nowhere to go when he bumped into the pile of rubble at his back.

So he studied the blade in Assindra's hand. She held it in a way that suggested she was more than competent in its use. Even so, he believed that he could hold his own against her.

But he was worried as well. He had faced a great many threats during his rise in Innsbruck. He had dispatched each one with a calm and focused resolve.

He was anything but calm now. He was agitated.

What he had just discovered made him feel as if he had fallen off the edge of the Crux and he was now being battered about in the Churn. Not knowing which end was up. Not knowing what was light and dark. Only knowing that he was lost.

Not a good position to be in when dealing with a Dark Magus. Particularly one who was also ...

He shifted his gaze away from the slowly approaching Assindra to the blade in his hand.

Could he use this artifact to make his escape?

If so, how?

He didn't have any ideas, but he needed to come up with something quickly.

The combat was about to begin.

Assindra was less than ten feet away from him.

And in truth he had little desire to cross blades with her.

Allowing his instincts to guide him once again, Mikel knelt quickly and slammed the hilt of the sword on the rocky floor.

The effect was immediate and more devastating than he could have possibly imagined.

A wave of pure white energy blasted out in all directions.

Assindra ducked away at the last second, creating a shield with the Curse that bore the brunt of the blast. Even so, she stumbled backward as she struggled to maintain control over her barrier, the immense power Mikel released taking her by surprise.

Then he did it again, slamming the hilt of the sword against the floor of the cavern. Harder.

Another wave of energy erupted from the steel and surged through the underground grotto. This one directed solely toward her.

The power of this blast stronger than the last, Assindra, shield still in place, failed to maintain her feet. She dropped to her knees, the aftershocks that rumbled through the cavern keeping her there. Several large stalactites and rocks broke free from the ceiling, forcing her to shift the position of her shield.

When the rumbling finally subsided to nothing more than

a soft tremble, Assindra pushed herself back to her feet. What he had done with the blade stunned her. What she saw now astonished her all the more.

He was surrounded by massive stones that must have weighed several tons. One large stalactite just a few inches to his side, half in and half out of the wide stream of lava that flowed through the center of the cavern.

Somehow he had survived the rockfall. How that was possible she didn't know. She assumed it was whatever power was contained within the blade. Not necessarily surprising when she thought about it, though definitely concerning.

It meant that he was more of a threat to her than she believed possible.

It meant that she needed to get that blade away from him.

Now.

The longer he had it in his possession, the stronger and more knowledgeable he became.

The more deadly an opponent he would be.

That was a possibility she had never considered and that she couldn't permit.

"How did you do that?" Assindra demanded. "Only someone skilled in the Talent should be able to call upon the power of the blade. But you do not have that skill."

Mikel had no answer for her. He didn't know if he was controlling the blade, the blade was directing his actions, or it was a combination of both.

Although at the moment he didn't really care because he was still alive.

What he did care about was that there was a catch.

As the energy contained within the sword surged through him, it warmed him, energized him, became a part of him, inscribed itself upon him. It felt like he was becoming one with the blade.

The entire concept seemed a bit ridiculous to him, yet that

was the only way to describe it. And he believed that was a good thing.

He realized as well that he needed to get away.

This instant.

Because no gift was ever granted without an attached cost.

Mikel was completely and utterly exhausted.

The blade had gifted him the power to drive Assindra backward, perhaps even destroy her if she had not defended herself so quickly, but he sensed as well that to do that the blade demanded his strength. The merger requiring a contribution from both parties.

He and the blade could work together. But it was a true partnership. Both needed to give in order for both to receive.

A fair trade, but a dangerous one for him when he really didn't know what he was doing.

And he feared what might happen if Assindra forced him to call upon so much of the power once again.

That wasn't quite right.

He feared when Assindra once again forced him to call upon so much of the power contained within the blade.

It was inevitable.

There was no chance that she would allow him to escape her now that he had demonstrated what he could do with the sword.

His desire to escape foremost on his mind, he combined some of what Kaduna had taught him when he was younger with his impulses that were now accentuated by the power granted to him by the sword.

On his own, he could not touch the Talent.

A limitation of his birth.

The sword removed that restriction.

With the scimitar, the Talent flowed through him like it had been there all along. Locked away. Just needing a key to be released. The hole within him filled. Making him feel more alive than he ever had before. The world around him sharper. The world around him more than what it had been.

Mikel slashed with his blazing steel, slicing through the reality to his front. Revealing a small office lit by several lanterns just on the other side. He stepped through the rip and disappeared, the fold in reality weaving itself back together in a heartbeat.

Silence descended in the chamber then, only interrupted by the gentle rumblings that continued throughout the cavern, small stones still falling from the ceiling and the walls.

Assindra ignored it all, staring at where Mikel used the Talent in a way that no Magus had done in millennia.

None strong enough.

None skilled enough.

Not even her.

He had folded space.

Connecting where he was to wherever he went.

Bringing two distinct locations right next to each other and then releasing them once he was gone.

And she had no way to follow him.

More than just impressive.

Worrisome as well.

She dusted off her dress. She was less than pleased that she didn't have the artifact. But she took some solace from the fact that she would find it again.

He would not be able to hide from her.

Not after what he had revealed.

She was more angry with herself for not recognizing her thief sooner. His true identity had teased her ever since she watched his fight against the Drude in the fog.

She should have known at the time. For it was the only explanation.

She had been distracted, however, not certain of all that happened because of the smothering mist. Impressed that he had survived. Not quite understanding how he had managed it. Believing that there was a great deal of luck involved.

Until now.

Finally she understood what truly happened.

Realizing that Mikel Stahlherz was a rare breed indeed.

She had thought he was dead.

He should have been dead, in fact.

And she could blame only one person for that failure.

But she was dead, of that Assindra was certain, so there was little point in doing so.

The question now was how to turn Mikel toward her purposes.

How to make him her own.

Then how to steal what he had taken for himself and make it hers.

Because somehow he had unlocked the power of one of the most potent weapons ever crafted by the Giants of the Rime.

That was what dominated her thoughts when she crafted a portal of spinning black, stepping through into a chamber that resembled a throne room that was several hundred leagues to the east and atop the Tor.

13

GAME OF CHANCE

"I'm glad that we haven't been interrupted this morning."

Lucius flicked his arm forward aggressively, as if he were throwing a ball, the dart a blur until it struck the board fifteen feet away. Though just barely. The sharp tip hanging at an angle. The tail gradually sinking toward the floor.

"You mean by the Sergeant?" Drin asked, not bothering to call out Lucius' score. A four. A poor throw. Then again, she couldn't say that she was surprised.

He was not one for finesse when he believed that power was the answer. And, as she had learned, he seemed to believe that power was the answer to most challenges or, in this case, a game of sport.

"Of course I mean the Sergeant." Lucius muttered a curse just under his breath, less than pleased with the result of his latest throw. Falling even farther behind Celindria. "How did he get so close to you without anyone noticing?"

Drin didn't reply right away, instead concentrating on her throw. With a quick flick of her wrist, the dart punched into the board.

Bull's-eye.

Again. The third in a row, in fact, the center of the board becoming a little crowded. All with her darts.

"How do you keep doing that?" demanded Lucius. Rather than being pleased by her success, he was peeved.

That bothered her. Although it was illuminating as well and not all that surprising.

It hadn't taken Drin long to learn that Lucius' success was his and her success was a threat. Under other circumstances, she might have pointed out that weakness to him. She had little patience for such behavior.

Yet now, with the pressure building upon her, the Coronation to be scheduled in the next few days and rumblings about the call for a Search growing stronger by the hour, she had no choice but to grin and bear it. No matter how much doing so disturbed her.

The good of the Crux before her own.

Her uncle had reminded her of that. Thus her decision to invite Lucius to a friendly game. Smooth his ruffled feathers and perhaps come to an understanding that wasn't based on their past relationship.

"A great deal of practice." She offered Lucius a smile, perhaps a bit too big.

"More like luck," Lucius grunted as he stepped up to throw.

She could have let it go, but she couldn't help herself. "Also, I've found that in certain matters a delicate touch often proves most effective."

"I doubt that very much." He moved his arm forward a few times, getting the range, staring at the board with one eye closed. "A weakness that you will need to correct once we assume the throne, because ruling the Crux will require strength and a firm hand. Especially at the beginning. To set the tone." Lucius snorted softly. "Delicacy has no place. It will do little to ensure our successful reign."

Drin ignored his many insults. The two most obvious being

his talking down to her and his assuming that she would allow him to claim the throne with her upon her ascension. Of course, with respect to the latter, she might not have a choice. Not if she was to claim the throne in the first place.

To soothe her irritation, she considered turning Lucius into a dartboard, having already decided exactly what feature she would aim for first.

A useless hope, of course, nothing more. As was her desire to tell Lucius that his presence was no longer required in the Citadel.

He could insult her all he wanted, although he likely didn't view his words or his behavior as inappropriate. He was simply being who he was.

And she couldn't afford to insult him no matter how much he deserved it.

Not without putting at risk all that she was working toward.

For just a heartbeat, she wanted to shout at the top of her lungs. Cursing her luck. Cursing whoever murdered her father. Hating the unfairness of the almost impossible situation she was in. Yet knowing that all of that would be no more than wasted breath.

She needed to focus on what was real.

She needed to focus on what she could do.

Not on what she wanted.

She had spoken with the heads of several First Families in the last two days. All of them had offered her their condolences and support. All of them ended the conversation with a threat veiled in advice.

To avoid the Search, ally with the Hanovers.

Based on that, she had no doubt that when she met with the Lords Vercengian and Karlonia later that afternoon they would say much the same.

Lucius had done an excellent job of penning her in, and she assumed that he wouldn't free her until she accepted his proposal. However, she feared that as soon as she did she would be walking into another cage, one from which she wouldn't be able to escape because Lucius would hold the key.

That's why she sought to delay. Citing her father's murder. Claiming the need for time to grieve.

Yet that had gotten her very little sympathy and only a reprieve of a few days.

The First Families cared primarily for the First Families.

Who ruled the Kingdom of the Crux was an important variable for ensuring the success of their endeavors, business and otherwise.

Thus, their insistence that the ascension take place on their terms. Not hers.

Just thinking about that angered her in a way that little else could. In a very real sense, Drin was no more than a chip to be played. Just as Lucius made plain time and time again.

To him, she was a means to an end. And she offered a few additional, more personal benefits as well.

"Perhaps a little less power next time," Drin suggested, unable to stop herself when Lucius' dart landed on three, clinging precariously to the board just like all his other throws.

"I don't need your advice," Lucius growled softly.

"I agree in part." Drin needed to tread carefully with him. She understood that. But that didn't mean that she couldn't bite at the edges if she was careful about how she did it. "There are times when power is required. However, I have learned after sitting on the dais with my father for so many years that delicacy is not a weakness. Rather, it's a skill."

She threw before Lucius could reply, assuming that he would miss entirely the several barbs she just offered him. The reminder as well. She had already sat on the dais. He had not.

"I have never seen anyone enjoy such a streak of luck," Lucius murmured, shaking his head in wonder, unwilling to give Drin any credit for her success. Another bull's-eye.

"Perhaps there is more to it than luck," Drin suggested, offering him a cunning smile even though she was certain that he would miss the hint.

"I doubt it," he replied with a haughty confidence. "Did you ever find the Sergeant?"

"No. Despite a search of the entire Citadel, he disappeared."

"How is that even possible?"

"A good question," Drin replied, and one that she had been contemplating ever since her uncle reported that not a single soldier had seen the Sergeant. In fact, not a single soldier knew a Sergeant like the one she described.

"You have no idea who he might be?" wondered Lucius. He found that hard to believe. A man somehow acquiring the uniform of a Crux soldier and then wandering around the Citadel with impunity? To him, that hinted at a conspiracy.

"A few guesses, nothing more."

"Nor how he got into the Citadel?"

Drin shook her head. Although less in annoyance and more in curiosity. After her brief interaction with the man who played at being a soldier, she viewed him as less of a threat to her than Lucius.

She did, however, want to know who he was. Because she wanted to speak with him again, believing that he might prove useful if her suspicions were correct.

And she did want to know how he got into the fortress. Although she already had a strong suspicion as to how he accomplished it.

"Perhaps I can help you with that then."

Drin gave Lucius a discerning look. "How so?"

Lucius stepped back from the line, offering her a broad smile. "Celindria, I can't reveal my sources."

"I didn't ask you to, Lucius." He was enjoying this much too much. "If you're unwilling to provide information, shall we continue with the darts? Based on the tally, I believe you're behind by ..."

"It was most likely the King of the Underworld," Lucius offered, interrupting her, not needing to be reminded how far behind he was. That thought more annoying than the Sergeant who had interrupted them right when his last interaction with Celindria was getting so interesting.

"The King of the Underworld?" Drin scoffed. "Really?"

"The one and only."

"Based on whose knowledge? The spies you have in the city and the Citadel?"

He didn't bother to deny it, although his pride added a spark to his dark eyes. "My eyes and ears are the best in the business. They are one of the reasons the Hanovers are the first of the First Families."

"Some of the other First Families likely would disagree with you."

"They would be fools to do so."

"Perhaps, but they are proud."

"Celindria, I need you to remember this, because it will be important for us going forward," Lucius said, one hand on a hip, dart in his other hand. "Power is all that matters. With power, you can be as proud as you desire. Only a fool wouldn't believe that."

"And of course your family is the proudest of them all." Drin laced a heavy dose of sarcasm into her voice.

"We are and we deserve to be," Lucius replied, once again either missing or purposely ignoring her barb.

Not wanting to go down this road with him, she gave in to her curiosity. "Why are you so certain that the Sergeant is the King of the Underworld? No one has ever proven that there even is a King of the Underworld."

"And therein lies the real power of the King of the Underworld," Lucius extolled. "No more than a whisper to most, yet all too real."

For once, Drin couldn't disagree with him. "What proof do you offer other than the reports of your spies?"

"Nothing substantial," he admitted. "Although the Sergeant did have some small resemblance to how the King of the Underworld has been described."

"A big man. A bit rough looking. Scars on his face. That could be more than half of the male population in Innsbruck."

"True," Lucius admitted. He was willing to give her that. "But I have it on good authority that he carries a mace that's more than a mace."

"A mace that's more than a mace? What do you mean?"

"There's a blade on the end of his weapon of choice."

Drin wasn't convinced. "I'm sure other people have a similar weapon."

"Perhaps, and perhaps not. It is a rare choice, don't you think? How many times have you seen a weapon like that?"

Just once, Drin thought, and recently. At the edge of the Frozen Waste. Choosing to keep that information to herself.

"I have my eyes and ears scouring the city for him even as we speak."

"The King of the Underworld?"

"Yes, of course," Lucius frowned. "Don't you see the opportunity this gives us, Celindria?"

"The opportunity?" She wasn't really listening to him, playing back in her mind her interaction with the Sergeant who had helped her the last time Lucius visited her. She had seen a flash of steel in a sheath at the small of his back that could have been a mace. But she couldn't be sure. Her thoughts on other matters then.

She looked up when she felt his hand on her arm, pulling her from her thoughts. She gripped the dart like she would the hilt of a dagger, her initial instinct to stab him with it if he reached for any other part of her. Strange. Several years before such a touch from Lucius would have pleased her.

"Of course the opportunity, Celindria." Lucius chuckled softly as he shook his head from side to side. Amused. Not surprised that she wasn't as quick on the uptake as he was. Another reason she would need a strong hand guiding her when she took the throne. "Once we eliminate the King of the Underworld, we take over his world. There will always be a black market in Innsbruck. There always has been. Once we seize his businesses, we will control that market. No one will be able to challenge us."

"You're putting a lot of faith in a rumor, Lucius." Drin withdrew her arm from his grip with a gentle tug.

"Only because it's deserved," he replied, giving her a wink as he said it.

"And I take it that you're mentioning this because you require something from me?" She could see it in his eyes. An almost inestimable greed.

For that was the only truth there was when it came to Lucius Hanover. He was never satisfied. He never had enough. He led the first of the First Families, he may gain the throne of the Crux through her – assuming she couldn't wiggle free from him, and he had a wealth with which few could compete. Yet for all that, she concluded that what should have been strengths actually were some of his greatest weaknesses.

"I will, yes," he replied, giving her a sly smile. "Just not yet. I will call upon you when the time is right."

"I can't wait."

Once again, Lucius missed the sarcasm that thickened her voice. "Best of all, I believe that he might be Caledonii."

Drin's gaze narrowed. "Doesn't that worry you? If he is, that means he can use the Talent. He won't take kindly to you mucking about in his business."

"That doesn't worry me." Lucius' expression became both hopeful and malicious. "I have ways to deal with Magii."

Drin didn't doubt him. You could buy anything in Innsbruck, including a Magus or two if the money was right.

Her brows knit together when she glimpsed the rabid energy dancing in the back of Lucius' eyes. As a people, the Caledonii were looked down upon. They were blamed for a great many crimes stretching back thousands of years. Most of which they never committed, those who did using them as scapegoats since Caledonii tended to keep to themselves and the power they exercised incited fear among those who didn't understand it.

She found it hard to comprehend Lucius' hatred for the Caledonii. It was personal in nature, of that she was certain. Though based in reality or on the rhetoric that had become attached to one of the original tribes of the Realms, she didn't know. And, in truth, with all that was going on, she had little desire to pursue it.

"Shall we finish this game?" Drin suggested. He would never admit that she was better than him at darts. Better than him at most anything actually. Still, it would be fun to beat him. Just to put a seed of doubt in the back of his mind regarding his own perceived omnipotence. And potentially a kernel she could use in the days ahead.

"Yes, but let's up the stakes."

"A wager?"

"Indeed."

"And if I win?" Drin asked.

"Whatever you ... desire."

She couldn't miss the suggestive tone in his voice. The yearning. Strange how quickly Lucius' moods changed. From angry to serious to disappointed to conniving and then back around the wheel once again all in a matter of minutes. With the expression he was giving her then, she had little doubt as to what was on his mind.

"And if you win?"

"A dinner in my mansion," he replied. His smile too broad. His eyes too bright. "Alone. No Sergeant appearing out of the blue."

"I hope you don't expect anything more beyond dinner."

"One can always hope," Lucius purred, giving her a sly grin that made her feel slightly sick to her stomach. "Besides, I doubt that you can resist me for long."

"You forget that I'm well ahead of you on points," Drin warned, "and there are only three throws left. You have little chance of beating me."

Lucius bit back the sharp reply on the tip of his tongue. His mercurial personality shifting in a heartbeat. He didn't care to be reminded of his failures. "Then let's make it one throw. Highest score wins."

Drin thought about that, understanding the risk, seeing as well the opportunity she was seeking. "If I win, you give me more time. You get the First Families to back off."

"I don't know that I ..."

"I deserve at least a few days to grieve." Her expression was hard. Her tone forceful. Her eyes red and beginning to water.

Lucius' gaze sharpened. He didn't like her request. Nevertheless, as he considered her proposal and all that was currently in play, he decided that a delay of a few days, if it came to it, would have little bearing on his plans. And it might actually make her more malleable, which was exactly what he wanted.

"Fine. But if I win, you accept my proposal, and we move forward faster."

Drin opened her mouth to reply, then closed it just as quickly. She had gotten what she wanted, although with a catch. A dangerous one.

One throw …

Drin had no doubt that she could beat Lucius.

But one throw …

That was a lot of pressure. A lot could happen when all rested on just one throw.

Luck might play a larger role than skill in one throw.

She was torn, then she realized that she had little choice if she wanted to gain the breathing room she desired. "Done."

Lucius smiled, pleased that he had cornered her so easily. "I'll throw first." He stepped forward, removing all of the darts, sweeping his from the board so that they clattered on the floor.

He handed Drin one, taking another for himself.

Stepping up to the chalk on the floor, he winked at her. "Are you sure you don't want to just admit defeat now? I perform extremely well under pressure."

Drin ignored his hidden meaning. "Prove it."

Lucius chuckled softly, then lined up his throw. Once again there was little delicacy to his effort, throwing the dart with a vicious energy. But this time luck was with him.

The second most centric ring. A single bull. A difficult score to beat.

Clearly he was quite pleased with himself. "As I said, Celindria, there is something to be said for moving through the world from a position of power. Opportunities," his smile becoming a rapacious grin, "open up for me when least expected."

Drin ignored his insinuation. Not thinking. Not looking. Knowing. Feeling. Throwing.

The dart striking the center ring.

Double bull.

The highest possible score.

"I guess you'll have to wait a little while longer." She said it with an inherent coldness, wanting him to understand what she thought of him and his perspective.

Once again, he missed her point, his smile broadening, growing warmer, the menace gone. "I will allow you to claim your victory, Celindria, but darts have little meaning in the real world."

"Is that so?"

"It is," he replied with a nod. "In the real world, often the only thing that matters is steel. A sad but true fact. Steel of heart. Steel of blade."

"Really? You mean like this?"

In a flash, a small dagger appeared in her hand. And just as fast it was gone, Drin flicking it with her thumb and forefinger.

Just as with her last throw, it hit the bull's-eye.

Lucius' eyes widened ever so briefly in surprise. He wanted to pawn it off on luck, but after watching her at darts, he couldn't. Clearly, she had a good bit of training.

He hadn't known that she was so skilled, and the wheels in the back of his brain already were turning. Focused on how to make use of her newly discovered talent when they assumed the throne together.

"You're quite good." Lucius offered her a nod of respect. She smiled in turn, surprised by the compliment, which was ruined when Lucius next opened his mouth. "Surprisingly so, in fact."

"There are a great many things you don't know about me." She meant it as a warning.

He didn't take it as such. Instead, he took it as a challenge.

"Apparently so," Lucius purred, one eyebrow raised. "I can't wait to find out about all of your secret talents."

His suggestive tone and wink soured all the more Drin's already sour mood. She had gained a little extra time. She didn't know that it would prove helpful in the end. Still, it had to be worth something.

"Although we don't have to wait, now do we?"

Drin took a step back when Lucius took a step toward her.

It was his eyes that worried her. She saw what he intended.

Worse, she saw that he believed he was entitled. That despite her small victory, their arrangement meant nothing to him. Because he didn't feel the need to keep to the terms. He could do as he wanted, just as he always did.

Because for him, just as he said, it was all about power.

He had it.

He had her where he wanted her.

And he believed that he could do whatever he wanted with her.

Drin took another step back and then one more. Lucius staying close.

Then he was right in front of her, his slightly stale breath on her cheek, his chest just a knuckle away from hers.

She had nowhere to go, her back up against the wall.

Under other circumstances, she knew exactly what she would do.

The Talent raced through her, demanding to be released.

But she couldn't do as she wanted.

Not now.

Not with all that was at stake.

"A fun game we play, Celindria," Lucius murmured, his hand reaching up, his fingers twisting a curl of her hair that hung over her ear. "But not as fun as the new game we can play."

"You promised a few more days," she said. Her voice cracked, revealing her nervousness.

That excited Lucius all the more. "I did," he replied with a nod, even as he leaned in closer to her. His lips about to touch hers. His other hand now on her hip and sliding slowly across to her belly. "And you still do. But the proposal has nothing to do with what we're doing now."

"I disagree." Her words were hard, unyielding, matching her eyes. And the steel dagger pressed against his groin.

Lucius looked down. "You really want to …"

"As you said, Lucius, darts have little meaning in the world. Steel of heart. Steel of blade. And as we both know, steel can be very, very final."

"Celindria, you understand that there is really no reason to be so difficult. Our union is no more than a formality. Just a continuation of where we left off before. Why delay the fun that we can ..."

"We had a deal, Lucius. I expect you to uphold your side."

Lucius pursed his lips. Studying Drin's eyes for any weakness. Seeing not a crack. The redness and tears replaced with purpose. "Is this really how you want to play this?"

"I'm playing the hand you dealt me. I won. I have a few more days to respond to your proposal."

Lucius snickered. Then he shook his head in disappointment. "I see that there is a great deal that I will have to teach you once we're together, Celindria. And based on your current display of resistance, the first lesson will be that I can do to you whatever I want. Because as I explained earlier, all that matters in our world is power. Even in our bedroom."

Hearing those words, the sick feeling in Drin's stomach became a slow boil of acid. She didn't want to think about the future. Not yet. Not when she still had a chance to change that future, slim though that chance might be.

"I give you leave to go, Lucius. I have some other matters that require my attention this morning."

"Celindria, we don't have to part this way," he murmured in a more soothing tone, hoping that he could convince her that she was overreacting. He tried to press against her, then pulled back, the dagger pressed more firmly against his groin confirming that he would need to wait awhile longer before he could surrender to his carnal desires.

"You're right, Lucius, we don't," Drin agreed, although she didn't remove her dagger. "We could part on worse terms. The choice is yours."

"Lucius, I understand you have somewhere else to be?" The voice was strong. Commanding. Brooking no argument. Because the comment wasn't a question.

Lucius turned, his upper lip curling into a tiny snarl before his smile returned to hide what he was truly feeling. Another interruption. This was getting more than tiresome.

But he would survive. And there were other ways to relieve the tension within him. Besides, soon, when he spent time with Celindria, there would be no interruptions. And the fun they would have then ... that only broadened his smile.

"A pleasure to see you, Battle Lord." Lucius offered Henri Dengannon a smile and a nod of respect. He was about to suggest that it was Henri who had somewhere else to be until he saw the squad of soldiers march past their commander and take up positions along the walls of the chamber, having eyes only for him. "And you're right, I do."

He turned toward Drin, reaching down, grasping her hand, lifting it so that he could brush the back of it with his lips. "Remember the proposal I made. You have earned a few extra days. After that, your succession is dependent on offering me the reply that I expect to hear."

"Do you want to hear what you want to hear or do you want the truth?"

"From you?" Drin asked. "When do I ever have the choice?"

Henri chuckled softly at that. "Fair enough."

"Out with it, uncle. I assume that Lucius Hanover is not my only problem."

He smiled knowingly. His niece was quick. Smart. Clever. She had a good head on her shoulders.

Celindria would make an excellent Queen of the Crux if she were given the chance.

"Correct. Lucius is a problem, but there is more going on in the game we are playing."

Drin thought about that for a moment. "Another player?"

"Yes."

"The King of the Underworld?"

The Battle Lord frowned. "Why would you suggest the King of the City Below?"

"So it is true." She grinned, having thrown out the name just to see what kind of reaction she got. "I have heard rumors, and Lucius is fixated on this criminal, but I never was certain if he was real. Not until now. So thank you, uncle."

Henri's frown deepened, less than pleased to be played so easily by his niece. "He is real, you're right. But we can talk about him later. He rarely involves himself in politics unless those politics affect him directly."

"And a possible Search and Coronation don't affect him?"

"They do, just as they affect everyone in the Kingdom. But when it comes to the King of the Underworld, you must understand that in many ways he is much like a First Family."

"How so?"

"He is a businessperson first and foremost. It just so happens that his businesses tend to be much more diverse compared to those of the First Families. And because of that a Search and Coronation provide both opportunities and risks at which he is quite adept at navigating."

"You sound as if you're almost impressed by him?"

"Impressed, no. But I do respect him. Because unlike the First Families, what he does, he doesn't just do for himself."

"What does that mean?"

"It means we will talk about him later. What we need to talk about now can't wait."

Drin nodded. "Malor Dragoran."

"Correct. I believe the King of the Tor has a hand in all that is happening in Innsbruck."

"He's to blame for my father's murder?" Drin's eyes flashed, her desire for vengeance almost palpable.

"I don't know that yet, although I wouldn't be surprised if he was involved."

"You have yet to find any evidence?"

"Not yet. But the investigation has just begun. The timing of what Malor is doing at our eastern border suggests that he was aware that the assassination was coming."

"Why else would he have sent so many troops to the Splintered Bridge? Just a few days before, in fact. Certainly not a coincidence."

"Exactly."

"I know that look, uncle. You want me to do something that I don't want to do." She stepped closer to him, tilting her head as she studied the man who had always had a strong presence in her life. Even convincing her father that she needed to visit Haven so that she could learn how to refine her skill in the Talent. "Out with it. Malor has always been a problem, and we will deal with him. At the moment he has little chance of crossing the Splintered Bridge, so we must deal with the more immediate threat first."

Henri sighed. His niece had not had the chance to grieve for her father. And now he was pushing her on this.

"How do things fare with the young Hanover?"

"You just saw," she grumbled, her anger rising.

"He is pushing hard."

"He is. Just as you would expect. And if I don't accept his offer, the First Families will ..." She didn't feel the need to complete that thought.

"I'm sorry, Drin."

"For what?" She didn't understand the remorse in her uncle's voice.

"For pushing you to find a suitable partner these last few years."

"I don't blame you for doing that, uncle. My father was as well. You were both seeking to strengthen my claim."

He nodded, thanking her for understanding. "It's just that when it comes to Hanover ..." He sighed. Not sure what he wanted to say or how to say it.

"Tell me, uncle."

"Do you really want to know? Once revealed it can't be put back in the box."

"From you, uncle, I only want the truth. Only ever the truth."

"Don't trust him, Drin."

She smiled. He had nothing to fear in that regard. "Why do you say that?"

"He has a very high opinion of himself."

"He's the head of a First Family, uncle." She sensed in an instant that he was holding back a critical piece of information, not yet certain how to share it.

"He came to the role sooner than anyone ever anticipated. Sooner than he should have, in fact."

Drin frowned as she thought back to when Lucius was raised to the high seat of his House. His father had passed away. A wasting sickness that had struck quickly. And the former Lord of House Hanover had been in excellent health. He also had been one of her father's strongest allies. Which brought to mind Malor and his soldiers playing their games on the far side of the Splintered Bridge.

"There's no proof?"

"None that I can find," Henri replied. "That doesn't mean there isn't proof."

"What does he want?"

"I fear he wants more from you than just your throne."

"What are you suggesting, uncle?"

"We know where matters stand with the First Families."

"We do," Drin replied, clearly not pleased by what she had to admit. "They want me to ally with the Hanovers."

"Because the Hanovers offer the greatest chance for stability."

"That's the argument they're presenting."

He nodded sagely at that. "The First Families' desire for stability makes sense, Drin. Particularly with Malor causing problems at the Splintered Bridge."

"What are you not saying, uncle?"

He smiled again. He wished that his brother was still here. Charles would be so proud of his daughter. "I'm saying that instead of seeking some way to escape Hanover, you should seek some other way that can give the First Families what they want. Stability."

Drin frowned, but then it hit her like a lightning bolt. "An ally who might have more power over the First Families than Lucius does."

"Exactly so."

14

A NEW GAME

"Our plan is not moving at the pace I desire, Assindra." His voice was commanding and as cold as the grave. "I do not like delay. I do not like excuses."

"I am quite aware of what you like and do not like, Malor." Her tone hinted at matters other than strategies and schemes.

Assindra kept to her slow pace as she walked around the throne. The King of the Tor sat stiffly on the heavy chair made from lightning-crafted glass. He struggled to stoke his pique as her fingers trailed across the back of his shoulders and then his chest, making him shudder, until she vanished behind him only to begin her teasing once more.

Malor Dragoran ruled the Tor with an iron hand. No one dared to challenge him.

Except for Assindra. Because despite all his trappings, despite all his accomplishments, in her eyes, he was no different than any other man.

He had a clear weakness that she could exploit whenever she wanted.

He didn't always think with his brain.

"I am trying to be serious," he huffed. "You're making that quite difficult."

Assindra's light touches distracted him from the issue between them. Brushing her leg against his knees. Reaching out and twisting his long hair and even the long whiskers of his beard around her fingers. Trailing a hand across his belly.

"We have been away from one another for far too long, Malor." Assindra offered him a disappointed frown. "Should we not focus on renewing our acquaintance first before conducting business?"

"Business first, Assindra."

She stopped then, right in front of him. Glaring. "Do you view our relationship as nothing more than a business deal, Malor? An arrangement to be negotiated and nothing more than that?"

"Isn't it?" he asked.

Assindra grunted her displeasure, placing her hands on her hips. Posing in a way that she knew from experience Malor would find not only appealing, but also irresistible. "I thought I meant more to you, Malor."

Malor's harsh gaze softened, though only a fraction, and not for long, his expression becoming shrewd. "We have known each other for quite a long time, Assindra."

"I'm beginning to regret that now."

"You don't regret it in the least because what we both want is almost within our grasp."

Assindra shrugged, although her eyes sparkled in delight. "I'll give you that."

"You also don't regret it because we both know where we stand with one another."

"Fair enough," she agreed, giving him a wink. Then she walked toward him with a seductive sway of her hips and sat down on his lap, running her hand across his chest, then down to his belly before brushing right below. "Still, should we not take a few minutes for ourselves?"

"Are you enjoying having your fun with me?" Malor growled, his dark eyes flashing dangerously. Working hard not to give in to the temptation she offered.

"Immensely," she replied with a husky chuckle. She nodded toward his groin. "You seem to be as well."

"You're a beautiful woman, Assindra. There's no point in denying it." Yet despite his physical reaction to her ministrations, he made no move to respond to her very open display of affection.

"But business first," she grumped.

"Business first," Malor confirmed.

"Your loss, Malor," Assindra sighed. Pushing herself off his lap, she made sure that she placed her left hand in exactly the right place as she did so to earn a small though satisfying groan for her efforts.

"Do you have it?" Malor needed to adjust how he was sitting because of his temporary discomfort that was also all too pleasurable.

"Almost. It fell through my grasp."

Malor was out of his seat and looming above her with a dizzying speed. "You said you had a way to claim it."

"I did," Assindra replied sharply, her anger rising at Malor's attempt to intimidate her. Would he never learn? "And I still do. The blade is free from its centuries-old protection. I can claim it whenever I choose."

"Then why don't you?"

Assindra's flinty gaze somehow became even harder. "Because it doesn't suit my purposes ... yet."

Malor leaned down, his black eyes catching hers. It was a battle of wills now, as both radiated a power that the other respected yet also craved for their own. "I thought we were working together on this, Assindra, because our goals are the same. Has that changed?"

Assindra's lip curled up into a slight, crooked smile. "Nothing has changed, Malor. Our goals remain the same. We will gain what we both want."

"I'm supposed to believe you, Assindra?" He scoffed at the notion. "You allowed the blade to slip through your fingers."

"For good reason, Malor."

He leaned even closer. Curious as to whether she would step back. "I would like to know that reason, Assindra."

She laughed then. Throatily. Holding her ground. "Do you really believe that you can intimidate me, Malor?"

The King of the Tor didn't reply. It was his turn to glare. After almost a minute passed, he leaned away from her. Although he did not step away. That he would never do. He would never give ground. "There are few who dare to stand toe to toe with me, Assindra. Why do you?"

She reached up and patted his chest, much as she would a pet dog. "Because we are more alike than you can possibly imagine, Malor."

"That's not an answer," he growled.

"It is for me," she replied. "Besides, my mother was very thorough with my training. And of all the lessons she taught me, one always stood out."

"That would be?"

"Never back down," Assindra explained. "You see, before I lived in the Spine with my people, my brother and I were born in the Murk."

Malor took a step back upon hearing that. Surprised by her revelation. His hard eyes softened for just an instant. Revealing several emotions all at once. So fast that they could barely be tracked. Although Assindra could.

Hatred. Greed. Disappointment. Betrayal. Anger.

And the most powerful of all. The desire for vengeance.

She knew as well that those emotions were not directed toward her. An interesting discovery. Could she make use of it? Only time would tell.

"You are familiar with the Wraiths?" he asked.

"I am indeed, Malor. More familiar than most."

He nodded at that. His eyes were hard when he looked down on her again. Needing to cover up his unease, he barked, "You know you're useless to me if you don't get the blade."

She fired right back at him, giving her temper free rein. "I keep my promises, Malor. You will get the blade. And you will give me what I want as well. If you don't, then you will regret your failure."

"If I get the blade, Assindra," Malor confirmed. Hearing the threat in her words, he chose to ignore it. Not in a position to make an example of her. Not yet. "Blade first, then I will fulfill my promise to you."

"You will have your blade, Malor. Even if I have to stick you with it myself."

"Careful, Assindra," Malor warned in a lethally quiet voice. "Do not overstep."

Assindra's gaze narrowed, reading several meanings in his words. Not surprised in the least by any of them. Unconcerned as well. Perceiving them as no more than reminders that she would need to be ready to act when the time came. "Malor, please, give me a little credit."

"I think I give you too much credit, Assindra."

Assindra ignored the jab. "Not enough credit, actually."

Malor grunted at that, then turned on his heel. "I have business to attend to. I suggest that you acquire the blade before I lose patience with you. And my patience is wearing thin."

Assindra watched him go as he strode between the columns of lightning-crafted glass that ran along both sides of the throne room, a miniature of the Barbed Path that led to the main gates of the Tor. Lightning striking the road of sand with a power and frequency that left behind masterful creations.

She was less than pleased with that interaction. Angry because Malor rejected her. Angry because just as he said she had lost the blade. Angry because there was more to Malor's desire for the blade than he was letting on, and she had yet to determine what that was.

But Malor was a problem for another day.

The thief first.

Mikel.

The King of the Underworld.

She had been able to think of little else except him since their encounter deep beneath the Crux.

She was angry with him as well. He presented a challenge that she had not experienced since ... well, she couldn't quite recall, actually.

She also was impressed with him. She knew that Mikel Stahlherz was capable. But she hadn't anticipated that he would prove to be as capable as he demonstrated.

Assindra snorted. Was that a spark of pride rising up in her chest?

She savagely crushed that emotion and her curiosity.

She needed to stay focused.

She needed the blade.

And now that it had merged with him, she had two choices for obtaining it.

Only one appealed to her.

15

HOSTILE TAKEOVER

"Seems like all is going as it should, Millie."

"It is, Mikel. You know I run a tight ship."

"That I do," he replied, flipping through the account book on her desk. Murmurs of conversation drifted through the open doorway, every so often a scantily clad woman passed by with a man or woman in tow.

"Teddy usually comes by to check on things. Everything all right?" Millie leaned closer to Mikel. She was dressed more elegantly than any of the other women in Mikel's employ, and she wore a great many more layers, yet she exuded a sexuality that none of the other ladies had yet to learn how to match.

"It is," he replied, offering her a small smile. "I just needed to get out for a little while is all. Clear my head."

Millie reached out, placing a warm hand on top of his. She leaned down even closer, whispering into his ear. "I can help you clear more than your head, Mikel."

"I know you can, Millie," he replied with a warm smile and a soft chuckle. "Thank you for the offer." He closed the book then, patting her hand with his.

"But you won't take me up on it?" When she first began

propositioning Mikel, Millie had been disappointed when he refused. Her disappointment vanished when she learned what held him back. And she had little doubt that he would never take her up on her offer. Still, what was the harm? Eventually she might get lucky.

He shook his head. "Sorry, but no. You know how it is."

She smiled sadly, nodding. There was a reason she was where she was, and she thought about it every day. "You know I'm not going to stop trying, Mikel."

"I appreciate that, Millie. And thank you."

She nodded. "Just don't let it get out that I couldn't entice you into my bed. That wouldn't do well for business, the madam of The Silken Pleasure unable to lure her boss between the sheets."

"Partner."

"Partner?" Millie pulled back. Frowning. She didn't understand. "What do you mean?"

Mikel smiled. "You've been working for me ever since we started The Silken Pleasure."

She nodded, confused, Mikel catching her off guard.

"Seven years now?"

She nodded again, remembering when she first met the purported King of the Underworld. Not really believing that it was him because he didn't appear to be as cruel or bloodthirsty as he was said to be. She was grateful that he had taken her in and given her a steady income that had only grown larger year over year.

"Do you remember what I said that day when we first met?"

Millie frowned as she searched her memory. "You said that you saw a drive in me that you saw in few others."

"I did," Mikel confirmed. "I also said that the nature of our business would change when the time was right."

He handed her several sheets of folded paper. Not yet

having caught up, she began to read through the thin stack, her eyes widening as she did so. "You can't be serious."

"I never kid about business, Millie. You know that better than anyone."

"Yes, but Mikel, I never thought ..."

"You don't want to do this? I know it's more responsibility, but I wouldn't offer you the chance if I didn't think that you could handle it."

She stared at him, at a loss for words, trying to regain her bearings. When she did, she spoke rapidly. "Yes, yes, yes. Of course I do. It's just that I never thought you meant all this."

"It's deserved. The Silken Pleasure is the most profitable of all my brothels. You will continue to manage it, but you will also take on an oversight role for the other six brothels I own in the city. Do you think you can manage that?"

Millie gulped, then nodded quickly. "Yes, I can."

"Good. Did you read the last page?"

She shook her head, then quickly flipped to the back of the document. This time, her eyes threatened to bulge out of their sockets. "Mikel, you're not playing with me? This says ..."

He nodded. "We are partners now, Millie. You own twenty percent of The Silken Pleasure. Each year going forward that percentage will increase if certain goals are met until we reach a fifty-fifty split. Fair?"

"More than fair," Millie breathed, unable to catch her breath, her smile broadening. Not knowing what to say, she lunged for Mikel. Pulling him toward her. Hugging him. Overwhelmed by his generosity.

"Good," he said when she finally let him go and he could breathe again. "All you need to do is sign once you've had a chance to review all the documents when you're thinking a bit more clearly. If you have any questions, you can ask me or Teddy."

She nodded. "I will."

MIKEL ENJOYED the touch of cool air as he walked down the street. It had been warm in the bordello. For obvious reasons.

He smiled, remembering how shocked Millie had been. Pleased by her reaction. Happy that she was happy.

They had been friends for a long time. She was a good person who had been dealt a bad hand, and she had made the most of it. Never complaining. Never giving up. Simply working hard. Demonstrating an exactness and single-mindedness that few could match.

Although there was one aspect to their encounter that bothered him if only a little bit.

Had he been a fool?

Millie was a beautiful woman, and the attraction between them was obvious. Her touching his hand had sent a wave of heat rushing through him. Turning his mind down a path that he had not traveled in quite a long time.

Yet still he had turned her down.

Again.

Why did he not surrender to what would have been an enjoyable temptation? Her interest in him obviously wasn't just business.

Pondering those questions was a waste of time, because he already knew the answer.

The memory of the woman he loved kept him out of her bed.

The memory that, try as he might, he couldn't seem to escape.

Because he felt her death hanging over him whenever his mind wandered.

He waved to the men and women working the doors to his many businesses in this section of the Fifth Ring. Two more of his brothels. A very successful gaming house. Three taverns. A small theater in the round. All of them busy that evening just like most every other.

Thanks to his reputation, it wasn't really necessary to have so many strongarms. Nevertheless, it was good to offer a visual reminder for anyone too deep in their cups or looking for trouble that it was best to steer clear of his establishments.

Before he took the curl that would take him to the Ring below, he stopped to talk with Curtis and May. They stood outside the Thirsty Pig, one of his most profitable taverns. The ale just as good as the roasted meats, the quality pulling customers from throughout the city, thus the long line that ran out from the front porch and formed daily well before the doors opened for business.

He liked to speak with as many of his employees as he could. He wanted them to understand that they were important to him, not just to his businesses. Moreover, that he was there for them. No matter what they might need.

Curtis, May, Millie, and all the others working with him seemed to appreciate his efforts. Their length of service confirming it, since few people working for the King of the Underworld ever left, at least not by choice. The pay was good as were the additional perks. The guarantee of quality physicks already paid for them and their families anytime day or night, schooling for their children, as well as a host of other benefits, most important a promise of safety.

No one bothered someone tied to the King of the Underworld, not if they wanted to continue to draw breath.

He stopped as well because he wanted to get a better feel for all that was around him, a faint hint of warning sounding in the back of his brain.

He shook hands with Curtis and May before continuing on his way. Taking his time as he worked his way down the street, he greeted several more people until he found his way back to The Fox's Lair.

Tapping the fox carved above the door as was his habit, when he walked through the entrance, Teddy was waiting for him.

"They're here?"

"Just arrived," Teddy confirmed.

"Ready?"

"Always."

"Do you think they'll take the risk?" Mikel appeared to be hopeful at that prospect, although slightly distracted as well.

"Makes it easier for them," Teddy replied, as if it were only common sense. "They've been trying to muscle in on us for a while."

"True."

"But that doesn't seem to be what's bothering you," Teddy prodded.

Mikel clapped his friend on the shoulder as he moved past him. "It isn't. You're right. Just a feeling, nothing more."

"And what is this feeling telling you?" Teddy had learned that it was always best to pay attention to Mikel's premonitions.

"That trouble is coming. And not just our friends waiting in the other room."

A SLIM FIGURE stayed deep within the shadows of the closed market. It would be a busy spot before the sun rose that morning. Now, however, near midnight, it offered her the perfect vantage point for keeping an eye on the entrance to the tavern.

She was supposed to do this quickly. The person she was indebted to demanded it.

So if she decided to make her move now, all the advantages had to be with her. She couldn't afford to fail.

And she wouldn't. She promised herself that.

She had watched him enter just a few minutes before, her

eyes sparking in recognition, delight, and then a hint of trep-idation.

It had been a long time.

In some respects, much too long.

In others, not long enough.

She needed to decide what to do.

Was it better to wait and see how events played out? Or should she move forward with her original plan?

Usually, she never doubted herself.

She blamed her hesitation on him.

He had always made her slightly uncomfortable. Often in a good way. Now ... not so much.

She conducted a quick internal debate. Considering what was expected of her. Knowing as well that there were other parties in play.

Perhaps too many.

A little chaos shouldn't hurt, however. If she was quick and she was smart she could use any distraction they created to her advantage.

She grasped onto that possibility.

Particularly since she was taking a massive risk by accepting him as her target.

Not just because of the threat he posed.

More because she knew based on first-hand experience that he was quite a bit more than he seemed.

"WE'VE HEARD a great deal about you."

"Most of it good, I hope." Mikel offered a crooked grin to the brawny fellow standing before him, noting the scar on his chin that left his beard wanting.

Jerad turned to look at the handful of men at his back. They mirrored his expression of confusion. "Why does that matter?"

Mikel shrugged, as if the answer was obvious. "It's important to have a good reputation in this business."

Jerad grunted in reply. He didn't care about having a good reputation. He only cared that the people he did business with feared him.

He had learned from an early age that fear went a long way to ensuring that no one cheated him. He had made examples of those few who foolishly tried to do so, never shying away from the bloody work that was required from time to time. Enjoying it, actually. Believing that it allowed him to let loose his creative side.

"You want the truth?" Jerad asked.

"I'd prefer it," Mikel replied.

"I've been told that you're a thief, a smuggler, and who knows what else," Jerad said with a shrug of his own, clearly not all that impressed by the so-called King of the Underworld. "What I found most interesting was that you're a thief and smuggler with principles."

"That bothers you?"

"It doesn't bother me," Jerad snorted, only partially feigning his amusement. "It simply suggests that you're weak."

Mikel nodded. He had expected as much. "And because of that you believe you can take advantage of me. Perhaps even carve out my business as your own."

"That was the hope."

"What else did you learn?" Mikel asked. "I'm sure you dug deeper than that."

"That you won't do business with a certain type and, based on that description, I've been wondering why you agreed to meet with me. Also, I learned that you won't deal in certain products."

"All true so far. But I can see that there's more you want to say."

Jerad stared at Mikel. He got the feeling that he was being

played. "Clearly you're quite intelligent. Your success demonstrates that."

Mikel waited, his grin still amiable, believing there was more Jerad wanted to express.

"And knowing all that, one question keeps coming to mind. One question that's been bothering me ever since I set foot in what has proven to be a very nice establishment."

"What question would that be?" Mikel prodded, believing that he already knew what it was.

"Why would you choose to meet with me even though you have no intention of ever doing business with me?"

"I like to meet new people," Mike replied casually.

"I find that highly unlikely," Jerad replied. "From what I've learned about you, you keep a very tight rein on your many businesses and trust only a handful of people."

"That's true. You found me out again."

"Then why did you allow me to come here today? Why even bother meeting with me when you have little intention of doing business with me?"

"I thought I would try to make it easier for you." Mikel's expression changed when he said the words, his eyes frosting over.

"Make what easier?"

"You already know." Mikel's good humor was gone, his voice flinty.

A tension clung to the room. Jerad looked back over his shoulder, gaining confidence and courage from his men, as well from the knowledge that he was facing off against only the Fox and his giant.

The numbers favored him. The giant might be a problem, but all of the men he had brought with him were experienced in the close work that would be required to neutralize the man said to be the Fox's accountant.

And that would leave the Fox for him. Exactly the way he wanted it.

Feeling better about his plans, he turned his attention back to Mikel. "You know that we came here to kill you."

"It's the smart play," Mikel agreed. "Besides, it makes it easier for me to achieve my goal."

"What would that be?"

"I thought it would be easier to kill you here and now rather than having to chase after you in Graz." Mikel's smile became menacing then. "Having to do that not only could be exhausting, but also time consuming. And if you know anything about me and my business after all your research, and clearly you do, then you know I like to be as efficient as possible."

"You've got quite a pair, you know that?" Jerad chuckled, using the laugh to cover the nervousness that tickled his large belly. He had assumed that he would do the deed with a knife in the back. Catching Mikel when he least expected it. But it didn't appear as if it was going to play out that way.

"I'll take that as a compliment." Mikel nodded over his shoulder. "Teddy, you've heard from all of Jerad's seconds?"

"I have," Teddy confirmed with a sharp nod. His hands rested on his belt. His cudgels within easy reach.

"My seconds?" Jerad demanded. "What are you talking about?"

"A hostile takeover, Jerad." Mikel smiled at his guest's look of surprise. The master of the Graz underworld was a smart man, but he had a fault that wasn't unique in their business. His ego often got in the way of good decisions. "You mean to say that you never thought about this possibility? Looks like that mistake is going to cost you."

"What are you talking about?"

"Teddy, would you care to explain?"

Teddy spoke in a calm tone, not a hint of emotion in his voice, as if he were simply rattling off a series of numbers. "All of your lieutenants – Scraggy, Hemp, Layla, Gertrude, and Bert – have agreed to partner with us going forward. We heard from Bert just this morning to confirm that our partnership deal is in place and effective as of midnight tonight, which is right about now."

"Partnership deal?" Jerad demanded in a shocked tone. "They work for me. They know what happens if they disobey me."

"Yes, they do," Teddy replied. "Even so, they believed that they had a better chance of success by partnering with us. Full partners, in fact. In this way we take over your business interests in Graz with a minimum of fuss."

Jerad didn't know what to say. He thought he was going to Innsbruck to eliminate a rival. But somehow his rival had gotten the better of him without him even knowing.

"That's the value of having a reputation like Mikel's," Teddy explained. "Your seconds preferred stability and security because both are essential to ensuring the flow of future revenue. They understand they can't get either from you. They believe they can gain that by working with us. Thus, their decision to sever ties with you. It didn't take much to convince them. Not after what you've done to some of their family members to prove your intentions."

"You know what that means, Jerad?" Mikel asked. He didn't wait for the criminal boss to reply. "It means that the only thing in the way of our starting this new business partnership is you."

Jerad's eyes widened. Finally beginning to understand why Mikel allowed him to come here.

Business wasn't his focus. At least not entirely.

With respect to him, it was blood.

"You made a mistake, Jerad." Mikel stood just a few feet away from him, having backed the visitor from Graz up against the wall.

He held his mace lightly in his hand, the head just as bloody as the blade. Mikel having no choice but to eliminate two of Jerad's thugs before taking on the boss himself. Jerad shoving his men out in front of him. Not the bravest fellow when being challenged directly, which might explain why he was still alive in the rough and tumble Tor criminal under-world. Although not for much longer.

"What was that?"

Jerad was lightheaded from the loss of blood and in a great deal of pain. He had tried to come at his competitor before he finished with one of his men, hoping to sneak his long dagger into Mikel's back.

It hadn't worked out the way he wanted, Jerad's attack unleashing a martial display from the King of the Underworld that he couldn't stand against. The many wounds crisscrossing his body and the crushed bones in his right hand, which forced him to fight with his weaker left, attested to that.

"Believing everything you heard about me." This wasn't the first time Mikel had faced a situation such as this one. A rival seeking to take over his business. That rival believing that because he treated people fairly, earning their loyalty rather than demanding it, that he was weak, then finding out that he was anything but. "That's going to cost you."

"You know what?" Jerad grumbled.

"What?"

"You talk too much."

"I've been accused of worse," Mikel said with a smile. "Let me put you out of your misery then."

Mikel lunged, Jerad moving to meet his attack. The Graz criminal not realizing that it was a feint until it was too late.

Midmotion Mikel knelt, bringing his hammer down on the

top of Jerad's foot and crushing the bone. When Jerad knelt, howling, reaching for his latest injury, Mikel brought the blade around in an arc when he rose up from the floor.

Jerad kept falling until his head smacked against the wood. Mikel cutting his throat. Jerad's blood pooling around him.

Mikel shook his head. Frowning. This wasn't the kind of work that he enjoyed. Still, it proved necessary on occasion.

He had learned from his many sources in Graz that Jerad planned to increase his interests in Innsbruck. To do that meant he would need to take down Mikel first.

Mikel, who had been working to expand his own interests in Graz, decided to take advantage of the opportunity Jerad presented to him and accelerate his own designs to expand his presence in the Tor capital.

Satisfied now with Jerad out of the way that his plans would move forward as he wanted, he turned, ready to go to Teddy's aid. Realizing just as quickly that there was nothing for him to do.

Teddy had everything well in hand. Two men dead at his feet and one man still standing against him. Sort of. The thug was down to one leg and one arm, his right side no longer of use to him. It wouldn't be long now before Teddy finished the thug.

Mikel took a deep breath then. Glad that this confrontation had ended without him having to pull any of his soldiers into the fight. He didn't like putting his people at risk if he could avoid it and there were already too many combatants in his cramped office. Or rather there had been.

Yet the hint of unease that had been bothering him all night remained, having nothing to do with Jerad and his heavies, and just then it crackled between his shoulder blades.

Sensing the air moving behind him, Mikel whipped around. Based solely on instinct, he brought his mace with him at shoulder height.

He grunted with relief when the clash of steel on steel sounded loudly in his office, taking the slash of the dagger across the hilt rather than across his throat.

He took a few steps backward. Having a very difficult time making out who he was fighting, he raised his mace with an annoying repetitiveness, each time grateful to parry another slash or jab. He had no other option except to focus solely on the shimmer of the black steel because there was little else for him to see.

Except for the dark purple eyes that were a part of the shadow that was trying to kill him.

Those eyes the giveaway.

A man -- or woman, he couldn't tell which – bred since birth to do one thing and one thing only.

Kill.

An assassin who supposedly never failed.

A Seeker.

A shiver of concern ran through Mikel.

He quickly crushed it, not having the time to listen. Able to do nothing more than give free rein to his instincts, he defended against the Seeker's seemingly ceaseless and increasingly creative assault.

The black dagger swept toward Mikel from angles that he didn't think were humanly possible. He would have been impressed with himself for withstanding the onslaught if not for the fact that his circumstances were so dire.

This certainly wasn't what Mikel was expecting this evening. And it certainly wasn't what he wanted to deal with now.

But what he wanted was of little concern.

Slashing and slicing with a mesmerizing efficiency, the Seeker compressed Mikel's world to one simple task.

Staying alive.

And for the next few minutes, Mikel did.

Concentrating on those purple eyes and the black blade.

Responding as best he could to the shift in the air as the assassin moved around him.

He was more than willing to take a few shallow slashes now and then if it meant staving off the killing blow.

Mikel knew that his strategy wasn't sustainable over the long term, however. That if he didn't change the game ... and swiftly ... the Seeker was going to win.

So that's what he tried to do.

Taking a step forward and faking a swing with his mace, the Seeker hesitated for the first time. Those few heartbeats were all he needed, Mikel reaching down and grabbing the scimitar lying on his desk.

The effect of his fingers grasping the hilt was immediate.

The Giant-crafted blade blazed to life, illuminating in a blinding light the shadow that had been trying to kill him.

The man's purple eyes – Mikel now certain that it was a man – flashed in surprise, though not concern.

And why would the Seeker be concerned?

He had never failed on an assignment before, and he wouldn't fail now.

Mikel could read all that in the assassin's purple orbs.

He didn't care.

All Mikel cared about was continuing to draw breath.

Thanks to his newly acquired blade, which didn't allow the Seeker to slip back into the shadows, he was able to do that.

A weapon in both hands now, Mikel danced forward, feinting with his mace, attacking with his sword.

Falling into a regular rhythm.

Feint.

Slash.

Feint.

Stab.

Mace.

Sword.

Mace.

Sword.

Feint.

Slash.

Feint.

Stab.

It's when Mikel saw the recognition in the attacker's purple eyes that he adapted his approach.

The instant the Seeker shifted his footing, believing that he knew what Mikel was going to do next, he did the opposite.

Rather than feinting with his mace, Mikel continued with his swing, smashing the bloody hammer into the Seeker's extended knee, cracking the bone.

The assassin dropped to his good knee, grunting in pain, Mikel finishing him with a hard smack across his temple.

This time, Mikel didn't breathe a sigh of relief.

Because he sensed another presence at his back, and he knew that it wasn't Teddy. His friend never would approach him from that direction right after a combat.

Turning to face his next challenger, gleaming blade already moving in a sweeping arc to defend himself, he was caught by the woman's eyes.

Not purple. She wasn't a Seeker.

Rather a deep blue.

A color he had not seen for several years.

A color he had never thought he would see again.

Mikel froze when she moved out of the shadows, her cowl slipping down to her shoulders as she stabbed with her long dagger.

Too stunned to move.

Too stunned to do anything but stare.

He thought she was dead.

She should be dead.

Then Mikel realized that he was about to die.

Her dagger aimed for his heart.

She had broken it once. Now she was poised to do it again ... and this time for good.

Resigned to his fate, he turned away at the last second, a blast of energy sizzling right over his shoulder and smashing into the wall, ripping apart the finished wood.

Knocked from his trance, Mikel pivoted swiftly, prepared to take on the ghost from his past.

But when the smoke cleared, he realized that she was gone.

Teddy approached warily, cudgels at the ready. "Was that ...?"

Mikel nodded, scanning his office just to make sure there were no more dangers lurking along the edges. "It was."

"How did she ...?"

"I don't know."

"Neither do I," Teddy murmured, his analytical mind already turning toward this new problem, "but I'm going to see what I can find out. And get these bodies out of here." Clapping Mikel's shoulder, glad that his friend was still alive, he headed toward the door.

For several breaths, Mikel didn't move. Trying to make sense of what had just happened.

The Seeker couldn't have been Jerad's doing. His competitor had wanted the pleasure of killing him all to himself.

Besides, Seekers were incredibly expensive and well beyond the means of most of his enemies. That could mean only one thing.

One or several of the First Families had decided to make a play for him.

One Family in particular standing above the others.

That bothered him.

If he was right, it complicated his life in a way that he didn't want it complicated.

Though that wasn't as problematic as the evening's second surprise.

Liria.

He gripped the hilt of the blazing sword a bit more tightly, sensing another presence coming up on his left side.

Seeing her in his peripheral vision, he relaxed, releasing the tension from his shoulders and loosening his grip on the sword.

"You have got to stop doing that," Mikel warned.

"What? Saving your life?" Nat asked with a heavy dose of sarcasm.

"Yes. No. I have no problem with you saving my life. But you need to exercise more control over the Talent."

"I did have control," Nat replied testily.

"Barely. You're raw. It's dangerous to do what you're doing without training. You stopped the woman from killing me, but you almost killed me as well while doing that."

"But I didn't," Nat challenged with a bright smile. "Besides, if you would stop putting yourself in positions where I have to save your life, then I won't." She shrugged. "You saved me. I saved you. It's only fair."

Mikel couldn't argue with Nat's logic. Besides, her spark appealed to him.

"Why do so many people want to kill you?" Nat asked.

"I told you that deciding to stay with me wasn't the best idea."

"Stop trying to avoid the question."

Mikel smiled at that. She was sharp. She was tenacious. And she was a pain in the ass. All reasons why she had grown on him so quickly. "Because in my business, there is always someone waiting in the wings to take my place."

"At the end there was more going on here than just that," Nat challenged.

"You're right."

"What was it? Business or personal?"

"That's a good question," Mikel said with a smile.

"I know it is," Nat agreed with a tinge of irritation in her voice. "Now answer the question."

"You really can be difficult, you know that?"

"I do. Now answer the question."

He smiled then, unable to contain his amusement. "I'll let you know when I know. Deal?"

"Deal," Nat agreed, realizing that was the most she was going to get out of him in that moment.

"And I want you to get training."

"I don't have time ..."

"You have time," he replied. "If you're going to keep working with me, then you will make the time and get training."

Nat frowned then scowled when she realized that he wouldn't relent. She nodded reluctantly. "You really can be difficult, you know that?"

"I do," Mikel replied with a soft laugh. Then he wrapped an arm around Nat's shoulders, pulling her close.

16

UNWANTED ADVANCE

"It is a fair arrangement, Queen Heir. Both Kingdoms prosper. That much is obvious."

"I fail to see how allowing several companies of Tor soldiers on the western side of the Splintered Bridge is a fair deal, Gregorius. It benefits no one except Malor Dragoran."

"Queen Heir, I assure you ..."

"You assure me?" Drin cut in, having little patience for these rhetorical games and deceptions. Understanding their value. Despising them all the same.

Her uncle stood by her side, frowning just as deeply as she was. They had been skirmishing against Tor soldiers for the better part of the week atop the Splintered Bridge. Ever since Drin's father had been murdered. A coincidence that could not be discounted. "I am tired of your assurances and those of your liege, Gregorius."

"Queen Heir, please. King Dragoran seeks nothing except for peace and prosperity between our two Kingdoms."

"He has a unique way of demonstrating that desire."

To say that she was angry was an understatement. Drin was enraged, having little doubt that her father's murder could be linked back to the King of the Tor. Somehow. She simply hadn't found the evidence to support her suspicions. Yet.

And it was her father's murder that put her in her incredibly precarious position. Not yet declared Queen of the Crux, though still required to serve in that role until the Coronation. Whether hers or someone else's yet to be determined.

The current unrest in the top rings of Innsbruck aided Malor Dragoran, thus his attempts to take advantage of the tension roiling through the Crux, as well as his desire for that tension to continue for as long as possible.

"He seeks only to help you, Queen Heir Dengannon," Gregorius replied in as placating a tone as he could manage. "You face dangers from beyond your borders. That much cannot be denied."

"I am looking at one now," Drin said quietly, though loud enough so that Gregorius heard her.

Dragoran's emissary avoided the hook set for him, continuing with what he was tasked with saying. "You face dangers as well from within your borders. Some of the First Families are considering calling for a Search. That could place you, and your Kingdom, in even greater peril." Gregorius shrugged, as if what he was about to say next was nothing more than common sense. "Having a few companies of Tor soldiers on your eastern border ready to assist could prove beneficial to you. Perhaps even secure your place."

"How so, Gregorius?" She couldn't wait to hear his reasoning.

"If matters here in the capital take a turn for the worse, I have been authorized to make those soldiers available for your use. To fight or ... as a means of escape. The Tor stands open to you even in your time of greatest need."

"Is that so?" She wasn't surprised by the offer. She was surprised that he was able to make the offer sound appealing while keeping a straight face.

"Indeed, Queen Heir Dengannon. My liege has only your best interests at heart."

"Your liege has only his best interests at heart. Your liege has designs on my throne, Gregorius."

The ambassador from the Kingdom of the Tor smiled thinly, then offered her a brief shake of his head. "Not your throne, Queen Heir. At least not yet."

A tense silence descended on the throne room then.

Drin didn't say anything for quite some time, eyes boring into Gregorius. The ambassador did an excellent job of holding her gaze at the beginning, though it wasn't long before he began to wilt.

"That sounded like a threat, Battle Lord."

Her uncle, standing just to her side, one hand on the hilt of his sword, nodded slowly. "It did, Queen Heir."

"I do not care to be threatened, Gregorius." Her eyes blazed with an angry fire.

"Queen Heir, I didn't ..." Gregorius realized that he may have overplayed his hand. "I didn't ..." And now he didn't know what to say, caught in a trap of his own making. "I was just trying to offer the assistance of my liege, Queen Heir. No more than that."

He bowed his head respectfully, quite aware that all of the soldiers lining the walls of the throne room, the stained-glass skylights above sending colorful images dancing across the floor and their armor, had a hand on the hilts of their swords. It seemed that they were of the same mind as their mistress.

"I know quite well what you were doing, Gregorius," Drin stated in a withering tone.

"Yes, Queen Heir. Of course." He was beginning to sweat, a slow drip down his scalp as well as his back. It wasn't a feeling that he enjoyed. "I simply wanted to offer what assistance that I could, knowing that you face some challenges here that must be addressed delicately."

"The challenge I'm thinking of addressing now, Gregorius, doesn't require any delicacy in my opinion." She leaned forward on the throne. "It requires a demonstration of power. And right now, you might be the best person to … play a role in that demonstration."

Gregorius gulped, not liking the sound of that at all. He had come to Innsbruck within hours of Charles Dengannon's murder. The timing required by his liege. Suspicious to all, he knew, just as Malor Dragoran wanted.

And Gregorius had done as his liege required of him. Yet now he feared that he had misplayed the cards his master gave him. His mistake about to come back and bite him in the ass.

He had only himself to blame, although he certainly wouldn't admit that to anyone. Particularly Malor Dragoran.

He had underestimated the young woman sitting on the throne. Believing the deceased king's daughter callow and easily swayed. Inexperienced and unwise to the ways of power. She seemed exceedingly comfortable in her seat, however. Worse, she was angry … and vengeful.

"I don't know whether that would be the best path to take," Gregorius stammered. Seeking some way to extricate himself from what he realized had become a very dangerous situation.

The Queen Heir stared at him for several seconds longer, making him feel as if he were nothing more than a chip to be played on a board. And he realized that, in fact, was exactly what he was.

"I do, Gregorius. I do." She leaned back into her throne abruptly, crossing one leg over the other. "Leave us, Gregorius. Return to Malor Dragoran."

Gregorius nodded in thanks, sighing with relief, maintaining a hold on his fear, as he backed away as quickly as he could while keeping his eyes on Celindria Dengannon. "Thank you, Queen Heir. And if I may, is there a message you would like me to provide to my liege? He asked that I invite you to visit him in Graz. He promises you safe passage and safe return. And if you know nothing else of my liege, he is a man who keeps his promises."

She waited until Gregorius was at the two doors at the very back that ran from floor to ceiling, a soldier on each side holding them open for the ambassador from the Kingdom of the Tor.

"I will take all that you have said under advisement," Drin replied. "And I will consider King Dragoran's offer. Before that, however, he must do something for me."

"What is that Queen Heir?" Gregorius' tone was hopeful. Perhaps he had made some progress after all.

"Pull his companies back from the Splintered Bridge. A league. As a show of good faith. I have never dealt with your liege. Only my father, who was murdered." Her gaze sharpened just as her words did so that Gregorius did not miss her point. "Then I will consider his last request." Her tone made it seem like doing so was much the same as considering the request of a felon sentenced to death.

"Yes, Queen Heir," Gregorius nodded emphatically, feeling like he had just slipped the noose himself. "Thank you."

Then he was gone, exiting the throne room quickly, the soldiers at the doors pulling them closed.

"Well done, Celindria," Henri Dengannon said, smiling, clapping his hands together a few times in applause. "You played him well."

Drin snorted softly. "I did pick up a few things while my father forced me to sit here with him for hours on end."

"It seems that all of your discomfort and discontent paid off."

"We'll see," she replied, smiling softly as a kaleidoscope of memories passed through her mind. Not only of her sitting next to her father while he conducted the business of the Crux, but also of the conversations they would have afterwards that lasted just as long as the sessions in the throne room. Her father wanted to make sure that her instruction was as complete as could be. "I'm sorry, what did you say?" Her uncle's comment pulled her out of what had been a sad but pleasant reverie.

"We need to consider it," Henry repeated.

"Consider it? Malor's offer of a visit? Are you serious? After all that we've learned about him?"

"He's a threat, yes."

"He's likely responsible for my father's death." Her voice rose as she said it, her disbelief plain.

"I don't disagree, but I won't agree until we have hard evidence."

"Diplomatic as always, uncle," Drin grumbled. "I don't know that I like that about you."

"Not diplomatic. Realistic. Until we know who murdered your father, we must conduct the business of the Crux in a certain way."

"And if Malor Dragoran was responsible for my father's murder?"

"Then we go to war." Henri's eyes were just as cold as those of his niece.

"There's the Battle Lord I know and love."

"I am not suggesting that you actually visit the Tor. If you did, we would never see you again."

Drin nodded, now understanding what he meant. "It's another card to play."

"Exactly. A way to earn us some more time."

"Fair enough," Drin replied. She studied her uncle, seeing as much hidden in his expression as was revealed. "You don't believe that this is over?"

"No," Henry confirmed. "I think the murder of your father was just the start."

"And you believe that Dragoran will take other measures to gain what he wants?"

"I do."

"That puts the Crux in a very difficult position."

"It already was with the pressure Dragoran is applying at the Splintered Bridge."

Drin thought about that challenging reality. "Can we hold them back if it comes to it?"

"If Dragoran pushes his soldiers across the Splintered Bridge, not for very long."

"That's never happened before, uncle. Dragoran himself has tried three times, the last before I was born, yet the soldiers of the Tor have never set foot in our Kingdom."

"I know," Henri said, "and I'd like to keep it that way."

"But still you're worried."

"I am. I have been receiving word from our eyes and ears that Dragoran might have some surprises up his sleeve that could cause problems for us."

Upon hearing that, Drin's worry intensified. "Then let's make sure they don't make it across the Splintered Bridge."

"Yes, Queen Heir." He bowed then headed toward the doors, the soldiers already opening them. "To that end, that's where I go now. I will accompany Gregorius and his party out of the Crux and see what can be done to strengthen our defenses."

Once her uncle left, Drin remained on the throne for more than an hour. Thinking. And not doing a very good job of it.

Too many memories played through her mind and not enough ideas.

And she knew why.

She did her best thinking when she wasn't stuck in the palace.

The question was where to go.

Or rather who she should visit.

17

BRIGHT BLADE

"How could she have survived?"

"I don't know."

"She was badly wounded yet she still made it out when she shouldn't have," Teddy murmured, shaking his head. He didn't like saying that. Because he didn't like surprises. Even more, he didn't like things that he couldn't explain. "We both believed that she was going to die. A wound like that? A death knell."

Mikel nodded, his thoughts still on those deep blue eyes that had almost cost him his life. He had hesitated when Liria appeared before him. Understandable considering how they parted ways. Still, by all rights, he should have died because of that mistake. If not for Nat looking out for him, he would have. "We did."

"It all seems like a bit too much to be a coincidence."

"It does," Mikel agreed.

"It's been what? Almost ten years?"

"Just about."

Teddy nodded, thinking about that. "And she appears within a day of you snatching the scimitar?"

Mikel smiled as he strode next to his friend. They were

working their way through the crowded streets of Innsbruck's First Ring, every available inch on both sides blanketed by vendors of various licit and illicit goods and services. "The wheels turning, Teddy?"

The giant nodded again, lost in thought for a few seconds more. "It's all a bit too convenient, don't you think?"

"That thought had crossed my mind. You think she came for the blade?"

"Definitely not you," Teddy replied without even having to think about it, ignoring Mikel's frown. If his friend didn't want to acknowledge the truth, that was his right. That didn't change the truth, however. Whether Mikel wanted to believe it or not, Liria had only always cared about Liria.

"That hurts, Teddy."

"You'll get over it," he grumbled. Watching in amazement when Mikel grasped the scimitar to fend off the Seeker, weapons such as that exceedingly rare and unmistakable, when Mikel explained what he had to do to acquire the blade -- from where and for whom – it only confirmed his suspicion. "It seems like you fell into a nest of vipers again."

"Not by choice."

"It's never by choice." Teddy barked out a laugh. "Yet still it happens to you much too frequently. And you escaped the nastiest viper ... at least for a time."

"I got lucky." Mikel wasn't going to lie to himself. If not for the blade, the Seeker would have killed him. And if not for ...

"The little miss saved you."

"She did." Mikel admitted that readily. Liria would have killed him if not for Nat's intervention. He was pleased by and grateful for that but also not.

He was grateful for the risk she had taken for him. Even more, he was pleased that Nat had chosen to stay with him.

She had proven her worth. That was undeniable. More importantly, he enjoyed having her around. She brought him back to a time when he wasn't focused on providing for so many people in Innsbruck. To a time when he cared only about providing for his family.

She didn't know it, but Nat was helping to fill a hole in his heart that he never thought could close. That he never wanted to close. Until perhaps now.

Still he worried about her. Because he feared what could happen if she got too close the next time someone made a play for him. Someone more skilled than she was. He didn't want her to pay for his mistake.

Teddy laughed softly, remembering the look on the girl's face after she drove Liria away. A grim satisfaction. And a warning for the woman who dared to attack the man who had taken her in. "Strong-willed. Hog headed. Sounds like someone I know."

Mikel didn't bother to argue against the claim. "Are you enjoying yourself, Teddy?"

"I am." His grin broadened, then faded as they entered a more rundown section of Innsbruck. There were fewer people on the streets and many of the buildings that hung over the avenue they trod on were in poor condition or boarded up. A few were marked with the red slash of the plague. Although that illness had last visited the city five years before, the neighborhood hardest hit had not yet recovered. And this one likely never would if Mikel couldn't fit the necessary pieces together just so. "Does he know that we're coming?"

"If he knew, he wouldn't be here." Mikel took the lead, Teddy right behind him, one hand on his belt, close to a cudgel. Everyone in the lower rungs of the city knew the Fox and the Giant. Still, better to be safe than sorry.

They had reached the very edge of the island, the waters of the Southern and Eastern Rivers coming together with a thunderous roar just on the other side of the dilapidated warehouse blocking their way.

"Fair enough."

Mikel strode through the alley to their left, Teddy following. The deeper they went, the spray of the rivers breaching the breakwater visible every so often, the colder it became.

And not because they were so close to the Churn. It felt as if the path they were on had taken them underground to a hidden tomb that never should have been disturbed.

A musty smell assaulted their nostrils. One of decay and death, bones and blood.

A sense of terror rose unbidden in both of them.

That's when the flashes of light and hints of movement began. Always at the edge of their vision. There but not there. More memory than truth.

Then the touches. A faint hand on a shoulder.

A whisper in the ear. A promise of death.

A maggot-filled breath caressing the cheek.

Understanding what they were up against, Mikel and Teddy ignored it all ... or at least tried to.

They looked over their shoulders every so often. Hurrying a bit faster down the alley. Glancing to the side. Despite knowing the cause of their unease, still affected by it. Finally they came to a stop in front of a large oak door wrapped in steel that didn't appear to have been opened in decades.

That's when the images started to appear with greater frequency and clarity. There than not. Whole then ripped apart. Deaths of the most horrible kind. Creatures of the most terrible sort. Loved ones become wights or worse. Spirits risen from the grave demanding that Mikel and Teddy join them.

The sense of dread that boiled up in both battle-hardened fighters threatened to take hold.

To stay where they were meant certain death and a terrible eternity. Better to flee. Now. Before they became spirits themselves. Several of the specters shooting toward them. Reaching for them. Craving them. Seeking to merge with them. To take possession of their bodies.

Mikel and Teddy ignored the compulsion and what was happening around them. Focusing on the door that stood in their way.

Kneeling down and pushing in on a small chip in the wall that was even with his ankle, the door opened on silent hinges. Teddy slipped through. Mikel closed the door behind them when he applied pressure on a similar latch on the inside wall.

As soon as they were in the warehouse, the overwhelming sense of terror vanished along with the spirits.

Both breathed easier, enjoying the quiet. The sound of the Churn muted by the structure's thick stone walls.

"His apparitions are getting better. Much more intense."

Mikel nodded, moving through the gloom with sure steps. Finding another latch in the far wall, he stepped out of the way and motioned with his hand. "They keep most everyone else away. Just as he likes it."

"You want me to go first?" Teddy asked.

"Why not?"

"The last time we came here we didn't leave on the best of terms. He holds grudges, particularly against you."

"You're worried that he's going to turn you into a frog? It was only a threat. He hasn't done that to someone in centuries." Mikel meant it as a joke. Teddy didn't take it that way.

"Something worse than a frog," Teddy muttered. "He's a tricky one. A snail?"

"Forget it. You have nothing to worry about." Mikel growled in frustration then stepped into the gloom. He began making his way up the circular staircase, a dim light at the very top beckoning to him. "We didn't leave on the best of terms not because of something we did, but rather because he failed again."

"And you don't think he holds that against us?" Teddy was

afraid of very few people in the world. One of them waited above.

"We located the books he wanted. If he didn't find what he needed in them that wasn't our fault."

"Maybe not, but ..."

"But he holds grudges. Which is why I'm out in front."

"Exactly," Teddy replied.

"Like a human shield."

Teddy shrugged, though not challenging the analogy. "Let's hope that it doesn't come to that. Nevertheless ..."

"Better caution than a foolish courage," Mikel murmured. "I get it. Come on. Quietly from here on out."

Mikel stopped abruptly, Teddy almost catching his friend's heel with his foot. "Seriously?"

"Sorry, I just don't want to get caught in a snare."

Mikel couldn't fault Teddy for his logic. Staying close to him should give Teddy some protection if the man they sought had left a few traps crafted from the Talent in their path. Those traps would have no impact on Mikel, Teddy hoping the same would be the case for him.

As they drew near the top of the staircase, Mikel slowed his pace. There was more light than dark now, an open doorway just a few flights above calling to them.

He didn't think he had to worry about the Magus they were visiting. Still, better to take his time and avoid any surprises that might be waiting for him.

When he reached the open doorway, he stopped. Savoring the heat emanating from the large fireplace on the far side of the room.

More like ballroom.

Finn had been busy, turning the top floor of the warehouse into his own personal library, shelves of books running from floor to ceiling along all of the walls, the only breaks the windows cornering the fire that offered a glimpse of the Churn far below.

Mikel walked on quiet feet into the room, dodging around the various piles of scrolls and texts blocking his way, intent on the man sitting at a small reading desk, long grey hair tied loosely at his shoulders with a black leather strap.

"Always need to make an entrance, don't you, Mikel?"

The older man, his raspy, worn-down voice sounding inappropriate in what appeared to be such an erudite space, didn't bother to turn around when he felt the touch of cold steel at his throat.

"Only when the person I'm looking for is trying very hard not to be found."

"Good point." He flipped the page of the large tome spread across the table. Teddy, who had come up behind Mikel, couldn't read it. But he knew what it was because of its distinctive, almost mesmerizing script. That and the fact that Mikel was perusing the page just as the old man was.

Caledonii.

"How are you, Teddy?"

"Doing well, Finn. Yourself."

"Could be better. There's a blade at my throat."

"Sorry," Mikel said. "Brief moment of distraction." He pulled his dagger away and sheathed it.

When he stepped back, Finn spun around on his chair. He didn't appear to be upset by the interruption. Rather, his craggy features suggested that he was pleased to see them. "You do realize that I'm here because I want to be here. Otherwise, you wouldn't have found me."

"I'm well aware, Finn."

"What did you think of the apparitions?"

"They're quite impressive," Teddy nodded. "If not for Mikel's unique ability I'd probably still be pissing my pants while running for the Second Ring."

"Exactly what I want to hear," Finn said, clapping his hands together in delight. He pushed himself up from his chair. "Come along. It's been too long."

Finn strode directly toward the fireplace, the mantle rising well above his head.

"Finn ..." Teddy began to call.

His concern proved unnecessary. The fire parted, leaving a path right down the middle of the hearth.

"It only lasts for a few seconds," Finn called over his shoulder. "You better hurry. You really don't want to get caught."

Mikel and Teddy hustled after him, the illusion molding itself around them as they trotted between the flames and then right through the image of the ash-covered back wall.

Finn was waiting for them there, a huge grin breaking his usually grim expression. "Not bad, don't you think?"

"Not bad at all," Mikel agreed. Not knowing if the Magus was referring to his use of the Talent with respect to the fireplace or the terraced garden he had constructed on the roof of the warehouse, the clash of the rivers far below them a dull roar.

Mikel took a moment to appreciate the view. The Churn resembled a boiling pot of water, the breakers taller than some of the tallest waves in the Silent Sea.

"Any of those yours?" Finn asked, nodding toward the large gondolas sailing to and from the Crux, thick chains looped through closed hooks at bow and stern preventing the vengeful current from releasing its wrath.

Mikel didn't reply, giving the Magus a grin of his own.

Finn nodded. "The ones above as well?"

The wealthier citizens of the Crux could leave and return to the island without having to brave the turbulent water that served as an effective defense against any would-be attackers, and at certain times of the year left most of the Crux's residents stranded on the island, even the larger gondolas that matched in size the vessels that sailed the Burnt Ocean unable to bear the force of the waves.

Mikel didn't reply, just giving the Magus a shrug and a wink.

"I thought as much."

"How did you manage this?" Mikel asked, waving his arm to encompass the terrace, not having any desire to discuss his business interests with the Magus. And he knew that Finn was curious. The last time he had visited, Finn was facing some hard times and required some assistance that Mikel would have hesitated to provide to anyone else.

"I'll explain later." Finn wore a pleased smile as he walked over to a long table near the railing. "Can I see it?"

"See what?" Teddy asked.

"We're going to play this game?" Finn grumbled. Teddy had the good manners to appear chagrined. "I sensed it when you arrived at my door. I take it that's why you're here."

"You sensed it?" Mikel asked.

"You know what that means?" Finn asked.

Mikel pulled the scimitar from the scabbard across his back and placed the weapon on the cloth Finn had waiting on the table.

"I do." Mikel hadn't considered that possibility. If Finn could sense it, then any Magus worth their salt could.

"Good. You need to take care."

Finn ignored Mikel and Teddy for several minutes after that. Not touching the blade. Simply studying it. Every so often he ran his hand a few inches over the top of the finely crafted steel.

"How are you feeling?" Mikel asked. Finn looked more haggard and worn than the last time he had seen him. Finn's skin taking on a greyish tint, a few streaks of black appearing on the back of his hands. That worried him. Mikel knew what it meant.

"Why are you asking?" Finn grunted, not bothering to lift his head.

"Because I care."

Finn grunted again, though because he appreciated Mikel's comment or didn't believe him was up for interpretation.

"What you found for me didn't help," the Magus explained in a gruff voice. "Just another miss."

"I'm sorry."

Finn nodded. "Let's focus on what I might actually be able to do something about."

"Do you know what it is?"

Finn didn't reply for several more minutes. Mikel and Teddy exchanged a look. The dull roar of the Churn strangely soothing.

Mikel and Teddy were shocked from their daze when Finn's eyes widened and he stumbled backward.

"What's the matter?" Mikel reached out and grabbed the Magus' arm before he fell over a stool.

"I never thought it was possible. It disappeared I don't know how many centuries ago."

"What is it?" Teddy asked.

"The Blade of Light," Finn said very softly, a touch of reverence in his voice.

"Giant crafted?" Mikel asked. He knew the answer. He just wanted to confirm it.

Finn nodded. "A blade like that could only be made by the Giants of the Rime."

"What's the Blade of Light?" Teddy asked.

"A trap," Finn explained so quietly that Mikel and Teddy needed to strain to hear.

"What do you mean a trap?" Mikel was more worried now than he had been when he stole the blade from the deepest cellar in the Citadel.

Finn pulled up the stool he had almost knocked over and

sat down, leaning his elbows on the table, still staring down at the weapon. "You know why the Giants of the Rime created weapons such as this one?"

Mikel nodded. "For use against those who turned to the Curse, monster and man."

Finn nodded. "That's more than most know."

"I had an excellent instructor."

"That you did," Finn agreed, offering Mikel a small smile before returning his gaze to the gleaming steel. Finding it hard to pull his eyes away from the weapon for more than a few seconds. "You better than anyone know how the Giants make weapons such as this one. How they merge the steel with light and the Talent."

"That's why the sword is called what it's called?" Teddy asked.

"In part, yes," Finn nodded. "There's more to it than that, however, and there's not enough time to go into it now."

"Since when have you avoided telling a story?" mused Teddy.

Finn snorted softly at that. Finally able to look up from the steel, he locked onto Mikel.

Mikel saw a sadness there that he had not expected to see in the Magus. "What's the matter, Finn?"

"It's not for me to tell, Mikel. I'm sorry."

"Finn, if you know something, you need to ..."

Finn held up his hands, quieting Teddy. "I'm sorry, but I'm not the best one to tell you all that you need to know about the Blade of Light."

"Cadmus?" Mikel suggested.

The Magus nodded. "Yes."

"At least tell me why you're scared."

Finn smiled thinly at the request. He should have assumed as much. Mikel didn't miss a thing. "You've used it before?"

Mikel's eyes tightened. "How did you know?"

"Give me a little credit. I am a Magus."

Mikel didn't reply right away, reliving the combat in his office. What it felt like with the blade in his hand. Battling the Seeker. The energy surging not only through the blade, but through him. An experience he never thought possible. "Unwittingly. It was the only weapon at hand. I didn't know what I was doing. Or rather I didn't know how to stop whatever the blade was doing."

Finn frowned, then nodded, clearly not surprised by the information Mikel shared. "You need to speak with Cadmus. He can tell you more about this weapon than anyone else. But until then, know this."

"That sounds ominous," Teddy rumbled.

Finn ignored him. "The Blade of Light is many things. Why it chose you, I do not know."

"Chose me?"

Finn nodded. "Chose you. The blade decides who it will partner with."

It was Mikel's turn to nod. What Finn described was exactly how it felt when he held the blade in hand.

"For whatever reason, the Blade of Light has selected you. But you need to be exceedingly careful until you talk to Cadmus, because I don't know how to defend against what this weapon does to its bearer."

"What do you mean?" Mikel didn't bother to try to keep the hint of worry from his voice.

"The Blade of Light is a devastating weapon against creatures of the Curse, but its use comes with a cost. The Blade is a catalyst. An amplifier."

"Of what?" Teddy asked.

"Energy, and it has a gluttonous appetite. The user of this blade can expand their power a thousandfold."

"And what if the user doesn't have the capacity to use the Talent?" Mikel wondered.

"Now that's a good question," Finn said, the touch of sadness in his eyes taking hold, "and that's why I'm worried about you."

"Ominous indeed," Teddy murmured.

"Not very helpful," Mikel grouched.

"It wasn't meant to be." Teddy offered his friend a sympathetic shrug.

Mikel shook his head in frustration. He had come to Finn hoping to get answers, yet he had only acquired more questions, along with a seed of worry burrowing into the back of his brain.

"You know where you need to go to get the answers you require. Don't delay," Finn advised. "If the Blade of Light drains you dry ..." The Magus shrugged, not feeling the need to finish that thought. "How did you acquire it?"

"I stole it."

Finn was quite aware of Mikel's unique skills and many businesses. "For whom?"

"A client," he shrugged.

"Why are you always so obstreperous?"

"That's an excellent question," Teddy mumbled just loud enough to be heard.

"Just my nature," Mikel replied, ignoring his friend.

"Who was the client?"

"A woman."

"Mikel, stop acting the child," Finn growled. His eyes, dull, sometimes glazed, sparked dangerously as his temper flared. He did not enjoy being played with.

Mikel smiled. "Glad to see that you still have some fire, Finn."

Finn glared at Mikel, then laughed softly. "Yes, I guess I do look a little worse for wear."

"You're managing?"

"I'm managing. Now answer the question. Who is the woman?"

"I don't know. I never met her before, and I assume the name she gave me is false. All I know is that she was a Magus."

"How can you tell?"

"Does it matter?"

"I guess it doesn't," Finn admitted. "What was the name she gave you?"

"Assindra."

Finn nodded a few times. "Doesn't ring a bell." He hoped that Mikel couldn't read him as well as he feared that he could. Wanting to avoid what could be a series of uncomfortable questions, the Magus locked eyes with Mikel. "Like I said, the Blade of Light is a part of you now."

"What does that mean exactly?"

"That's all I can tell you. You and the Blade have come to an agreement of sorts. Why? I don't know. How? You know better than me. For more answers, talk to the Frost Lord."

Mikel's eyes narrowed. He knew that Finn wasn't telling him everything. But then again, the Magus rarely did. "Before I go, I have a favor to ask."

"You've got some nerve. We should be square after this."

"Actually, it's for a young woman who has some skill in the Talent."

That caught Finn's attention. "She just came into her power?" He couldn't hide his interest.

"You would have to talk to her about that."

"Yes, I would."

"Although I need to make one thing perfectly clear." Mikel leaned in toward Finn, his turn to catch the Magus' eyes. "I'm very fond of her. She's almost like a daughter to me. Do we understand one another?"

Finn nodded slowly. This is why he liked doing business

with the King of the Underworld. There was never any lack of clarity. "We do."

18

CALM AND COOL

"Would you just stand still?" Nat demanded in a low growl.

She spun back around, thinking that she could take a swipe at Mikel before he was prepared for her next attack. Mace at the ready, however, Mikel was nowhere to be found.

She felt a light tap on her shoulder and a whisper in her ear.

"Too predictable."

Nat pivoted quickly, swinging with her mace as hard as she could. Believing that her speed would make up for her poor footwork. Realizing just as quickly that she was wrong, already feeling herself getting pulled off balance.

Mikel helped her on her way, giving Nat a slight nudge to her hip that sent her stumbling through the small courtyard in the center of The Fox's Lair, sprawled on her hands and knees.

"That was good work," Mikel said.

"How could that be good?" Nat pushed herself up, not bothering to brush herself off. "I was a sitting duck when I fell. You could have finished me whenever you wanted."

Mikel nodded toward her right hand. "You're still holding your weapon."

"Small victory," Nat grumbled.

"You need to take what you can get."

"I'm not getting much," Nat replied. "I've yet to gain a touch on you."

"I've been doing this longer than you have." He wasn't teasing her. He was just stating a fact.

"You mean I can't master this mace of yours in just a few days?" Nat wondered, giving Mikel the grin that always made him smile as well.

He began to shrug, but stopped mid-motion, gliding backward instead. "Clever."

His smile grew even bigger as he raised his mace to parry her blow. Nat used his moment of hesitation to attack, seeking to take advantage of his desire to explain how she could have avoided her ignominious fall.

He didn't give her the chance she sought as he moved slowly around the courtyard. Though Nat's play failed, he liked her aggressiveness and how she approached the training session. Always thinking. Always searching for that angle that would give her the opening she desired. Never giving up.

"I thought so," Nat mumbled, shaking her head in frustration. Despite her attack not working as she wanted, still she kept pressing forward. Not swinging as wildly as before, however, understanding that was only a recipe for disaster. Instead she controlled her slashes and punches. Fast and sharp movements only. More precise in her decision making and her maneuvering.

"Well done," Mikel said as he defended against her attack. "Right foot forward just a few inches more. That will improve your balance. Good. Elbow up higher on the backslash. Perfect. Don't leave the steel in place. Always moving just like you are."

The practice combat continued for another ten minutes.

Mikel allowed Nat to guide the session now that she was demonstrating much of what he had taught her. Her emotions under control. Her thinking clear and precise.

"Let's call it a day," Mikel suggested. He was barely breathing. Nat was gasping for air, sweaty hair matted to her forehead, her shirt soaked through.

"I can keep going," she protested even as she fought the urge to bend at the waist and rest her hands on her knees.

"It wouldn't do any good. It's too easy to fall back into bad habits when you're tired. Better to end the session on a high note."

"High note? I still haven't gained a touch on you." That fact clearly irritated her.

"But I haven't gained a touch on you either since we started again."

Nat halted her advance. Thinking about that. A smile beginning to form. "That's true." She was pleased. But clearly she wasn't done.

Mikel was expecting Nat to try it. In fact, he had thought that she would give in to her mounting frustration earlier than this. Her desperation to gain the touch of steel that she craved almost too much to ignore. But she hadn't. So all credit to her for holding out this long.

He viewed her patience as a good thing. And he didn't mind when a small ball of energy shot from her palm, streaking right toward his chest. They needed to have this conversation, and now was a good time for it.

He didn't move. He didn't flinch. When the Talent struck him, it did nothing at all. The white-hot sphere fizzled out like it was no more than a few sickly sparks.

Disappointed, Nat was about to utter a curse she had heard in the tavern the night before. She never got the chance, her disappointment warring with her shock when she felt the light touch of Mikel's blade against her throat.

"I could kill you now with barely a cut. You understand that?"

Nat nodded slowly, not wanting the steel to slice into her flesh.

"But that would defeat the purpose of what we're doing. Do you understand the mistake that you made?"

Mikel pulled back his weapon so that she could answer. "I made a lot of mistakes."

Mikel smiled. "At the end. Your last one."

"Attacking you with the Talent even though it has no effect on you?" She sighed. "I was just trying to distract you. That's all. I didn't mean to make you angry."

Mikel frowned, not understanding why Nat thought he might be angry until he realized that she was interpreting his precise tone for that. "I'm not angry. And using the Talent as a distraction wasn't your mistake."

"Then what was it?" she asked, her confusion evident.

"I saw what you were going to do in your eyes. I knew you were going to use the Talent, so I was already moving toward you before you threw the sphere at me. You gave yourself away and I used that against you."

"Intuition," she murmured.

"More like instinct," he clarified.

"How could you have seen that?"

"I have more experience than you."

"So I'll always be at a disadvantage when fighting you?"

Mikel shrugged. "If you keep training, keep thinking, keep learning, maybe not."

"So there's hope?" she asked brightly.

"Only if you learn to control your emotions."

"That's what you saw in my eyes? My excitement?"

He nodded. "What did you see when you were looking in my eyes during our combat?"

"Purpose? Clarity? A coldness? No more than that." It was

Nat's turn to nod. "Another lesson for today that applies to more than just learning how to use steel as a weapon."

Mikel's smile broadened. "There you go. There are many types of combat. Steel. Wits. To name just two. In both, the ability to control your emotions is essential to your success, because your life likely will depend upon it."

"Reveal only what you want to reveal."

"And on that note we're done for today." He led her over to the bench set against the wall, sitting down and leaning back into the wood. Hands behind his head, he tried to stretch out his back. It had been bothering him ever since his duel with the Seeker.

"You're enjoying these lessons?" Mikel asked.

Nat gave him a worried glance. "You want to stop?"

"No," he replied with a gentle laugh. "This is the best part of my day."

"Good," she sighed, breathing easy again. Mikel and Teddy rescuing her had given her a new life that after only a few weeks she valued in a way that she never believed possible. Still she feared it could be taken from her just as fast as it had been given, not yet comfortable with her good fortune. Not certain if she ever could be.

For the first time since coming to Innsbruck, she was safe. Fed. She had her own room and bed. And she was learning. From the minute she woke up until the minute she went to sleep. About fighting. About running a tavern. About managing multiple businesses. About anything and everything. Mikel and Teddy always had something new for her to master.

"I'll continue to teach you how to fight with steel, but you need another tutor."

"Another tutor?" Nat was confused. Mikel and Teddy seemed more than capable of instructing her in everything she needed to know, whether steel, mathematics, accounting, strategy, risk, decision making, how to use a lockpick ... the list just kept getting longer. "For what?"

"The Talent."

She considered his response for several seconds, finally nodding. That made sense. "Who?"

"An old friend."

"You mean a Magus," she corrected.

"I do," Mikel chuckled. He liked her precision in all things. If she could bring that into her steelcraft, she would be a truly formidable opponent. "What's the matter?" He didn't understand why Nat was frowning.

"Why do you want to help me?" She kicked at an imaginary stone from where she was sitting on the bench. "You've been helping me ever since you set me free. No strings attached."

"And you're not used to other people helping you." Mikel sighed. Not an uncommon occurrence in their world.

"Not without them getting something in return. Usually something I don't want to give."

Mikel glimpsed some dark memories hidden in the back of Nat's eyes. He wasn't going to ask about those. If she wanted to talk, he would listen. But he sensed that now wasn't the time.

He smiled sadly. "Because I was once in the position that you're in now. A position where just a little help meant all the difference with respect to the life I've been able to lead."

"And someone helped you so that's why you want to help me?"

"Actually, many people didn't help me. Many people who had the chance to help me chose not to." He shook his head, clearing it of the memories that strained to break loose. "But yes, finally, someone did help me. And that person never expected anything in return other than an honest effort on my part."

"And that's all you want? An honest effort?"

Mikel nodded, his expression serious. He spoke with the

solemnity that he usually reserved for when he was negotiating a business deal. Nat noticed. Sitting up a little straighter. "That's all I ask for. An honest effort on your part. There will be times when you succeed. There will be just as many times when you fail."

"Just like a few minutes ago," Nat grumbled, not enjoying that memory.

"Just like a few minutes ago," Mikel agreed, "but whether you succeed or fail has no impact on the bargain we make today." He turned toward her, catching her eyes. "I promise you that so long as you make an honest effort, so will I. That's no more and no less than we can ask of anyone."

He held out his hand then. Waiting. Hoping.

Nat stared at what he proffered, recognizing the gravity of the situation and what her accepting his hand would mean. "One person helped you, and you want to help me in return?" In the world that Nat had grown up in, the concept of a fair deal held little meaning.

Mikel nodded again. "That's why I want to help you. I wouldn't be where I am today without the help of one person. Perhaps I can give you a nudge in the right direction as well."

Nat bit the inside of her cheek. Considering. Weighing. Then she reached out and grasped his hand. Shaking it firmly. "Then we have a deal."

"We have a deal," Mikel confirmed. He released her hand and leaned back into the bench, linking his fingers behind his head as he stretched his back again.

Nat smiled then. She felt lighter and she didn't understand why. Perhaps it was because it seemed like the weight of the world had been lifted from her shoulders. She had a path now. One that she had been testing since she met Mikel. One that she liked. And one on which she could continue. All she had to do was try her best.

"Thanks for your help in the tavern." Mikel leaned forward.

Placing his forearms on his knees, every so often he reached down with his fingers toward the dirt beneath his feet. Still trying to stretch the muscles in his back. "I owe you my life. If not for you, the woman would have killed me."

"You're welcome." Nat's smile broadened, pleased with herself. "You're in a dangerous business."

"Sometimes, yes," Mikel admitted. "Not always."

"But more dangerous than not."

"It can feel that way sometimes, yes." Mikel sighed. Then he smiled. Nat had shifted closer to him on the bench. Leaning against his shoulder. "It comes down to trust. Most of the people I work with I can trust. The one you saved me from, I can't."

"I'd like to help you with your business," Nat stated, though it was more a request. Despite their agreement she was uncertain about how far she could push.

"You already have," Mikel said.

"You know what I mean," Nat chided, adding a hint of exasperation to her voice.

"I do. That's why I brought these." He reached down next to the bench and pulled up a small stack of books wrapped with leather belts. He placed the package on the ground in front of Nat.

"What are these?"

"If you're going to be successful in business, you need to have a good education."

"You're going to teach me?" She could barely contain her excitement.

"I am."

"Are you a teacher?"

"We'll find out," Mikel said with a bark of a laugh.

"Who taught you?" She reached down, running her fingers across the leather binding of the book on the top of the stack.

"Kaduna."

"Who was Kaduna?"

"She was the one who gave me a chance when no one else would. She helped to put me on the path that has brought me here to you." There was so much more that he could say about Kaduna. About everything she did for him. How she put herself at risk to keep him safe. More times than he could remember, in fact. Always thinking of him first. Teaching him all that she could, and when she couldn't, finding someone who could.

"Kaduna was your mother?"

"I didn't know my mother," Mikel replied quietly, although his voice didn't contain even the faintest trace of sadness.

Kaduna had told him his parents died shortly after he was born. Learning that, and needing to give his full attention to dealing with the challenges he faced when he was younger, he never wasted much time looking at the past. He was always focused on the present and every so often he turned his sights to the future. Just as he was doing now. "Kaduna was more like a very kind and very tough mother. But we weren't related."

"We're not related."

"No, we're not."

"So Kaduna wasn't your mother, but she was like your mother."

"She was," Mikel confirmed.

"And you're not my father, but you could be like my father?"

Mikel sensed the tension radiating off Nat. He understood the importance of her question. Just as much, how important his answer was. "I could, yes."

"That's good to know." A small smile broke out on Nat's much-too-often serious visage. Breathing easier once again, the stress that she had been feeling faded swiftly.

"Why all these?" She pointed toward the books.

Mikel's eyes sparked in delight. He loved how Nat's mind jumped from one topic to the next. Never settling in one place for too long. Her curiosity knowing almost no bounds.

"Can you read?"

"Yes." She reached down and loosened a strap. Picking up the thin book on top, she flipped through the pages and then rattled off a few sentences, Mikel following along with her.

"We start with those tomorrow. He picked up the next book on the pile and handed it to Nat.

"*The Art of War*," she read.

"Read the first five chapters tonight. Tomorrow, after our session here in the courtyard, we'll talk about the book. The lessons within apply to more than just combat."

"What does war have to do with business?"

"More than you might think. Read the chapters tonight and you'll see what I mean when we talk tomorrow."

She nodded, holding the book to her chest. He doubted that she would let it out of her grasp until she finished the assignment. And knowing her, he wouldn't be surprised if she read the entire text by tomorrow.

"So what's the matter with your leg?"

Mikel stopped rubbing his right knee and thigh. During the training session he felt good, the activity helping to loosen the scar tissue. Just as always, however, his old wounds tightened up again and began to ache when he was done.

"An old injury," he shrugged. "It bothers me from time to time."

"More like all the time," she judged, crossing her arms, book still held against her chest.

"You know, you notice way too much," he said with a raised eyebrow.

Nat shrugged. "If I didn't, you'd be dead. You said so yourself."

"Fair enough," Mikel sighed.

"Who gave it to you?"

"Is there a question you don't like?"

She frowned. "If I don't ask, I don't get answers. If I don't get answers, I don't learn."

"I've unleashed a monster," Mikel said in an amused tone.

"So who gave it to you?"

"You don't let anything go, do you?"

"No, but it's only fair, because neither do you."

Mikel worked hard not to snort out a laugh. He didn't want to give Nat the satisfaction. "I received one of the wounds from the woman I loved. Or at least I thought I loved."

"The woman you loved?" That caught Nat's attention.

He ignored her question. "No one really asks me about my leg."

"Why not?"

"I assume because they don't want to pry." He didn't say anything more, waiting to see if Nat would get the hint. She didn't. She continued to stare at him expectantly. "Or that they're afraid to," he added.

"Not even Teddy?"

"Teddy doesn't need to ask. He was there when I was wounded the second time."

"Why would people be afraid to ask you about it?"

"You mean other than the desire to not pry?"

"Yes, other than that." Once again, Nat missed the hint. Or she caught it and chose to ignore it, Mikel believing that she might be practicing their last lesson from the combat. Hiding her emotions. Although in this current circumstance her newfound skill irritated him.

"Apparently I can be intimidating."

"Says who?" It was Nat's turn to lift an eyebrow, registering her disbelief.

"Says pretty much everybody."

"I don't think that you're intimidating," Nat stated unequivocally, not even needing to think about it.

"Then you're one of the few. But that's good."

"Why is that good?"

"Because I don't want you to be intimidated or afraid of me."

"Well, I'm not."

"You said that," Mikel confirmed with a smile. "Like I said, that's good."

"Why is that good?"

"Because I like you. We're friends." He noticed how she was beginning to frown. "And maybe we could be more than that as we just talked about, more like a family."

Nat's frown quickly transformed into a small smile. "Friends shouldn't be intimidated by their friends."

"Agreed."

"Now will you tell me what happened to your leg?"

"I thought that you might have let that go." Mikel's tone suggested that he hoped that she would.

"I don't let anything go."

"I've noticed that. You're tenacious. That's what I like about you."

"That's the only thing you like about me?"

Mikel laughed. In many ways this was the most difficult conversation he had engaged in for quite a long time. And he was enjoying it in a way that he had enjoyed very little for quite a long time. "No, there are other things that I like about you. Many things."

"You can tell me about all those other things later."

"That's kind of you." Mikel doubted that she missed his sarcasm.

"Now tell me about your leg."

"I thought I might have gotten you off that topic."

"You said it yourself," Nat said, offering him a sweet smile. "I'm tenacious."

Mikel laughed again, deciding to give her a piece of what she was asking for. She would have to work harder for the rest. "I hurt my leg twice. The first time was the worst of the two."

"What happened?"

"I was in the Bitter Heights. Hunting."

"In the Bitter Heights?"

"Yes, that's where I grew up. I lived there until I was a few years younger than you are now. Until I needed to get out. Start a new life."

Nat nodded, locking away that information for future use. "Continue."

Mikel gave her another raised eyebrow, but he did as she ordered. "I was hunting in a valley surrounded by snow-capped peaks that rose several thousand feet, almost touching the sky. Tracking an elk. It had taken most of the day for me to find it and then get close. Downwind, of course, so the animal wouldn't find me out."

"The elk gored you?"

"No, right before I was about to release the arrow on my bow, I realized that while I was hunting the elk, I was being hunted as well."

"By what?" Nat's eyes widened, caught up in the tale.

"A Grim." When he saw Nat's frown, Mikel explained. "They're common in the Bitter Heights. It's a wild hound that looks much like a wolf, only bigger and more vicious. It kills to eat. It also kills because it can."

"The Grim attacked you?"

Mikel nodded. "It did. I sensed the Grim just a second before it pounced on me. It came at me from behind. I turned fast enough to shoot an arrow at it, though it didn't do anything more than irritate the beast for just a heartbeat." He leaned in toward her, giving her shoulder a nudge with his own. "Your next lesson for today. A Grim's hide is very thick. Arrows don't punch through very deeply. If you want to have any chance against a Grim, you need to strike it in the eye or the throat."

"And you didn't?"

"I didn't. I didn't have the time."

"Then how did you survive?"

"The Grim didn't take me down from behind like it wanted to. If it had, I'd be dead. When the animal leapt at me, I was facing it. I used my bow to keep its jaws away from me, pushing the wood into its maw."

"That didn't work?"

"Not for long." Mikel replied. Speaking about that incident now, years having passed, he considered once again whether he could have done anything differently. He concluded that he couldn't, other than identifying the Grim stalking him sooner than he did. "A Grim's jaws are strong enough to chomp on rocks. Once the animal snapped my bow in two, it reared back to bite again and I tried to scramble away."

"You didn't get far."

"No. The Grim ripped open my thigh, taking out a good-sized chunk."

"What did you do?"

"Screamed in pain."

Nat snorted. Then she nudged him with her shoulder. "I meant how did you survive."

He pulled free the mace he always kept sheathed at the small of his back, twisting it around so that the blade on one end, the blade that had been at Nat's throat just minutes before, caught the light streaming into the courtyard. "While the Grim was enjoying the flesh it stripped from me, I drove the blade into the beast's eye."

"You killed it."

"I did. And then I almost died anyway, because no one from my tribe would hunt with me and I was several leagues away from my village. But that's a story for another time."

"You were Caledonii?" Nat asked, satisfied for now, though wanting clarification on one item. She remembered Mikel referencing the Bitter Heights. One of the tribes original to the Realms was said to live in those desolate mountains. No one else ventured there. The tribe ostracized.

"Yes, I am."

"Why are you here then?"

"I was Caledonii, I am Caledonii," Mikel corrected quickly. "The other Caledonii, however, didn't view me as Caledonii. So eventually I ended up here because they didn't want me there. Another long story, and now's not the time to go into it all."

Nat sensed Mikel's discomfort, and this time she let her line of questioning go. At least for now. "That's not a very nice way to be treated."

"No, it's not. But as you've learned, you can't always change the world. And when you can't, you have to find some way to navigate through that world. That's what I did. With Kaduna's help."

Nat nodded, hearing the truth in his words because she had lived through much the same herself. "I wouldn't do something like that to you."

"I know that you wouldn't." Mikel reached over and placed an arm around her shoulders. She leaned into him, so he assumed that she appreciated the gesture. "Thank you."

"We're family," Nat said softly, having come to the decision she had been mulling ever since she started the conversation. "Family doesn't do that to family."

Mikel smiled, hugging Nat to his shoulder.

They stayed there until the sun began to set.

Nat reading *The Art of War*.

Mikel trying to keep the tears he felt welling up in his eyes from rolling down his cheeks.

19

A NEW WORLD

"That's the one?"

Millie nodded toward the far side of the street. The madame of The Silken Pleasure stood on the front porch, greeting her customers. Keeping an eye on who came and went. Always smiling. Always calculating. Business was just as good as it always was. Better, in fact, which was why she was looking forward to speaking with Mikel in a few days. "She needs to be more careful about the questions she's asking. I've received several offers regarding her that I thought best ignored."

Teddy looked toward the tavern that fronted the brothel. Catching sight of the young woman beneath the softly glowing lanterns, he frowned. Then he shook his head. He didn't need this aggravation.

She wore a cloak with a cowl to hide who she was. Clearly, though, she didn't belong in this part of the city. She radiated a mild arrogance and authority that was usually reserved for the upper rings of Innsbruck. An expectation as well that whatever she required would be delivered to her without question.

A failing of her upbringing, Teddy believed. An unrealistic way to approach the world she had entered that evening.

Millie was right. The woman didn't belong.

Her coming here could lead to only one thing.

Trouble.

He shook his head again then sighed. He didn't have time for this. There was other business that he needed to deal with on this night. He didn't have a choice, however. He couldn't just leave her there.

As he had learned, no matter how much he might want, trouble rarely left on its own. Best to deal with it sooner rather than later. Because if he didn't, it only grew bigger left unchecked.

"Thanks Millie," Teddy said in a warm rumble. "I'll let Mikel know that you were looking out for him."

He stepped off the porch and strode toward the woman who was looking up and down the street. Likely trying to decide which way to go next. Because there were few people in these Innsbruck neighborhoods willing to give her the information that she desired.

And for good reason.

Their lives depended on their discretion.

"You're a pretty one."

Drin turned, coming face to face with several men exiting the tavern. Clearly well into their cups and with only one thing on their mind.

By the look of them, chainmen. Big. Brawny. Rough with scarred hands. A few missing fingers. Charged with bringing the gondolas through the Churn.

"Not as pretty as you," she replied, hoping to throw the man off. Having no doubt as to what he wanted. Her hand already on the hilt of the long dagger hidden beneath her cloak.

"You think I'm pretty?" The chainman frowned. He wasn't

sure what to do with that comment. Not happy that his friends at his back were snickering and chortling away at his expense. Therefore, the chainman did what he usually did when he was confused or became embarrassed. He got angry.

"Are you making fun of me?"

"I think she is, Eddi," one of his friends agreed.

The chainman took a menacing step toward Drin. His intentions clear in his posture.

Eyes widening in alarm, she had her dagger halfway out of the sheath on her hip when a deep, calming voice at her back startled her. She watched as a hand reached over her shoulder and came to rest on the chainman's chest, stopping him cold with barely a touch.

"I don't think you're pretty. I think you're ugly. And I can make you even uglier if you don't leave the lady alone."

The chainman's eyes boiled with rage as he lifted his gaze from the woman. He followed the hand up the long arm to the giant standing behind her. Fear smothered his bad temper in a flash, much like a top being placed on a grease fire.

"Teddy, I didn't know ..."

"No harm done ... yet." Teddy removed his hand from the chainman's chest. "I suggest you and your friends go back into the tavern, book some rooms, and sleep it off ... or maybe have a little fun before doing that." With his other hand, he held out several golds that Eddi was more than happy to accept. "With our compliments, of course, Eddi. For your discretion and good sense."

Eddi nodded. "Of course, Teddy. Thank you."

The chainman stepped back then, nodding his apologies to the woman before scampering back up the steps and into the tavern, his friends following right after him, all silent as mice.

"You didn't have to do that."

Teddy looked down. The woman who barely came up to his chest had turned on him. Puffing herself up like a peacock. "I did. If he tried to do something to you, the soldiers of the Crux would have come down from their perch on high. They wouldn't ask the right questions and they'd make the lives of the people living in this neighborhood miserable. No one wants to deal with that. Too much time. Too much hassle. Too much bad blood. And all because you chose to come to a place that you shouldn't be."

Drin scowled, still not placated. "I was simply explaining that I can handle myself."

"I have no doubt that you can," Teddy agreed, not wanting to get into it with the petite spitfire who stood there as if she owned everything she set her eyes upon. Of course, in some ways she did, though he chose to ignore that inconvenient fact. "But you're asking questions that will get you into trouble."

Drin's expression changed then, becoming more than just curious. "You know who I'm looking for?" After suffering through her work for the day – if endless dialogue with the First Families that led nowhere and meeting after meeting with no clear solution to the issues dominating the Crux could be described as honest work -- Drin snuck out of the Citadel, using a tunnel known only to her that took her down to the Seventh Ring.

As soon as she exited the printing shop, free of her many responsibilities at least for a few hours, she breathed easier. Walking the streets of Innsbruck as she made her way toward the lower rings, she felt energized.

Her goal?

To locate the sergeant who wasn't a sergeant.

She believed doing that was essential to keeping the promise she had made to herself. She would find out who was responsible for her father's murder, and she would mete out the justice deserved for assassinating the King of the Crux in such a heinous manner.

She wanted answers.

She needed answers.

And she believed that she could only obtain those answers from the man who saved her life against the Drude. The man she was certain was also the sergeant who had interrupted Lucius Hanover before he could press his case with her any further.

Just as much, she needed guidance. She felt lost. Doing what was required of her. But not doing what she believed was necessary.

Why she thought the man she was looking for could help her with that last part, she wasn't quite sure. Still, she held out hope that he could.

Even as the energy that pushed her forward when she began her hunt slowly fizzled as the night drifted toward early morning. Her many inquiries leading her right into one brick wall after another.

As the hours slipped by without any success, her belief faded. Frustration setting in. Until now.

"I do," Teddy admitted reluctantly. "That's why I'm here. Remove the cowl."

"Remove the cowl?" She didn't understand her request.

Teddy nodded. "Before I decide what to do with you, I need to see your face."

"Why?"

"Because we've had problems with cowled women the last few days."

Drin considered his demand, curious, at the same time a small spark of hope reviving her belief that she was on the right path. Then she nodded. Believing she knew of one instance to which he might be referring, she dropped the cowl to her shoulders.

"Do you believe that I'm a problem?" Drin asked, a challenge in her tone.

Teddy muttered to himself. It seemed that this evening was

only getting worse. He didn't like the path that he was mulling. Not one bit.

Nevertheless, he didn't think he had a choice, because he doubted that he could convince the woman standing before him to turn around and go back from whence she came.

He knew who she was. And he knew of what she was capable.

"Of that, I have no doubt," Teddy grumbled. "I'd bow, but that would bring too much attention to you. And you don't want that here. Not after the fog."

Drin's eyes narrowed, then she smiled thinly. He recognized her. And thanks to his last few words, she recognized him. "I'm sorry to have unsettled you. I am not demanding that your friend meet with me for long. I simply request a few minutes of his time."

"Just a few minutes?"

Drin nodded. "No more than that. Then I will leave you and him be."

"I doubt that," Teddy muttered softly, though loud enough for Drin to hear, which only served to deepen her scowl.

Teddy saw it, but he didn't care. The Citadel was a long way from the Fifth Ring, and even farther from where they were going. "Come on."

He headed down the street, not bothering to look over his shoulder, certain that she would be dogging his steps. Knowing as well that she recognized him as one of the shadows who helped her against the men sent to kill her in the murk.

"Is it always like this?" Drin asked. There was barely room to stand. The only reason she was able to push inside was because of her escort.

She followed Teddy, a path opening behind him as he

pushed his way through the crowd and then passed the bar, his wake closing quickly.

The Fox's Lair.

She had caught the name on the swinging placard above the entrance before they walked in. Certainly an appropriate appellation from what she had learned of the man she wanted to meet.

Teddy nodded as they continued down the hallway. It was a busy night. Just like every other night. "It is. Ale. Beer. Wine. We serve the best in the city."

"Even better than ..." She stopped herself, not wanting to insult her guide.

Teddy lifted an eyebrow as he looked over his shoulder. "Better than what's served in the higher rings?" He smiled then. "Where do you think they get their ale, beer, and wine?"

Reaching the end of the hallway, he pushed open a door for her. Drin hesitated for just a moment.

"You have nothing to fear. You should know that by now."

Drin smiled at that. The giant was right. She did know that.

Stepping by him, a sense of satisfaction raced through her.

She had found her quarry.

He was sitting on a bench reading in the moonlight, just a few lanterns lighting the small courtyard. She assumed it was a practice ground, though in each corner there was a garden carefully laid.

Herbs in one. Flowers in another. No, not just flowers. Edible flowers. She was too far away from the gardens on the far side, but she assumed they were much like the two on this side. Growing what was used in the tavern's restaurant.

When her eyes came back to the reason she left the Citadel, Drin realized that she had disturbed him. The sounds of the common room carried through the open door, and he didn't appear to be pleased by the interruption.

"What are you reading?" she asked, hoping to remove the frown that marred the sharp features of his battered face.

He didn't reply right away. Not looking at her. Looking at her guide instead.

Glancing over her shoulder, she read the silent communication that occurred between them.

The bear of a man was less than pleased by the interruption, even more so that she was the cause of it. Her guide shrugged, using his eyes to relay to him that it was necessary.

Her guide said a bit more as well with his expression. Most obvious to Drin, that the man sitting on the bench was to talk with her and then get rid of her as quickly and as quietly as possible.

She wasn't insulted by that suggestion. If she were in their position, she'd want the same.

Returning her gaze to the man she had come to see, she almost took a step back. She stopped herself at the very last second.

He had risen so quietly and approached so swiftly that he stood no more than a few feet away from her now, and she hadn't even heard him move. Just another reminder as to why he had proven so dangerous in the fog.

"You two play nice." Teddy stepped back into the hallway and allowed the door to close. As soon as it did, a welcome silence settled around them, the noise from the common room gone.

Drin found it more and more difficult controlling her nerves as she examined the hulking fellow in front of her who hadn't yet said a word. He was big. But not heavy. Almost all of his bulk muscle. Yet that certainly didn't hinder his speed, as she had seen.

He wasn't handsome. Though his weathered visage revealed a character that she had only come across a few times before. In fact, his expression now reminded her of her uncle. The only real distinguishing characteristic, other than his nose that she was certain had been broken several times, was his eyes.

Cold. Calculating. Certain.

Although she didn't believe they were always like that. At least she hoped they weren't.

A spark of discomfort shot through her when she realized that he was studying her. Not only measuring her, but also seeking a sense of who she truly was.

She was startled from her thoughts when he snapped the book closed and held it out so that she could read the title.

The Art of War.

"Just reviewing," Mikel said in response to the puzzled look she gave him. "I have to teach a lesson tomorrow and my student is smarter than I am. So I can't afford to make a mistake. If I do, she'll never let me hear the end of it."

Of all the things that Drin expected him to say, that wasn't it. Her eyes crinkled. Her smile genuine. A sense of relief flooded through her. His cold eyes weren't as cold as they had been just a moment before.

Against her better judgment, she realized that she liked the man. Even though she had a good sense as to exactly who he was and what he did.

"So you're a teacher," she prodded, seeking some way to begin the dialogue that might offer a good avenue for her to get to the primary reason she was there.

"At times."

"But not always?"

Mikel shook his head. "No. Not always. I take on many roles depending on the circumstances. Just like you do."

Crow's feet appeared below Drin's eyes, her look cunning. Matching his.

He was telling her that he knew more about her than she

knew about him. Also that she was on his ground now. That here he made the decisions.

A useful reminder, she acknowledged. Because he enjoyed advantages here that she didn't, having given up most of those as soon as she left the Citadel on her own.

"And you are?" Drin started.

"You know who I am," Mikel replied, seeing the recognition in her eyes. He didn't feel the need to help her get to where she wanted to go, even though Teddy wanted her gone as quickly as possible. "And you're trouble." His last two experiences with her testified to the truth of his statement.

"That seems to be the assumption that most are making of me today," Drin replied calmly. She decided to seek the upper hand, just as she would if she were back on the Royal Ring. "Are you always this difficult?" She was not used to interacting with people in this manner. There wasn't disrespect in his tone or what he said. There was ...

She wasn't quite certain how to define it. A challenge? Or perhaps there was more to it. Rather a test?

"This isn't difficult," he replied. "This is just me."

A test for certain. "You never gave me a chance to thank you, Sergeant ..."

He didn't reply right away, taking the time to decide what he wanted to reveal. "You know I'm not a Sergeant."

"Yet you were in the Citadel."

"I was."

She expected more from him. Not gaining it, she pushed again. "How did you get into the Citadel if you're not in service to the Army of the Crux?"

"I imagine the same way you exited the Citadel this evening."

She realized then that he was going to make her work for her answers. And instead of being irritated by that, she was pleased. Not just a challenge or a test, but also a game.

So be it.

She was used to games, as she viewed the politics of the Crux as no more than that, although one of high stakes and serious consequences. And if she could manage the First Families and all of their demands, then she could certainly manage the man standing before her.

"You and your friend aided me in the fog."

"Guilty."

"You knew who I was when you did so."

"At the end, yes," Mikel confirmed with a nod.

"Why did you help me?"

"The same reason as I told you before."

"Because I needed help." Drin still found it difficult to wrap her mind around what he was saying. He and his friend placing themselves in danger when there was no cause to do so. He could have left her to her fate and no one would have thought the worse of him. Except perhaps himself. She smiled then, beginning to understand him just a little bit more.

He shrugged. "I was taught to expect nothing in return when doing a good deed, although sometimes, in the rarest of circumstances, it would be paid forward."

"You're not telling me everything," Drin challenged, believing that she was right. He was holding back. Not revealing his true motivation.

"I'm not, you're right."

Drin stood there expectantly, waiting for him to say more, then realizing he wasn't going to. Her hard stare that worked on most everyone else had no impact upon him. Restraining the growl of irritation that begged to be freed, she picked up on what he last said. How doing a good deed could lead to something in return.

"Since you knew who I was, why didn't you ask for a reward?"

"I don't need a reward."

"You don't need a reward?" Once again he caught her by surprise. Who in their right mind would turn down a reward from someone of her standing?

"No. Like I said, I helped you because you needed help." He smiled, then gave her a wink. "Although I might need a favor. At some point in the future."

And there it was, she realized. Her suspicions confirmed. "You're the one my uncle was telling me about."

"I can't say that I know the Battle Lord."

Drin nodded her head slowly, eyes locked onto his. Finding the game they were playing much more enjoyable than she anticipated. Because she realized that he could have added a few words to the end of that sentence. *Very well*. But he didn't, not feeling the need, knowing that she would figure it out on her own.

"What should I call you if not Sergeant ..."

He admired her persistence. "I have many names. Some earned, some not."

"You're being difficult again."

"I'm just being myself."

"Difficult, you mean?" Drin replied, refusing to budge.

"I tend to be," he admitted finally with the hint of a smile. "At this point in my life I have little cause to be anything other than who I am."

"Perhaps just this once you could be more forthcoming. It would get me out of your hair that much faster." It was her turn to shrug and then give him a raised eyebrow. "That's what you want, isn't it?"

He smiled, fingers intertwined behind his back, book still in his grasp. "You can call me Mikel."

"Just Mikel?"

He nodded. "No more than that is needed."

"You're also called the Fox."

"On occasion."

"The Knife."

"That too."

"The Broken Bear."

"That one is actually my favorite."

"The Shadow?"

"I don't know how I got that one," Mikel admitted. "It doesn't really fit when you get a good look at me, now does it?"

"I beg to differ. From your work in the fog, it seems the perfect choice." Drin bit the inside of her lip, trying not to laugh.

She didn't know what to think of him.

He represented everything that she opposed. He was at the center of much of what she wanted to stamp out in the Crux. Crime. Corruption.

Yet here she stood, having a conversation with him, because her personal beliefs had no relevance. The requirements of her position took precedence. The simple truth being that she needed him.

"I should throw you into a cell." She placed one hand on her right hip, left leg extended forward.

Mikel didn't miss how her hand was now only inches from the long dagger on her belt, but he wasn't worried. If she was going to come at him, it would be with the Talent. "For what crime? Helping you?"

"I'm sure there are a host of charges that I could bring against you."

He shrugged, not bothering to deny it. "But you won't."

She bit the inside of her lip just a little harder. Eyes narrowing further. Almost a squint.

She didn't want to back down. Instead, she found another way to extricate herself, even though she was reluctant to do so, chafing at what was demanded of her. She remembered one of her father's lessons, told to her after a particularly difficult session with an ambassador from the Cape.

You didn't have to like your allies. You just needed to be able to trust them so long as you were working with them. And she got the sense that she could trust Mikel. Even if she didn't want to.

"I won't. At least not right now."

"That's very kind of you," Mikel replied, a hint of sarcasm in his voice.

"You're gloating." Drin's eyes flashed.

"I don't gloat. Ever." His voice turned frigidly cold in an instant, matching his eyes. What little warmth that had been creeping in at the edges gone.

She believed him. "What you do doesn't bother you?"

"Why should it?" he shrugged. "It's the same as you do. The same rules apply. I just do it in a world different from yours."

Drin had an immediate, scathing reply on the tip of her tongue. She held it back, instead thinking about his argument. There was some logic to it. Besides, now wasn't the time to get into a quarrel. Not when she needed something from him and she already owed him a debt.

"And what people call you doesn't bother you?"

"You mean the names other than the Fox or the Knife or the Broken Bear?"

Drin nodded.

Mikel shrugged. "Does it bother you?"

"What do you mean?"

"Does what some people call you bother you? It's not always pleasant, I'm sure." Mikel lifted his hands, as if to say there was little point in worrying about what you couldn't control. "It's just the way of the world, isn't it? Especially when someone else wants what you have."

Drin's left foot began to tap the ground. She still wasn't sure what to make of Mikel. "You come across as more erudite than I anticipated."

"You expected that after speaking with me I'd reveal myself to be no more than a thug."

He didn't appear to be insulted by that conclusion, in fact he seemed almost pleased, so she was just as blunt. "Yes, I did."

"My apologies for destroying the illusion."

"I don't get the sense that you are."

"I'm not," Mikel said, grinning, then returning to what they had been talking about just a minute before. "Like I said, I have many names. Some earned. Some not. In the end, what I'm called doesn't matter. All that matters is what I do. Because a name doesn't make the person."

"What do you mean by that?" Drin couldn't help herself. She was too intrigued by what he said not to ask.

"Names are useful, I've found, and they don't always have to be accurate to get the job done."

"Get what job done?"

"Depends on the day," Mikel replied. "Would you care to sit?"

He motioned toward the bench. Drin hesitated, then offered him a small dip of her head as she settled back against the smooth wood as if she sat on the throne in the Citadel.

Mikel didn't seem to notice, or if he did he chose not to comment as he leaned back in a slight slouch and crossed his legs in front of him.

"You're purported to be the King of the Underworld." Drin felt no need to dodge around the topic. She sensed that he preferred a direct approach, her attempt to come at what she wanted to discuss in a roundabout manner leaving her no closer to her objective.

"That's what people say about me, yes."

"So you are?" She leaned in toward him briefly. "I know you're enjoying this game, but better to speak plainly. It means I leave you all the sooner."

"Music to my ears," Mikel replied in a surprisingly gentle

tone for such a big man. "Yes, I am the King of the Underworld. A useful name at times. And sometimes not."

"You do realize this is my Kingdom." Her eyes were just as sharp as her tone, almost as if she wanted him to challenge her.

"It is," he agreed. "For now."

A spark of red shot across her cheeks, her chest tightening. When she looked into his eyes, however, she realized that he was referencing the fragility of her current circumstances. He wasn't throwing down the gauntlet.

But he was pushing her. Still measuring her. Wanting to test her mettle. She refused to bite.

"For now," she confirmed, "and well into the future. Of that I can assure you."

"I like your confidence," Mikel replied, offering her a nod of respect. "You're going to need it in the days ahead."

"You don't believe me?" Drin demanded, feeling feisty.

"I didn't say that."

"I don't like having another ruler in my Kingdom. That can lead to confusion ... or worse."

"I'm not a threat to you, Queen Heir Dengannon. Your father understood that."

So it was true. Her father had dealings with the King of the Underworld. She mulled that revelation for a time. A small smile cracked her lips when she recognized the significance of the title he gave her. "You seem the type of man where losing to a woman in a game of sport wouldn't bother you."

"Why would it bother me?" Mikel wondered, not understanding why she moved the conversation in this direction. "I already know you're better at throwing a dagger than I am. Woman or no, the only thing I care about is that you're not throwing daggers at me. Stick to the dartboard and we'll get along fine."

Drin smiled at that. For the first time in a long time she felt good about herself. Mikel's compliment helping to rebuild the fortitude within her that had been weakening, the difficulties that came up during the day's almost endless dialogues with various First Families chipping away at the very precarious foundation of her rule.

The only conclusion she could reach after wasting most of the day making her case for the throne was that her odds of reaching the Coronation had worsened drastically. More upsetting, it seemed that the only real option for maintaining a hold on her father's seat required acceding to a proposal that, though on the surface seemed like the right course of action, she wasn't certain she wanted to accept. A vague premonition of concern souring the concept.

"So why did you really come down here? I know you were asking about me."

"When did you find out? Your friend didn't say anything to you when he brought me here."

"I knew you were in the streets as soon as you left the printing shop. I knew you were looking for me as soon as you asked at the bake shop not far from where we met the first time about the, and I quote, 'scary looking fellow with the big shoulders and bigger attitude whose face has seen better days.'"

"I'm sorry," Drin apologized, heat rising in her cheeks and revealing her embarrassment, unable to stop the soft chuckle that escaped. "I didn't know how ..."

Mikel held up his hands, more amused than insulted. "Don't worry. I've been described in much more colorful terms than those."

Drin nodded at that, thankful to be let off so easily.

She should have assumed as much. Mikel could not be who he was if he didn't have eyes and ears everywhere in the city. And the fact that he revealed all this to her confirmed that he was confident in his position. A quiet way of reminding her that she couldn't touch him. Though perhaps if she were smart she could use him.

"You and your friend helped me in the fog."

"Teddy," Mikel nodded.

"Teddy?" Drin considered that, perplexed for a moment. "That's his name? It doesn't seem to fit ..."

"Someone of his size?" Mikel laughed softly. "Yes, it is a little deceptive, isn't it? But as I said, names have their many different uses. For example, there is quite a big difference between Queen Heir and Queen."

Drin pursed her lips. Another hint from a very clever fellow. He did resemble a Broken Bear, yet he had the cunning of a Fox. Reminding her that he would not be played. If she wanted something from him, she would need to speak plainly.

So she started again. "You and Teddy helped me against the assassins and then the Drude."

"We did," Mikel replied, seeing no reason not to confirm what she already knew to be the truth.

"You know what a Drude is."

"I do," he confirmed.

"That's uncommon knowledge." Her gaze was insightful and demanding, locking eyes with his, seeking a clue he might not be willing to divulge.

"I had an excellent education."

Drin waited for him to say more. Hoping that he would. Not surprised when he didn't. "I can count on my fingers the number of people in Innsbruck who might have knowledge of a Drude. And you wouldn't be one of them."

"There are surprises all around us, Queen Heir. You need only look with open eyes to find them."

She ignored his subtle dig, although she didn't miss what he was telling her. That a broader perspective might do her some good. That how the Crux worked on the Royal Ring wasn't how the Crux worked there in The Fox's Lair. "Yes, and you were there when the Drude appeared."

Mikel grinned then. He sat straighter, curling his right knee beneath him, kneading gently the joint and leg that bothered him constantly. Thankful that now it was no more than a dull ache. "You're a Magus, Queen Heir. You can tell that I have no skill in the Talent nor in the Curse."

"You're right, I can."

He nodded then, his smile curling into the grin of a fox. "You know I had nothing to do with the Drude, but you think I know who sent it."

"I think you might suspect since you know what a Drude is." Her eyes sharpened, becoming shrewder than they already were. "I can make it worth your while if you have information to share. The Drude was there for me, and I believe that same Drude killed my father."

Mikel didn't reply right away. The Queen Heir reminded him of Nat. Sharper than the edge of a blade and just as driven. "I suspect you're right about that. And you want to know who sent it because you feel the need for justice."

"Vengeance," Drin corrected in a fierce whisper.

"A dangerous road, Queen Heir."

"Why do you say that?" she demanded, pulling back from him slightly. Not understanding his comment. "Vengeance is my right. It is my responsibility."

"I understand why you feel this way. But believe me, seeking revenge has a way of changing a person, and not always for the good."

"You have some experience in this?" she accused.

"More than I would like, in fact."

Drin's gaze turned hard. She had no desire to discuss the merits of her decision with a criminal. "What I do and why is of no concern to you. I came here because I believe you know who might have sent the Drude."

"You believe that I have connections such as that?" Mikel snorted out a soft laugh. "That's quite an ask even for me."

"Yet I'm asking because I believe I'm right."

Rather than getting irritated, Mikel's expression turned thoughtful. She didn't back down. He liked that. And he believed that it would serve her well in the hard days to come. Because if she lost the throne there was a strong likelihood that she would lose her life as well. "I suspect, but I don't know it for the truth. Once I know it for the truth, I'll deal with it."

"What do you mean you'll deal with it?" Drin demanded, barely able to control the anger that flashed through her like a wildfire. "The Drude killed my father. The Dark Magus that sent that monster belongs to me."

If she expected the anger of the Queen Heir to intimidate the King of the Underworld, she was mistaken. Mikel spoke in a quiet, gentle tone. "I understand your desire for revenge, Queen Heir, but I suggest respectfully although strongly that you focus your attention on the future. I suggest that you focus on ensuring that you can remove the term *heir* from your title. That's a job in and of itself and one more worthy of your attention." He leaned closer to her, willing her to understand. "The time to do that is passing quickly. Don't allow it to pass you by."

"You are not in a position to tell me what I should and should not be doing."

"I am quite well aware of who you are, Queen *Heir*." He hoped that his emphasis on that last bothersome absolutely essential word forced her to acknowledge his point. "The Dark Magus has tried to kill me twice now. She broke a deal as well. I have just as much right to her as you do."

"And you believe that trumps the murder of my father?" She got the sense that indeed he did believe the Dark Magus had committed a higher crime against him, though not the attempts on his life. Rather the fact that a deal brokered between them had been broken. She didn't know how to make sense of that logic.

"I'll deal with the Dark Magus," Mikel said again, his tone

suggesting that on this topic they had nothing further to discuss.

"The Dark Magus ..."

"Don't you have enough to worry about?" Mikel asked, his patience fraying, the tone of his voice confirming it.

"I can manage all that I must," she replied, trying to infuse an arrogance in her voice that didn't come naturally. "And I will."

Mikel smiled, appreciating the effort that she was making. With all that she had been compelled to deal with during the last few days, he was impressed.

She had a spine made of steel. Of that he was certain.

He just hoped that when she realized her success might require making accommodations and allowances that she didn't like that same spine didn't break, because he didn't sense any bend in her.

"If you keep telling yourself that, you'll find yourself in the Churn ... Queen Heir." Mikel hoped the imagery he provided slowed her down long enough to think rather than argue. "You know it just as well as I do. Your position is precarious at best. The First Families are nervous, and they exercise much too great an influence in this city to begin with. They want stability because stability is good for business."

"And do you want stability?" She said it almost as a provocation.

"I've worked hard to diversify my businesses. They benefit from stability. They benefit from chaos as well. And sometimes a little chaos is a good thing. It's just a matter of whether that chaos comes at the right time and by whose hand."

Drin frowned, not sure what he was telling her. "Are you saying you don't want me on the throne?"

"No, I'm just answering your question." He frowned. She was getting angry, her emotions rising, the tell her reddening cheeks.

"And you feel no loyalty to the Dengannons?" Her voice became a touch louder, her emotions threatening to get the better of her.

She was unused to being challenged in this way and so frequently. The First Families never talked to her in such a direct manner. Their words always veiled and carrying multiple meanings.

Yet, strangely, in one sense she appreciated the fact that Mikel didn't mince words. He told her what he thought, not caring how she might react. She couldn't remember the last time she had engaged with someone in such a challenging and honest conversation.

"Why would I feel any loyalty to your family?" He appeared to be genuinely baffled by her question.

"We've ruled the Kingdom of the Crux for almost four hundred years."

"Dynasties come and go, Queen Heir. That's the way of history."

Drin's eyes bulged. She was barely able to control the fury rising within her. Did he not understand all the good her family had done for the city and the Kingdom?

"The Dengannons are the reason Innsbruck and the Kingdom became such a commercial success," Drin stated with a barely restrained fervor. "Before my family's rule, there was little here to speak of. Just a small town that served as a waypoint for traders. Keep in mind as well that we are the reason Malor Dragoran has not conquered the Crux. Can you imagine what it would be like here if he ruled? What do you think he would do to you and your businesses?"

"The city would have developed as a trading center whether or not the Dengannons sat on the throne," Mikel replied evenly, not swayed by her passion or her argument. "That all began well before your family unseated the Hanovers and gained control of the Crux."

"I disagree with that perspective most vehemently. All the histories say ..."

"The histories written during the time of the Dengannon rule? Convenient, don't you think?" Mikel continued before Drin could offer another defense, which he was certain she was about to do. "Also, and this is a key point, the Splintered Bridge is doing the hard work against Malor Dragoran right now. Not you. And if I told the Battle Lord that, he'd agree with me."

Drin lifted her hands to the moon, closed her eyes, then took a deep breath. She spoke calmly, even though doing so was a struggle.

"The Splintered Bridge is essential to our defense, I'll give you that. However, I must point out that the Army of the Crux plays a critical role as well."

"I don't deny it."

"That's good to hear," Drin replied, hoping that he didn't miss her sarcasm. "At least we can reach some kind of partial agreement in that regard."

She offered Mikel a smile, though it faltered quickly. He appeared to be more amused than anything else. Refusing to be knocked off balance, she continued. "However, I must challenge your belief regarding the success and prosperity we've experienced here in Innsbruck. Much of it is built on the decisions made by my ancestors. That is a truth that cannot be denied."

Mikel didn't reply right away. Instead, he studied his sparring partner.

He understood why this was difficult for her. They were coming at the matter from two different directions. Two competing perspectives. She looked at the city from the top down. He from the bottom up. Therefore, rather than hit back directly, he decided to take a more subtle approach.

"In terms of the city's commercial success ... well, define success."

"What do you mean?" Drin didn't anticipate his question, expecting an all-out assault on her argument.

Mikel leaned forward. "Are you speaking of the First Families and their financial success? Their wealth?"

"Of course. How could I not? That's an obvious example ..."

"That's an obvious example of the rich getting richer. The real commercial success of this city comes from the hard-working people the rich living in the top rings don't see, don't want to see, or only want to see when necessary. The artisans and craftspeople. The merchants and traders. The innkeepers and ..."

"Owners of the houses of ill repute?" Drin cut in with a sanctimonious frown, believing she might have cut him off at the knees. Much to her chagrin, she didn't.

"It's a business like any other. I'm simply meeting a market need. And, in my houses of ill repute as you call them, the men and women working for me are free and protected. They're guaranteed a good living and the chance to leave the life they're leading if that's what they desire. I always have other options for them. The same can't be said for many of the other bordellos on the Crux. Many of those bordellos visited by members of the First Families, including the gentleman seeking to catch your eye and join you on the throne."

For just a moment, Drin didn't know what to say. Was that the truth? She had never thought that ... "You may seek to justify what you do however you like. That will not change my belief that you engage in an inexcusable practice."

Mikel had no interest in getting into the fight she had begun between them, certain that with her he couldn't win. "I don't have time for this, Queen Heir. You look at the world around us by gazing down from your ivory Citadel. Even with your frequent secret visits into the city you see only what you want to see. I see the world around us for what it is. Because I live in the real world. Not one shrouded in power and privilege."

"Now who sounds all high and mighty. You're just trying to deflect because you know that I'm right."

"I offer you my perspective, Queen Heir, based on what I do, not what I want to be. I have businesses to run. I have people who rely on me." He pushed himself up from his seat despite the pain in his leg. He felt the need to move, requiring some way to release the agitation building up within him, his desire to continue this conversation gone. "Instead of getting on my back, instead of believing that you are essential to the success of the city, perhaps you should focus on the real challenge you face. Perhaps you should direct your attention toward why the First Families are so nervous."

"They're nervous because ..."

"They're nervous because Lucius Hanover is making them nervous. He is the one blocking your path to the Coronation."

That statement stopped Drin in her tracks, the righteous anger that had been driving her draining away in a flash. "How do you know ..."

"I know because I know this city, Queen Heir. I know what's going on in every ring. That's why I'm successful. That's why I worked with your father on occasion. In fact, that's the only reason he worked with me. I could provide him with what he needed when no one else could."

Drin shot out of her seat, fingers gripped tightly into fists, knuckles white. She wanted nothing more than to scream at the top of her lungs, angrier than she had been since ... she didn't know when.

What was most galling, however, was that she wasn't angry with him. Although she believed that she had every right to be. No, she was angry with herself.

Because she was scared. She feared that he spoke the truth about Lucius Hanover. She feared what might happen if the

First Families called for a Search. She feared what she might need to do to avoid that. She feared that the King of the Underworld was correct in the advice he gave her.

"Clearly we do not agree on several issues," Drin said in as calm a voice as she could manage. Realizing that she should not have given her emotions such free reign. "Nevertheless, I am still the best person to rule the Kingdom of the Crux."

Mikel didn't reply right away, and that only stoked her anger once more. Why his opinion mattered to her, she couldn't explain even to herself.

"If it's between you and Lucius Hanover, I agree. But what does that matter?"

"What do you mean what does it matter? Of course it matters."

"From what I understand, he's trying to force your hand. If he marries you, he still gains the throne. He'll then use his family's power and wealth to consolidate his position. Doing that will come at your expense. He'll either brush you aside or get rid of you through some convenient accident. Probably during the birth of your first child. That would make the most sense for him politically."

"You can't possibly think that he would do that." Drin was shocked. Primarily because she hadn't come up with that scenario first.

"And you can't?" he asked, his expression revealing his disappointment with her naivete.

It was justified, she had to admit. But only to herself. She refused to appear weak in front of him.

Drin shook her head in annoyance. He really did seem to know all that was going on. "Well, then, if you understand the politics of the First Families so well, what would you have me do?"

"Kill him."

"Kill him?" Drin asked, incredulous. "Are you serious?"

"It's a time-honored tactic," Mikel said with a shrug. The idea of spilling the blood of arguably the head of the most powerful of all the First Families of little concern to him. "Kill him and be done with it. Problem solved. More than one problem, in fact."

"I can't just kill him."

"The Battle Lord is your uncle. You have the Army of the Crux at your back. Kill him. Show the First Families who rules. As long as business continues as usual after that, the First Families will settle down and get in line." He shook his head, surprised that she hadn't thought about this before. An easy solution to a complex problem. "You might need to make a few more examples of anyone who's too vociferous, but in the larger scheme of things what does that matter?"

"I can't just kill ..."

"Sure you can. Your family, which as you said is so critical to the success of the Crux, has done it before. Just read the history your family wrote. Besides, the First Families allied with the Hanovers are only allies because they believe that they have no choice. Kill Lucius Hanover and those alliances disappear. You'd be doing those First Families a favor. They'll be the first to support you."

"I can't believe you're suggesting this," Drin murmured. "That's a very harsh perspective."

"It's a realistic perspective, Queen *Heir*. And it's the only perspective that gets you to the throne and keeps you there."

"CAN I offer you one piece of advice?"

Mikel walked next to Drin, her hood up and hiding her face. He was leading her back up to the Seventh Ring, the curl of the incline beginning. Teddy and several of Mikel's other men shadowed them in the busy street to ensure that they weren't accosted ... and to see if any of the First Families had watchers watching.

"Can I stop you from doing so?"

One side of Mikel's face curled up into the hint of a smile. He appreciated her humor. "Watch your back. One Drude destroyed doesn't mean another isn't lurking in the dark waiting to strike."

"I'm well aware of that possibility, Mikel," Drin replied with a forced calm, speaking in a tone that she usually reserved for when she was sitting on the Crux throne. She wanted to test him. Just like he had been testing her. "But I do value your concern. Thank you."

"Of course, Queen Heir. I live but to serve."

"Serve yourself you mean." Drin said it before she could stop herself, his sarcasm poking her the wrong way.

Regretting her lapse. At least a little bit. He had helped her twice already. And at no small risk to himself. Still, she was irritated. He had refused to accede to her demands, and she wasn't used to that.

He ignored the bite in her words, understanding where the friction was coming from. "More often than not I do what I must. Not what I want. Just like you."

Drin growled softly. Why was he so good at deflecting her anger? Offering her these quippy sayings that rang more true than not. Thoroughly annoying her, though intriguing her at the same time. And perhaps that's what bothered her the most.

Not wanting to give up just yet, she decided to try one more time to gain what she wanted before she left him. "You still plan to go after the Dark Magus?"

"I'm already going after the Dark Magus." Mikel nodded to a few of the folks he passed, all of them nodding to him to demonstrate their respect.

Maddie, who had started a dress shop thanks to his small investment. Gully needed a little assistance to expand his smithy, and Mikel provided the labor and materials for free in exchange for a small interest in the business. Beatrice required help obtaining some rare flowers and herbs for her apothecary, and Mikel ensured the only trade route that brought in her necessaries remained open despite the difficulties to the south.

He knew quite well that most, particularly those living in the higher rings, defined a successful business based on the numbers. Profit and loss. The net.

Mikel didn't disagree, but he viewed that as only one of several key variables to be used when making decisions regarding his many interests in Innsbruck and beyond.

From his perspective, often the most crucial variable was whether the prospective business opportunity benefited his potential partner and, more importantly, the larger community. Because he understood that for him to be successful, he needed those working with him and those relying on him to be successful as well.

"I would still prefer that you leave this to me. I have a strong interest in the outcome."

"Yes, you made that quite clear. Several times in fact."

"And yet you still won't acknowledge that the legitimacy of my claim takes precedence over your own."

"That's a matter of perspective, Queen Heir."

Drin shook her head in aggravation, out of ideas on how to make him change his mind. "You can truly be a frustrating ..."

"You've made your position known, Queen Heir." He said it quietly so that none of the people walking up and down the street could hear what they were discussing. "My position has not changed. Nor will it."

"We can do it together," Drin suggested in a hopeful tone. "I can bring a great many resources to bear that would prove beneficial. In fact, several that I'm sure you can't access without me."

"I'll consider it," Mikel replied vaguely.

A movement on his left caught his eye. Under an awning for a spice shop, he saw two men he didn't recognize who appeared to be tracking them through the crowd.

Of course, Mikel didn't know everyone in the streets of Innsbruck, but he never ignored the warning bell that had a habit of going off in the back of his head at times like this. That and the fact that the two men were trying much too hard not to be noticed. All the while wearing leathers and fur-lined cloaks that reminded him of his encounters in the lowlands of the Bitter Heights with those tied to Malor Dragoran.

Perhaps a coincidence. Perhaps not. Better to assume the worst, though.

A subtle nod from Mikel sent three of his men to explore the wares being sold from three different shops lining the street. All of them close to the suspect duo.

They would stay with the pair for now. Then, at the right time, they would introduce themselves so that they could discover who these two were, where they were from, and why they were in Innsbruck.

"You don't want my assistance?" scoffed Drin, trying to infuse as much disbelief into her voice as she could. "A mistake, Mikel. There is much that I can offer you that others can't."

Mikel understood the value of what Drin was extending to him. Still, he understood as well the danger of accepting. Moreover, he didn't want to tell her that she'd only get in his way, having no doubt as to how she'd react. "If I need your help, I'll let you know."

"And you'll let me know what you learn?" she prodded. She had asked him this several times already, his response the same each time.

"I will," he confirmed with a nod. He refused to say when he would tell her, however. He would do what was required first, then allow the circumstances that followed to dictate the timing.

"If you succeed in taking the Dark Magus and bring her before me, I will owe you a favor. Do not forget that. I always pay my debts."

"You already owe me a favor, Queen Heir. Regardless of what happens with the Dark Magus, I'll come calling when I need to collect."

With a light touch on the small of her back, he directed her through a break in the crowd and off the street right to the printing shop from which she had emerged only a few hours before. He sensed her tension at his touch.

Mikel understood that she wasn't entirely pleased with how he was leaving matters with her. He didn't care, however.

Business was business. And this business was his to accomplish whether she liked it or not.

"One more piece of advice?"

Drin turned toward him. Face still in shadows. She wouldn't remove the hood until she was off the street, just as she promised. "Do I have a choice?"

He shrugged. "It's up to you."

She sighed. She couldn't stop a small smile from curling her lips despite his recalcitrance. "Tell me."

"The Splintered Bridge. It's not as strong a barrier as everyone believes."

"You know this how?" Drin challenged.

"Does it matter?"

Drin's eyes narrowed. Difficult as always. And she had learned that there was no point in trying to push him. He would only tell her what he wanted her to know. "If I say yes, will you answer?"

"No."

She closed her eyes briefly, working hard to ignore her flaring annoyance. Which was only made that much more difficult when she opened her eyes again and she realized thanks to the spark in his eyes that he enjoyed putting her on edge.

Another way to gauge her, she assumed. "If the Splintered Bridge is compromised, what would you suggest that I do?"

"Talk with Leonardo Vinicius about how to improve it as a defense. He can help, and he's not hard to find. Just look for the smoke and fire."

"Thank you," Drin replied testily. Smoke and fire? She could ask, but she didn't. She didn't want to get pulled down a rabbit hole. He had already given her more than enough to think about. "I'll keep that in mind."

"It was a pleasure ... my Queen."

With that, Mikel turned, stepping back into the street, walking off with the slight limp that she noticed when they left The Fox's Lair. The same leg he had been rubbing during their conversation.

She watched him go until he was swallowed up by the crowd. Not missing the critical hint he gave her upon his leaving.

She didn't gain all that she wanted from him, and she wasn't used to failing. Nevertheless, she still felt good about her encounter with the man said to have his hand on the very pulse of Innsbruck.

Turning on her heel, she used a thin stream of the Talent to open the door to the printing shop. Locking the door after she walked through, she made her way deeper into the store's recesses to the hidden tunnel in the back that would take her to the Citadel.

Ever since her father was murdered, in addition to battling her grief, she had been battling the vultures circling around her. All of them intent on gaining something for themselves. Lucius Hanover the most grasping of them all.

Mikel wanted something from her as well. That didn't surprise her. But at least with him it was a fair exchange. She could live with that.

A give and take. Not just a take.

Now the trick was to discover what he might want before he asked. That and thinking about how she might be able to turn the pragmatic King of the Underworld into more of a willing ally.

~

"ANY UPDATE FROM THE BOYS?"

Teddy slid right next to Mikel as he walked down the street, heading toward the ring below. "They'll let us know as soon as they find out anything useful."

"You know where those two are likely from."

"The Tor would be my guess."

"That was my fear," Mikel confirmed.

"Here for you or her?"

Mikel shrugged. "Too early to tell. Dragoran has an interest in us both. Though I'd lean toward her."

"You want the boys to bring them to you so you can have a quiet word yourself?"

Mikel shook his head. "Let's see what they get out of them first. Then we can decide."

Teddy nodded. "So what did you do?"

"What do you mean?"

"I know that look." Teddy wasn't taken in by his friend's expression.

"What look?"

"When you try to appear innocent. It doesn't work, you know. It never has."

"Sure it has."

"You keep telling yourself that," Teddy snorted.

"I will."

"Now what did you do?"

"I haven't done anything."

"You promised the Queen Heir something," Teddy sighed.

"We talked about this before you met with her. You said you would only go so far."

"And I did only go so far. I made it clear that the Dark Magus is ours for the taking. Once we have her, we can decide how to bring in the Queen Heir."

"You told her that?" Teddy's eyes widened. An uncommon occurrence. Mikel rarely surprised him. But this? Telling the Queen Heir what he planned to do without her on a matter that touched her deeply? Risky didn't even begin to describe it.

He could have just lied to her. But of course that wasn't Mikel's way. Honest to a fault.

"I did." He and Teddy headed down the curl that would take them off the Seventh Ring, a small street market blocking off a good section of the boulevard.

"We're going after the Dark Magus?" Clearly, Teddy was less than enthused by that prospect.

"We are."

"Despite the risk?"

"Because of the risk."

"Because of the risk? What do you mean?" Teddy's initial confusion quickly shifted to one of understanding. "You're going soft again."

Mikel snorted. "I'm not going soft. It's a business decision. No more than that."

"The Queen Heir is already in debt to us."

"She is," Mikel agreed.

"Yet you feel the need to do this for her?"

"We're doing this for us," Mikel replied. "The Dark Magus broke a contract with us. We can't allow that."

"We can't? Why not?"

"It's bad for business."

"I beg to differ," Teddy challenged. "That sounds like good business. Let the Queen Heir go after her. We've got other matters to attend to. Less dangerous matters."

"We can deal with those matters and the Dark Magus at the same time."

"Like I said, you're going soft, and all it takes is a pretty face."

"There's more to it than that," Mikel replied.

"Well, at least you've admitted it," Teddy said in a deep chuckle.

"I've admitted to nothing. Making an example of the Dark Magus is good business. And if it earns us another favor from the Queen, then all the better."

"We don't know if she's going to be the Queen. Not with all the rumblings among the First Families."

"Thus the decision to take the Dark Magus off her plate. Now, she can focus on what she needs to do to ensure she can take the throne."

Teddy shook his head, more amused than anything else. He should have assumed that this was going to happen. "Why? I know it's not just because she's a pretty face. And it's not just because it's good business. You're picking. And as we both know, when it comes to politics, that can be dangerous. If we pick wrong, we've got water rougher than the Churn ahead of us."

Mikel shrugged, having a hard time putting into words what went into his thinking. "It just feels right."

"You and your overdeveloped sense of what's right," Teddy snorted.

"It's because of my overdeveloped sense of what's right that you're still alive," Mikel countered.

"Fair enough. In the future, though, I'd suggest sticking with thieving and our many other enterprises, because I fear that this strange desire of yours to do good will be the death of you."

20

WALKING THE BRIDGE

"I s this wise, Celindria? You being away from the Crux at a time like this?"

"You worry too much, Uncle Henri."

"That's my job."

Drin couldn't disagree with him. The responsibility for defending the Kingdom of the Crux from all threats was his primary responsibility as the Battle Lord. Both external and internal.

"I would suggest focusing more on Malor Dragoran rather than on what's going on atop the Crux. You can leave the rest to me."

"I don't doubt your abilities, Celindria. Nevertheless, leaving Innsbruck even only for a day without a date set for your Coronation offers the First Families who might wish to challenge your claim ..."

"I'm aware of the risk, Henri. Have no doubt of that. Keep in mind, however, that my leaving the city can be interpreted in another way."

"As you already having taken on the role of Queen, putting the interests of the Kingdom of the Crux ahead of all else. Just as if you already sat the throne." A small upturn at the side of his mouth suggested a smile. A rare occurrence for him. Deserved though. A gutsy move by his niece.

"Exactly, uncle. Rising above the politics of Innsbruck for the greater good."

"A risky strategy, Celindria."

"With all that I'm dealing with, I believe that it's a necessary strategy."

"I hope you're reading the situation correctly."

"I hope so as well."

"Watch your step there, Celindria. That's a new sinkhole."

The soldiers of the Crux had cordoned off the gap that extended for twenty feet in all directions. Two men stood guard, focused not on what might be occurring on the far side of the bridge, but rather on what might be happening beneath them. A heavy gloom shading the edges of the gap in the span that revealed the grey clouds hiding the Trench below.

The Zaroi that nested beneath the Splintered Bridge usually didn't come out of their lairs until full dark. Their large eyes overly sensitive to sunlight.

Usually.

"It seems that the bridge is splintering all the more," Drin observed as she avoided the obstruction and followed her uncle toward the center of the span that connected North Lienz to South Lienz.

The Splintered Bridge was the only link by land between the Kingdom of the Crux and the Kingdom of the Tor, allowing for a steady trade between the two competing realms.

Traversing the span was far from simple, however, and fraught with danger. The bridge once could manage ten large wagons one right next to the other. No more.

The surface of the Splintered Bridge was pockmarked by gaps. Holes bigger than the one that Drin had just avoided, which made travel across not only perilous, but also ever-changing.

And repairing the bridge wasn't a possibility. Not with the Zaroi.

Besides, with the greedy Malor Dragoran always looking toward the west and the riches of the Crux, there was little desire on the part of Drin and her Dengannon forebears to make crossing the Splintered Bridge easier since the arch served such a strategic role in her Kingdom's defense.

"I understand that you found several corpses not far from here."

Henri nodded, stopping at the very center of the bridge that spanned the Trench. A mile long, on the far side he could just make out a company of Tor soldiers examining the caravans moving in that direction, their ultimate goal Graz, Malor Dragoran's stronghold and former capital of the Splintered Empire.

"Pieces of corpses," he corrected. He pointed toward a large hole just a hundred yards farther down the bridge. "Only what the Zaroi left for us. Just as always they were quite thorough."

"The Tor soldiers came across at night?"

"They tried to," Henri said. "Whether they were making their way toward our line or already had done their scouting and were on their way back I can't say."

"They're growing bolder," Drin murmured, unhappy with her conclusion.

"They are. Mostly scouting missions, true. But a few raids as well. They never get far, but it is concerning. It hints at what might be coming our way."

"Testing us."

"Testing you," Henri clarified. "This didn't begin until your father was murdered."

Drin bit her lip. She understood what that meant. The message that Malor Dragoran was sending her. "Our defenses are in good shape. But we won't have much warning. Especially if they risk the darkness."

"And our forces are spread thinly here," Henri said. "We do not have a large army to begin with. Having to send several companies back to Innsbruck until the Coronation is over puts us at a further disadvantage."

"Which means the longer it takes to get to the Coronation, the more time Malor Dragoran has to do whatever it is that he wants to do."

"Exactly."

"I was speaking with a new friend in Innsbruck before coming here," Drin began.

"A new friend?" Henri asked with a trace of skepticism.

Drin nodded. "Specific to the challenge we face here, he suggested that we seek out a promising inventor who might be able to help us."

"What's his name?"

"Leonardo Vinicius."

It was Henri's turn to nod. He decided to hold back what he knew about the eccentric young fellow. "Your new friend told you about Leonardo?"

"He did."

"And who is this new friend?"

Drin laughed softly. "No one to worry about, Uncle."

"Of course not." Henri examined his niece with a jaundiced eye. "That's all you're going to tell me about this new friend?"

"There's nothing else to say," Drin said with a shrug. "I don't know him all that well. However, from the little time I've spent with him, it has been time well spent. I believe that his advice in this matter is worth pursuing."

"You don't know him all that well, yet you're taking seriously his suggestion with respect to how to protect the Kingdom?"

"Instinct, Henri. You taught me about how there were times

to go with my gut. And, in this instance, my gut is telling me to heed my new friend's advice."

Henri was stuck. Because he had, indeed, spoken with her about the importance of relying on her instincts when the time was right.

And who was he to question her instincts?

In fact, he couldn't. He needed to do all that he could to support her. To build her confidence. Because the days ahead would only get harder for her.

"I'm not promising that we're doing anything other than speaking to this Leonardo," Drin continued. Then she shrugged. "What do we have to lose by talking to him? Perhaps he proves helpful. Perhaps he doesn't. There's only one way to find out."

Henri studied his niece for a few seconds more. He sensed that there was a great deal more that she wasn't telling him. Pressing her now, however, would be a waste of time.

"I will send a few good men to find this Leonardo. Then we can talk with him and perhaps make him an offer he can't refuse to join us here. How do we find him?"

"Smoke and fire apparently."

21

DISAPPOINTED CLIENT

Assindra watched, mesmerized, as the rough water of the Churn smashed against the Crux's coast with the power of a tempest, salty spray blasting up and over the seawall. So strong that it was visible even from where she had taken up residence in one of the mansions just below the Royal Ring.

She had a great deal of work to do after her meeting with Malor Dragoran. Yet her thoughts remained fixed on a woman who had once been her friend.

A woman who had tried to kill her.

A woman Assindra had killed instead.

Kaduna.

She hadn't thought of her in years.

Peculiar that she would pop back into her mind now of all times.

Something had to have triggered the memories, but for the life of her she couldn't determine the cause.

They had been the best of friends.

Until Assindra had taken a path that Kaduna refused to walk.

Despite that, Kaduna had agreed to raise Assindra's child. Refusing to blame the babe for Assindra's choices.

More than a decade after giving birth, believing that she was safe from those hunting her, Assindra had searched for Kaduna and her son.

She had found Kaduna. Not her son, however. He had died. An illness when he was quite young.

Assindra still didn't know what to think about that. She had the weakest of connections to him to begin with and barely any memory of the babe.

What's more, she hadn't thought about the child she had given up until she realized that same child could be of use to her with her studies regarding the Curse.

Besides, what was the point of hoping for what she couldn't have?

She wasn't entirely disappointed that he died. Assindra knew that she had little in the way of motherly affection or instinct.

In truth, she was disappointed that her child never had the chance to gift her what she required from him.

"You came very highly recommended, Liria. I did not expect you to fail."

Liria closed her eyes, scrunching up her lips, holding in the sharp reply she craved to release. She did not like being reminded of her failure. The taste bitter.

"You did not tell me that I would need to defend against another Magus," Liria countered, refusing to back down.

"Magus?" Assindra scoffed. "You mean the old man who is counting down the last of his days squirreled away somewhere in the city? He got in your way?"

"Not an old man," Liria countered. "A girl."

Assindra turned away from the Churn upon hearing that, focusing her dark eyes on her thief. She studied the woman for a time, seeking some semblance of a lie. Identifying none.

"There are no other Magii on the Crux other than the old man. If there were, I would know."

Liria shrugged, doing her best to hide her unease. "If not a Magus, then a girl with the potential to be one."

Assindra's eyes narrowed. An interesting development. And information that she might be able to use for her own benefit. Assuming that she could find whoever Liria was speaking about.

"You couldn't stand against an untrained girl?"

"An untrained girl only needs to get lucky once," Liria replied with as much certainty as she could marshal.

Lips pursed, Assindra nodded slowly. "I concede the point." She stepped a few feet closer to Liria. "Our contract remains in place despite your failure."

"He knows I'm here. He'll be looking for me."

"And that worries you?" A small smile graced Assindra's thin lips. "I did not take you as one who ran at the first sign of adversity."

Liria frowned, not liking how the Magus challenged her. Even more so, not wanting to admit the truth. "He'll be on his guard. It just makes my task that much more difficult."

"Then you should have killed him when you got the chance," Assindra replied in an exceedingly cold voice.

"I would have if the girl didn't get in the way," Liria almost hissed, fighting to restrain the anger rising within her. Understanding that it would do little good against a woman of Assindra's power and intention.

"If the task you've agreed to is too much, I can release you from your contract, though you won't like the attached penalty. That I can assure you."

"I'll meet the terms of our contract," Liria replied quickly, her face paling just a touch. She had agreed to work with Assindra despite knowing her reputation, unable to ignore the purse to be earned once she completed the required task. Even more so knowing the penalty of refusing her. "Have no fear of that."

"And yet I do worry," Assindra replied. She stepped closer to Liria, now just a few feet separating them. She studied her nails for a few seconds, tiny sparks of black shooting up from her fingertips. Nothing dangerous. Just a reminder.

"As I said, you have nothing to fear. I will meet the terms of our contract." Liria said the words with as much heat as she could infuse within her voice, which wasn't much. The Magus' display unsettled her, just as she knew it was meant to.

"I need what that man has, Liria. You should have taken it from him when you had the chance, whatever the cost."

"You'll get it," Liria replied with a sharp nod. "That's a promise."

"Why should I believe you?"

"You know my work. I've done what ... eight, nine jobs for you already."

"You have, and quite well in fact. Without any difficulties along the way, which is indeed impressive. Yet now you have failed. And now I have learned as well your history with the man you were supposed to kill. You didn't tell me that before I gave you this job."

"The past means nothing in the present."

"Really? Then why should I take your word? Why should I not focus more on the maxim you're only as good as your last job?"

"What are you suggesting?" Liria didn't know if she should be insulted or worried.

"You know exactly what I'm suggesting." Assindra's eyes flashed dangerously, the sparks from her fingertips shooting a bit higher into the air, causing Liria to take a few steps backward.

"I have no feelings for him. Those died a long time ago."

"So you say."

"I don't. I swear it." Liria forced herself not to swallow, desperate for Assindra to not hear the lie.

"I own you, girl," Assindra reminded after a much too long period of time passed, Liria's nervousness increasing all the while. "Remember that. I should kill you for your failure, but I won't. Get the blade from your former love. Whether he lives or dies doesn't matter to me. The only thing that matters is the artifact. I can do nothing else without it."

22

QUICK VISIT

"We don't have a lot of time today, Finn. I've got other business to attend to."

"Would you stay quiet for just a minute so I can think?"

The Magus ran his fingers just above the scimitar Mikel held in his hand. He had been doing some research on the weapon at Mikel's request, unfortunately finding very little and wishing that he still had access to the libraries at Haven and the Aeyrie. Therefore, he had asked Mikel to come back to his hidden apartment.

Finn hoped that a second inspection of the blade might offer him some new insight. So far, however, his efforts ensured nothing more than continued aggravation. A reminder of his own failings, which Finn really didn't need. He was already well aware of all his weaknesses and could do without the added disappointment.

"I'd prefer that you were doing something other than thinking." Mikel enjoyed the feel of the scimitar's hilt in his hand. Like it was meant to be there. The steel, vibrating so softly that only he could feel it, seemed to agree.

He tried to ignore the dim glow of energy that ran along the inscribed steel.

It made sense, of course. Finn said the artifact he had stolen was the Blade of Light.

Still, that dim glow unsettled him. The blade only glowed when Mikel wrapped his fingers around the hilt. Not Teddy. Not Nat. Not Finn. Not even when Finn tried to infuse the weapon with the Talent, the artifact rejecting his effort.

The Blade of Light only came to life when Mikel grasped it.

He really wanted to know why that was the case, particularly after how bone-weary he had felt when forced to make use of the blade in his office. That was an experience he wanted to avoid in the future.

"I would if I could," grumbled Finn, "and any business you might have pales in importance compared to finding out what's going on between this Giant-crafted weapon and you." Finn growled a few curses under his breath while shaking his head, his exasperation rising. "Will you be visiting with Cadmus any time soon?"

"I'm not scheduled to meet with him for a few weeks, and you know how the Giants of the Rime are."

"That I do," Finn murmured as he continued to study the glowing blade.

On pain of death no one was permitted to enter the Frozen Waste without the Frost Lord's permission. Mikel was the only person who had earned the trust of the King of the Rime. The only one in centuries, in fact. But even then, he only made use of the gift granted to him at prescribed times. Because the Frost Lord did not like surprises and Mikel did not want to overstep.

"Can you do it?"

Finn was quiet for a few seconds, then he shook his head with even greater vigor, having no choice but to admit defeat. "You can feel the blade?"

"I can," Mikel replied. "It's like a presence in me. Stuck in the back of my head."

"You talk to it?" Finn was trying to understand, and he needed to begin somewhere.

"No, nothing like that. We more ... sense one another." That was the best explanation that Mikel could offer.

"That I can understand," Finn replied. "From what I've been able to piece together, it's much like a remora and a shark."

Mikel gave the Magus a puzzled expression. "You lost me."

"A symbiotic relationship," Finn explained with a shrug. "Just like a shark and a remora."

"And which one am I?" Mikel asked, remembering what happened when he made use of the Blade of Light. Or rather the sword made use of him. He wasn't sure which. But he was certain of the exhaustion that had settled deep within his bones. An exhaustion that could have proven dangerous if he didn't break the link with the blade when he did.

"Now that's an excellent question," Finn chuckled.

The Magus leaned back, shaking his head, trying to think of some other way to approach this dilemma. A mix of displeasure and curiosity surged through him. The first satisfied. Not the second.

In all his time in the Order of the Magii, he had never come across a situation such as this one, and that was despite having knowledge of some of the most powerful artifacts ever crafted by the Giants of the Rime.

The Blade of Light was a mystery to him, and he had few ideas on how to obtain the answers that he wanted.

"You're not offering much help, Finn. And like I said, I have other more pressing matters to deal with."

"More pressing than ensuring you stay alive?"

Mikel frowned, wanting to ignore the truth in his friend's words, yet knowing that he couldn't. Understanding that the sword easily could have drained him not only of his strength, but his spirit as well. Leaving him a dried out husk on the floor of his office and doing Liria's job for her.

He took a deep breath, then let it out slowly. "If we don't really know what this is," Mikel said, waving the sword in the air a few times – it really did feel like the hilt belonged between his fingers, "any suggestions on how to deal with this?"

"Other than speaking to Cadmus about it?"

"Other than that. To get me to when I can speak with Cadmus."

Finn crossed his arms over his chest, staring at the blade. His eyes narrowed as he studied the steel. It was gleaming more brightly now. He leaned forward then, noting how Mikel's brow was scrunched up.

A small smile creased Finn's lips, Mikel nodding slowly to himself. It was possible. But there was only one way to find out.

Pushing himself up from his stool, the Magus walked away from Mikel until he was at the far end of the terrace.

"Where are you ..."

Mikel never had the chance to complete his question. The ball of fire Finn shot his way came so swiftly that for a heartbeat Mikel couldn't quite understand what was going on.

He recovered quickly, however. The Blade of Light flashing with a blinding energy, Mikel slashed with the steel, cutting through the Talent thrown his way. The remnants of energy caught on the blade swirled around the steel until they were absorbed by the weapon.

"What in blazes are you ..."

Mikel slashed again with the blade. Once more. A fourth time. And a fifth. After the seventh attempt, Finn finally stopped.

The Magus strode toward him, a broad smile breaking his craggy features.

"Explain, Finn." Mikel's voice was cold. Dangerous.

Although he was curious as well. Because with each attack the same thing happened. The Giant-crafted weapon took in what pieces of energy remained after Mikel defended himself. "Just like Cadmus, I don't like surprises. Particularly ones that can cost me my life."

"Look." Finn nodded toward the blade. "You were never in any real danger."

Mikel did as the Magus bade. Eyes widening. A better understanding coming to him. The scimitar shined so brightly that he couldn't look at it without squinting. "It's playing off my need."

"Not just your need," Finn said quietly.

Mikel nodded. The Magus was right. Need was only a part of it. "My intentions. The blade responds to my need based on how I want to use it."

"There's more to it than that," Finn prodded, smiling broadly. He felt a lot better about himself, believing that he had solved the puzzle placed before him. At least most of it anyway.

Mikel nodded again, allowing Finn to play the role of instructor. "My desires, my intentions, are the key to using the blade."

"What do you think you're doing?" Finn jumped backward, tripping over a stool and falling hard on his buttocks. He avoided Mikel's slash, which would have cut across his throat if the steel connected, and now was staring at the tip of the blade, centered right between his eyes. "Mikel, I'm just trying to help you. There's no need ..."

Mikel pulled the blade away from Finn, then offered a hand, helping the old Magus back to his feet. He held the steel out for Finn's inspection. There was nary a glow to be seen, the steel a faint grey.

"If the blade perceives my intention as good or right, such as defending myself, it responds to what I need. However, if the blade perceives my desire as bad, like attacking you for no good cause, it won't respond."

"Intriguing," Finn murmured, Mikel's assault forgotten, "and not all that surprising considering who crafted the weapon and why."

Mikel nodded as he turned the blade this way and that, examining the steel. His discovery did make sense. It also worried him. Because it suggested that the connection he felt with the weapon was a deep one and potentially unbreakable. The blade didn't stop him from taking a swipe at Finn, but it certainly didn't approve.

"Limiting."

"That's one way to look at it," Finn said.

"What's another way?"

"You've already experienced it, the power that can be employed through that blade." Finn nodded toward the steel that was glowing dimly once again. "That much power can easily corrupt someone with a weak will."

"So a safeguard of sorts," Mikel suggested.

"Yes, that's my take. You are so entwined with the blade that you are one and the same. What you feel, what you experience, the blade does as well. In essence, it also functions as a sort of conscience."

"As if the one I already had wasn't bad enough," Mikel grumbled.

"Funny." Finn gave his friend a commiserating pat on his shoulder. "But like I said, not necessarily a bad thing."

"You're suggesting the blade has a consciousness all its own."

Finn shrugged. "Maybe it does. I don't know."

"I don't know if that's good or bad."

"I don't know either. I think you're the only person who will be able to determine that."

Mikel snorted, shaking his head. "It seems that all we've

done, Finn, is create a knot of additional questions that we need to untie."

"I'll give you that. Although I think I might have at least one solution for you."

"With respect to?"

"You said that when you used the blade you were drained. You lost your strength. You barely had any energy. You were so weak that you were close to unconsciousness."

"Not a feeling I enjoyed, I can at least tell you that."

"I doubt the blade did as well."

"What are you getting at, Finn?"

"If we're right that the blade is linked to you in some deep, inextricable way, and that it's tied to your desires and intentions, perhaps controlling the blade is much like controlling your emotions."

"Controlling my emotions? What does that ..." Mikel thought about what the Magus was proposing. Perhaps he was right.

Finn's comment brought Kaduna to mind. She had been quite insistent while he was growing up.

She had spent hours with him, teaching specific techniques to maintain control over his emotions. To ensure that he was always balanced, much as if he was running with ease, without fear of a slip, on a log floating in the Churn. No matter how much his emotions roiled within him, she wanted him to exert control over himself.

Why?

Other than saying that it was necessary. That he was unique. Though she had never explained why that was the case.

She had told him that as a Caledonii who didn't exercise the power of a Caledonii, he still needed to be a Caledonii. That meant he had to master all that a Caledonii graced with the Talent would, short of actually employing the Talent.

Hours upon hours of lessons late into the night followed after his chores and other training was done. Not only how to control his emotions, but also how to think. How to balance risk and reward. How to make split-second decisions while needing to take into account more than one competing variable. And so much more. Honing his mind. Honing his control.

He had viewed all that effort as no more than Kaduna being Kaduna. She felt bad for him, so she demonstrated a kindness that none of the other Caledonii were willing to show to him. Because to them he was just a waste of their time.

Was there more to all that Kaduna had required of him than that?

Was all her training, all that she demanded of him, done with another purpose in mind?

A purpose that she never had the chance to reveal because of her death?

That sent Mikel's thinking down a road he had never explored before. Because he didn't want to. Also because there had never been the need.

Was she also teaching him how to hide what he really was by suppressing his true self?

If so, why?

What was she afraid of?

Him?

What he might become?

Or what might be coming for him?

That last thought had the ring of truth to it, though he had no evidence to support his theory.

Other than the fact that he and Kaduna tended to avoid Caledonii when they left the Bitter Heights and then did their best to disappear in Innsbruck, not a hard thing to do in such a large and busy city. Until Kaduna's sad demise, of course.

"Is the blade pulling on more than just my strength?"

Finn didn't reply right away, his wild eyebrows scrunched

together, making it seem as if a single, large caterpillar had nested on his brow. "I don't know. But just because I don't know doesn't mean you might not be right. All I can say with any certainty is that the Blade of Light isn't a reservoir of energy like some of the other artifacts crafted by the Giants of the Rime."

"What do you mean?"

"There are some artifacts, such as the Seventh Stone and the Blood Ruby, that serve as reservoirs for the Talent and the Curse. They hold the energy for use by those who can draw from those artifacts."

"But not so the Blade of Light?"

"No, the Blade of Light functions solely as an amplifier. A catalyst of sorts. Adding to the power that a Magus can employ, but dependent on the power of the Magus to function."

"Then how do you explain the blade deciding to link with me?"

"I can't." Finn shrugged, wishing that he could say more than that. Knowing that it was wasted breath if he did.

"Are you suggesting that I can access the Talent?" Mikel snorted.

Although even as he scoffed at the notion, memories of his time with Kaduna continued to flit through his mind. Pieces here and there. From different ages and when they were living in different places.

But all focused on one thing and one thing only. Looking inward. Focusing on some quality within him that after all these years he had almost forgotten.

"I wouldn't go that far because I don't sense the Talent. And with you just a few feet away from me, I would know if you could touch that natural magic."

"Then what could it be if not the Talent?" Mikel had always wondered about his resistance to natural magic, both the Talent and the Curse. Perhaps there was more to what Kaduna had explained was a unique ability among the Caledonii only seen once every thousand years. Perhaps the reason for this attribute was more obvious than what Kaduna let on. Teaching him not only to control his emotions, but also how to hide this attribute. Not just from others but also from himself.

"I don't know, lad," Finn growled. His temper beginning to simmer. Though not at Mikel. Rather because of his own rising frustration, his lack of knowledge grating. "If I knew, I'd tell you. All I know from what little research I was able to do is that the Blade of Light requires a source of power to function. Apparently, you are a source of power."

"I don't know how to make sense of that."

"Neither do I, lad. I'm sorry. You need to speak with Cadmus. It's as simple as that. He's the only one who might be able to enlighten you."

"And until I speak with him what do you suggest?"

"You mean in terms of maintaining control?"

Mikel nodded.

"My initial advice is don't use the blade again until you speak with Cadmus."

"Not very helpful."

"That doesn't make it bad advice, however." Finn offered his frustrated friend a wry grin.

"Assuming that isn't possible?" Mikel prodded.

Finn's smile deepened. Trouble did have a way of finding Mikel. "Assuming that isn't possible, clearly you know how to control your emotions. Probably better than anyone else I've ever come across."

"The skill was forced upon me."

"Really?" That caught Finn's attention. "We should talk more about that."

"Perhaps, but not now." Mikel's expression confirmed that he had no desire to engage in another experiment with the Magus.

"Right. Well, all I can suggest is that you try to exert the same control you've learned as a Caledonii over the sword as well. Perhaps it functions in much the same way."

"Like a hose," Mikel said with a nod, one of his earliest lessons with Kaduna returning to him.

"A hose?" Finn didn't understand the reference.

"A hose," Mikel repeated. "You control the flow of water through a hose by squeezing on it."

Finn smiled at the analogy. "I don't see why that won't work if you think you can do it. I would simply counsel that you do it slowly and carefully. Whatever power is in play ... well ... it's stronger than any power I've ever come into contact with before. You should not have been able to do what you did when I attacked you. If you squeeze too hard ..."

"I'll keep that in mind," Mikel replied.

"One other thing I'd suggest you keep in mind."

"That would be?"

"As I said, the Blade of Light doesn't give power or share power. It uses power. It makes a power stronger. Perhaps it does something else as well."

"I'm afraid to ask." Mikel tried to interject a touch of humor in what was a much too serious conversation.

"You should be," Finn confirmed. He wasn't smiling when he said it. "Perhaps the Blade of Light also unlocks the person it's chosen to bond with."

"Unlocks?"

"Their power or potential," Finn continued. "You need to understand, Mikel, that the Blade of Light is neither good nor evil. It just is. It's a tool designed to fight those who can employ the Curse."

"Then why would it pick me if I have no skill in the Talent?"

"I've asked myself that question many times since you showed the blade to me. I'm at a loss. All I can suggest is that perhaps the blade sees something in you that you don't see in yourself." Finn gave Mikel a more discerning look. "Or that you can't see."

"I'm a thief, Finn. No more and no less than that."

"You are what you are, Mikel. All I'm saying is that perhaps the blade sees more in you than you do."

"You do enjoy being cryptic, don't you?"

"More than you can possibly imagine," Finn replied with a laugh. He turned serious just an instant later. "Think about what I'm telling you, Mikel. Maybe the blade sees something more in you than what you see. Maybe the blade believes you have something more to offer."

"I find that hard to believe, Finn."

"Have you not thought that there could be more to your life?" Finn asked. The Magus understood that trying to persuade Mikel of anything was a useless effort. Nevertheless, he could plant the seeds that could take his thoughts down new paths he might not have considered otherwise. "Have you not thought about what you could do if you shifted your skills in a different direction?"

"I'm not trying to be a hero, Finn. Like most everyone else, I'm just trying to survive."

"I can understand that. I'm simply suggesting that perhaps in your case that's not enough. Perhaps more is required of you."

23

UNINVITED GUESTS

"You sure you have time for this, Gully? Business seems better than either of us imagined."

"Business is good thanks to you, Mikel." The blacksmith led Mikel through the forge, looking over the shoulders of the two journeyman smiths and three apprentices who were working for him. Thanks to Mikel's investment, his previously one-man shop was growing at a rate he found both thrilling and terrifying. "And yes, we can manage it. How many again?"

"One hundred."

With a set of tongs, Gully picked up the dagger one of his apprentices was working on, turning it this way and that so that he could examine the glowing steel with a keener eye. Satisfied, he nodded, the apprentice sighing with relief, even daring a brief smile.

Gully was an exacting boss, though a fair one. He demanded the highest quality work from those he employed, just as his clients demanded the same from him.

That in large part was why Mikel decided to invest in his smithy. He didn't doubt Gully's integrity and skill, two qualities he looked for in all his business partners.

Of course, it didn't hurt to have control over the supply chain that could provide him with however many weapons he might need at a moment's notice. That was only good business after all.

"We can do it, but I don't have enough of the steel you want me to use. An order from the Hanovers almost wiped me out."

"The Hanovers?" Mikel grinned like a fox. He couldn't say that he was surprised. Not with some of the rumors that were circulating through the Crux.

"Yes, our largest yet. Swords, daggers, axes, a couple dozen spears. I delivered them just yesterday."

"Sounds like we made a good profit."

"We did," Gully replied with a rare grin. "They wanted me to rush the work."

"So they paid a premium."

"They did," Gully confirmed. "I wouldn't have taken the job otherwise."

"Good man." Mikel offered the smith a friendly slap on the back. "I've got a shipment coming from the mainland tomorrow. I'll let you know when it will be delivered."

"How did you manage that? From what I understand there's a shortage and only ..." Gully stopped himself, his grin growing wider. With Mikel, there was no such thing as obstacles. There were only opportunities. "Once I receive the steel, I'll get started immediately. Does that work?"

"It does, Gully. Thank you."

"You getting ready for a battle with these short swords you want?"

"Hoping to avoid one actually," Mikel replied with a smile of his own, although his good humor didn't reach his eyes. A fact that Gully didn't miss. "How long once you get started?"

"A few days if I push a few orders."

Mikel understood what Gully was saying. Pushing a few orders would push back some of the revenue they would earn.

Still, this was more important. "Thank you. I appreciate you doing that for me."

Gully nodded. "As I've said, anything for you, Mikel. I owe you more than you know."

"All you owe me is one hundred short swords."

"Fair enough," Gully laughed. "Now let me get back to it and see if I can put a dent in our back orders so I don't have to push off too much other work when the steel arrives."

Mikel watched Gully lose himself deeper in the forge, the large man moving with a deceptive grace as he picked up the biggest hammer Mikel had ever seen and then placed a length of steel into the fire, waiting for it to reach the temperature he wanted before he began his work.

"You seem worried, Teddy. What's the matter?"

"How can you tell I'm worried? You're not even looking at me."

Mikel turned around, giving his friend a lift of his eyebrow. "It radiates off you, Teddy. I could sense your worry from a block away."

"Funny," Teddy muttered, failing to see the humor.

"One of us has to be."

Teddy couldn't help himself, barking out a laugh. "You keep telling yourself that."

"I will. Now what's got your knickers in a knot."

"Don't press your luck."

"Sorry, couldn't resist." Mikel lifted his hands as an apology.

"Our eyes and ears have been giving me much the same information the last few days. Small groups of men coming into the city. Trying not to draw any attention to themselves."

"There are always people coming into Innsbruck. Why does this worry you?" Mikel wasn't going to dismiss those reports. He did want to know what Teddy was thinking.

"It feels wrong. Looks wrong too."

"Soldiers?" He had learned to trust Teddy's instincts. Doing so had saved both their lives more times than he could count.

"Maybe. Maybe something worse."

Mikel nodded. "We know where some of our guests are?"

"We do," Teddy confirmed in a forbidding tone, already knowing what Mikel had in mind.

"Let's pay them a visit."

24

NO JOY

"How'd they get across the Churn?"

Mikel knelt next to Teddy, looking through the bottom of a dirty window that gave them an excellent view of the alley that led toward the abandoned warehouse built right up against the seawall.

It was quiet. They hadn't seen anyone since Mikel snuck in more than a half-hour before upon receiving Teddy's message. They were in a neighborhood destroyed in the last flood that was yet to be rebuilt. Possibly never to be rebuilt, although Mikel had not given up hope. Several ideas playing through his mind even as he focused on the task at hand.

"Hanover's private gondola," Teddy reported.

"Other locations?"

Teddy nodded. "At least ten. I have crews searching for more. Just in case."

Smart. Thorough. But Mikel expected nothing less from his friend. "How many do you think?"

Teddy scowled. He was an accountant by trade. He preferred precision. Guessing always made him feel slightly sick to his stomach. "Fifty that we can be certain of." He shrugged. "Based on when we first identified how the Hanover gondola was being used and how frequently it was making the trip above the Churn, I'm certain there are more."

Mikel was certain of that as well. Call it an instinct. And he tended to listen to his instincts.

"When was the last time the Hanover gondola came across?"

"Late this morning."

"So it's been sitting for most of the afternoon."

"It has," Teddy confirmed. "You think Hanover has all the men he wants in the city?"

"That would be my guess."

"Which would mean that he'd want to put in play whatever he has planned soon. He wouldn't want to wait. The longer he waits the greater his chance of being discovered."

"I would think so," Mikel confirmed. "Particularly if our assumption about where these men are coming from proves accurate."

"What do you want to do?"

Mikel thought about Teddy's question. Despite this new challenge having potentially dire consequences for the city and the Kingdom, actually he was pleased. It allowed him to focus on something other than his encounter with Finn, the weight of the scimitar in the scabbard across his back feeling unduly heavy thanks to their latest conversation.

"When was the last time anyone came in or out?"

"An hour ago. He was carrying several pails."

Mikel nodded. "Street food."

"Yes. Likely bedding down for the night. They need to keep out of sight."

"Then perhaps we should introduce ourselves before they say their goodnights."

"I was afraid you were going to say that," grumbled Teddy, even as a malicious smile cracked his grim visage.

"Weapons first?"

Teddy stood on the catwalk above the floor of the ware-house, a cudgel in each hand.

The warehouse was dark except for the northeast corner that was well away from the doors. A small fire burned in a large metal bin. Five men with their bedrolls laid out around it were talking quietly.

"Weapons at the ready," Mikel said.

"You want to talk to them first?"

"That was my hope."

"And if they don't want to talk to you?"

"That's where you come in," Mikel explained with a grin.

"Wonderful," Teddy grumped, watching as Mikel stepped silently down the elevated walkway to the far end and disappeared into the darkness. Not appearing again until he was at the very bottom of the ladder and visible at the edge of the firelight.

"Gentlemen, a few minutes of your time?" Mikel requested.

Five heads turned as one in his direction. Staring. Shocked. Then concerned. Not quite sure what to make of the man standing across from them with a mace in one hand.

"What in blazes are you doing here?" Harald demanded. The self-appointed leader of the group because he was the largest of the five pushed himself up from where he was lying down, stomping toward Mikel with a dagger in his hand. The other four were quick to follow, spreading out so that their visitor had little chance of escape.

"I just wanted to ask you a few questions."

"You want to ask us a few questions?" Harald demanded, not quite believing what he was hearing. "Are you serious? You want to talk when we've got you dead to rights with drawn steel?"

Mikel frowned, then shook his head. Realizing that this was going to be a lot more difficult than it needed to be. "Yes, just a few minutes of your time. That's all I require."

Harald didn't reply at first. Frowning. Trying to make sense of the man who clearly had no ability to perceive the peril of his current situation.

"Who are you?"

"Mikel."

Harald waited for more. He didn't get it from the strange fellow.

Yet, what was even stranger, Harald was getting nervous, and he didn't quite understand why. Maybe it was because their visitor, facing off against a fist of trained soldiers, didn't appear to be nervous. He appeared to be curious. As well as much too comfortable. As if he was the one controlling the encounter.

Harald thought about sending his men at Mikel. He held them back, however. Curious himself. Also, his worry was becoming more tangible, thus his decision to delay and think more about how to remove this problem from their midst. "What do you want to know?"

"You came across on the Hanover gondola?"

"How could you possibly know that?" demanded Harald.

"Thank you for confirming that for me," Mikel replied with an appreciative nod.

"I didn't ..." Harald stopped himself, realizing that he did.

"And from what I understand there are twenty teams just like yours?"

"Less than ..." Harald shut his mouth before he could reveal the truth.

"Thank you. I thought as much."

Harald snorted then, trying to regain control of the discussion. Beginning to understand that engaging in a conversation with this fellow would only give him a headache and make his life that much more difficult. It was time to put in play his initial thought for eliminating this distraction. "It doesn't matter what you know. I can tell you everything we have planned."

"And why is that?" Mikel was expecting Harald's response.

"You won't be leaving here alive."

Mikel smiled. Certain that his new friend could give him more than he anticipated before it was time for them to part company. "You know, I was thinking much the same about you and your friends."

"You were ..." Harald couldn't quite believe what he was hearing. Even more, he was tired of this conversation. His nerves only getting worse. "Kill him."

Harald's men made it only a few steps before a huge shadow, gripping a cable that extended down from the ceiling, swung into the light, allowing his momentum to do his job for him.

One of Harald's men flew backward into another of his soldiers, both of them crashing against the far wall before the fight really even began. And neither of them appeared capable of regrouping as they lay there motionless. Broken, battered, and unconscious ... if they were lucky.

Harald's immediate thought was to get out of the warehouse so that he could warn the other teams. He never got the chance.

As the giant with a cudgel in each hand strode toward what was left of his men, Harald had his own worries.

Mikel.

The man who desired nothing more than a conversation stalked toward him with a deceptive yet purposeful calm, mace held against the side of his leg.

$\sim$

"Did you believe him?"

"No reason not to," Mikel replied. "You did stick a dagger into his ear, so I doubt that he was lying."

"Good point," Teddy grunted, unable to argue with his friend's logic. Then he chuckled, enjoying his own humor.

Once Teddy eliminated the last pair of soldiers and Mikel incapacitated Harald, it hadn't taken long to extract the information they wanted. Harald was more than willing to answer all their questions and more as he gazed upon the bodies strewn about the warehouse floor. Desperate to not join them, yet at the same time inevitably a small part of him understanding that he could not escape his fate.

"He didn't really tell us anything we didn't suspect."

"True, though confirmation certainly doesn't hurt."

"It doesn't," Mikel agreed.

"Although we still face something of a challenge."

"You worry too much, Teddy. What we have in mind shouldn't be too hard."

"You can't just walk up to the gate and demand an audience with her."

"You don't think so?"

"Seriously? No, I don't think so."

"You're probably right about that," Mikel agreed, "so I had another possibility in mind."

25

UNANNOUNCED VISIT

"Did you really have to do that?" Ronnie rubbed his cheek. It was sore, but not too sore.

It should hurt worse than it did, Mikel only giving him a glancing blow and pulling back before he connected fully with Ronnie's jaw. Mikel realizing just in time that Ronnie was trying to pull him out of the ruckus that had taken up a good section of the street.

Ronnie appreciated Mikel's restraint. He had no desire to feel the full brunt of the power Mikel could bring to bear with a single punch. The last fool to suffer that hadn't regained consciousness for several days, and it had been touch and go for a time.

"It wasn't my intention to strike you, Ronnie. Truly. I'm sorry." Mikel stood on the other side of the bars. The cell in the basement of the Citadel was small but dry. A stream of moonlight shone down from the grate set in the wall to provide more illumination than the torch just beyond the door. "You just happened to walk where my fist was going."

"I find that very hard to believe, Mikel. I've seen you in a fight. I know what you can do."

"In my defense, it was more a brawl than a fight, so I was a little distracted."

Ronnie nodded. A fair point on Mikel's part. More than a hundred men had taken part, so it was a wonder that Mikel hadn't laid him out.

It was strange, though. As soon as he and a few squads of the City Watch appeared, the fight ended with barely any fuss.

He wasn't complaining. Ronnie had served during the riots that followed the last major flood, and he had no desire to relive that experience. Nevertheless, it was quite peculiar.

"Just a little fun, Ronnie. A good number of the boys letting off a little steam was all. No more than that."

"I'm sure you can convince the magistrate of that," Ronnie suggested, then nodded toward the cell. "I hope you don't mind the accommodations." He had done what he could, separating Mikel from the rest of the men brought in to be arraigned and placing him in a private cell. They were friends after all.

"Not in the least," Mikel replied. "This will do nicely." He placed his hands through the bars and leaned his forearms on the crosspiece. "How's the family?"

Ronnie brightened at the question. "Everyone is doing well. Emma wanted me to thank you. She's been working at the apothecary. She loves it. She can't get enough of all that Vanessa is teaching her. Thank you for that."

"It's the least I can do, Ronnie. Don't give it a second thought."

"It's more than you should have done, Mikel," Ronnie said with absolute certainty. He had mentioned to Mikel in passing the last time he visited The Fox's Lair that his daughter was interested in the healing arts and particularly holistic care. Within days, Vanessa was at their door inter-viewing Emma and then accepting the young woman as her apprentice. "And Amos asked that you stop by when you can. He wants to share some of his latest paintings with you. I think he has one in mind for you before he puts the next few up for sale."

Mikel nodded with pleasure. A minor lord loyal to one of the First Families had been trying to take advantage of the young man and his much-in-demand skills.

Amos had a unique way of looking at the world, not really having a keen eye for the dangers lurking on the Innsbruck streets, and therefore not knowing how to extricate himself from the lord's grasp. Mikel had put a stop to it quickly. And permanently.

"I'd be happy to, as soon as I put this experience behind me."

It was good to hear that Amos was doing well and that he was back on level ground. His talent as a painter was second to none, all of the First Families vying for his work. He also had a chronic illness that required a medicine that was difficult to acquire and was well beyond the means of Amos and his family ... until Mikel stepped in.

"And Charlene would like you to come over for dinner. She says the last time she saw you in the streets you looked too thin. She thinks you need more meat on your bones. A woman won't want you unless she has something to hold onto." Ronnie coughed softly, realizing he might have overstepped. "That's just Charlene talking. Not me. You know how she is."

Mikel laughed at his friend's discomfort, Ronnie joining him. "Charlene thinks everyone needs a little more meat on their bones."

"That she does," Ronnie replied. He then patted his rather good-sized belly. "Except for me, of course."

"And that's why I don't come over for dinner so frequently. If I did, I'd look like you, Ronnie."

"You've got the right of it, Mikel," Ronnie agreed, laughing heartily. The Sergeant of the City Watch looked over his shoulder, scanning the cells along the other side of the hallway. All of them were filled with the men who participated in the brawl. All of them, he was certain, were men who worked for Mikel. Recognizing quite a few. "You know it's kind of strange. How quickly the brawl came to an end when we arrived. Just two squads to put a stop to a tussle between a century of hardened fighters. Usually it's quite a bit more difficult to break up a clash that takes up most of a block."

"You know how it is, Ronnie. You never know how things are going to play out in the streets of Innsbruck." Mikel leaned forward, giving the Sergeant a smile. "It was probably that natural authority of yours that did the trick. As soon as you arrived, we realized that it was better that we be done with it."

"Right," Ronnie agreed with a slow nod, not satisfied with Mikel's explanation. Not believing him for a second. He studied the men over his shoulder. None of them seemed to be the least bit concerned that they had been placed in holding cells. In fact, several were already sleeping, others playing cards quietly, a few even reading books that they had brought with them. Why would they bring books? "From where I'm standing, it's almost like you wanted these men here."

Mikel's eyes glittered with mischief. "It does, doesn't it."

Ronnie didn't say anything more, just nodding and then placing a finger to the side of his nose. He had assumed as much. Mikel never did anything unless there was a reason for it.

"I'd let you go if I could, Mikel. You know that."

"I know, Ronnie. Don't worry about it." Mikel's warm eyes turned cold in an instant. "You do what you need to do. I'll do what I need to do."

"And should I worry about what you need to do?" A flicker of concern passed across Ronnie's craggy face. He was well aware of who Mikel was. He didn't care. Mikel was a friend. More than that, actually, as the King of the Underworld looked after the people of the Crux that those living in the Royal Ring didn't want to see or failed to see. People like him.

"No need to worry ... yet. If you need to, I'll let you know. Fair?"

"Fair," Ronnie agreed. Shaking Mikel's hand through the bars, he stepped back. "I need to get home to Charlene. I'll stop by the magistrate's home and give her a nudge to get all this behind you."

Mikel shook his head. "Don't bother, Ronnie. Go home to Charlene and the kids. Give my best to Emma and Amos. Let the magistrate sleep. There's no need to rush anything. A day ... or two ... won't matter."

Ronnie stared at Mikel, eyes tightening. "I don't need to worry?"

"I'll tell you when you need to worry. Have no fear of that. Just tell the boys at the gates to keep a sharp eye."

"Anything specific?"

Mikel shook his head. "No more than rumors. You know how it is."

Ronnie nodded at that. "Have a good night, Mikel. The magistrate likely won't be here until the end of the day tomorrow. Perhaps even the day after. I'll make sure." He headed for the door.

"That works just fine, Ronnie. And if you don't mind, please let the boys know that I've got breakfast coming this morning for all the lads with me. They're more than welcome to join us. They'll be plenty for all."

MIKEL PUSHED his cell door closed with a soft click, placing his lock pick back into the hidden cache in the sole of his boot.

"All good, Samuel?" He walked down the hallway to the far end, nodding to his men as he made his way toward the exit.

The whip-thin man nodded, giving his employer and friend a broad grin. He pushed on the door closest to the stairs that led up from the basement. It opened smoothly and without making a sound, Samuel applying a little oil he had secreted away to the hinges before he tested his work. He then pulled it closed again, though he left it unlocked. "Child's play."

Mikel had assumed as much. Samuel led Mikel's team of thieves. The man could get in and out of a privy guarded by a phalanx of soldiers without any of them noticing. Nor would the lord sitting upon it. "I'll be back soon."

Samuel nodded. "Nothing more on the timing?"

"Not until Teddy finishes his side of things." Mikel had sent the giant after a few more of the infiltrating teams hidden throughout the city, hoping to acquire the one piece of information that Harald had been unable to give him. The timetable.

"No worries." Samuel clearly was quite comfortable in a cell. That's where Mikel had found him, in fact, beginning a partnership that had lasted for more than a decade, much to the benefit of them both. "We'll be ready."

"Of that I have no doubt."

Mikel headed up the stairs on silent feet. Although he didn't make for the main door at the very top. Instead, he picked the lock on the small armory that was just to the right of the exit. Leaving that door unlocked for Samuel when he closed it, Mikel strode to the back of the large storeroom.

Pushing down on the small notch in the floor at the very back, the wall slid open to reveal a dark tunnel. Stepping through, he grabbed the lantern placed in the metal sconce bolted into the wall, lit the taper with a few scrapes of flint and steel, then closed the door behind him.

Now it was just a matter of getting to where he needed to go.

Mikel could have entered the Citadel with little difficulty

and without anyone knowing, having done it many times before.

By himself, however.

Doing so with a hundred men at his back would have presented more of a problem.

Better to use another way to get Samuel and the boys where he suspected that he would need them.

Ready for what was to come.

Just not knowing when.

"You have the temerity to sneak into my apartment?" Barely able to contain herself, Drin's face was red with rage. She understood that Mikel worked along the very border of legitimacy, but in this he had gone well past the line. "It's well within my right to take your head here and now."

"A pleasure to see you again, Queen Heir Dengannon," Mikel replied calmly. He pushed himself up from where he sat on the stone slab, closing the book he had been reading and slipping it into a back pocket.

"How dare you!"

Mikel gave her a quizzical expression, trying to understand the true source of her anger. "Are you more upset that I snuck into your chambers without being discovered or that I left you a note asking you to join me here?"

Drin stepped up close to the bars, crumpling in her hand the piece of paper that requested that she meet with him at her earliest convenience in the cells beneath the Citadel. Written in a script that would have shamed the calligrapher assigned to craft the invitations for all royal functions.

"I am the Queen of the Crux, Mikel," she stated with a quiet heat. "No one summons me or requests my presence. It works the other way around. Always."

Mikel maintained his smile, understanding her ire. He would have been disappointed if he hadn't drawn her fire. "My apologies, Queen *Heir*."

His use of her current title again and his emphasis on the last word stopped her cold. She growled softly beneath her breath. No matter how much she didn't like it, she needed to maintain control over her temper. And she needed to find out why the King of the Underworld had taken such a risk just to speak with her.

"Why place yourself in this position, Mikel? There are other ways to get my attention."

"Yes, but none so effective and efficient. I dropped off the note less than an hour ago."

She ignored the spark of pride she heard in his voice because of his success. "You could escape any time you want, Mikel." She was well aware of his knowledge of the Citadel and its many secret passageways. "Why haven't you?"

"I needed to speak with you, Queen Heir. That's the truth."

"Here? Seriously?"

Mikel offered her a faint shrug. "Where no one would see us, Queen Heir, and where no one could overhear or interrupt us."

"What about all of them?" She motioned toward the scores of men locked in the cells behind her, all of whom were making a much-too-obvious effort not to pay attention to their conversation. Even more, Drin realized, men who seemed to be quite comfortable in their cells. It was almost as if it was no more than a day's work for them. And if they were working for Mikel, then perhaps that's exactly what it was. "You had to bring all of them into this?"

"I must deal with the world as it is, Queen Heir. Not as I want it to be."

"More cryptic advice from the King of the Underworld," she grumbled, not in the mood to hear it.

"Not advice, Queen Heir. No more than the truth."

There was so much that Drin wanted to say. But what was the point?

It would only extend the amount of time that she would be down in the cells, and she had other matters that required her attention. More rumblings from the First Families about the need for a Search. Lucius Hanover seeking to have dinner with her so that he could push once again to join her on the throne. Another emissary on the way from Malor Dragoran just a few days after she sent the other one packing.

She didn't have time for Mikel's games. Just as he had said, she needed to concentrate on the real world.

"Tell me," she sighed, wanting to hear why he was there so that she could leave him to his fate.

"You need to be careful, Queen Heir."

"I'm always careful, Mikel," she replied with more exhaustion than heat. "I have no choice. Until I sit on the throne after the Coronation, I'm more pawn than queen ... as you so like to remind me."

"I only remind you, Queen Heir, when you need to be reminded."

"My threat still stands, Mikel." Drin's eyes narrowed, her cheeks reddening as her anger took hold once more. He had no right to speak to her in this way. Not now. Not when so much was at stake. "I can take your head whenever I desire."

"Then you'd never gain the information that could be essential to you assuming the throne, Queen Heir."

That stopped her. She studied Mikel's expression for several seconds. Yet again, much to her frustration, his hard countenance revealed absolutely nothing. "What information would that be?"

"For the last few days small groups of soldiers have been entering the city."

That got Drin's attention. She hadn't been expecting that

from him. Rumors relating to machinations put in motion by some of the First Families, perhaps. Certainly not this. "How did you get this information? Your eyes and ears?"

"Eyes and ears, yes. And then my own eyes and ears."

"Explain." Drin placed her right hand on her hip, extended her left leg, then began to tap her foot softly against the stone floor. Her favorite posture, Mikel had learned, for when she was both irritated and inquisitive.

"A few nice gentlemen who entered the city secretly were kind enough to tell me some of what was going on, and it all seems to be tied to you."

"Me?"

"Do I really need to explain?"

Drin frowned. She wanted to be angry with Mikel for his familiarity and how he challenged her whenever he could. But she couldn't be. In his own way, he was seeking to help her, and she couldn't ignore that. "No. There's only one reason they would be here."

"Thus why I'm here to talk with you."

"These soldiers spoke with you willingly?"

"The Giant can be very persuasive," Mikel explained.

The Giant? Then she got it. His partner in crime. Teddy. "What did he do?"

"Nothing you need worry about, Queen Heir. Nothing that wasn't necessary."

"And where are these men? I would like to speak with them myself."

"Unfortunately, they are no longer taking questions."

"You didn't?" she exclaimed. Drin was appalled. Although she couldn't say that she was surprised.

Mikel shrugged as if it was a matter of little concern. "Interrogations can be difficult exercises. Pressure needs to be applied at times. The more pressure that needs to be applied, the more severe the consequences." He smiled apologetically. "We needed to make certain, and we did."

Drin didn't know whether to be disappointed, disquieted, or both. She knew only that there was no point in pursuing that thread any further, in large part because arguing with Mikel was a waste of her breath and her time. Instead, Drin picked at another thread that was more relevant to her more immediate concerns. "Who are they working for?" She wasn't quite ready to use the past tense when speaking about the infiltrators Mikel caught.

"All indications are they came from the Tor, Queen Heir."

"Malor Dragoran is sending another embassy. From what I understand, they'll be here by the end of the day. Do you think these soldiers have anything to do with this embassy?"

"We didn't get into that," Mikel shrugged again. This time an apology. He would have pursued that line of questioning, but he had been in a bit of a rush. "Although in my experience I have little faith in coincidence."

Neither did Drin. "Did you kill them?"

"No, *I* didn't."

Drin chose to ignore how Mikel phrased his reply. "How did they get across the Churn without being identified? You didn't smuggle them across, did you? Is that how you discovered them?" There was a tinge of regret and disappointment in her voice at that possibility.

"Of course not," Mikel scoffed, clearly insulted by her suggestion. "That's bad for business. As I mentioned the last time we spoke, I prefer to keep politics well away from my business interests."

"Of course, Mikel, my apologies." She chose not to point out that his coming here to warn her very much put him right in the middle of the Crux's politics. Why he had chosen to take such a risk, she wasn't quite sure. Although she really wanted to know. Because he wouldn't have done so without good cause. "I'm sorry I insinuated as much."

"Apology accepted, Queen Heir."

Drin bit her tongue, holding back the smile that threatened to break through her stern demeanor. Mikel certainly did have a knack for both making her teeth hurt and then pulling her back from the edge. "How did they get across?"

"Private gondola." He gave her a knowing look and a nod of encouragement. Clearly, he expected her to figure it out on her own.

"It had to be Hanover," she murmured quietly. Thinking now. Her anger gone. Replaced by the political acuity her father had worked so hard to instill within her. If Lucius was involved, then that could mean only one thing. And it wasn't good for her.

Mikel didn't reply. Not feeling the need to do so. He simply gave her a slight nod.

She looked at him then. Really looked at him.

She had done more digging after her last encounter with the King of the Underworld, wanting to get a better feel for the man said to exercise a power in Innsbruck and beyond that rivaled if not surpassed that of many of the First Families. What she learned surprised her. Frightened her. Pleased her as well.

"Are you picking a side, Mikel? Is that why you're here?"

Mikel had spent just as much time during the last few days studying Celindria Dengannon. In many ways, she reminded him of her father, which was to be expected. But in other ways she was clearly her own person. Those aspects of her personality intrigued him.

There was a promise there. A possibility that might be good for the Kingdom of the Crux.

But he was still unwilling to throw his weight behind her based on that. Just a hope. Because he had seen the same spark in other people before, only to be disappointed when they allowed the power they exercised to become more than a tool. That power becoming a goal instead.

"As I said, Queen Heir, I avoid politics when I can."

"Yes, I remember. Business first. Always."

Mikel nodded, smiling, though that smile never reached his eyes. "Yes, business first. Because a business cannot succeed without people. And my main concern is the people of Innsbruck. Because my success is their success."

"How very noble of you." Drin didn't say it scornfully, though it could be perceived as such. Rather, she offered her comment as a challenge.

"Not noble, Queen Heir. Realistic. Learned from hard experience. No more."

She snorted softly at that. She should have anticipated just such a response from him. "Why should I trust you, Mikel?"

"You mean despite the fact that I've helped you twice now and asked nothing in return?"

Drin nodded then, her smile broadening, believing that she had discovered the answer. "That's what this is about? You want me to owe you another favor?"

"That's a short-sighted perspective, Queen Heir." Mikel's voice was almost as frigid as the Frozen Waste.

"Although not necessarily inaccurate." She wasn't put off by his mild indignation. She was beginning to understand who he was, which meant that she was beginning to understand how he needed to function to achieve his objectives.

"Not necessarily," Mikel admitted. His smile was a bit warmer, almost as if he was enjoying the game that they were playing.

"I appreciate you bringing this information to me, Mikel. And you're right, I should give you the benefit of the doubt because you've helped me in the past. But as we both know, the past is the past. In business and politics, all that matters is the present and the future."

"Another short-sighted perspective, Queen Heir."

"Perhaps," Drin admitted, "and perhaps not. I ask again, why should I trust you?"

"You shouldn't trust me. I've told you that already. But you should listen to me. What's the harm of checking into the information I've provided you? What's the harm of increasing the number of guards in the Citadel and around you? What's the harm of keeping a close eye on this Dragoran embassy? If I'm lying, no harm is done. And if I'm not, hopefully any potential harm can be mitigated."

Drin didn't say anything for several heartbeats. Her eyes locked onto his. Her foot tapping on the stone floor.

Interacting with Mikel was both exhilarating and exhausting, and she hadn't decided yet if that was good or bad. "You know, I have no idea what to do with you."

"Why do you need to do anything with me?"

"You already know the answer to that, Mikel." She turned quickly on her heel, stepping out into the hallway, heading toward the stairs that would take her out from the holding cells and back into a world that was more dangerous than the one she was leaving. "Do not summon me again. And I suggest you find some way to make yourself scarce, because I'm still of a mind to take your head."

LOST in thought after Celindria Dengannon left, Mikel remained standing in front of the bars for quite a long time.

She was strong. Tough. Focused. Certainly not someone to take lightly.

All that might be enough to get her through to the Coronation.

Then again, it might not.

He let out a deep breath. There was only so much he could do.

He could advise.

He could provide her with information that would benefit her.

She would decide what if anything to do with what he gave her.

Although she did raise a good question. Why was he getting involved in political matters?

He never had before. He never had any interest or desire.

By doing so now he was breaking one of his cardinal rules and possibly putting his businesses and, more importantly, the role he played in the Innsbruck community in jeopardy.

Reaching down, he began massaging his knee and thigh. His old injury was acting up again, though that only made sense.

It had been a long day.

And he still had a great deal more to do.

He smiled then, shaking his head, wondering if he was going soft.

Had he taken a liking to Celindria Dengannon?

Or was she the least worst of the options for the Crux throne?

Then again, perhaps there was another reason for his decisions and actions that he didn't want to consider.

A reason that could prove to be a disaster for him, his line of work not kind to such entanglements.

Mikel pushed on the cell door, which opened on silent hinges. "You heard about the embassy?"

Samuel nodded. "We'll be ready."

"Good." Mikel pulled the book from his pocket and handed it to Samuel, who nodded his thanks for new reading material. "I need to take care of a few things. You know what to do?"

"We do. And we will. Have no fear of that."

26

BLOOD ON THE SHEETS

"What are you doing here?"

"The Battle Lord asked that I stay in the suite with you, Queen Heir." The soldier bowed respectfully. "Just in case."

"He did, did he?" Drin grumbled. She stood in the alcove that was just off to the side from her bedroom. Slightly distracted as she sifted through the papers on her desk. All of them appearing seemingly out of thin air in just the few hours since she had left her suite for the throne room.

Apparently her father was right. A Kingdom was run on parchment. Writs. Proclamations. Laws. Codicils. Entreaties.

Just the thought of having to work her way through this new stack made her sick to her stomach.

"Yes, Queen Heir." The soldier shifted his shoulders. Not so much nervous to be having a conversation with someone of her rank, but rather as if the fit of his tunic wasn't quite right. He slunk forward a few feet as he did so, offering her a smile and a conciliatory nod.

"And what else did he say?"

She picked up another piece of paper. This one a request

from the Hanovers and a few other First Families who were tied closely to Lucius' House. She shook her head. Her annoyance becoming something more.

Another request for a few hours of her time later this evening. This was getting tedious. What more could Lucius and his allies say on their behalf that she hadn't heard already?

"What do you mean, Queen Heir?" The soldier appeared to be surprised at her question. Concerned as well.

She made it a point to know every man serving in the Army of the Crux, if not by name, then at least by appearance. A difficult skill when there were thousands, yet made easier by her use of the Talent. And with this soldier ... she was drawing a blank. Either he had joined her service in the last few weeks or ...

Drin smiled disarmingly then, seeking to put the man at ease. Not wanting him to realize that she had noticed how he shuffled a few feet closer to her desk. That his uniform didn't fit him as well as it should. And that there were a few tiny spots of blood on his cuffs.

"I appreciate my uncle's concern for my person, but there must have been more to it than that. A cause for his concern. And his need to send you out of all the soldiers loyal to the Crux."

"I don't understand," the soldier replied, having taken two more steps closer to the desk while the Queen Heir reached for another stack of papers to peruse.

Drin looked up then, her smile anything but disarming now. "I just find it curious that he would send you all the way from the Splintered Bridge with nothing more than a desire for you to look after me. Especially with all the soldiers already standing guard here in the Citadel. Soldiers I have known since I was a child." She nodded toward the closed door to emphasize her point.

The soldier frowned. When he had arrived with the

message, the men at the door had let him through with barely a second glance, satisfied by the uniform he wore. Just as he assumed they would be. Because who in their right mind would make a play for the Queen Heir while she was in the Citadel?

"The Battle Lord was quite busy, Queen Heir." He shrugged then offered a sly look. "I can only assume that he selected me because I have certain skills that most other soldiers don't."

"I'm sure that was why," Drin agreed. "My uncle keeps faith with a heavy and unforgiving burden. Seeking to hold the Splintered Bridge and protect the Crux from the soldiers of the Tor." Her expression hardened, eyes becoming flinty. "Soldiers like you."

"Exactly, Queen Heir ..." The soldier froze, the rest of what he was going to say stuck in his throat. The Queen Heir's unyielding expression trapping him. Her small smile as well.

Clear that she had caught him in his lie, he pulled the long dagger from the belt on his hip.

"You think you can take me, soldier?" She noticed how the steel flashed in the lamplight except for the tip. There was a greyish substance rubbed onto the sharpened end. She wasn't surprised. Only a scratch would be required. Although she doubted that her death was his aim.

"Only one way to find out," he replied with a chilling indifference. "Of course even with your unique skills, I'm not all that concerned by a woman barely out of adolescence."

Drin snorted softly at that. "Perhaps you should be."

The soldier's demeanor shifted in a heartbeat. The respect gone. Replaced by an arrogance that was revealed by his lunge, only the desk keeping him away from her.

That's as far as he got. Shock coloring his features.

With a quick flick of her right wrist, a small dagger she used to open her letters streaked through the air. Her kidnapper hadn't noticed her picking it up the last time she reached into the stack of papers atop her desk.

The grunt and gasp that followed confirmed that her aim was true. The soldier's hand went to the hilt, the blade embedded in his neck.

"You bit ..."

The soldier loyal to Malor Dragoran didn't have a chance to complete his complaint. Stumbling backward as blood stained his shirt, he dropped the poisoned dagger and then struggled to pull free the short sword on his hip.

When he finally succeeded and looked up, he took a few more staggering steps backward, seeking to put a wall at his back.

The Queen Heir advancing toward him with a predatory glare.

"FASTER! WE'LL LOSE OUR CHANCE."

"We might not even be needed, Kurik," Wendel replied in a quiet hiss. "We're the second option, remember? The backup. If all goes as it should, Derek will have the package already wrapped and waiting for us in the tunnel."

The Captain in the Tor Guard gave his second in command a hard look, though he didn't slow his pace. In fact, he shifted from a jog to a trot, forcing the men at his back to do the same. "I'm well aware, Wendel. I helped to develop the plan, remember?"

Wendel offered his commander a respectful nod. There was no point in pushing Kurik when he was like this. Strung tight as a bowstring. "I'm not questioning you."

"Seems like it," he growled.

"I'm just wondering if the risk of discovery is worth it. Perhaps slow is better right now?"

Kurik sighed, much of his anger at being challenged fading. Wendel was right. They needed to be careful. The longer they remained undetected, the better their odds of success.

They were making their way through a tunnel within the walls of the Citadel, relying on information provided to them by people they didn't know and they certainly didn't trust.

Moreover, they had only a few torches to light their way. Just beyond the reach of the flames anyone could be waiting to waylay them.

Kurik didn't say anything to Wendel, giving him a quick look before slowing his pace. He wasn't going to admit to the validity of his subordinate's advice. However, if he saw any hint of a self-satisfied expression on Wendel's buck-toothed countenance, he'd kill him now just to make a point to the other men he had selected for this mission. Despite the fact that would reduce his already reduced numbers.

King Dragoran had given him a hundred soldiers for this assignment. All of them thoroughly trained in how to enter Innsbruck without being noticed. Even more important, how to get into the Citadel right under the noses of the Crux Guard.

Yet as he engaged in the most important and dangerous part of his mission, he had only fifty men with him.

What had happened to the others he had not a clue. And that bothered him a great deal.

He didn't like the idea of walking into a trap. Yet there was nothing for it now. And, so far, all had gone as planned as soon as he gathered the men who made it safely across the Churn to the Crux.

Besides, even if the pathfinder sent ahead to capture their target didn't complete his task, Kurik still should have enough men to complete his.

Yet if that was the case, why was he so unsettled?

Why did he feel a heavy urgency pressing down upon his shoulders?

This wasn't the first time Kurik had been handed an assignment like this one. They never went off without a hitch. There were always unanticipated obstacles to be addressed. Surprises always got in the way.

And always, in spite of all that, he and his men pushed through and achieved their objective.

Perhaps it was because the stakes were so high. His King's larger strategy depended almost entirely upon the success of this mission.

And Kurik knew exactly what would happen if he failed and had the temerity to show his face once again on the Tor.

"We're here, Captain."

Wendel stood where the corridor they had been following ended. Turning toward his right, his torch illuminated the faint outline of the sliding door hidden in the wall. Exactly where they were told it would be.

Kurik understood what his deputy was trying to do by using his rank. Make amends.

Fair enough. He would allow Wendel's previous indiscretion. They were where they needed to be and no one in the Citadel was any the wiser.

Just as important, they were adhering to their timetable. If they could get her out of the Citadel and then to the ambassador, who was scheduled to come across the Churn in a private gondola within the next hour, they could be well on their way to the Splintered Bridge before the Queen Heir's kidnapping was discovered.

The only issue that gave Kurik any concern was that their pathfinder wasn't here waiting for them. Just as he promised he would be.

Though Kurik couldn't say that he was shocked. Promises only went so far on missions such as this one.

Hoping that their luck would continue to hold, Kurik nodded to Wendel.

The soldier knelt down and searched for the latch that was supposed to be right near the base of the door.

Wendel breathed a sigh of relief when he found it. He looked up and over his shoulder. His Captain nodded.

Wendel pushed down on the latch, then slid out of the way. Allowing Kurik to slide the door a foot to the side and push his head part of the way out into the hallway.

Empty to his right.

But not to his left.

Several squads of soldiers milled about at the other end of the hallway. Right in front of Celindria Dengannon's suite.

Had his pathfinder failed to ...

"Guards!"

The angry cry that erupted from the Queen Heir's suite answered Kurik's question for him.

So much for their luck holding.

Now it was time for a more direct approach.

Exactly the way he preferred it.

Because he doubted that these few squads of Crux soldiers would be able to stand against his men.

He stepped out into the hallway, waiting a few seconds for his depleted company to join him. The soldiers at the end of the hallway were focused on what was going on in the suite. Not on what was occurring in the hallway.

After his entire force emerged from the hidden tunnel, Kurik pulled the sword from the scabbard across his back and stalked down the corridor, his men following his example.

He had one job.

Kidnap Celindria Dengannon and get her to the Tor.

He would do whatever was necessary to make that happen.

Even sacrifice himself.

Because he refused to pay the penalty his King would mete out for failure, finding that option much worse.

"HOLD THE LINE!" Drin ordered. She stood just outside her alcove, her suite a battleground.

Bloody dagger in one hand to match the bloody short sword in the other, two men lay dead at her feet. Thankfully neither men of the Crux. Both believing that they had greater skill with their blades than she did with hers. Discovering much to their regret the price of their arrogance.

Unfortunately not all of the soldiers of the Crux were enjoying the same success as she was. Many of the dead crumpled on the thick carpets of her entryway and living room loyal to her.

"Hold the line!" she repeated, jumping into the fight yet again. Sword and then dagger flashing as she cut across an attacker's forearm, the man stumbling back, hissing in pain.

Her soldiers redoubled their efforts at her command, all of them certain as to what would happen if they allowed the invaders from the Tor who had somehow found a way into the Citadel to push them out onto the terrace.

They would have no room to maneuver. They would have no options for getting the Queen Heir to safety. Not with a drop of more than a hundred feet at their backs.

Nevertheless, Drin sensed the truth of the clash. Her soldiers' efforts could last for only so much longer. Ten defenders remained from the original twenty. They were putting up a valiant fight, however they could do nothing more than retreat. They were facing five times their number, the crush of bodies the only variable slowing their certain defeat.

Drin leapt forward, short sword extended. She knocked away an attacker's sword before it cut across the shoulder of the soldier fighting in front of her. Unfortunately she wasn't fast enough to prevent the Tor soldier on the other side from skewering the poor fellow, who dropped to his knees and clutched at the bloody wound in his belly.

For the next few minutes, the larger clash was lost on her. Her focus solely on the fight swirling within a few feet of her.

She didn't know how many men she was battling. All she knew was that she needed to hold her ground. Her dagger and sword flashing through the tight space with a relentless ferocity.

Several times she considered using the Talent if for no other reason than to relieve the unabating pressure that she and her men were under.

She decided against it each time the thought passed through her mind.

Drin had just as much chance of harming her own soldiers with natural magic as she did the Tor soldiers.

"It's done, Dengannon. Step forward and surrender yourself. Otherwise, your men, what's left of them, die."

The sharp command brought Drin out from beneath the haze that had settled over her, realizing that the Tor soldiers had stepped back, creating a space of a few feet between her and the three Crux soldiers who continued to fight by her side. The last of her defenders. The rest dead.

"It's not done until I say it's done," Drin replied in a heated voice. She sheathed her dagger, a sphere of energy forming above her palm. She no longer believed that there was a need for caution.

"I know what you can do, Queen Heir," Kurik replied in a much-too-calm tone. "It will do you little good here."

"And why is that?" Drin hoped that by engaging in a conversation, she might be able to give more defenders of the Citadel the opportunity to join the clash, assuming the sounds of the battle had drifted down from the top floor.

"Because I have archers, Queen Heir," Kurik stated with a deserved conviction, "and they are targeting you." The commander of the Tor raiding party stepped forward then, pushing through his men until he stood right in front of her. Only a few feet separating them. "You may kill some of us, but not before the arrows strike home. Wasted effort on your part."

"I don't view killing a few more Tor soldiers as wasted effort."

"Perhaps not," Kurik replied in a shockingly amiable tone. "But if you do that we'll slaughter the last of your men. Do you want their unnecessary deaths on your conscience? Because we will shoot to wound you. You will be leaving here with us. Have no doubt of that. The fact that you are a Magus cannot save you from that reality."

Drin looked to her right and then her left. Three men still alive from the twenty. All determined yet all wounded. A painful truth. Even worse, she had no cause to disbelieve this Tor soldier. She knew they weren't there to kill her. They could have done that already with the archers. They wanted to take her alive.

Decision made, she released her hold on the Talent, the sphere of energy dancing above her palm winking out.

She was about to offer her surrender no matter how bitter the words tasted, but she hesitated. Eyes drawn to a faint rustling just beyond the entryway to her suite.

Her eyes widened as a stream of fighters burst into her suite.

Slamming into the Tor soldiers from behind.

Daggers. Cudgels. Maces.

All weapons best employed in tight spaces.

All being used with a practiced efficiency.

All of the men just minutes before residing in the holding cells beneath the Citadel.

～

Drin was astonished but thinking about it just a second more she realized that she really had no cause to be. She should have assumed that this would happen after his warning.

"You work for the King of the Underworld," Drin stated when the man who had been reading in the cell across from Mikel's appeared by her side.

He wielded his twin daggers with a deadly efficiency, clearing the space around them. The rest of his men were herding more than attacking, seeking to force the Tor soldiers deeper into the suite with the goal of creating a clear lane to the doorway.

"I do." He glided forward with a fluid grace, leaving a bloody stripe across a soldier's neck with a delicate slice, then allowing the man to collapse to the carpet. Stepping back so that he was right next to his charge. Pleased by the efforts of his men, who were enjoying just as much success as he was. "Samuel, Queen Dengannon."

"He knew this was going to happen. Didn't he." She was ready to reach for the Talent once again, her dagger still sheathed. The mad scramble in front of her made her hesitate. She didn't want to harm any of the fighters aiding her and shift the momentum back in favor of the Tor soldiers.

"He was hoping that it wouldn't, but he wanted to be prepared."

"Why?" Drin was about to lunge with her short sword. She restrained herself. The Tor soldier she was going to attack forced to retreat by three men from the holding cells.

"Because that's what he likes to do," Samuel replied.

"What do you mean?"

"He likes to be ready for as many possibilities as he can be. That's why he's so good at what he does."

"So he suspected," Drin murmured, all the while watching as Mikel's fighters demonstrated a surprising discipline for what she had taken initially to be no more than a band of brigands.

It was almost as if they had trained for the maneuver they were conducting, driving the Tor soldiers exactly where they wanted them to be. Focusing their efforts first on the archers, removing them from the clash, before applying their deadly skills to the other invaders.

Thanks to their efficient work, there were just a few stragglers, including the Tor commander, blocking the path they were seeking to create.

"He as much as told you, Queen Heir. You just needed to listen."

"I was listening. I just didn't think that ..." She was going to say more. Samuel interrupted her.

"You can take me to task for overstepping if we get out of here. Sheathe your sword and take your dagger."

She did as he ordered without a second thought, already understanding what he had in mind.

He nodded toward the smaller blade she now held in her hand. "Can you use that?"

"Better than most," she replied without a hint of arrogance.

"Good. Stay right behind me. Only use it if you need to."

Drin nodded, almost stepping on Samuel's heels as he headed toward the door.

"Clear the way boys! We need that tunnel."

Mikel's fighters moved as one. Shifting their positioning, they surrounded Samuel and Drin, ensuring that the Tor soldiers couldn't stop them from breaking out of the apartment.

Once they were in the hallway, a wedge of fighters darted into the tunnel, guaranteeing that the way was clear. Ignoring the sounds of the fighting that was taking place on the floor below them, the clash of steel striking steel echoing in the staircase at the far end of the corridor.

Samuel and Drin were right behind the point of the wedge.

The other fighters at their backs. Disengaging so quickly that it took the Tor soldiers a few seconds to catch up to what was happening.

As soon as they reached the darkness of the tunnel, a handful of torches came to life.

"Bolt it," Samuel ordered.

The man tasked with that responsibility and closest to the hidden doorway did just that, slamming a steel wedge into the mechanism so that it couldn't be opened from the hallway.

And just in time.

Tor soldiers slammed ineffectually against the hidden door.

Unwilling to give up their prize so easily.

Experiencing no joy, however, the door holding.

"Stay close, Queen Heir," Samuel said, giving Drin a nod and a crooked smile. "We still have a long way to go before you're safe. This wasn't the only raiding party sent into the Citadel."

27

TRAP OF THEIR OWN MAKING

Drin moved as swiftly and surreptitiously through the streets of Innsbruck as she could. Samuel guiding her. A few of his fighters stayed with them, keeping an eye out for threats.

The rest of Mikel's troop broke off one by one as they worked their way down the rings of the city built atop the Crux, allowing themselves to be absorbed back into the rhythm of Innsbruck. Although Drin doubted that they had gone far. Knowing Mikel, those fighters were probably still tracking them until Samuel got them to wherever they were going.

"Not The Fox's Lair?" Drin spotted Mikel's tavern on the corner, but they didn't make for the welcoming establishment. Samuel kept on his present course, continuing toward the lower rings and going right past with barely a glance the one place Drin thought might offer her sanctuary.

Samuel had given her a cloak as soon as they exited the Citadel to mask her from any hidden watchers. And based on the fact that Samuel's focus shifted this way and that, never stopping for long on any one person or movement that caught his eye, at least not yet, clearly he believed that his caution was warranted. That they were not yet free of the Tor soldiers seeking to abduct her.

"No, too obvious," Samuel said with a shake of his head, sharp eyes scanning all around them in search of the slightest hint of trouble. "Won't be long now. Don't worry."

Drin frowned but didn't say anything. Not liking the position she was in. Primarily because she wasn't in control.

This wasn't her show. In fact, it had never been her show.

Mikel had orchestrated it all as soon as he got a whiff of Tor soldiers sneaking into the city. She was certain of that. The one concession he had made was warning her of the danger she faced, and she hadn't taken it as seriously as she should have. That had been her mistake. Because if she had perhaps she wouldn't be in her current predicament.

Drin continued in silence for the next several minutes as Samuel wove unerringly through the maze of Innsbruck's side streets. The handful of men still with them ensured that no one bothered them, though at this hour there were few to worry about.

"Are you sure about this?"

Drin had rarely come down here before. Having little cause to do so.

The First Ring.

Several neighborhoods on this level where the seawall fought the Churn still abandoned because of the devastation caused by the last flood. The reconstruction work yet to begin.

It seemed odd. She recalled her father signing the documents to begin the rebuilding and discussing the plans with the city's master engineers.

She forced herself to clear her mind. Now wasn't the time for that question. It would have to wait for when her sole concern no longer was escaping her hunters.

Still, she found it difficult not to be distracted by what she saw.

There were only a few houses. All of them empty. The shops closed.

Most of the homes were apartments, constructed for the less fortunate residents of the Crux. No more than a handful appeared to be in use.

Those apartments were built one upon the other, much like steps in a staircase, giving the people living here -- used to live here she corrected – a faster route to the safety of the Second Ring when the rivers breached the breakwater.

The emptiness bothered her in a visceral way. She remembered the one time her father had brought her down to the lowest level of Innsbruck to inspect the gondola stations.

If not for the soldiers surrounding them, they would have struggled to make any headway through the crowd. People everywhere. Businesses prospering. Children going to school. Taverns bustling.

Now ...

There was nothing except for silence.

There was no one in the streets and the moon had just risen.

She found every aspect of trotting along the ring road disconcerting, consumed by a sadness she had never experienced before.

"Completely sure, Queen Dengannon," Samuel replied, he and his men demonstrating a keen wariness as they navigated their frequent stomping grounds. "Have no fear. I would never lead you astray."

"Because I'm the Queen or because you work for Mikel?" Drin couldn't resist asking, meaning it as a joke to lighten the tense mood.

Samuel answered quickly and with complete seriousness. "Because I work for Mikel, of course. He's fair, more than fair, but you don't want to get on his bad side."

Drin didn't have a response. Not surprised though still

humbled to discover that even in her city she was not always the top dog.

They were close to the gondola docks where the Western and Southern Rivers met when Samuel brought them to a halt a few minutes later, the massive towers and winches that worked the chains crossing to the far shores rising just over the apartments to their left.

"Why have we ..."

Samuel raised his hand, asking for quiet.

She obliged. Drin sensed it then. They were no longer alone.

A shadow flitted by in the alley just to their right.

Then a few more.

A gang of thieves perhaps?

Drin discarded that idea immediately. All the thieves in Innsbruck worked for Mikel. They were already helping her.

So if not a gang ...

"We need to move, Queen Dengannon." Samuel urged her down a side street and away from the alley with lurking shadows, more of those shadows appearing in the ring road behind and in front of them.

"Tor soldiers."

Samuel nodded as he and his men led her off the main boulevard, past a row of what had once been shops, and then into the warren of alleys closest to the seawall. "Has to be. Come on."

Samuel picked up the pace, Drin staying with him.

"There! I see them!"

Drin broke into a run at the shout, sensing their pursuers closing behind them. For the next few minutes, it was a race. Samuel leading them this way and that, attempting to evade their hunters. Yet just when they thought they had broken free, it wasn't to be. More shouts sounded along the abandoned streets as the Tor soldiers tightened the noose.

"Samuel, we can't go this way." Drin reached out, grasping his arm, pulling him back as they all skidded to a stop.

He had led them down an alley scarcely large enough to walk through without turning her shoulders that opened to a deserted courtyard, boarded up apartment buildings rising up around them, the seawall at their backs.

It was too late.

They were trapped.

The shadows that had been chasing them materialized out of the gloom, streaming down the alley and spreading out into the plaza, seeking to flank Drin and her small band of guardians.

Drin reached for her sword, mimicking the actions of Samuel and his men, all of whom now held steel in their hands.

"Have no fear, Queen Dengannon," Samuel said in a quiet voice meant only for her as they watched more Tor soldiers stride confidently into the courtyard, all convinced that their hunt was over. "Remember what I said. Mikel is all about options."

Drin could only hope that was the case. Because at that moment she saw few options other than a fight that wouldn't end well for them.

There were too many Tor soldiers. And there was no avenue for escape, nothing except for battened up buildings on all sides. Their only means of egress back through the thirty, maybe even forty, men who flooded into the square through the narrow alley.

"He wanted this to happen?" Drin found that hard to believe. Then again, though she didn't know him very well, thanks to her several engagements with him she had discerned quickly that Mikel never did anything without a good reason.

"He did." Samuel nodded to the men on each flank. They shifted a few feet farther out in each direction, giving them more room for the inevitable clash to come, though not so far as to allow their attackers to break through their makeshift line easily.

"He wanted to flush them out?" Drin shook her head, biting the inside of her lip. She should have assumed as much.

"He did," Samuel confirmed with a sharp nod. "Time was short, and he didn't think that he'd found them all. He believed that this would be the easiest way to force the worms out of the woodwork."

"He used me as bait!" Drin exclaimed in a whispered hiss. She couldn't believe it. "I'm the Queen of the Crux, and he used me as bait?" Her building anger knew almost no bounds.

"Perhaps you could take it up with him?" Samuel requested in a placating voice, his nerves tightening. "I just follow orders."

"But not my orders." Drin's eyes blazed with fury. How could Mikel have done this to her? Why would he dare to take such a risk? Without even telling her? After all ...

"A man can serve only one master honestly, Queen Dengannon."

She couldn't argue that point with him. "You can count on me taking him up on this, Samuel. Assuming that we can ..."

"You've run as far as you can, Dengannon." A Tor soldier dressed like a commoner stepped out of the gloom, visible thanks to the bright light of the full moon that bathed the courtyard. The rest of his men took a few steps toward Drin and her defenders, holding their ground when he raised a hand.

"Keep him talking," Samuel urged in a whisper.

"Why would I want to do that?"

"Buy us some time if you can."

Drin gave Samuel a questioning look.

"Trust me," he urged. Then he gave her a wink. "I got you this far."

"You got me right into a trap."

Samuel smiled, proud of that fact. "Just as I was supposed to Queen Dengannon. A trap of our own making."

Drin growled in anger, then turned to face the Tor soldier. "Your name?"

"Captain Marcellus Montesarian Mandrake."

"That's quite a mouthful, Captain."

"I have a long and proud heritage, Queen Heir."

"As a soldier or as a kidnapper, Captain."

Mandrake took a few steps closer, revealing an oiled mustache and beard, the tips twisted into sharp points. His scalp was shaved. A thin white scar around one ear visible. "I am simply doing my duty, Queen Heir."

"You are invading my Kingdom, Captain Mandrake."

He smiled then. "Again, Queen Heir, I am just doing my duty." He motioned toward Samuel and the other men with her. "There is no reason for this to end badly for all of you. As you've likely surmised, we are here to escort you to the Tor. No harm need befall your companions."

Drin snorted. "Escort? Interesting choice of words."

Captain Mandrake shrugged. "The right choice. King Dragoran would like to speak with you. He believes that he has a way to ensure that the enmity between our two Kingdoms is brought to an end."

"With me sitting on his lap like a good little girl I take it?"

Captain Mandrake did not reply right away, slightly shocked by the Queen Heir's response and the image it created in his mind. Flustered, he cleared his throat before offering a temperate reply. "Of course not, Queen Heir. I believe he has an alliance in mind. From what I understand a fair one."

Drin smiled then. "We should speak plainly, Captain Mandrake. Doing otherwise is a waste of time. You know quite well that Malor Dragoran's definition of fairness means that he gets what he wants. First, foremost, and always. Simple as that."

Captain Mandrake smiled again, offering the Queen of the Crux a nod of respect. "It seems that you know him well."

"Well enough. And speaking plainly, you have no intention of allowing my men to go free. They're witnesses."

"I was simply attempting to soften the blow, Queen Heir."

"Wasted effort, Captain Mandrake. I'm not a fool."

"I would never think you a fool, Queen Heir. But I must insist that you come with me now."

At his nod, several of Mandrake's soldiers stepped forward, swords drawn. Samuel and his men tensed, preparing for the fight they had been anticipating.

A confident voice that sounded from right behind Drin delayed that inevitability, stopping the Tor soldiers in their tracks.

"I'm sorry, Captain. But the Queen Heir has a previous engagement. With me, in fact. She won't be able to join you."

Mikel stepped past Samuel and next to Drin, Teddy coming up on her other side.

"Took you long enough," Drin grumbled out of the side of her mouth. Where he had come from she didn't know. She was simply glad that he was here, finding his presence both comforting and uncomfortable.

"Timing is everything," he replied just as quietly before turning his full attention to Captain Mandrake and his soldiers.

"And you are?" the Tor Captain demanded. He was done being polite, feeling the pinch of time. Wanting to be off the Crux as quickly as possible. The ambassador and his troop of soldiers who would take them to and then over the Splintered Bridge were waiting on the far shore. The sooner they began that journey, the sooner they would be back on home soil.

"No one of consequence," Mikel replied. He pulled the scimitar from the scabbard across his back, the steel gleaming brightly. He hoped that cheap theatrics might put the Tor soldiers, already unsettled, slightly more off balance before the real fun began.

"You made a mistake then," Captain Mandrake said, infusing his voice with a confidence that he didn't really feel. Worried about the glowing steel. There was some aspect to this new player that made his teeth hurt. A sense of menace radiated from him despite his calm appearance and smile. "As the Queen Heir so rightly noted, we can't have any witnesses. You and your friend are now nothing more than dead men walking."

"Actually, you made the mistake, Captain," Mikel corrected.

"What mistake would that be?" Mandrake shifted his gaze briefly to the giant standing on the Queen Heir's other side. He was rolling his shoulders and moving his neck. Stretching. Then the giant gave him a wink. Mandrake forced himself not to take a step backward, his worry only intensifying. He felt as if he was losing control over what should have been a straightforward snatch and grab.

"Most of your comrades in arms are gone, Captain, or soon will be," Mikel explained. "I suggest that you leave now while you still can."

"Not without the Queen Heir, friend." Mandrake pushed his cloak to the side and pulled his sword from the scabbard on his hip, his expression grim. Eager as well. "You think you can stop me?"

Mikel smiled fiendishly at the challenge the Captain offered him. "I don't think. I know." He whispered to Drin. "Now would be a good time to show some of what a Magus can do."

Drin smiled then, finally having a release for her anger, more than happy to accommodate Mikel's request. Reaching for the Talent, she watched as the Captain's eyes bulged at the sight of the sparks dancing across her fingertips.

Before Mandrake could order his archers to fire, the men brought there specifically to prevent the Queen Heir from employing the power she could summon, streaks of energy shot from her palms, blasting into the cobblestones in front of Mandrake and his soldiers. A massive cloud of rock and dust erupted, the ground shaking slightly, as the first line of soldiers flew backward.

Before the Tor soldiers not killed by the blast could push themselves up from the shattered courtyard, all of them unsteady on their feet, ears ringing, vision blurred, a swarm of Mikel's men surged out of the gloom, leaping down from the supposedly empty buildings that surrounded the courtyard, a handful of archers taking up positions on the balconies to ensure that none of Mandrake's archers who might have survived could take a shot at the Queen Heir.

"Not much of a fight," Teddy rumbled.

"It wasn't meant to be," Mikel replied.

When the last of the cloud cleared, the only men standing were Mikel's. The Tor soldiers not killed in Drin's attack eliminated just as fast with daggers.

"That kind of takes all the fun out of it."

"When did you become so bloodthirsty?"

Teddy shrugged, then kicked at one of the broken cobblestones that had ended up near his foot. "I just need a little exercise, that's all."

Mikel nodded in understanding. "Spending too much time in the books today?"

"Not that. Nat wouldn't let me step away. Question after question. Even when I offered a few sweet treats, they kept coming. I just needed ..."

"Excuse me," Drin interrupted in a sharp tone. "Perhaps you could continue this conversation later at a more appropriate time."

"Of course, Queen Heir," Teddy replied, taking a step back while offering her a nod of respect.

She turned her attention to Mikel, her eyes blazing with

anger. "Bait? You used me as bait? How dare you? I'm going to put you right back into that cell and make sure you can't get out this time." She made several other promises as well, each worse than the preceding one. Each dealing with a punishment she was going to administer to her rescuer at her leisure.

Mikel smiled, weathering the storm. "Queen Heir, perhaps we could continue this in a safer location. Now, we need to get off the streets."

He stepped back toward the seawall, Teddy following him.

Drin stood there for a moment, not done with her harangue. Shocked to find that she was alone in a courtyard full of dead men. Samuel and all of Mikel's other fighters already gone.

He used her as bait and now he left her presence without so much as a by your leave?

She moved quickly to catch up to him as he approached a door in the breakwater that she never would have noticed if Mikel wasn't heading straight toward it.

"Why the rush?" she demanded. "Captain Mandrake is no longer a concern."

"True, but there are others like him still searching for you in the city."

"Then we should go back to the Citadel," Drin said with as much certainty as she could muster, a sense of unease filling her as she stared into the darkness of the doorway.

"You can't go back to the Citadel. Not yet."

"Why not?"

"How did the Tor soldiers get into the Citadel?" Mikel asked, not slowing down.

"Well, if you didn't help them ..." Drin stopped, the truth striking her like a slap across the face. "A traitor."

Mikel nodded, one foot in the courtyard, one past the open door. "Or more than one. We have yet to determine who and how many. Though we have a few good ideas."

"Still, at the Citadel ..."

"Who can you trust there if your uncle is still in command at the Splintered Bridge?"

Drin tried to answer his question, but she couldn't. Because she didn't like the answer.

No one.

Mikel nodded. Understanding how hard this was for her.

Queen of the Crux meant exercising a great deal of power. It also meant a great deal of loneliness.

"Would you care to join me, Queen Heir?" He beckoned for her to step through the doorway.

"Where are we going?"

"Somewhere safe."

"Which would be?"

"The City Below, of course."

28

A FEW GOOD BOOKS

For the first time since the attack in the Citadel, Drin was able to relax. Briefly. The adrenaline that had been keeping her going the last few hours draining from her body. Now she desired nothing more than to close her eyes and take a nap.

But she couldn't.

There was too much to do.

She needed to figure out her next steps.

Tor soldiers in the Citadel.

Malor Dragoran attempting to kidnap her.

Traitors on the Crux.

She would have found all that hard to believe if it was not all too real.

"Are you certain we're safe?"

"Quite safe," Mikel replied. He sat across from her at the table placed in the back of his bookshop in the City Below. She had asked that same question several times in the last few minutes. Understandable considering what she had experienced. "No one can get beneath the Crux without my approval."

"You say that as if it's a fact," she snorted, still uneasy. Still not yet willing to trust.

"It is a fact." He said it without a hint of arrogance. Simply stating the truth.

"We need to get moving." Another topic that Drin had raised several times since gaining the refuge of the bookshop.

"You said that already," Mikel continued. More times than I care to recall he wanted to add. But he chose not to. Not wanting to aggravate Drin. At least not any more than usual. What she was dealing with not easy to work through.

"Because we're still here," she said tartly.

"We're still here because we need to be here," Mikel explained calmly. Although Celindria Dengannon was settling slowly, she was still on edge. Nervous. It would do her little good in that moment. Nothing would do her any good until she found the calm she needed once more.

"When are we going to move?"

"When the time is right."

"When will the time be right?"

"I can't tell you that yet. But I will when I know."

"Mikel, I am the Queen Heir. Need I remind you that ..."

"And need I remind you, Queen Heir," Mikel said, interrupting her, his voice exceedingly quiet, though still forceful, almost commanding, "that at the moment I'm the only person you can trust on the Crux. Need I remind you that you're not bundled off and on your way to the Tor because of me. Need I remind you that you're here at my pleasure. So perhaps a bit more patience and a lot less attitude."

The sharpness of Mikel's tone stopped Drin cold. She couldn't remember the last time anyone had spoken to her in such a way. In fact, she couldn't recall anyone ever talking to her in such a way.

Rather than responding in a placating tone, she pushed back, adding to the boil of the pot. "You would dare to speak to

me in this way? You may be the King of the Underworld, but
..."

"Celindria, you need to stop." Mikel's voice was cold. Just
like his eyes. What little patience he had left gone. "I don't dare.
I do."

He leaned closer to her then, feeling slightly sorry for her.
She had been placed in an almost untenable position. One that
she had never anticipated.

Mikel understood why it was so hard for her to wrap her
mind around what was happening. Nevertheless, she needed
to. For both their sakes.

Because he was taking a risk that for most anyone else he
would have avoided.

"I am sorry that you have to deal with all this," he continued. "I understand that you have not yet even had time to
grieve the loss of your father. Nevertheless, if you are to rule the
Crux, then you must be able to put your emotions aside. You
must be able to perceive the world through a calculating eye.
You must be able to make good decisions. Because if you do
not, becoming a guest of Malor Dragoran will be the least of
your worries."

Stunned, Drin stared at Mikel. Not sure what to do. Not
sure what to say.

She wanted to lash out. All the while understanding that
would do her little good.

She was angry with herself more than she was with him.
Because everything Mikel said was the truth.

She took a deep breath, trying to gain better control over
her frazzled nerves and the exhaustion that was creeping
into her.

Drin nodded then, hoping that Mikel took it as an apology,
because she refused to say it out loud. "How do I ensure that I
make good decisions?"

Mikel didn't reply right away. Instead, he studied the

claimant to the throne. He understood how hard it was for her to back down. Going against her character. Her natural tendency was to push back when someone pushed her. If she didn't, she couldn't rule the Crux, now could she?

But that wasn't the question in that moment. The question wasn't how she was to rule the Crux. The question was how to ensure that she did rule the Crux.

"With good information." He offered her a smile that she took as acceptance of her apology.

"And where do we get good information?"

"We already are getting good information," Mikel replied. "Teddy is analyzing the reports that we're receiving now."

Drin sat back then. Realizing just how big a fool she had been. Or perhaps it was more that she wasn't thinking as clearly as she needed to. Forced to acknowledge that an attempted kidnapping in her own city could do that to her.

She should have assumed that Mikel was already well aware of what was going on in the Citadel. And he would know even more in the next few hours.

He had more than just a hand on the pulse of the city. He had eyes and ears everywhere. Nothing happened on the Crux without him knowing about it.

"And when will you be sharing this information with me?" Drin asked her question in what she hoped was a reasonable tone.

"When it's actionable. And once you've had a chance to rest."

"I don't have time to rest," Drin stated with a sharp edge.

"And that right there proves that you need to rest. You can't expect to make good decisions otherwise. You can't make decisions based on emotion or what you want. You need to make them based on what is. And we don't know what is just yet. Give it a few hours and then we can move. Fair?"

She didn't respond right away, pursing her lips. Examining

Mikel. Looking for ... she didn't know what. "You sound like my father."

"I'll take that as a compliment," he said with a dry grin.

"You should." No longer wanting to argue, she shifted her focus in a new direction. Seeking some way to take the edge off. "Why are you so calm?"

"Because I'm not the one who wants the Crux throne."

Drin stared, mouth open. Not sure what to say. Startled by his response. Then she laughed, and she couldn't stop laughing. All the pressure that she had been feeling, all the tension, all the fear, released from deep within her belly.

"Better?"

"Better," she confirmed once she was down to a low chuckle.

"Good. Glad I could help."

She smiled wryly, shaking her head. He had a way of making her feel that she wasn't quite sure what to make of -- at ease one moment, on edge the next; thankfully now the former -- so she decided not to put a lot of effort into doing so. Not yet. Not unless they survived what came next.

More relaxed, she examined the well-kept shop, her eyes scanning the hundreds, more like thousands, of titles all around her.

Upon leaving the City Above, Mikel had led Drin to his bookshop in the belly of the Crux. Empty because of the late hour.

She had noted the quality of the texts as she walked down the main aisle, just as good as what she could find in some of the shops closer to the Royal Ring. And here in the back the shelves and tables all around them were covered in books. All assiduously catalogued.

"I never took you for the owner of a bookshop. It seems a bit staid compared to all of your other endeavors."

Mikel didn't bite. "I cannot live without books."

"You came up with that?" she asked with a raised eyebrow.

"No. I read it somewhere," he said with a grin. "So I took it. Just as I would with some of my other endeavors."

"I deserved that," Drin acknowledged with a quiet snort.

"You did."

"So what is this place?" She motioned with her hand to all that was around her. The comfortable chairs, carpets, and lamps gave the space an inviting warmth, making her think that he spent a good bit of time down here. It was an excellent location to hide away when you needed some time to yourself. Or when you were being hunted by your enemies.

"A shop, yes, but primarily storage for my other bookshop in the City Above. I can't put everything on the shelves. The more valuable items are by request only, so I keep those books and scrolls down here."

She shouldn't have been surprised. Though it seemed that after connecting with Mikel, each encounter brought her something new and unexpected. And the fact that he owned a bookshop wasn't even the biggest revelation he had offered her that night.

The City Below.

She had only heard of it.

Whispers, no more.

Always having the desire but never the chance to find some way to explore what was said to lie within the Crux.

Walking through that door in the seawall had opened her eyes. No more than a hundred yards beyond, through a rough-cut passageway with pointed stalactites reaching down from the ceiling, they had come to a steel door that already was opening for them. Teddy leading the procession.

She was astounded by what greeted her. The monstrous cavern extended off into the gloom. Illuminated by the thousands of lanterns hanging down from chains fixed to the huge stalactites above. The noise of the people moving to and fro within the underground space creating an inviting buzz that confirmed for her that the small metropolis was just as vibrant as the one above.

A web of tunnels, ladders, walkways, and bridges connected homes and businesses built from wood or carved out of the caves, all painted in bright colors that caught the light. Elevators reached deeper down into the dormant volcano to the many levels that extended below.

Looking over one of the railings in search of the bottom, Drin marveled at the colors, the energy, and the prosperity.

What really took her breath away was the engineering integrated into the City Below's design. The aqueducts and massive drains and sluices the most obvious examples.

Truly remarkable. The people living within the Crux did not have to worry about the flooding that occurred above. When the Churn breached the seawall, the excess floodwater would be carried away and have no effect on these people's lives. And she was absolutely certain that her family as rulers of the Crux had nothing to do with it. She would have known otherwise.

That realization unleashed a host of questions. The most prominent being, who had done all this work?

But she didn't have the time to ask. Struggling to control her curiosity, she held her tongue as Teddy guided them quickly through the crowd until they reached the bookshop, which, though it wasn't too far away, still took a good bit of time.

All along the way the people living here nodded to Mikel, murmured a few kind words, even bowed their heads in respect. Mikel always offered a kind word in return, never failing to stop and provide a few sweets hidden in his pockets whenever the groups of children running and climbing through the streets surrounded him.

What she saw didn't match what she had heard about the King of the Underworld. At least not entirely.

Mikel exercised a great deal of power in the Crux. That much was obvious. Yet it appeared to be based more on trust and respect rather than fear or the threat of punishment for failing to obey.

The image that he had crafted for himself, at least in certain circles, was at odds with how he presented himself here. A strange contradiction that intrigued her.

Then again, she had not yet seen him in circumstances that might require him to adhere more closely to the persona put forward in the City Above. And she had no doubt that he could adhere to the image and reputation of the King of the Underworld if required to do so.

"Why the interest in books?" She leaned forward, lifting her hands as a way of apology. "I'm not trying to insult you. I'm just naturally inquisitive."

"No offense taken." Drin's worry amused Mikel. "The woman who raised me taught me to read at an early age. The only way she'd let me stay up late is if I had a book open. It was my favorite time of the day."

Drin smiled. "The chance to escape."

"Exactly," Mikel nodded. "I couldn't escape physically from the world that surrounded us. But I could mentally. So I relished those opportunities."

Before Drin could ask her next question, curious as to what he might be referring, a sharp voice cut her off.

"This is her?"

Drin turned, taking in the young woman standing behind her. Pretty. And clearly not pleased that Drin was there based on her frown and the hard set of her features.

"Be nice, Nat. This is the Queen Heir."

"I'll try to keep that in mind," Nat growled unconvincingly.

Having no desire to deal with Nat's bad mood or the tension between her and the Queen Heir, and feeling the urge to get moving himself, understanding that time was of the essence just as the Queen Heir noted, Mikel pushed himself up from his chair.

"Celindria Dengannon, this is Natalya. Nat to her friends. She'll be staying with you while Teddy and I are out and about."

Drin reached over quickly and grasped Mikel's forearm, holding him in place. "Out and about where?"

"Like we discussed, we need good information to make good decisions. The best information is the information Teddy and I can dig up."

Mikel pulled away from Drin gently, heading for the front of the shop.

"I'm going with you, of course."

"No, you're not. That's why Nat is here."

"To keep an eye on me," Drin accused.

"Putting it bluntly ... yes." Mikel gave Drin a broad smile.

"I have every right to go with you. You can't keep me here."

"I'm not keeping you here, Queen Heir," Mikel replied, hoping that his use of her formal title might snap some sense into her. "You can go anytime you want. But not with Teddy and me."

"Why can't I ..."

"It's not safe, Celindria," Mikel said in a softer tone. "For you and for us if we're caught with you. Until we know what's going on up above. Once we have a better picture, we can discuss next steps that make sense."

Drin sighed, unable to argue with his logic no matter how much she wanted to. "It's not good that I'm not seen. That can damage my prospects just as much as my being taken across the Splintered Bridge."

"I won't argue the point."

Drin closed her eyes, nodding reluctantly, understanding that she wouldn't be able to budge him. She was smiling when she opened her eyes again. Although it wasn't a warm smile. "You're doing it again."

"Doing what?" Mikel asked innocently.

"Using me as bait."

"Not you specifically," he replied with a shrug. "Just the fact that you're not in the Citadel and no one knows where you are."

"You're still using me."

"I am."

"Is he always this honest?"

Nat frowned and nodded, not expecting the Queen Heir to engage her in conversation. "He is. It'll cost him in the end."

"Probably," Drin agreed. She turned her attention back to Mikel. "You want to see what happens in my absence."

"I do," Mikel confirmed.

"You'll be gone how long?"

"Back by dinner," he answered with a broad grin, almost as if they were a family, Mikel wanting the food to be warm when she put it on the table.

Drin nodded as if she were giving him permission. A small but noticeable attempt to exercise some of the authority that she was accustomed to. "Back by dinner."

"I wasn't asking for your approval, Queen Heir."

"And yet I was giving it to you," she replied with a self-satisfied smile.

Mikel looked at Nat. "What are you grinning about?"

"I'm beginning to like her."

29

LAY OF THE LAND

"You all right?"

"What?" Mikel asked.

"You all right?" Teddy asked again.

He nodded. "I'm fine."

"You sure?"

"I'm sure," Mikel confirmed, his voice taking on a keener edge.

"Because it looked to me like you were lost." Teddy lifted an eyebrow, clearly not convinced by Mikel's claim.

Mikel snorted softly. "You trying to get under my skin or are you bored?"

"A little of both."

"Perhaps a little more focus?"

Teddy shrugged. "I'm always focused. You just don't want to answer my question honestly."

"I don't want to answer your question at all," Mikel said as he and Teddy walked through the backstreets of Innsbruck's Seventh Ring. Sticking to the shadows. Both of them wary. Sensing how the mood of the city had changed during the night. And not for the better.

"Because you're lost."

"Teddy, now's not the time," Mikel stated a bit more sharply. He knew what his friend was pushing toward. He really had no desire to go there.

"You can't ignore this, Mikel."

"I'm not. I'm just trying to focus on what's directly in front of us."

"And you don't think what's causing you to feel lost connects to what's directly in front of us?"

Mikel and Teddy had spent the last few hours working their sources, seeking to clarify and build on the information Teddy already had acquired and pick up anything else that could help them chart the right path through what they both anticipated would be rough seas on the Crux. Risky though it would be, they had concluded that there was only one place to go to find the answers they were seeking.

The Citadel.

"It does, Teddy, of that I have no doubt." Mikel smiled when he saw his friend's broad grin, Teddy clearly pleased that he had read him correctly. "And not lost. Just thinking."

"That can be quite dangerous," Teddy warned.

"Don't I know it," he grumbled.

He and Teddy were about to head into the belly of the beast, yet Mikel couldn't get Liria out of his head. Their brief encounter, what could have been a deadly encounter, had stuck with him. And not in a good way.

That, in itself, didn't surprise him. He just didn't understand why of all times she consumed his thoughts now.

Maybe the shock of it all was finally catching up to him.

Mikel had thought that she was dead.

He thought that he had been the one to send her to the other side.

He thought that his heart had hardened toward her, her betrayal too much to ignore.

Yet even after all that had occurred between them, he still had feelings for her.

Buried deep down.

But still there.

He didn't understand it.

And he wasn't certain that he liked it.

Then there was Celindria Dengannon.

Another complication, though this one of a different type.

What was he supposed to do about her?

He had been enjoying a good life before she forced her way into it.

That wasn't quite right, now was it?

He had allowed her into his life because he decided to help her in the Frozen Waste against the Northern Trolls.

Why had he done that?

Why hadn't he just left her to her fate?

Thanks to that decision, now he couldn't seem to be able to get away from her. And worse, why was there a small part of him that didn't want to get away from her?

He shook his head. Frustrated. Annoyed. Confused.

Ever since Liria had tried to kill him, several of these and other questions had been tormenting him. In large part because he didn't want to answer them, knowing the truth but not wanting to deal with it.

Not yet.

The time wasn't right.

Because just as he had told Teddy, he needed to focus on what was right in front of them. He could worry about Liria and Celindria Dengannon after he and Teddy completed that night's work and laid out a path that didn't lead to both their necks laid out on the headsman's block.

Mikel stopped under an awning, allowing the shadows to settle around him and Teddy, his friend right next to him. They had been making for a small butcher shop at the corner of the alley that he used from time to time when wanting to enter the Citadel unnoticed. A path into the fortress that he believed was known only to him. Apparently a mistaken assumption.

"You think they know about the tunnel?" Mikel nodded toward the handful of men loitering around the entrance to the shop. If these men were trying to fit in with the neighborhood, they were doing a terrible job of it. They were dressed a bit too well. Their clothes too well cut. Their cloaks not hiding their swords, the hilts too shiny to be those of someone who might do business in this part of the city.

"Wouldn't put it past them."

"Friend or foe?"

"Do you really want to find out?" Teddy shrugged.

"Not particularly."

Without another word, Mikel and Teddy slipped down a side street. Keeping a close eye on anyone who paid too much attention to them. Making sure they weren't being followed.

After the attack on the Queen Heir, Mikel was certain that there were soldiers guarding many of the rat's nest of tunnels that cut through the Citadel. Whether those soldiers were loyal to the Dengannons or the Hanovers didn't matter. They couldn't afford to be found out.

"This the spot?"

Mikel nodded. He had led Teddy down an alley then turned to the right, passing through a surprisingly large stable that opened to a corral before he continued through and into another barn, a few of the stable hands nodding to him in respect as they passed.

"I assume there's some trick to this?"

"There always is, isn't there?"

Mikel stopped in front of the back wall. Placing his back against the stones, he walked toward Teddy. Seven paces exactly. Then he turned to his right. Three more paces. Once there, he took two big steps backward. He then bent down, wiping away the hay that covered the floor.

"Don't worry, Lew and Roo will cover everything up once we're gone. They've done this before."

"You use this route often?"

"Only when I need to. That's why I think it will be clear."

"You wiped the records?" Teddy asked.

"What records?"

Mikel looked up and grinned. Having dug up a piece of rope that was ingeniously hidden in the wooden board beneath Mikel's feet, he pulled.

Teddy jumped back quickly, the floor giving way.

"You could have warned me," Teddy grouched.

"Where's the fun in that?"

Ignoring Teddy's scowl, believing it was only fair to have a little fun with his friend since Teddy had been pushing him on topics he had no desire to discuss, Mikel carefully climbed down the steps that were revealed.

Teddy followed. Once they were at the bottom, Mikel pushed in on a small knob set in the wall, the floor closing above them.

"Where will this take us?" Teddy asked, lighting with flint and steel the oil lantern that Mikel handed to him.

"You'll see."

"You just have to be mysterious, don't you? You can't help yourself."

"One of the small pleasures in life," Mikel admitted.

For the next hour, Mikel led Teddy through the walls of the Citadel. He took his time. Believing that the way would be clear. But preferring caution until his hope was confirmed.

He stopped when he reached the alcove carved out of the passageway, small streaks of light shining through slits cut into the stone at an angle that illuminated the floor and allowed them to hear what was being said on the other side as if they were in the chamber as well.

Mikel put a finger to his lips, then nodded.

The throne room was on the other side.

"You don't want to acknowledge the truth. I understand that. But you can't ignore ..."

"I can ignore whatever I choose to ignore, Hanover." The Battle Lord's voice was brittle, sounding like steel scraping across stone. He wasn't pleased with the topic of the conversation, and he cared even less for the person he was speaking to.

"Henri, don't allow your emotions to ..."

"You presume too much, Hanover. You will address me as the Battle Lord or as Lord Dengannon. Do you understand?"

A long silence followed. Lucius Hanover frowned, eyes narrowing. Forgetting for just a moment that all wasn't yet as he wanted it to be. Beginning to understand that one of the obstacles to making that happen was standing before him. Even more, fighting to control the rage roiling in his gut, unable to recall the last time anyone, even the Battle Lord's late brother, had spoken to him in such a way.

"Of course ... Lord Dengannon." Hanover offered the Battle Lord a slight nod of apology. "I did not mean to insult you."

"That remains up for debate."

Hanover ignored the Battle Lord's challenge. "The Coronation can no longer be delayed, Lord Dengannon. We do not have the time."

"Of course it can continue to be delayed, Hanover," Dengannon growled. "It will be delayed. The Queen Heir must be found and returned safely to the Citadel."

Hanover nodded with a false understanding, then offered the Battle Lord a supercilious smile. "I'm sorry, Lord Dengannon. But I am here today wearing many hats. Primarily as a man desperately worried about the woman he loves."

Henri Dengannon's face somehow tightened even more at Hanover's statement, not believing a word that left the scheming highborn's mouth. Though he kept his mouth shut. He knew that what he wanted to say would do him little good and only aggravate what was a difficult and delicate situation.

"But also as a representative of the First Families. We have not seen or heard from Celindria since that dreadful attack earlier this evening. We have not located her within the Citadel, despite a thorough search of the keep's many tunnels. She could have been taken without our knowledge. She could be dead ..."

"She is not dead," the Battle Lord rebutted with absolute confidence. He was certain that she wouldn't have gone without a fight, and from what he had seen upon examining her suite and then piecing together the stories told by the soldiers who fought against Dragoran's raiders, he believed that there was a good chance that she had gained aid from an unexpected source. Although he would keep that possibility to himself for the time being.

"We hope that she is not dead," Hanover said with a commiserating nod. "I can't bear the thought of anything happening to Celindria. She was so vibrant. She was so beautiful."

So useful to your purposes, the Battle Lord could have added, though he kept that to himself. "Is."

"I'm sorry?"

"Is. You said was." The Battle Lord's eyes blazed fiercely. "My niece is not dead, Hanover."

"Yes, of course," Hanover agreed, giving Dengannon a self-deprecating smile. "My mistake. My emotions are threatening to get the better of me. I just can't stand to think of her ..."

The Battle Lord stood solid as a stone in front of Hanover, his expression darkening. He was a fighter. He always had been. He had no time and no patience for the politics and machinations of the Crux court and the First Families.

Yet there was little that he could do about the wheels that Hanover had set in motion. And he could only push so far with all that was in flux. So best to allow Hanover to say what he wanted to say despite most of it being fictitious prattle so that Dengannon could get on to the more important task of finding his niece.

"Still, we must be realistic," Hanover continued, "and that is why the First Families have asked that I speak with you. To protect the Crux, the Coronation must take place as swiftly as possible."

"Is that so?" The Battle Lord smiled thinly. He always had been aware of Hanover's greed and ambition. Right then, it was being put on full display.

"Isn't it, Lord Dengannon? The needs of the Crux must come first. Always. We must have stability. We must have firm rule. Especially in these difficult times."

"I desire only to serve. Agreed." Henri's hands rested on his belt, closer to the hilts of his dagger and sword. His expression darkening. "And you're the one to provide that stability with my niece in danger?"

"That will be for the Council to decide, Lord Dengannon."

"The Council is in your pocket, Hanover."

"The Council members act independently, Lord Dengannon. They will decide what is best for the Crux in Celindria's absence," Lucius clarified quickly, the Battle Lord making him nervous. "What we hope is just an absence."

At that moment, Henri Dengannon's driving desire was to slide his dagger through Hanover's throat. He restrained himself, if only barely. "Very convenient for you, Hanover."

Lucius smiled then, beginning to lose patience with the Battle Lord. The man held a great deal of power within the Crux. Until the Coronation. At which point the Dengannons would be nothing more than a footnote in history ... and Henri Dengannon would be fair game.

"It is not a matter of convenience, Lord Dengannon. It is a matter of necessity."

"Necessity? You're going to use the excuse of ..."

"It's not an excuse, Lord Dengannon. It's a necessity." Lucius stepped in closer to the Battle Lord. Wanting to demonstrate that the hardened military man didn't frighten him. Dengannon's lips curling into a smirk as the distance closed between them angering Lucius. That wasn't the response that he was looking for. "The First Families all agree. We all hope that Celindria is alive and well. But we can't rely on hope. Not with all that is at stake."

"For you, you mean?"

Lucius ignored Dengannon's challenge, although behind the mask his guts churned. "For all of us, Dengannon. We cannot delay with Malor Dragoran pushing at the boundaries of the Crux. The risk is too great."

"Malor Dragoran will not cross the Splintered Bridge, Hanover. I pledge my life to that."

"Let's hope you don't need to make that sacrifice, Lord Dengannon. However, I do appreciate your fervor and your loyalty to the Crux. And I will hold you to your word." Lucius was pleased to see the creases around the Battle Lord's eyes tighten. His poorly veiled barb striking home. "But we cannot trust in hope. We can only trust in ourselves. We must have a ruler on the throne who can stand up to Dragoran, because Malor Dragoran will not wait. He will take advantage of our weakness."

The Battle Lord didn't miss Hanover's implication that

Celindria was not the person best suited to oppose the King of the Tor.

"We must have a ruler on the throne so that Dragoran cannot work from within the Crux to take it for himself."

Dengannon worked hard not to snort at Hanover's last statement, because he had no doubt that Dragoran's strategy in that regard already was well underway. In fact, perhaps right at that moment. Right before his eyes.

"We cannot allow Dragoran to attack the Crux directly," Hanover finished, speaking in a deeper tone. A tone he had been practicing for when he ascended to the throne.

"His attack with raiders on Celindria here in the Citadel isn't direct enough for you, Hanover?" Dengannon didn't bother to ask Hanover how it was that so many raiders had made it into the city undetected. He already had a good sense as to what happened, and he knew how to confirm his suspicions.

"It is a cause for war, Dengannon. I fully admit that. But we cannot afford a war. Not until we have someone on the throne who can stand up to Malor Dragoran. Not until we have someone on the throne the people of the Crux support and trust."

"And you believe that you're that ruler, Hanover?" The Battle Lord almost barked the words out in a laugh. But he couldn't, because what Hanover was suggesting regarding his niece soured his stomach.

"I do." Hanover ignored the slight, then gave his conceit free rein. "But only because we lost Celindria. Besides, none of the other First Families can do as I can."

"That can be taken many ways, Hanover. Many of them not good."

"Now is not the time for humor, Lord Dengannon."

"It's not," the Battle Lord agreed. "It's also not the time for greed."

"You make a heavy charge, Lord Dengannon." Lucius' hand went to the dagger on his belt, his eyes flashing with an angry fire.

The Battle Lord ignored him. If Hanover pulled the blade, he'd kill the upstart without a second thought. Not caring about the consequences. Actually relishing the opportunity that Hanover might so foolishly present to him. "The truth can hurt, Hanover. You should know that by now."

Lucius struggled to control his temper. Eyes locked onto Dengannon's. He glanced down. The Battle Lord already had his hand wrapped around the hilt of his dagger. Quickly calculating the odds of success, he decided that it was best not to take the risk. So he moved his hand away from his weapon. "We need to appear strong, Lord Dengannon. Prepared. That means a ruler who can stand up to Malor Dragoran. I can do that. No one else from the First Families can."

"We don't know that my niece is dead, Hanover. You overstep."

"We don't, you're right," Lucius confirmed, "and I'm pleased to admit that. It gives me hope for her safe return." His cold eyes filled with avarice argued against his words. "But based on the assassins that we found dead in her suite as well as those in other locations around the city ..." Lucius didn't feel the need to complete his thought.

"You can make your argument in front of the Council tomorrow." The Battle Lord had tired of the conversation and wanted to shift his focus to more immediate matters. The first, of course, determining where his niece could be. "They will decide."

"They already have, Lord Dengannon."

Henri's face became a thundercloud. He had been so consumed by his fears regarding his niece that he had not paid close enough attention to the schemes already in play.

The Council decided the Succession.

Once that was done, the Coronation was no more than a formality.

And as soon as Drin disappeared, the sand started flowing through the hourglass. Hanover taking full advantage.

"You've wanted this all along," the Battle Lord accused.

"With Celindria at my side, Battle Lord. Without her, the Council must do what is required. You know that just as well as I do."

"YOU'RE NOT SURPRISED?" Teddy asked. He already knew the answer, but he wanted to hear it from Mikel anyway.

"No, I'm not surprised." He and Teddy had assumed that Hanover had a hand in how the Tor soldiers crossed to the Crux. Everything that they had just heard simply confirmed their belief that he was an active participant in the plot, the grasping bastard allying himself to the greatest threat to the Crux.

"Now it's just a matter of what we do."

Mikel nodded. "It is."

"We're already involved in this," Teddy stated. And they were. That truth held ramifications for them and their business interests on the Crux as well as on the Tor.

"We are."

"The question is how much more involved we want to become."

"That's one of the questions," Mikel agreed.

They were heading back through Innsbruck on a roundabout route, making for The Fox's Lair first and then to the City Below. They were taking their time as they worked their way down the city's rings. Wanting to ensure they weren't being followed. Leaving anyone who might be so foolish as to do so to Mikel's trackers, who were keeping an eye out for just such a tail.

Mikel smiled briefly, amused. There was a great deal that he needed to decide, yet in that moment he found it funny that his primary thought was that he would be back by dinner, just as the Queen Heir required.

He assumed that this was what having a family might be like. He didn't have much experience with that. Not since Kaduna gave her life for his.

Yet for some reason he didn't quite understand, the thought of sitting down to eat with the Queen Heir appealed to him. Despite her unique ability to aggravate him, whether because of her high and mighty behavior or her expectation that he would follow her lead in all things.

He decided that he would allow her this small victory. He had used her as bait after all ... twice. So it was only fair.

"What are you thinking?" Teddy asked.

Mikel stayed quiet for a few hundred yards, eyes sweeping all around them, not catching anyone or anything that gave him cause for concern, before replying with a shrug. "Business is business and politics is politics."

"Is it though?" Teddy's tone carried the whiff of a challenge.

Mikel sighed, then smiled. His friend had him. If he couldn't convince Teddy, then there was no way that he could convince himself. "In this case, no, it's not."

"What are you thinking, Mikel?" Teddy asked again. He could tell that the wheels were turning in his friend's calculating mind. Mikel considering various schemes and strategies, taking into account risks, opportunities, and potential results, both good and bad.

"It's all been a bit too easy."

"Easy?" Teddy frowned. "It wasn't easy finding the Tor soldiers. And we didn't catch them all."

"No, it wasn't, and we didn't. You're right about that. Maybe easy isn't the right term. Maybe the better word is straightforward."

Teddy took a moment to consider what his friend was suggesting. "The King of the Tor isn't known for making things simple, now is he?"

"He isn't," Mikel agreed. Based on their business dealings on the Tor, some of them with the Crown, he had learned that things weren't always what they seemed in that Kingdom. Even when the terms were set out in an airtight contract. "Dragoran has more than one play going."

"What makes you say that?"

"It's what I would do. With all that's at stake, I'd want to enhance my chances of success."

"Then what ..." Teddy smiled, nodding slowly as it came to him. "Kidnap the Queen Heir to gain a say in the Crux Coronation." A simple play. But Mikel was right. There was more than one strategy at work. "Holding her might not be enough. Marrying her might be required. He could decide that once the dust settles."

"But Hanover wants the throne, and he has the means to take it, whether or not he has the Queen Heir at his side."

"And there's no guarantee that the First Families would allow the Queen Heir's claim to go forward regardless because of Hanover's maneuvering," Teddy nodded. Games within games. "So Dragoran is really just trying to keep her out of the picture until he sees how events play out on the Crux once Hanover makes his claim."

"Correct. The Queen Heir is a chip to be played when the time is right. No more than that. Dragoran wants to see if the horse he is backing can make it to the Coronation."

"And if Hanover does, Dragoran's got a patsy doing his work for him," Teddy concluded with a small smile, having no choice but to appreciate the nuance of the scheme. "In time, he gains what he wants. Hanover is weaker than the Queen Heir would be and in his thrall. With Hanover on the throne, Dragoran's chances of bringing the Crux back together with the Tor improve." Teddy nodded thoughtfully. "Hanover is just arrogant enough to give Dragoran the access he wants to the Splintered Bridge. Once he does, Hanover has signed his own death warrant, though he likely won't realize it until he feels the steel at his throat."

"And if his patsy doesn't take the throne ..." Mikel prompted.

"Dragoran ensures no one does while keeping Celindria Dengannon under wraps."

"A weakened Crux improves his odds as well. For the First Families, it will come down to power and influence. They all have interests on the Tor as well. If they gain more with Dragoran than they do supporting the Queen Heir, then it's an easy decision for them to make."

"You have to give Dragoran credit."

"You do," Mikel agreed.

"He has multiple plays going just as you said."

"That he does."

"So what do we do?"

"The more plays, the more opportunities to throw a few obstacles in his way to trip him up," Mikel said, The Fox's Lair coming into view just a few blocks down the street.

"Where do you want to start?" Teddy's smile changed, becoming more dastardly. Clearly, he was looking forward to the next act in the performance. This was the kind of work that he enjoyed the most.

"We deal with Dragoran's patsy. That will take most of the King of the Tor's options off the board."

"And you have a plan for doing that?"

"I do," Mikel confirmed with a sharp nod. "When we get

back, grab your spectacles and find Nat. I need you two to do some research for me."

"Into what?"

"House Hanover."

"What do you want to know?"

"How to hurt them," Mikel replied with a wicked grin. "Badly."

30

MORE THAN JUST NUMBERS

"What are you doing?" Drin peered over Nat's shoulder. She was tired of reading. Even more, she was tired of waiting. Although Mikel still had a few more hours before she expected him to return. Intensely curious as to whether he would keep his promise and not sure why it was so important to her that he did.

"Reconciling the accounts." Nat didn't look up as she scribbled in a large notebook, matching various bills and statements to the line items and then adjusting the numbers as appropriate.

"The accounts?" Nat couldn't be more than fifteen, yet Mikel trusted her with his books? Drin found that hard to believe. "To Mikel's businesses? Really?"

"That and other entities," Nat murmured, tongue between her teeth as she worked through several calculations then checked her work. "Teddy will go over everything to make sure I didn't make a mistake."

"What do you mean other entities?"

Nat leaned back, forcing Drin to move. The Queen Heir

stepped to the side and then sat down next to Mikel's apprentice bookkeeper.

"I'm trying to work." Although Nat really didn't mind the break. Her hand was beginning to cramp, and she wriggled her fingers to loosen them. She just didn't want the Queen Heir to think that she did. "That's hard to do with all your questions."

Rather than getting testy at being spoken to in such a way, Drin smiled. Amused. Clearly the young woman didn't care who Drin was. Just as Mikel didn't seem to care. And clearly the young woman had taken on several of Mikel's characteristics while working with him.

"My apologies. It's just that I'm curious."

"You're bored," Nat corrected.

"That too," Drin admitted.

"Why are you so curious about Mikel?"

"Because until just a few days ago I had no idea who he was. And since then I've spent more time with him than with anyone else. I find him ..." Drin shrugged, not certain how to say what she wanted to say.

Nat's eyes tightened, her gaze becoming more discriminating. Challenging too. "You're interested in him."

Drin leaned back, startled. "I'm not interested in him. I find him perplexing."

Nat smiled, refusing to be put off. She knew what the Queen Heir's much-too-quick reply meant. "You are. It's obvious."

Drin leaned forward, crossing her arms and resting her elbows on her thighs. Nat was sharp and much too observant. She could understand why Mikel trusted her with such important work. She didn't miss a thing. "I'm not interested in him. I'm interested in who he is."

Nat didn't reply right away. Finally deciding to allow the lie. "You think Mikel can help you gain the throne."

"Mikel has already helped me," Drin replied. "Several

times, in fact. But he can't help me gain the throne. That's something I need to do on my own."

"Because if you don't do it on your own the First Families will view you as weak."

"Exactly," Drin confirmed.

"You do realize, I hope, that after all the time you've spent with Mikel he likely could help you in ways that would not make you appear weak in front of the First Families."

"I'm well aware," Drin replied swiftly. Because she had indeed thought of that, concluding that was a path to be avoided if at all possible. Not wanting to be indebted to him or anyone else. "I'd still prefer to gain the throne on my own if I can."

"You should give more consideration to that." Nat never had much use for authority. That might even be what had gotten her in trouble in the first place, although she had little desire to think about that now.

Of course, the decisions Nat had made led her here. To a place where she felt comfortable and safe. So though her path may have been winding and painful, she had found a home.

And despite her ingrained aversion, no matter how much she wanted to dislike the Queen Heir, she couldn't. Rather than continue to be difficult, she decided to explain how Mikel not only owned a great many of his own businesses in Innsbruck, but also how he supported a variety of other businesses throughout the city. Just a broad brush, however. She'd keep the details to herself.

Listening raptly as Nat answered her many questions, Drin was shocked to discover just how deeply Mikel's fingers reached into the city and the Kingdom. It seemed that if he didn't own a business outright, then he had a partial interest in every major business on the Crux. Thanks to that diversification, Mikel was in a much better position to negotiate and manipulate the Kingdom's economy than any of the First Families.

Impressive. Also concerning. Because it meant that Mikel was uniquely positioned to exert pressure in places and ways that no one else could. Not even her.

"How does Mikel select the businesses he supports?" Drin was more than just a little curious. She assumed that there was a method to his madness.

"They have to be family run, of course. That's the first factor. And there are several more variables Mikel will review after that. At the top of the list is whether the employees can earn a stake in the business. If they can, that increases the likelihood that Mikel will invest."

"Smart."

"More than smart," Nat clarified. "Essential. It's the only way to ensure that these businesses have a good foundation and that they won't fall within the orbit of one of the First Families."

"Definitely something to be avoided." Drin knew how most of the First Families managed their economic endeavors, their workers no more than another cost. Necessary but expendable if it meant a higher profit.

"And based on the books, Mikel is making money. But he's making money so that he can invest back into those businesses to ensure that the people he's working with can make money as well."

"How so?"

"Mikel never takes a profit. He always puts what he earned from a business back into that business so that business will continue to grow and prosper."

"Which ensures that those families and the people working with them, the people who also have a stake in those businesses, grow and prosper as well."

"Exactly," Nat confirmed. "It's a good model."

"Remarkable," Drin murmured, although she really shouldn't have been surprised. Because if she had learned nothing else about Mikel in the last few days, it was that he was full of surprises. "And how is it that you came to work for Mikel?"

"Why do you want to know?" Nat's natural caution returned in an instant in the form of her abrasiveness, not liking it when people pried into her prior life.

"Just curious," Drin replied, lifting her hands to apologize. Not smiling. Knowing that doing so would likely make the young woman even more prickly than she already was. She attempted to mollify Nat, though she wasn't certain that she could. "From what you just said, Mikel is very selective with respect to the businesses he invests in. I assume that he is just as selective in the people he chooses to work with."

Instead of snapping at the Queen Heir, Nat thought about what she said. She didn't want to be, but Nat was pleased. Because the Queen Heir was complimenting her. "I got lucky." Nat offered a barebones explanation as to what happened, having no desire to share the most intimate and painful details of her life with a woman she barely knew and she had yet to decide was a friend, a foe, or something in between.

"Tough on the outside but a man with a soft heart," Drin murmured.

"Stay away from Mikel's heart," Nat warned. "If you hurt him, I hurt you. Do we understand one another?"

Drin studied the young woman, recognizing the strength in her. The determination. Even more, her loyalty to the man who had given her an opportunity for a better life. "We do. You have nothing to fear in that regard."

Nat nodded, then began to turn back to her work. Drin's next question delayed her.

"Why does Mikel do all this? Why is he helping so many people?"

"You'd have to ask him."

"I'm asking you." Drin said it without the commanding tone she might have used in another situation.

"Because he believes that what's good for the people of Innsbruck is good for him." Nat shrugged. "He hasn't said as much, but that's what I see. And I should know. Because all the other people I've come into contact with in this city are in it for themselves."

"Including the crime?" Fearing that the young woman might choose to end the conversation if she didn't like the direction it was going, Drin didn't ask her next question in a challenging way.

Nevertheless, Drin couldn't afford to forget that despite all the good that Mikel had done for the people living on the Crux, he had earned the title King of the Underworld, and that could only have been accomplished through more illegitimate and nefarious means. Thankfully, Nat didn't take it as such.

"It's just another form of business," Nat said with a shrug, as if the question wasn't worth her time. "Besides, Mikel regulates all that happens in the shadows of Innsbruck. Without him at the controls, it would be much worse."

"What do you mean?" Drin needed further clarification, because she didn't understand what Nat was implying.

"There are rules in business," Nat began.

"There are."

"There are also rules in the criminal underworld."

Drin leaned back then, nodding sagely now that she understood. She should have assumed as much. "If someone breaks these rules?"

"Then Mikel breaks them."

Drin expected just such a response. Mikel governed the criminal underworld wearing a velvet glove, a steel gauntlet beneath. "Would you like to take a break?"

"A break?" Nat didn't understand. "Haven't I been? I still have a great deal more to do."

A small ball of blazing white energy appeared just above Drin's palm, the Talent dancing from one finger to the next.

Nat's eyes widened first in alarm, then in delight.

"I can sense the Talent in you. Untamed for the most part. I thought you might care for a lesson. Think of it as a small payment for your time and knowledge."

31

HEAVY NEWS

"Thank you for taking the time to teach Nat. When she was telling me about what you showed her, she was quite excited. And that was nice to see, because she's usually too serious."

Mikel and Drin pushed their dishes out of the way once they finished their dinner. It hadn't been a heavy meal, a vegetable soup, which Drin viewed as a good thing. She needed to be able to think. To move. Because time was running out. She could feel it. An ache in her bones.

Even so, she needed to be patient as well despite the urgency tugging at her. She sensed that she couldn't push Mikel. He did things in his own time. Any attempt she made to use her rank and title against him would likely cause him to dig in, if only to demonstrate how obstinate he could be. And she couldn't afford any additional and unnecessary delays. Not with all that could be happening in the City Above.

"That's good to hear," Drin replied. Desperate to talk about matters more relevant to her current circumstances. At the same time understanding the value of radiating a calm and a certainty that she wasn't feeling. Another lesson learned from her father. Just because she wasn't in control didn't mean she couldn't make others think that she was. Especially since the next few minutes of conversation with the King of the Underworld likely would prove crucial to her cause. "Because at first I thought she was just as likely to stab me as she was to talk to me."

"A fair assumption."

Drin snorted out a soft laugh. Not forced, even though her thoughts still focused on her primary concern. "Nat told me a bit about how she came to work for you."

"Not an uncommon story unfortunately."

"You helping her how you have is uncommon."

Mikel shrugged. "Perhaps. That's for someone else to decide. I meant the circumstances in which I found her. There are many more just like her on the Crux. Forced into situations from which they can't escape."

"And you plan to help those who you can?"

Mikel offered Drin a sad smile. "I'll help those who I can, yes. But I won't be able to help them all."

Drin nodded, brow furrowing, beginning to understand that she was engaging more in a negotiation than a conversation. "Perhaps I could help you with that."

"Once you take the throne you mean." Mikel's eyes narrowed, anticipating the proposal.

"Once I take the throne," Drin confirmed with another nod. She studied Mikel. Waiting. Hoping. She had strung out her lure, offering him a chance to bite, but he hadn't taken it. So she decided on a new approach. "Nat has a lot to learn. She's strong and she's raw. She needs more instruction."

"She's getting it." Mikel had to give the Queen Heir credit. Her second snare in just as many seconds. He had no doubt that she was less than pleased that her lures had yet to draw him in, but he was impressed by how well she concealed her disappointment.

"You have a Magus teaching her?" Drin found that surprising, her aggravation at failing to reel Mikel in forgotten for just a moment. She wasn't aware of any other Magii living in the city. Then again, as she had learned, and much to her regret, there was a great deal happening in her city about which she knew very little.

Mikel smiled. "Only a Magus can teach a Magus."

"Why are you always so cryptic and annoying?"

"You're welcome," Mikel replied, giving her a lift of his eyebrows and a wink that made her smile.

Drin shook her head in mock frustration. "Nat is quite strong in the Talent."

"You can sense that?"

"That and other things," Drin confirmed.

"What do you mean by other things?" He was well aware that certain Magii had skills that were unique to them.

"There are times when I can see the truth," Drin stated without a hint of emotion. She was searching for another way to pull him in, and she hoped this might work, introducing a topic that she rarely talked about. Knowing how it could make some people uncomfortable.

"You mean you know when someone is lying?" Mikel asked, seeking clarification.

Drin shook her head. "It goes deeper than that."

"How so?" Mikel leaned forward then, placing his forearms on the table and clasping his hands in front of him. "And I know you're enjoying being cryptic and annoying, but I would ask that you refrain for a time so that I can understand better what you mean."

Drin snorted out another soft laugh, appreciating how Mikel sought to put her at ease. The sympathetic spark in the back of his eyes confirmed that he knew she was uncomfortable talking about this with him, yet she was still making the effort to do so. And he appreciated that.

"It's not that I can sense when someone is lying. It's that I can sense the truth in a person. I can see who they truly are."

Mikel considered that for a moment. "All the time? With every person you come into contact with? That would be more than exhausting I would think."

Drin shook her head. "No. This ability comes and goes. I don't know when it's going to hit me. It just does."

"So you can see who the person truly is. Their goals and desires. Dreams and motivation. What they truly want. What they truly hate. What they want to be. I'm assuming that's just the tip of it all."

Drin nodded. "It is, but you're going down the right path."

Mikel understood immediately how such a skill could prove useful, especially for someone sitting on the throne of the Crux. But there was another dimension to it as well. "A positive in many ways. Yet horrifying in others."

"You're right, it can be. I'm seeing the truth of the individual, and often the individual doesn't see it themselves. Often they don't want to."

"A skill such as that could come in handy in my line of work."

"You want to add me to your payroll?" Drin mused, realizing that he was making a joke and not an offer.

"Definitely not," Mikel replied. "Too dangerous. And I get the sense that you'd be a terrible employee."

Drin smiled then. "I don't know whether I should view that in a positive or negative light."

"What truth do you see when you look at me?" Mikel wanted to push the conversation farther along. Although the Queen Heir couldn't sense it, he was feeling the urgency of their present circumstances as well. Their time together, pleasant though it had been for the last hour, was rapidly coming to a close.

"As I said, it happens rarely."

Mikel didn't miss her brief hesitation. "Yes, but you've seen the truth with respect to me."

"I haven't ..." Drin began to protest.

"I can see it in your eyes. There's no point in trying to deny it."

Drin stared at Mikel for a time. Not angry at being found out. Simply examining him. Seeing more of him than anyone else likely ever had. Wondering if she could get out from his cold gaze without offering him the information he desired. Because she knew from experience what the impact could be on someone unprepared to hear what she had to say.

Then realizing just as quickly that she couldn't. That she needed to tell him if she was to have any chance at all of gaining his assistance.

"I see a man of honor and integrity. A man who values the truth. In himself and others."

"Thank you for that," Mikel replied after thinking about her admission, choosing not to question her veracity. Taking what she said as the truth and not as an attempt to blow smoke. "But that's not all."

Drin bit the inside of her lip. She should have assumed that he would find her out. She had tried to keep to herself some of what she saw, thinking she might be able to make use of it when the time was right. When she needed to give him that final nudge. Clearly that wasn't going to happen, however.

Because Mikel wouldn't give up the bone until she told him everything. And she sensed that he would be able to hear a lie just as well as she could.

"No, that's not all." Drin leaned forward then, so that she could look him in the eyes, less than a foot separating them. "I also see a power in you. One that I don't understand other than the fact that this power gives you the capacity to create or destroy. People. Cities. Maybe even kingdoms. That's all I can see." Drin frowned. Displeased that she couldn't determine any more than that. Concerned as well. Never having had such a reading before.

"That worries you?"

"It doesn't worry you?" Drin countered.

"I'll let you know once I have a chance to think about it."

Drin frowned. He wasn't telling her everything. And he hadn't been surprised when she told him what she had seen. Why? "I see something else in you as well. Do you want to know what that is?"

"No."

"Why not?" Drin was more than just slightly taken aback by his lack of interest.

"Because if I ask and you tell me than it might change my life in a way that I don't want it to. I like my life the way it is."

"You're a grouch," Drin replied, frowning. She had hoped to set another lure for him with what she had to offer, but once again he refused to take even a nibble.

"I've been accused of worse."

Drin decided to try one more time, coming at Mikel from a different angle. "You are Caledonii?"

"How could you ..." He stopped himself when he realized. She had seen the truth about him, so there was no point in trying to deny it. "I am."

"Is Stahlherz your Caledonii name?"

"No." Mikel wasn't pleased that she was able to pull his surname from him with just a look. "It's a close approximation. The Caledonii language doesn't always translate well to the common tongue."

"What does it mean? Stahlherz?"

Mikel didn't reply right away. Then he realized that there was no point in holding anything back. "Steelheart."

"That fits you well." Drin tried to add a little levity to what had become a heavy conversation. "It should be one of your nicknames."

"I have enough nicknames." His mumbled response suggested that this wasn't a topic that he wanted to discuss.

"And there's the grouch." Drin was pleased when Mikel smiled at her quip instead of snapping at her. "Wait. Steelheart. That's the name of the ..."

"That is no longer relevant to me."

Drin didn't ask her follow-up question. Clearly this was a sore subject for him, understandably so, in fact. Because he was Caledonii but not truly Caledonii. A difficult and painful position to occupy. So she let it drop. For now. "You're an enigma to me, Mikel."

"Is that a good or bad thing?"

"Right now ... bad." Drin's frown deepened. She had learned a few things about her rescuer during their conversation. But no more than that. And she didn't feel any closer to achieving her objective.

"Why do you say that?"

Drin ignored his question, having one of her own. "Why are you helping me?"

"I haven't agreed to help you yet," Mikel clarified, not wanting her to put words into his mouth.

"You have in the past," she clarified.

"I have," Mikel confirmed with a nod.

"Why?"

"Actually I'm beginning to regret helping you."

"I just proved to you that I can see the truth about you," Drin countered. "You're back to being cryptic and annoying."

"You claim to see the truth. Why so many questions? I would assume that based on this skill of yours that you know the answers before you ask them."

"Maybe I do," Drin replied, offering Mikel an enigmatic smile. "I know why you're *going* to help me."

Mikel smiled in turn, intrigued. Liking her confidence. "I can't wait to hear this."

"Because no matter how hard you try, you can't seem to avoid doing the right thing." She gave him a lift of her eyebrows and an annoyingly smug grin. "And you have a soft heart for strays and outcasts."

"Keep that to yourself," Teddy said, striding into the private dining room in The Bear's Den, Mikel's tavern in the City Below where he had taken Drin to eat. "It would be bad for business."

"That it would," Mikel agreed. "You have news?"

Teddy nodded. "The Council meets tomorrow at noon."

"To announce the Search?" Drin asked. She dreaded that next step, but she had steeled herself for it. She would do whatever was required to gain the throne.

Teddy shook his head. "No. To conduct the Coronation. They've already identified a candidate. It's unanimous."

"Hanover," Drin hissed, that sinking feeling that she had been experiencing twisting her guts into knots.

"Hanover," Teddy confirmed. "Just as we anticipated."

32

REQUEST FOR HELP

"Why would I get involved in this? Playing for power as you want me to isn't relevant to what I'm trying to do."

"You play for power every day," Drin challenged. "You know it just as well as I do."

"That may be," Mikel acknowledged, having no doubt that she would call him on his statement. Just as he intended. "Nonetheless, why should I care who has the throne? Chaos and confusion benefit me." He offered her a wink and a nod. "And I have absolutely no doubt that Hanover would be a much worse ruler than you would. Backing you could cost me a great deal of money and opportunities I wouldn't have otherwise."

"And what about all the other people living in the Kingdom of the Crux?" Drin demanded, seeking to expand her argument after having learned from Nat how Mikel invested in and worked with his community. "I understand what you're saying. I can't argue with your logic. But shouldn't you be looking out for them as well?"

"I already am," Mikel replied, his voice harder. Clearly not happy with her challenge. "Can you say the same?"

"What are you implying?"

"I'm implying nothing. I'm saying that for almost all of the time I've known you, your focus has been on the throne. Not on the people of the Crux."

"You overstep," Drin growled in an exceedingly cold voice.

"Do you deny it?" Mikel asked, not put off by her anger.

"The two are not mutually exclusive," Drin replied in a steady voice, her eyes still flashing with a white-hot anger. Not liking how Mikel questioned her intentions. Not having a good response if he chose to push her harder on the matter.

"Perhaps, yet I have not heard a single word from you bringing those two concepts together."

Drin bit her lip to keep back the sharp response on the tip of her tongue, realizing that showing nothing more than anger would only offer additional kindling to his argument. More damning, thinking back on their interactions, she couldn't dispute his claim.

Taking a few deep breaths, she settled on a calmer approach. "Consider what is happening here. Consider what could happen if Hanover ascends to the throne. Consider what could happen if I ascend to the throne as I should."

"Why should you?"

Drin opened her mouth to reply then closed it just as quickly. Her expression revealed her confusion as to why he would even ask that question. "My family has ruled the Crux for more than four hundred years. Is that not reason enough?"

"Dynasties don't last forever, Queen Heir," Mikel replied with a shrug, clearly not convinced by her argument.

"Are you trying to be annoying and cynical? Because if you are, you're succeeding." Drin snorted in disgust, angry with herself for losing her temper during this critical dialogue. But she was even angrier with Mikel. "Too much is at stake. You cannot throw away history and tradition so casually."

"I am simply stating the truth, Queen Heir. You have a claim to the throne. That's undeniable. But that doesn't guarantee that you should rule the Crux."

"Even after four centuries?" She couldn't understand why Mikel was being so recalcitrant.

"The past is the past," he said with such casual nonchalance that a shiver swept down Drin's spine, reminding her of their first meeting in the Frozen Waste. "What matters is what happens today. What happens tomorrow. And the day after that. Change can be scary. But change isn't necessarily a bad thing."

"Don't you want to ensure that the right person sits on the throne?"

"You, you mean? Again, Queen Heir, you have a claim. A strong claim. But still just a claim. You do not have a guarantee of your place despite centuries of tradition, which you know just as well as I do."

Drin closed her eyes, taking another deep breath, seeking to calm the conflicting emotions roiling through her. Recognizing that now all she could be was honest. It was her only option. "Mikel, I need you."

It was hard for Drin to get those words out. Still she did. Because she had nowhere else to turn. A man she had known for a very short time, a man with a reputation for ruling the shadowy underside of the Crux with an iron fist wrapped in velvet, a man who aggravated and surprised her on a regular basis, held her future in his hand.

"Queen Heir, please understand that ..."

"Mikel, this is not the time to hedge your bets. This is the time to pick a side." She hoped that pushing him might spur him into action. His response shocked her.

"Why?"

"Why?" Drin repeated. She couldn't believe how difficult he was being. It was easier dealing with an emissary from Malor Dragoran. "What do you mean why?"

Mikel leaned back in his chair, arms crossed. Teddy stood behind him. Both stone-faced. Both thinking the same thing.

Celindria Dengannon was used to getting her way. That was to be expected based on who she was. If she was going to survive the next few days, however, she needed to learn that expectation could kill you. She would need to think clearly and quickly. And she would need to look at the world from a different perspective. One in which her interests weren't the only interests that had to be considered.

"Why?" Mikel repeated, believing that it was a fair question. "Why do I have to support you? You could be right, but you have yet to say anything to convince me."

For several seconds, Drin didn't know how to reply. She understood that being difficult was in Mikel's nature. Nevertheless, she believed that when push came to shove he would do the right thing. Believing as well that supporting her was the right thing.

Then it struck her like a slap across the cheek.

He was right.

She hated admitting that to herself, but he was right.

She had told him what she needed from him. What she expected from him. She never considered what he might want or need from her. She never considered the possibility that this wasn't just a conversation. It was also a negotiation. And that going forward as she sought to claim the throne, that's what it was going to be. Always a negotiation.

She wasn't in a position where she could make a demand and expect to be obeyed. She was in a position where she needed to work harder for what she wanted. For what she believed was right. She was in a position where she needed to find a middle ground that worked for them both.

"You're going to support Hanover over me?" She found that possibility sickening, but she realized that she needed to approach Mikel in a different way if she was to have any chance of success. "The man cares only for himself. He cares only for what he can gain by taking the throne."

"No different than many a monarch," Mikel countered with a disinterested shrug. "Wouldn't you agree, Teddy?"

"I would," the giant standing behind Mikel's right shoulder nodded.

"No different ..." Her tone sharpened, Mikel once again knocking her off her stride. Not allowing her to build up any momentum behind her argument. "What are you suggesting?"

"I'm not suggesting anything, Queen Heir," Mikel replied in that very calm voice of his that only served to irritate her. "I'm stating that many of the people who take power do so for themselves and no one else. They don't care about the people they're responsible for. Those people no more than tools or playthings. You're absolutely right regarding Hanover. But he's a known quantity, and that's a quality that can be worked with."

"Manipulated, you mean."

Mikel smiled, ignoring her disdain. "Hanover's approach would be no different than many a monarch who came before him."

Drin leaned forward, squeezing her fingers together tightly. Straining to control the sharp emotions begging to be released. "Are you saying that my father was just like Lucius Hanover?" She could barely control the rage surging through her. Requiring some release, she smacked a palm on the table. "My father was nothing like Lucius Hanover."

"I never said he was, Queen Heir," Mikel responded in a voice just above a whisper. Not moving. Not giving any reaction at all. Except his eyes, which locked onto hers and held a gravitas that she had never seen in them before.

"Then what are you saying?" She bit off the words slowly, her tone one that would be expected if she were back in the Citadel's throne room.

Mikel didn't reply right away. He understood why she was acting this way. Why she was so on edge.

Teddy's news damaged her claim. Perhaps fatally. By setting the Coronation for tomorrow, the Council was revealing either their belief that Celindria Dengannon was dead or their lack of interest if she was still alive.

Worse, it suggested that Drin showing herself tomorrow no longer mattered. The decision was made. It would take a great deal to reverse it. Assuming, of course, that Celindria Dengannon even could make it to the Citadel without being cut down along the way by those preferring she not interfere with the transfer of power.

Mikel understood why the Council was acting as it was. Politics was nothing more than self-interest veiled in a shroud of governance.

The First Families were acting in their own best interests, just as they always did. They wanted stability. They wanted to build their power. They wanted to make money. And Hanover had promised them all that ... while also threatening them to get in line, Dragoran's club held over their heads.

But there was no point in trying to explain that to the Queen Heir, because she understood that just as well as he did. She just wasn't in the mood to hear it.

"Drin, can I speak bluntly?"

She was caught off guard by his familiarity. Mikel had never called her by her nickname. Rather than taking him to task, she permitted the transgression. "When have you ever not?"

Mikel smiled then, appreciating the subtle jab, though it didn't reach his eyes. The cold dominating. "The people of this city, the ones living well below the heights where you and the other lords and ladies of the First Families reside, don't care who sits on the throne so long as they have the capacity to live their lives as they wish. So long as they have the chance to make something of themselves. Feed their families. Stay well and stay healthy. Enjoy a future that doesn't involve those with power and privilege stepping on their necks whenever it's convenient for them to do so. It's as simple as that."

"And with me …"

"Drin, the people don't know you," Mikel cut in.

"But they know my father," she countered with absolute certainty. "And he is not a Hanover. I am not a Hanover. That should count for something."

"We do know your father. You're right. But that's not the magical elixir that you believe it to be."

"What are you saying?" Her father had been an excellent King of the Crux. One of the best to ever sit the throne.

"I'm saying that your father more often than not did what the First Families wanted. Not necessarily what was best for the people who relied upon him. That's why his problems looking down upon the Crux were so few. He never stuck his hand in the scorpion's nest."

"You have nothing with which to support that claim." She tried to sound offended, but she found it difficult. She doubted that he would raise the issue if he didn't believe there was some truth to it. The King of the Underworld shockingly honest with his assessments.

"Drin, the people of the Crux never had cause to love your father. They tolerated him. No more. He kept out of their affairs for the most part, and they appreciated that, but he certainly didn't help them when aid was required."

Drin didn't know how to reply to that. So she wracked her brain, searching for some example that put the lie to Mikel's argument. "What about after the last flood? Three years ago. Many of the neighborhoods that were destroyed in the lower rings were rebuilt in just weeks. That demonstrates a commitment that can't be ignored."

"They were," Mikel admitted. "You're right."

"My father released several million in gold from the treasury to do that. You can't just ignore that."

"He did. You're right."

Drin was confused, not understanding why Mikel was all of a sudden being so agreeable. Unless ... "Why are you looking at me like that? As if my father did nothing at all."

"Because barely a fraction of that money was used for its stated purpose."

"What are you talking about?" That couldn't be right. Her father wouldn't allow that to happen.

"Who owns the companies that would usually take on the task of rebuilding after a flood?"

Drin rattled off several names before she stopped. Realizing that she was doing nothing more than reciting most of the First Families. A cold lump of reality settled in the pit of her stomach as a result.

"They took the money, but they didn't use it as they were supposed to," Mikel explained. "They used most of it for themselves."

"How do you know that?" Drin's challenge sounded weak even to her.

"We have the records to prove it," Teddy confirmed with a sad nod. He felt some sympathy for the Queen Heir. Mikel was offering her a hard lesson. Forcing her to look at the world around her in a way that she never had before, because she never had to before. She had lived a sheltered life of a sort. Seeing what she wanted to see. Not what she needed to see.

Drin sighed, much of the energy that had been driving her now draining out of her. She felt utterly and completely exhausted. Lost as well when she realized that her world wasn't what she believed it to be. "Then how were the lower levels rebuilt so quickly?"

Teddy nodded toward Mikel.

"It was you?" Drin had a hard time believing that, failing

to keep the surprise from her voice. The money and resources required. Did he really exercise so much sway on the Crux?

Mikel shrugged, seemingly embarrassed by Teddy's admission.

"That's why everyone looks at you the way they do."

Mikel shrugged again. "In part. There are other reasons."

"You really are the King of the Underworld, aren't you? My father ruled the Citadel. You rule everything else beyond that."

"I wouldn't go that far," Mikel replied, having the good manners to appear slightly embarrassed. "Your father and I had an agreement of sorts. I stayed out of his way, and he stayed out of mine. And he did prove useful on occasion helping to derail certain plans that the First Families put in place that would have harmed my interests."

"Your interests? Not the people's interests?"

"With all due respect, Queen Heir," Teddy cut in, "I would think that by now you understand that more often than not Mikel's interests are the people's interests."

"Then why don't you take the throne?" Drin demanded, the fire back in her eyes. Thoroughly not enjoying the direction this negotiation masquerading as a conversation had taken. "Obviously, you're much better positioned to succeed than I am."

"I don't want it," Mikel replied without a second thought. "I like where I am. What I'm doing. I see no reason to change that."

"Some would argue that demonstrates a lack of ambition." Drin's edge was keener than she intended.

Mikel smiled at that. "And others would say it demonstrates a self-awareness that is lacking in most."

"I can't win with you, can I?" Drin was at her wit's end. Her efforts to convince him had failed to bear fruit, and she was out of ideas.

"Don't sell yourself short," Mikel replied very, very quietly, having little doubt that she would catch his meaning.

And Drin did. She locked eyes with Mikel, studying him once more. Her unique skill in the Talent coming into play once again. Unbidden. Revealing a new truth about him. One that gave her hope in what for her was a desperate time.

"I'm sorry," she said finally. "I didn't know my father demonstrated so little interest in all that was happening on the Crux. I didn't know what he wasn't doing and what you were doing." She reached out to him then, grasping his hands. Squeezing. Hoping that she believed him. "But I swear to you that I will put the interests of the people of the Crux before my interests and before the interests of the First Families. I will do what's right if given the chance."

"Even if it hurts?" Mikel didn't try to pull his hands free from hers.

"Even if it hurts."

33

GOING FOR A STROLL

"Do you really think this is a good idea?"

Mikel shook his head. "No."

"Yet still we're here."

"I didn't say it was a good idea," Mikel clarified, "but what we're doing is necessary."

His reply didn't fill Drin with the confidence that she so desperately sought. Because they still had a long way to go before they made it to the Citadel. And the longer it took, the greater the chance that they didn't make it there at all.

"Why is this necessary? That's one part of your plan that you failed to explain to me."

"Best for those seeking to stop you to come at you directly. It helps to avoid knives in the back."

Drin shook her head in wonder, rolling her eyes. "Bait. Again." She couldn't believe that he would do this to her for a third time. Even more that she would allow it.

"If that's how you want to look at it," Mikel replied. "There's another perspective you could adopt that might take the sting out of it."

"And that would be?"

"You're laying a trap for those seeking to trap you."

"Nicely done," Drin grunted in reply. She had to admit, there was some logic attached to his strategy that she found hard to argue against.

"I have a good idea on occasion." His eyes swept around them. His mind clearly on other matters.

"On occasion," Drin admitted, although that was as far as she was willing to go. "You really think Dragoran's soldiers are still looking for me?"

"No, I wouldn't worry about them."

"Why not? I thought there were still a few squads left in the city."

"There were," Mikel confirmed. He didn't like it any more than Drin did. Striding down the middle of the street for all to see once they emerged from the City Below, the sun still sleeping. Taking their time. Appearing to be on a stroll. Ensuring that any eyes watching for them saw them. And now standing on the stage of an open-air theater just below the Fourth Ring. Seemingly without a care in the world.

"Were?"

Mikel nodded. "We were able to root out those few who escaped the Citadel or didn't make it there in the first place. Dragoran's soldiers shouldn't be a problem any longer."

"You didn't think telling me that was important?" Drin growled. She should have been angrier with Mikel for holding back that information. But she wasn't.

Drin pulled her eyes away from Mikel and looked out over the theater. The stone benches continued all the way up to the next ring. Empty now. No one to be seen. Not a sound to be heard. No threat to worry about.

They were alone.

Yet if that was the case, why did it feel like danger stalked toward them?

Why was her skin prickling as if natural magic was in play?

"Dragoran's soldiers weren't our only concern."

"If not Dragoran's soldiers, then …"

"Sometimes it's better not to question," Mikel interrupted. "Sometimes it's just better to do. Cuts down on the over-thinking."

Before Drin thought to take him to task for offering her a lesson that she didn't want or need, and refusing to admit that she actually was going to listen to his suggestion, she gave in to her instincts.

The prickling of her skin getting worse.

Becoming almost unbearable.

Reaching for the Talent, she extended her senses out into the amphitheater. What she discovered chilled her to the bone.

"How many?"

"Five," Drin replied, fighting the fear that was rising within her.

She realized then who had come for her.

Seekers.

And Mikel had known that they would.

Mikel pulled the scimitar from the scabbard across his back, the steel glowing brightly. As soon as he did, five figures appeared in the amphitheater, coalescing out of the shadows and light.

"How did you do that?" Drin demanded, her fear momentarily forgotten.

"Do what?"

She could see the assassins plain as day, whatever magic that had been hiding them gone. And she had nothing to do with it. "You can't use the Talent."

"I can't," Mikel confirmed.

"Then how did you …"

"Perhaps we can discuss this later," Mikel suggested, nodding toward the quintet of killers just a few rows away.

Gliding toward them with an almost inhuman grace that was more than just a little unsettling.

"If there is a later." She knew just how fast these assassins could move. Her uncle had been very clear when they spoke after her father's murder, wanting to make sure that she was prepared for any peril that might come her way.

Henri had been quite specific and quite laudatory. Seekers stung faster and more frequently than a wasp.

She might kill one with the Talent. Mikel might kill another. But that would still leave three Seekers left. And all the job required was one.

"Perhaps you could slow them down for just a few seconds?" Mikel glimpsed what was playing behind Drin's eyes. The concern. But not the fear. The fear was there, because he felt it as well, yet she had managed to lock it away. That was good. That impressed him and boded well for the future.

"Slow them down? You don't want me to ..." She realized then what was happening. He was doing it to her again.

The five killers had stopped for just a heartbeat. Their purple eyes fixed on Mikel and Drin. Realizing that their prey somehow had pierced their magical illusion.

Unaffected by that discovery. Focused on their task.

Moving as one, the Seekers streaked toward Celindria Dengannon. Mikel an afterthought.

The assassins made it no farther than another row before Drin struck.

A wave of energy blasted from both her palms.

Slamming into the Seekers.

Holding them in place.

Just for a few seconds.

That was all that she could manage.

But that was all the time that Mikel required.

The instant the Seekers froze in place, several dozen archers, hidden among the pillars rising at the back of the theater, released their arrows. The sharp twang of the bowstrings sounded exceedingly loud among the silence of the columns. The archers focused on accuracy with the first shot. Then they tried to put as many arrows in play as they could.

Seekers were successful in large part because they were infused with a natural magic that enhanced their skills and abilities, such as moving faster than any person had a right to or shrugging off a strike by the Talent.

These five, all veteran assassins, reacted as they had been trained to do.

Stuck in place, they used their gift to break free from Drin's snare, the Talent that she used against them slipping off them like rain sliding off an oilskin cloak.

Drin cursed. Angry that the killers had escaped her so easily.

Still, she took some small measure of pleasure when two of the men stumbled, caught by the first flight of steel-tipped shafts.

Yet even then the wounds didn't slow them down for long. The injured assassins weaving toward Drin with their peers somehow navigated the cloud of quarrels without further injury.

Drin looked at Mikel. Worried. Yet her ally didn't appear to be concerned in the least.

She understood why just a moment later.

The stomp of boots growing louder behind her explained why he was grinning like a cat that had caught a mouse. Or in this case five lethal Seekers.

"I can't believe you did this to me again!" Although Drin had a hard time infusing her voice with the required vitriol.

Mikel shrugged and offered her a chastened look that didn't fit well on his features as his fighters rushed past him. Crashing into the Seekers. Relying on their overwhelming numbers to kill men who were used to fighting with a single swipe of their daggers and fading away before they needed to use their blade again.

"I can't believe you did this to me again," Drin repeated, though in a calmer voice.

"It wasn't that I didn't want to tell you," Mikel said.

"But ..." She needed more of an explanation than that.

"But I needed you to act naturally. I didn't think our friend would give up. He's too interested in the throne."

"So Seekers seemed like the next logical step."

Mikel nodded. "After what happened in The Fox's Lair, yes."

"You wanted to make sure we caught them all." She had to give him credit for putting in play such an effective strategy.

"Exactly."

"And did we?" Drin asked, a touch of heat still in her voice. Her adrenaline running fast through her veins.

Mikel looked out across the amphitheater. Finishing the assassins with a practiced efficiency, his fighters were moving toward the top bench, the next ring just above. Prepared to climb higher. Ready to make for the Citadel. Leaving five dead Seekers in their wake. Just as many as his sources suggested would be coming for the Queen Heir.

Nevertheless, just to make sure, he turned slowly in all directions, holding the blade in front of him. The energy running along the steel glowed dimly. Not flaring as it had when the assassins first appeared.

"I believe we did," Mikel confirmed with a satisfied nod.

Drin frowned, giving Mikel the hard look that she had practiced ever since she joined her father for the first time on the pedestal in the Citadel's throne room. Then she growled softly.

It had no effect on him whatsoever as he offered her a nod and a smile, almost as if he was congratulating her on a job well done.

She promised herself that they were going to have a long

conversation about his penchant for putting her out on a line to see what would bite, but that would have to wait.

"Where did you get that?" she asked, transfixed by the power radiating from the steel blade in his hand.

"It's a long story." Mikel had no desire to explain who he had stolen the ancient blade for and from where.

"I want to hear it."

"We'll see," Mikel replied in a noncommittal tone. "I would think that now that the path is clear, you would prefer to visit the Citadel and have a say in the Coronation."

"You're with me?" Drin asked.

"For now."

Drin smiled. That was as much of an endorsement as she could expect from him, and she was happy to take it. "What made you change your mind?"

"Who said I changed my mind?"

Drin stopped herself before she asked her next question. She knew that this was how it could be with Mikel. How hard it could be to extract information from him. And she was willing to admit, at least to herself, that there were times when she enjoyed the game they played with one another.

But she couldn't afford to do that now. Because time was short.

"They belong to you?" Drin recognized many of the men and women who eliminated the Seekers, as they also played a part in her rescue from Dragoran's soldiers only yesterday.

"No, they don't belong to me," Mikel replied, unable to resist clarifying despite the frown he earned from the Queen Heir. "They all work for me. And today they work for you as well."

"What do you mean?"

"Today, until you're back on the throne, they're the Queen's Guard."

34

FOR THE THRONE

"You have no proof, Hanover," the Battle Lord growled.

"Neither do you, Lord Dengannon," Lucius replied in as hard a voice as he could muster without losing his temper. Understanding the importance of being perceived as under control. Always. And needing to do so without ceding any ground to the Battle Lord. "Should we not assume the worst? Is that not what you would do and advise if this terrible misfortune did not affect you so directly?"

"We should assume that my niece is tougher than you're giving her credit for, Hanover. I do not believe that she is dead. I do not believe that she is taken." He bit off the words as if he were chewing on hardened leather.

Lucius Hanover sighed then shook his head ever so slightly, seeking to convey a sense of sadness and resignation. They had been having this same argument for the last quarter hour, no progress made. The representatives from the other First Families looking on. Maintaining their silence.

Haratounian. Richterious. Ascelpan. Scipio. Tadari.

All the others.

All used to power.

All used to wealth.

All used to taking advantage of weaknesses when presented with the opportunity.

All hating the fact that their weaknesses were being preyed upon in that very moment.

They sat upon their chairs set an equal distance apart from one another.

Because here, in the Council chamber, they were all supposed to be equal.

Equal in power.

Equal in rights.

It was only in the throne room that teased them just to their front, accessible through the large doors covered by a plated gold that depicted scenes from the Crux's history, that they were supposed to be reminded of their place.

Yet they felt that inequity now.

Here, in the Council Chamber, and soon in the throne room.

Because the power that they craved was unattainable.

That power would reside with Hanover.

It was a foregone conclusion.

The other First Families understood that. They did not want to accept it, but they had no choice. They were beholden to him.

The only representative from a First Family yet to fall in line was the Battle Lord.

Henri Dengannon stood in front of his chair, arms crossed, his face red with fury, doing all that he could to prevent Hanover from claiming what belonged to his niece. Demonstrating the obstinance for which he was so well known.

The First Families respected, grudgingly, what Lord Dengannon was doing. Nevertheless, they wanted to get to the reason they had been summoned.

The Coronation.

They didn't like the position they were in. Being pulled between the two most powerful Families on the Crux.

Even so, they had made their deal.

If it could be called a deal.

Since they couldn't make a claim to the throne, they wanted this done. The change in leadership was a foregone conclusion in their minds. And they had no desire to be reminded of their own failings.

However, the Battle Lord was making it difficult. Pushing the man who would soon rule the Crux.

And they could see that Lucius Hanover was tiring of the Battle Lord's challenge.

His brow furrowing. Eyes tightening. Hands clenched into fists, knuckles white.

It had been amusing at first to Lucius. He believed that the Battle Lord's efforts to delay were simply the result of his inability or lack of desire to read the room accurately.

Now, however, his stubbornness was nothing more than annoying and, in his mind, leaning toward treason.

Worse, much to Lucius' irritation, Lord Dengannon's obstinance had set off a little bell of worry in the back of his brain, making him wonder whether the Battle Lord's efforts didn't result from his lack of comprehension but rather more from some stratagem he had put in play.

Thinking about it further, Lucius scoffed at the possibility of the latter.

Henri Dengannon was a military man. He always had been. He had no time for politics or schemes or machinations. He was direct. Always. Simply an uncle worried about his niece.

Lucius realized then that's how he needed to deal with the Lord of House Dengannon. As a commanding officer addressing a subordinate. Still, his concern didn't diminish.

"And we hope that you are correct, Lord Dengannon,"

Lucius cut in, earning a scowl and a hard look for his efforts and not caring a whit. "We hope that Celindria is alive and well. But we do not know. All we know is that she is not here."

"She is not here because it is not safe for her ..."

"Time is of the essence, Lord Dengannon," Lucius interrupted again, no longer having patience for an argument that had been decided before it had even begun. "We do not have the luxury of waiting. The Coronation must take place today. As soon as possible. The First Families have said as much. And, in this chamber, the First Families' words are law."

"WHAT ARE YOU DOING HERE?" Marak demanded. The Captain of House Hanover's personal guard, who stood watch in front of the Council Chamber, was used to being obeyed. Always. Without question. By everyone. "You're supposed to be at the main gate."

"I was," Ronnie replied. The Sergeant serving in the Army of the Crux snorted, both amused and perplexed by the dandy standing before him.

Hanover's Captain was dressed in the finest fighting leathers. The hilt of his sword was encrusted with several jewels. And he wore on his head a wide-brimmed hat with a droopy brim that was quite fetching though less than practical and most definitely a hazard during a fight.

Then again, Ronnie doubted that the man had pulled the blade from his finely wrought scabbard very often, so the Captain had little to worry about. He shrugged. "Now I'm here."

Marak wasn't pleased to see the Sergeant. He was even less pleased that the Sergeant, who clearly had disobeyed his order, had brought several squads of soldiers with him. And that was making him and the score of men at his back nervous.

"We guard the higher levels of the Citadel, Sergeant," Marak explained in a voice that he might use with an unruly child. "Not you. Lord Hanover made that clear. You may return to your post. Now."

Ronnie frowned at the Captain. Marak might lead Hanover's soldiers, but he had no authority regarding the soldiers of the Crux. Just because Lucius Hanover said that he did didn't make it so. Because Lucius Hanover did not yet sit on the throne.

"Does the Battle Lord know what you're doing, Marak?"

Hanover's Captain stared daggers at the Sergeant. Not used to being challenged, and not liking it. Shocked that his order was being questioned by a man who wasn't even an officer.

"It doesn't matter what the Battle Lord knows, Sergeant." Marak took a step closer to his irritant, placing a hand on the hilt of his sword. "He won't be the Battle Lord as soon as the door behind me opens. Best that you fall in with the new way of doing things before it's too late."

"Or what?" Ronnie was a man with an affable personality. Little bothered him, which was why he was such a good soldier. The constant aggravations of living a martial life, being told what to do and when, had little impact upon him. Except when he came across arrogant upstarts who looked down on those who had devoted their lives to defending the Crux and viewed him and his men as nothing more than tools to be put into play.

"Or you and your friends will find yourselves in the cells beneath the Citadel." Marak said the words quietly and with a menace that he had practiced many a time in the mirror. Quite pleased to have the opportunity to make use of his training. Even more so that he was playing his role exactly as he believed that he should. "If the new King of the Crux is generous. If not ..." Marak left the rest unsaid, not believing that he needed to complete his threat.

"You're so certain your master will be given the throne,

are you?" Ronnie squared up to Marak, completely at his ease, as were his men. His veterans stood calmly behind him while the Captain's soldiers fidgeted and shifted from one foot to the other, the tension of the confrontation getting to them. Just like Marak, they were not used to being challenged.

"More than certain, Sergeant. The Crux throne will be Lord Hanover's in no more than a few minutes. Now clear out or we'll clear you out."

"Did you hear that, boys?" Ronnie said over his shoulder. "The dandy and his fools are going to clear us out."

Marak's face reddened, body stiffening, when laughter and guffaws erupted from behind the Sergeant.

"You will leave this place ..."

"We can't do that," Ronnie interrupted. His good humor was gone, replaced by a seriousness rarely seen on the Sergeant's usually warm and welcoming countenance. His hand on the hilt of his sword.

"Can't do that?" Marak snorted, not quite believing what he was hearing. Never having been disobeyed in this way before. Having learned to push back when placed in a situation such as this, he gave little thought to all that was in play around him. "You will do that, Sergeant. You will do it now."

"The only people leaving here will be you, Captain." Ronnie's grin was one of satisfaction when he watched Marak's expression change from an overarching conceit to fear, the Captain gulping at the touch of cold steel to his throat.

Marak and his men had been so focused on Ronnie and the soldiers with him that they paid little attention to the shadows moving behind them and in the corridors on both sides.

Thanks to the distraction Ronnie provided, Samuel and his men emerged from the hidden tunnels with Hanover's troops none the wiser. Just as Mikel wanted.

"Close?" Ronnie asked once his men locked Marak and his

soldiers in a storeroom at the far end of the corridor with which they could become much more intimately acquainted.

Samuel nodded back down the hallway that led directly to the throne room.

Ronnie chuckled, smiling broadly.

There was quite a procession coming their way.

And not a drop of blood shed.

Yet.

"LORD DENGANNON, please. We understand your argument. You have made your point multiple times. But there is little that we can do. The rules of the Council are quite explicit." Lord Haratounian leaned forward, forearms on his knees, pleading with his eyes. Not wanting to be in this position yet feeling the need to interject. None of the other Lords and Ladies seated around him desired to engage with the irate Battle Lord. "Once a Coronation has been called, we must proceed. We cannot wait. We cannot delay. No one may leave the chamber until a candidate has been selected and proclaimed. That is the law. You know it just as well as we do."

"Exactly so," Lucius agreed. Pushing himself up from his chair, he approached Lord Dengannon with a false commiseration spreading across his face. An emotion that never reached his conniving eyes. He sensed that the other First Families were tired of the game just like he was. It was time to get down to the reason they were all there.

"You do not rule here, Hanover." Henri refused to be budged. Wanting to add that Hanover would never rule here. But he could not. Because at that moment, the scales tipped in Hanover's direction. Heavily so.

Henri had done all that he could to delay the proceedings. To get those Lords and Ladies of the Crux who were seated around them to rethink the alliances made. To consider other possibilities. And, most of all, to gain just a little more time. Yet no more. He had reached the end of his rope, and he was out of ideas.

"I do not, you're correct. But neither do you. No one does." Lucius lifted his arms to the stained glass above to emphasize his frustration. "That's why we're here, is it not? No one leads at what is a critical time and someone must."

Before Henri could begin a new argument for delaying the Coronation if only for a few more hours, Lord Scipio interrupted. "Please, Henri. We understand where you stand. We understand why you must do as you are. But we cannot wait any longer for …"

"For whom, my Lords and Ladies?"

Gaze pulled to the Council chamber's main entrance, double doors open wide, Henri smiled. Every eye in the throne room followed his.

"I'm sorry to keep you waiting, but as you know I was unavoidably detained. Now that I have dealt with those insurgents who sought to impose themselves upon our Kingdom, perhaps we could get to the reason that we are all here."

Smiling broadly, Celindria Dengannon strode into the room. Her eyes, sharp as a raptor's, took in the mood of the First Families in a flash, knowing exactly what was required of her. Stopping in front of the chair reserved for the Dengannons, her uncle assumed his place at her shoulder and placed a hand on the hilt of his sword.

"My Coronation."

~

"CELINDRIA! I was so worried about you." Lucius strode quickly to the Queen Heir. Before she could resist him, he had her in his arms. Wrapping her into a hug that drew more than just a scowl from the Battle Lord. "I am so pleased to see you with us."

"I'm sure you are, Lucius," Drin replied. She extracted herself from the much-too-familiar hands of the head of House Hanover with a not-so-gentle shove, cringing until she was free from his touch, though she kept her disgust from her placid gaze.

"You must tell us all that happened, Celindria," Lucius prompted. He had never anticipated this possibility, and he needed time to think of some way to turn this surprise to his advantage. All the while hiding the rage surging through him at how his plans, so close to completion, threatened to come undone. "We were all quite concerned about the attack upon your person, yet none of us could offer aid because we couldn't find you. We didn't know if you were dead or alive."

Drin smiled thinly. From Lucius' tone, clearly he preferred the former. "Obviously alive, Lucius. And the happenings of yesterday can wait until after our business is concluded." She shifted her gaze away from Lucius, catching the eyes of every Lord and Lady in the circular chamber, many of their countenances turning pale when she next spoke. "The retribution to be had will have to wait as well. Although it will be swift and harsh. An attack on the Crux, whether from within or without, cannot go unanswered."

"Of course not," Lucius replied hastily. Clasping his fingers together because he feared that if he didn't his hands would reveal his nervousness, he sought to play for more time. There had to be some way to correct this jarring shift in circumstance. "Yet how is it that you survived such a heinous attack?"

"As you and all the Lords and Ladies with us know, Lucius, having the *right* allies is essential to our success." None of the men and women listening so intently to what she said missed Drin's meaning. "I just happen to have an ally who can do things that none of the rest of us can. A friend who takes a very dim view of those who seek to betray the Crux."

"And this friend is ..." Lucius desperately wanted a name. That might give him a chance to regain control over a situation that was slipping rapidly from between his fingers.

"Not important to our larger dialogue," Drin stated unequivocally. "We are here for another matter of critical importance to the Crux, are we not?"

"Yes, yes, of course," Lucius said, stumbling with his words at first and failing to gain any traction as the mood in the chamber continued to deteriorate. And not in his favor.

He noted the nervousness on the faces of most of the Lords and Ladies of the Crux. Hating the fact that several of the heads of Houses, those he was unable to turn to his side, were grinning at him with a hint of maliciousness, clearly pleased, a few even staring daggers.

Fearing what would happen if the dialogue continued for much longer, and not liking the predatory look that the Battle Lord was giving him, Lucius decided that delicacy was less important than speed.

"If the Council permits, and I have no doubt that the Council will, we can move forward as *we* discussed." Lucius nodded toward Celindria to emphasize his point.

"As we discussed, Lucius?" Drin stepped back and sat in her chair, adopting the posture she used while occupying the throne. One knee bent, leg crossed over. Perfectly at her ease as she settled back against the headboard. Her face revealed nothing more than calm resolve. Making a clear statement that was not missed by the others in the chamber.

Because of her action, the shift in the dynamics of the room was palpable. The Lords and Ladies quieted instantly, captured by the drama playing out before them. The tension increasing.

Lucius opened his mouth, then closed it with a frown.

Momentarily confused. Uncertain of how to proceed. Not quite sure what had just happened. "Yes, I thought that we …"

"We what, Lucius?" Drin offered him a smile that could be interpreted as both beguiling and belittling, depending on the perspective.

"We …"

"We discussed what the options might be, did we not?" She leaned forward, posture straight as a steel sword. "Actually, no, that isn't quite right, is it? Rather you told me what the options were. Or what one option was. The only option in your mind. The option that you preferred."

"And the best option I still believe," Lucius replied, a hint of tension in his voice that almost led to a gulp.

"For you, perhaps, Lucius." She shook her head sadly. "But for the Crux … I'm not so sure."

"For the Crux?" Lucius snorted softly. "Celindria, for the Crux, I truly believe …"

"That a Hanover must be on the throne." Drin leaned back into her chair, spine ramrod straight, chuckling softly, her eyes revealing her disappointment. "Yes, I remember. You made quite a strenuous argument. Very hard to forget."

"Not an argument, Celindria," Lucius professed. "A necessity." Seeking to buttress his claim he tried to bring a few others into the dialogue. "Would you not agree, Lords Haratounian and Scipio?"

"I'm sure the Lords Haratounian and Scipio agree on the need for a strong hand guiding the Crux." She turned her sharp eyes toward the two men who sat next to one another. Their eyes widened, seeing something in her expression that they had never seen before, both realizing that it would be best to stay quiet and out of this duel. "And I have no doubt that they both agree on exactly whose hand that should be."

"Celindria, please. I understand that you've been dealing with a great many stresses. The last more than any person in your position should have to deal with. An attack on your person? Infuriating. But that attack demonstrates ..."

"That Malor Dragoran is afraid of me," Drin stated in a strong and clear voice that shut off the flow of Lucius' words.

Lucius smiled cheekily, feeling his grip on the throne slowly slipping away. "Celindria, I don't know ..."

"I'm sure the Battle Lord would agree. I'm sure as well that he, just like many of the Lords and Ladies with us, believes that a demonstration of strength will be required to ensure Dragoran's designs on our Kingdom are blunted."

Lord Dengannon nodded. His eyes flinty. "The *Queen Heir* is correct." He stressed his niece's title, wanting to remind those with them where the real power lay. "Why else would Malor Dragoran attempt to assassinate my niece if not because he viewed her as a threat? And is that not what we need right now? A strong leader? A Queen who will fight for the Crux? A Queen who will not bend to the will of a man who desires to subjugate us?"

Before Lucius could argue against her uncle's perspective, Drin spoke up. "What say you, Lord Tadari? Should we not have a leader who will always put the interests of the Crux before their own?"

Before the old man with the receding hair and muttonchops that got lost in his bushy mustache could reply, Drin shifted her focus to some of the other First Families. Picking certain ones because she knew where their true loyalties rested.

"And you, Lady Becera? Should not the leader of the Crux put the interests of the Crux before their own? And you Lady Kendillon? Would you not agree?"

"Absolutely right, Queen Heir," Lady Kendillon answered without a moment's hesitation, earning a sharp glare from Lucius Hanover and not caring. She had ruled her House for half a century. She didn't appreciate being pressured by a toddler who thought only of himself. "The Crux first. The Crux always."

"The Crux first. The Crux always." Drin smiled, giving Lady Kendillon a nod of respect. "Thank you for that, Lady Kendillon. I will use that saying if I may." Lady Kendillon nodded her approval, smiling. Pleased to grant her permission. Drin continued. "And I have no doubt that the Lords Haratounian, Scipio, Ascelpan, and everyone else privileged to serve on this Council agree with you. Don't you, Lord Richterious?"

For just an instant, Ethan Richterious stared at Drin like a deer caught by a lamplight. Frozen. Never expecting to be drawn into this. He had ruled his House for only a few years. Not liking how House Hanover lorded it over him. Nevertheless, stuck because his debts were immense, and he wasn't in a position to push back. Until now. Because though he was far from penurious, he did know how to read a room. And he sensed an opportunity.

"I do indeed, Queen Heir." He inclined his head as a sign of respect. "The Crux first. The Crux always."

"Thank you, Lord Richterious, for confirming what we all believe." Drin shifted her gaze back toward Lucius Hanover. Her eyes shrewd. "That is why the Coronation must be completed just as you say it must, Lucius. We must put someone on the throne who can stand up to Malor Dragoran. We must put someone on the throne who Malor Dragoran is afraid of."

"We must!" Lord Richterious agreed in a shout that was soon echoed by every other Lord and Lady in the Council chamber. Several of the men and women pounding their armrests with their fists. Caught up in the moment in part. Also sensing the opportunity to extricate themselves from the noose that had been slipped around their necks.

Except for one.

Lucius Hanover stepped back a few feet, only stopping

when the back of his legs hit his chair. He couldn't look away from Celindria Dengannon. Even though he wanted to. Because she refused to release his eyes with her own.

It felt like he was seeing her for the first time.

Somehow she had wriggled free from the trap he set for her.

Somehow she had turned that trap into a tool.

And she had used that tool against him to take the throne.

All on her own.

How was that possible?

After all that he had done to ensure his ascension.

It didn't make sense.

He had many of the other First Families by the balls, yet they had just reneged on their agreements with barely a second thought?

It just didn't make sense!

Lucius scowled when Drin finally let go of his eyes as she turned her shrewd smile into a warm one, sharing it with the Lords and Ladies who were up from their seats, surrounding her, and offering her their congratulations.

There was more than one way to take the throne.

And though violence wasn't his first choice because of the often messy consequences, he wasn't averse to its application. Because only the Battle Lord would stand in his way, and Lucius was certain that he could deal with him.

Believing in the need for drastic action, his hand drifted down to the sword at his hip. Fingers grasping the hilt, he was about to pull the blade free.

But he couldn't.

A large hand with a crushing grip took hold of his own, keeping his steel sheathed.

"A foolish play, Lord Hanover."

Lucius glanced to his right. Before he could look up and study the face of the man standing next to him, he gasped, the pain in his fingers intensifying. The man shockingly strong.

"Look around you, Hanover. Your window of opportunity has closed."

And he did when the grip on his hand loosened enough so that he could breathe again.

Soldiers had filed in and now lined the walls of the Council chamber, the doors thrown open once the First Families made their decision. All of the soldiers from the Army of the Crux. None of them from his guard. And mixed in were a dozen or more other fighters who, though they weren't wearing armor, looked just as competent if not more so than the soldiers standing with them. All of them staring at him.

"This is not right," he grumbled. He tried to look up at his tormentor's face. He couldn't. The man's large hand squeezed his fingers harder, causing him to gasp in pain.

"Right or wrong means nothing, Lord Hanover. You should know that. Here, in the Citadel, all that matters is who wins. And today, the Queen Heir wins. Not you."

"I should win. I should ..."

Lucius gasped again then moaned softly, bending at the knees. He remained crouched over, however, unable to reach the floor. The man standing at his side held him in place as his crushing grip sent a wave of excruciating agony through him.

"You should acknowledge and accept your new reality." The man locking him in place nodded, Lucius catching the movement and looking across the room toward Celindria, who, smiling broadly, offered Lucius a less-than-welcoming nod.

"You see it, don't you?"

"See what?" Lucius demanded, though he could barely get the words out because of the pain.

"She sees you, Hanover. The Queen Heir knows who you truly are. And so do I. So I suggest you tread carefully. Very, very carefully."

The man standing next to Lucius stepped back then, releasing his hold. The Lord of House Hanover dropped into his chair, holding his throbbing hand against his chest, groaning softly. When he was finally able to feel the blood flowing to his fingers once again, the sting bringing a new agony, he sought the face of his tormentor.

"And just who in blazes are you?" he demanded. He didn't know the hulking figure who towered over him, although he believed that he should. There was something familiar about him.

"A friend of the Queen."

35

NACHAHMEN GREETING

"I would like to be alone for a little while longer."

She'd didn't bother to turn around, listening as the door closed silently behind her.

Drin stood atop the dais in the throne room. One hand on the royal seat carved from a boulder-sized chunk of a heart tree that was ripped free by a lightning strike, she gazed through the open stained-glass window out onto the city that extended to the very rim of the Crux.

Even from here, she could see the Churn fighting with itself. Splashes of white froth caused by the massive waves surging up and over the breaker.

The Coronation itself hadn't been much of an affair. A swift acclamation of support from the First Families, even Lucius Hanover, before the Lords and Ladies of the Crux drifted away. All of them, she was certain, wanting to get right to the task of determining what her ascension meant to them and their fortunes ... and how they were going to manage her.

They would try. She was certain of that. And she would be ready. But she did not need to worry about that just yet.

She needed some time to herself. To reflect.

Drin had always wanted the throne. She believed that she deserved the throne since her family had ruled for four centuries. Yet she had never believed that she would attain the seat because of her father's murder.

Bittersweet didn't describe what she was feeling right then. And, in fact, for the first time in her life, she wondered if she had taken on more than she should have. She wondered whether she truly deserved the throne.

Because this wasn't how she wanted to take up the reins of power in the Crux.

Strange to have achieved what she desired the most only to question the validity of that desire and her new position.

Perhaps it was because the last time she had been in this chamber her father had been with her. Conducting the business of the Crux. Always taking a few seconds here and there to offer advice so that she would be prepared when it came time for her to assume his place.

A deep sadness welled up within her. She missed her father. She wished he was here with her now. She wished that he was sitting on the throne while she stood by his side.

But wishing for what she wanted didn't matter.

What mattered was what she did.

A lesson from her father.

She needed to think then do. Not worry.

And after the last few days, she had quite a lot to do.

Drin spun around, reaching for the Talent. A sphere of energy blazing to life above both her palms.

The door had been pulled closed, but she sensed that she wasn't alone. And the presence that joined her felt wrong. Tainted in some way. Making her think of rot and decay.

Drin gave a start. "Uncle Henri? I thought you were going to check on the ..."

Drin dove out of the way. Rolling behind the back of the

throne. Then scrambling toward the center of the chamber so that she had more space to maneuver.

The creature that resembled her uncle clearly wasn't. Same size. Same bearing. Same features. Yet not really him.

Though enough of him to get past the guards at the door.

It was the eyes that gave away her attacker.

Pure black.

That and the creature's remarkable speed.

Her attacker moved so swiftly that she could barely track the creature, forcing her to move based on instinct. Still, she did just enough to avoid the claws that sought her flesh.

The creature advancing toward her again, Drin didn't wait, though she feared that she already knew what was going to happen.

She threw one sphere of energy and then the other. One more. And another. So many that it appeared that streams of power shot from her palms.

Yet not once did she hit her attacker.

Whatever creature it was that had taken her uncle's shape glided about the chamber with an infuriating grace. Slipping and sliding out of the way. Moving like no human ever could.

"What are you?" Drin demanded.

"Your downfall," the creature replied in a sibilant hiss. "Your reign will be the shortest ever for the Crux."

Growling in anger, Drin sent a blast of energy directly at the creature. Then a second. And a third.

The monster evaded each strike.

Each time drawing closer to where she stood.

Closing the distance between them.

Drin realized that she had nowhere to run.

Yet she refused to show her back even for an instant despite her desire to put the throne between them.

Knowing that if she did the creature would take her down from behind.

That knowledge eating away at her, Drin's attacks became more desperate.

Blasts of energy erupted from her palms.

Drin did all that she could to keep the creature away from her.

Having no success, the monster continued to dance toward her.

Until the creature held both her wrists in one clawed hand.

"A valiant effort, Queen of the Crux. But your rule ends now."

Pulling back its free claw and preparing to drive it right through Drin's chest, the creature froze. Pure black eyes dimming. Frame shimmering.

Drin watched in astonishment as a sword of blazing fire slid through her attacker's body from back to front.

The effect was instantaneous.

The illusion that had been her uncle disappeared the instant the competing magics met, revealing a swirling black mist that was now just loosely formed into the shape of a man.

That mist sought to draw away from the energy flowing along the blade, but it couldn't.

Not fast enough.

Not strong enough.

The fiery power of the sword wrapping itself around the black mist, enclosing it, then compressing it in a white-hot light.

Burning it.

Destroying it.

A shriek of torment echoed in the throne room until every last speck of black burned away.

"What in blazes are you doing here?" Drin saw on Mikel's face the same shock that she was experiencing. His scimitar, once flashing brightly, now back to a dim glow.

"I just wanted to offer you my congratulations." He gave her a smile and a wink. "Good thing I decided to come back when I did."

Drin nodded, not in a position to disagree with him. She heard the pounding on the doors to the throne room then, the creature that had attacked her wedging them closed. Mikel having come through the hidden door that remained open at the back of the chamber. "What was that?"

"A Nachahmen," Mikel replied with a heavy sigh.

"A Nachahmen." Drin stared at Mikel, not understanding how he could be so calm after what had just happened. "What's a Nachahmen?"

"An assassin of the deadliest sort."

"I'm going to need more than that." Drin wasn't in the mood for anything less than a full explanation.

Recognizing the look she gave him, Mikel offered the more in-depth response that she desired. "A malevolent spirit much like a Drude forced into service by a Dark Magus. The key difference being they can assume the shape, the mannerisms, the voice of whomever they choose. A Nachahmen. The perfect assassin. Only their black eyes give them away, and the most powerful and skilled of those monsters won't reveal that much. Able to change eye color as well and control the evil flowing through them. Much worse than a Drude because as you saw they have skills of their own that are unique that even a potent Magus such as yourself struggles against."

"That's not what I wanted to hear." Drin frowned, walking to the throne on unsteady legs. Sitting. Leaning forward, fore-arms on the armrests. All the while fighting the urge to expel the contents of her stomach.

"Then you shouldn't have asked." Mikel sheathed his scimi-tar. He had reacted instinctively. Grasping his sword as soon as he entered the throne room.

Drawn not toward the Queen but toward the evil that was the Curse.

Feeling the power surge along the steel.

Feeling the power surging through him.

A joining of sorts.

A rough balance achieved.

Which was why he didn't feel completely exhausted.

Though he still didn't quite understand what he did to make that happen.

Drin couldn't stop herself from snorting out a laugh despite the trembling that had taken her, realizing just how close she had come to dying. Not wanting to think on that, she focused on how Mikel had saved her.

"When did you learn to do that?"

"Just now," Mikel replied with a shrug. Less interested in what he had done. More interested in who had sent the Nachahmen. One person in particular coming to mind. That person apparently tired of employing Druden.

"And you never told me about this power of yours?"

"I can't tell you about something I didn't know I had."

"You truly are a frustrating person to deal with," Drin chided. Leaning back into her chair, she took a deep breath, feeling a little better. For whatever reason, Mikel had a calming effect upon her.

"I'm well aware. But where's the fun if everything was always easy for you?"

Drin bit down on her tongue so that she didn't laugh. "We'll be having a long conversation about this."

Mikel didn't say anything, just giving her a smile. Based on the look she was giving him, he decided that it would be wise to make himself scarce for a time.

In part because of her interest in the blade.

Also because someone very powerful clearly wanted the Queen of the Crux dead.

36

PARTING SHOT

"I will see the Queen now."

Mikel frowned upon closing the doors to the throne room, Lucius Hanover squaring up to him. "She has other business. I suggest you make an appointment."

"And who are you to tell me what I can and can't do?"

"No one," Mikel replied, clearly unconcerned by the threat contained in Hanover's words. "But these fine gentlemen behind me can tell you what you can and can't do. In fact, I have no doubt that they'd be more than happy to do just that. Isn't that so, Sergeant?"

The squad of soldiers standing guard in front of the door held their spears competently in their hands. Their expressions hard. Almost severe. Clearly less than pleased by the attack on the Queen.

"We would indeed," Ronnie confirmed. The Sergeant stepped forward, hand on the hilt of his sword. The men at his back having eyes only for Lord Hanover. "The Queen was quite explicit. She is not to be disturbed for the rest of the day."

Lucius wanted to shout in fury, his rage all consuming. He had been so close to taking the throne himself. Celindria somehow surviving the attack that had been carefully planned and then turning it to her advantage.

This additional slight threatened to push him over the edge. Hanover almost unable to bear the collapse of his dreams. The fact that he was outplayed by a woman only making the pain of his loss that much more excruciating.

Yet understanding what would happen if he ignored the Sergeant and tried to force his way past. Not wanting to embarrass himself any further, he maintained control over his temper and stepped away from the doors, following Mikel as he walked down the hallway.

"I know who you are, Caledonii." Lucius sidled up next to Mikel. "You're the King of the Underworld."

"And I know who you are, Hanover."

"What in blazes do you mean by that?" Lucius' eyes flashed, his rage boiling just beneath the surface. Having no doubt that this was the man who had laid hands upon him, preventing him from acting when the moment was ripe.

"It means exactly what I said."

"You're a fool to threaten me. You may rule in the shadows, but I rule in the light."

Mikel stopped then, giving Lucius a sad smile and a shake of his head. "At the moment, Hanover, you rule nothing at all."

"How dare you!" Lucius' hand, bruised and aching, went for the hilt of his sword. Mikel's dark smile stopped him.

"I saved you from yourself not long ago. If you draw your steel, I'll kill you where you stand."

Mikel watched the conflicting emotions flash across Hanover's face. He understood the struggle the lord faced, Hanover's dreams burning up with the speed of a piece of parchment thrown into a fire.

A small part of him hoped that the man would demonstrate just a shred of courage and free his steel. But it wasn't to be.

Hanover decided to rely on the threats with which he was so familiar and comfortable rather than risking himself.

"You are an outcast in the city, Caledonii. You do not belong here. You do not belong anywhere but in the ground. You will pay for what you have done to me. Have no doubt of that. So I suggest that you enjoy what little time you have left because no one takes what belongs to me."

"Is that a challenge, Hanover?" Mikel stepped in close, eyes sparking with menace.

Hanover forced himself to hold his ground, refusing to back down. "It is more than a challenge. It is a promise. I will see you and all you hold dear swept into the Churn."

"If you know me so well, then you'd know that I don't respond well to threats." Mikel took a step forward, looming even more over Hanover. Reaching out, he grasped Hanover's hand. Forcing it open. Then he dropped five rings into his palm. One from each of the Seekers sent to eliminate Drin. The assassins earning the ring of their Order after their first kill. "These belong to you, I believe. You can return them to the one who gifted them."

Smiling as Hanover stared at the rings in his palm, dumbfounded, Mikel headed down the hallway, offering one last piece of advice. "There is one other thing you might not know about me, Hanover. I hold grudges." He offered the lord a wave over his shoulder without bothering to turn around. "I'll be seeing you again, Hanover. Likely when you don't want to see me. That's a promise."

37

MORE TO DO

"Your task is not done, my friend."

Cadmus stood atop the roof of his home. Semicircular in shape, much like an igloo, the top had been scraped down to create a platform that gave him a view of the entire valley, the mountains of the north surrounding the capital of the Frozen Waste. The landscape dotted by fast-running streams covered by ice that was dozens of feet thick.

His home was no larger than any of the others, his position as Frost Lord obvious because his home had been built on the tallest knoll in the valley. There wasn't much wood in the Frozen Waste. But there was a great deal of rock, snow, and ice, and the Giants of the Rime had mastered the skill of using those materials to stay warm even in subzero temperatures while a blizzard raged just beyond their doors.

After his last conversation with Celindria Dengannon, Queen of the Crux, Mikel felt the urge to get away for a time. Needing to gain some peace. Though apparently the Frost Lord wasn't going to allow him that.

"My task?"

"You thought that helping Celindria Dengannon claim the throne was all that was required of you?" asked Cadmus.

"Well, not really, but I kind of hoped."

Cadmus chuckled at that. A booming sound because of the giant's great size. "The folly of youth. Hoping. You cannot trust in hope. You can only trust in yourself and that the world around you will not move as you want it to."

"And that the world only will move as you want it to with a little help."

"Well said."

"And what are you not saying, Cadmus?"

"That though Queen Dengannon may have the throne, the threat persists and likely grows stronger and more aggressive."

"Malor."

Cadmus nodded. "And the Dark Magus, for a Drude could only come from a Dark Magus. A Nachahmen? That worries me more, because that calling would be beyond most Dark Magii."

"I didn't want any of this, you know."

"I know," Cadmus sighed in commiseration. "Nevertheless it often comes down not to what we want ..."

"But to what we must do," Mikel said, finishing the Frost Lord's thought for him. Having heard it many times before.

"Right again."

"And what must I do?"

"That is something that you'll need to figure out. Until then, someone wants to say hello."

Cadmus lifted his gaze to the sky at the exact moment a large shadow sped over them, a shriek blasting through the small valley.

Mikel looked up with a warm smile.

It hadn't been very long, yet she had grown since he had last seen her. She was twice as large as a draft horse now.

Eisa.

The ice dragon circled around them several times, blue and white scales flashing and then disappearing in the cloudless sky. Making her virtually invisible unless the light struck her in a certain way.

With a final shriek, she curled toward the mountains in search of prey.

"She comes by regularly," Cadmus said.

"Why?"

"She's looking for you."

"Me? Why would she be looking for me?"

"You have a connection with her. A bond. You cannot escape it."

"I'm not trying to escape it. But there's another bond that I wanted to speak with you about first."

"That would be?"

Mikel pulled the scimitar from the scabbard on his back. Cadmus' eyes widened upon seeing the Giant-crafted blade that glowed brightly in the sunlight. "Tell me of the Blade of Light."

"That is a story for the ages."

"You make it sound ominous," Mikel snorted. "As if I should be worried."

"You should be. Because the blade you wield is both a gift and a curse."

BONUS MATERIAL

If you really enjoyed this story, I need you to do me a HUGE favor – please follow me on Amazon and BookBub. And if you have a few minutes, consider writing a review.

Keep reading for two chapters from *Sacrificing the Queen,* Book 2 in my series *Legend of the Dragon Lord.* Order Book 2 from my author website PeterWachtBooks.com. Also available on Amazon.

SACRIFICING THE QUEEN

LEGEND OF THE DRAGON LORD

2

AN EPIC FANTASY FICTION SERIES

PETER WACHT

Sacrificing the Queen
By Peter Wacht

Book 2 of Legend of the Dragon Lord

Published in the United States by Kestrel Media Group LLC.

ISBN: 978-1-950236-66-4

eBook ISBN: 978-1-950236-65-7

Library of Congress Control Number: 2025905362

 Created with Vellum

1. ICY FORETELLING

"Where do matters stand between you and the Queen of the Crux?"

Mikel didn't have the chance to answer the question. He was too busy diving to the side and then sliding across the crusted snow to avoid the scythe that sang through the air where he had been standing.

It was a beautiful weapon. Mikel would be the first to admit that. The haft was made of the smoothest and strongest stone, the blade crafted from a steel that was easily mistaken for ice and never lost its edge. But that didn't mean he wanted that weapon cutting so close.

Mikel was back up in a flash, the steel spikes on the soles of his boots giving him a grip on the icy surface that allowed him to move with his customary speed. The only hindrance slowing him down was his damaged knee that tightened and ached in the cold of the Frozen Waste.

"Matters are no different than they were when last I saw her," Mikel finally answered. "Why?"

Mikel frowned as he slashed with his scimitar, the steel glowing dimly, and not because of the bright sunlight reflecting off the white of the Maze. He shook his head, trying to clear it of the woman sitting on the throne of the Crux.

He needed to keep his focus on his opponent. Otherwise, the Frost Lord would make him pay for his lapse in concentration.

He had little expectation of gaining the touch that he wanted. The best he could hope for was that he kept Cadmus on his toes, making his friend hesitate before he attacked again.

The Giant of the Rime held a distinct advantage. Since Cadmus stood almost twice as tall as Mikel, he enjoyed a much longer reach. He didn't need to risk getting in tight to Mikel to gain the touch that would give him the victory. Cadmus could poke at him from a distance for as long as he desired so long as he didn't make a mistake that Mikel could use against him.

However, for Mikel to gain the touch that would end this practice combat, he needed to get in close. A risky tactic, though a necessary one. And on this day a challenge he had yet to meet.

"Are you certain of that?" Cadmus asked, his deep voice rumbling off the circular walls of the hollow that was carved out of the snow and ice.

The Frost Lord had led Mikel to the Maze that morning. Supposedly seeking more of a test as part of his training regimen than he could gain against his Defenders while offering his friend a unique honor. To hone his skills as the Giants of the Rime did.

Rather than take on the many obstacles situated throughout the Maze that the less-experienced Giants needed to master before the final combat could begin -- tricks and traps, perils and hazards that changed regularly, from shifting walls and hidden pits to tusked mastodons and snowcats larger than draft horses – Cadmus had led Mikel right to the center of the training ground.

The Circle.

Bridges crafted of ice allowed the Rime Armsmasters to look down on all that occurred in the practice ring so that they could evaluate their students as they sought to pass the required tests to become a Defender of the Rime.

Neither Cadmus nor Mikel felt the need to add to the level of difficulty of that morning's exercise, preferring to climb down the ladder at the end of the bridge to take their places. Having little doubt that their adversary would test them in ways that no other challenge or opponent could. And the last hour had proven them right.

The Frost Lord and Mikel displayed an innate and ingrained ability that few could match. Since the practice combat began, neither had gained a winning strike, though it had been a near thing for each on a few occasions.

At the same time they engaged in a conversation that started with their mutual business interests and now had taken them to more delicate topics. Matters that Mikel had little desire to discuss.

Mikel stepped back a few more feet, wary of Cadmus' scythe as he circled around to his friend's left, the Frost Lord having taken up a position near the center of the Circle. Before he attacked again, Mikel wanted the sun streaming into Cadmus' eyes, the glare worse coming off the ice and snow.

"Why wouldn't I be?" Mikel asked. He frowned again at his friend's comment. What was Cadmus implying? It seemed as if the Frost Lord wanted to say something, but he wanted Mikel to say it first.

"Because I would think that after all that has happened circumstances between the two of you have changed."

"How so?" They had. Mikel couldn't deny that. How could they not after what had conspired on the Crux?

But he didn't need to admit that to Cadmus. If he did, he'd never hear the end of it. When Mikel felt the heat of the sun on the back of his neck and saw Cadmus squint, he rushed forward, slashing toward the Giant's hip.

The Frost Lord moved faster than someone of his size should be able to. Pivoting, the Giant took one big step backward. Then he ducked, allowing Mikel's blade to cut through the air above him.

Cadmus was about to push himself back up, wanting to target Mikel's vulnerable back leg, sensing that his victory was close, when he stopped abruptly. Or rather the touch of cold steel at his throat stopped him.

The Frost Lord growled. Furious. Though not at Mikel. Rather at himself. He had fallen for Mikel's feint, not even seeing Mikel pull the dagger from the sheath at his hip.

"You saved her life, Mikel," Cadmus rumbled, accepting his friend's hand as he regained his feet. Sighing. Disappointed once again. The same result as every other time he brought his friend here.

Cadmus had yet to defeat Mikel in a combat. Frustrating. And the reason he preferred to train with Mikel on his own.

Nevertheless, a good result in his opinion. His failure helped to keep him humble, and it meant that he had a goal to strive for the next time the two stepped into the Circle.

"And because of that you believe that she's in my debt?" Mikel asked in a soft chuckle. He sheathed his dagger, sword still in his hand. "I doubt the illustrious Queen of the Crux sees it that way. She's been quite clear about what her expectations are with respect to my business dealings. She's made quite a few pronouncements, in fact, about what I'm supposed to do and what I'm not allowed to do. Not even a conversation. Simply our great and august Queen of the Crux issuing a host of rules and requirements that are supposed to define the link between the Crown and the King of the Underworld."

"Do you intend to follow these rules?"

Mikel didn't even need to think about it. "Of course not.

There'd be no fun in that. Besides, I have a reputation to maintain."

Cadmus laughed, expecting just such a response. "You can't really blame her. She feels the need to exercise her authority. To solidify her position as quickly as she can because she does not want to rely on you to hold her throne. It only makes sense."

"Agreed," Mikel replied with a nod, "so I'm not taking issue with her motivation. I'm taking issue with her constant stream of orders. You would think that she would demonstrate at least a modicum of delicacy with respect to her approach."

Cadmus frowned again, this time his expression more a question. "You do understand that she doesn't just see you as the King of the Underworld, right?"

Now it was Mikel's turn to frown. "Why would she see me as anything else? That's what I am. What little interaction we've had since she ascended to the throne of the Crux has been focused solely on how she expects the City Above to interact with the City Below. As I said, what I am and am not permitted to do. All of it is more than just a little aggravating because it doesn't have to be this way between us."

"That's all that's been happening between you two?" Cadmus prompted with a raised eyebrow. He was certain that Mikel's unsaid complaint only partially had to do with the business between the Queen and the role he played behind the throne.

Mikel had a ready reply, though he didn't offer it. Instead, he thought about what his friend was implying. Had his relationship with Celindria Dengannon changed since he helped her claim the throne after her father's murder?

It was Cadmus' turn to chuckle. "You see it now, don't you?"

"I don't know what I see," Mikel grumbled, feeling the need to be stubborn at least for a little while longer. Not yet ready to acknowledge what Cadmus was hinting at.

"You do know. You just don't want to put it into words. If you do then it becomes real."

Drin had assumed the throne just a month past, and in that time Mikel had been busy. Not only with his own many businesses and dealings, but also in helping the Queen with some tasks best left to his particular expertise.

Mikel's expression changed then. Becoming harder. His frown solidifying and threatening to become a permanent fixture on his brow.

"You don't like it when I'm right, do you?" Cadmus asked, having little trouble reading his friend.

"In this case, no," Mikel growled, realizing how his friend trapped him. Nevertheless, he didn't want to give Cadmus all the satisfaction that he was seeking. "Although in truth I'm more surprised since you're so rarely right."

The Frost Lord's eyes tightened. Flashing once. Then he shook his head. "Always pushing, even when you know better."

"One of my better traits," Mikel replied, giving his friend a smile that did little to improve his rough appearance.

Cadmus snorted, then admitted the truth. "At certain times, yes it is."

"I've enjoyed my start to the day, Cadmus, but weapons training out in the middle of nowhere and then you grilling me about my connection to the Queen," Mikel refusing to use the word *relationship*, "wasn't the only reason, the primary reason in fact, that you asked me to join you here today."

Mikel motioned with his free hand at their surroundings. The snow-capped peaks that separated the Frozen Waste from the Kingdom of the Crux were several leagues to the east. Icehold, Cadmus' capital, was a few miles to the west. Besides the Maze that the Giants had carved out of the ice and snow on this frigid plain there was little to see other than the drifting white that danced and swirled at the whim of the gusty wind.

And there was little to feel other than a bone-breaking cold.

Although Mikel was grateful that he avoided the worst of the chill thanks to the clothes Julia had gifted to him several years before, Cadmus' daughter displaying a somewhat unsettling interest in him.

Made of the unique material that the Giants of the Rime wore, though in a smaller size, the thin layers allowed Mikel to conserve his heat and, since he didn't need to wear a heavy parka – several heavy parkas when the worst of the cold came during the darkest nights of the winter, not limiting his movement in any way. Best of all, the mix of white, blue, grey, and random specks of black allowed him to blend into the colors of the Frozen Waste. It served as a natural camouflage if he didn't move hastily.

Cadmus smiled. His bright blue eyes sparking as he ran a hand through his long white hair that resembled icicles. "You need to learn more about the scimitar. You also need to practice using the weapon."

"That's why we're really out here?" Mikel nodded knowingly. He had assumed as much. In fact, he hadn't expected Cadmus to take so long before inviting him into the Frozen Waste.

And that was a key point. Only those invited into the bleak, wintry landscape were permitted to enter. To do so without an invitation ensured a quick death. For the Giants of the Rime had only one punishment for intruders.

Cadmus nodded. "In large part, yes. I did want to put you through your paces, although it seems the opposite occurred. You put me through mine."

"I was happy to help in that regard."

"I bet you were," Cadmus confirmed, ignoring the grin Mikel gave him that was designed to get under his skin. "Moving beyond that, you need to learn how to partner with the Blade of Light."

"Partner?" Mikel had been hired to steal the scimitar from the very depths of the Citadel.

And he had.

But he had refused to relinquish it the instant his fingers touched the steel.

Mikel never broke a contract. And he didn't view holding back the ancient weapon from the person who hired him as doing that. Because the woman never revealed prior to their agreement that she was a Dark Magus. He found that out on his own, and to his way of thinking that voided the deal.

He didn't do business with people touched by the Curse.

Ever.

He understood the cost of doing so.

Cadmus nodded. "Partner."

Thinking about what his friend was telling him, partner made sense to Mikel. The few times that he had used the power contained within the Blade of Light, he hadn't demanded it from the ancient weapon. Rather the blade crafted by the Giants of the Rime had gifted him the potent energy. As if they had come to a meeting of the minds.

Perhaps that was the trick. Just like any good business deal, two parties coming together based on mutual interest or need.

"The blade and I work together," Mikel mused. "Based on the little experience I have, it's strange. It's almost as if it has a consciousness all on its own."

"Exactly," Cadmus confirmed. "In fact, some believe that the Blade of Light does have a consciousness just as you said."

"But you don't know?" That was a line of thought that piqued Mikel's interest. It would make learning the properties of the ancient weapon much easier.

Cadmus shrugged, shaking his head sadly. "We have lost a great deal of knowledge over the centuries, in large part because of the War of the Brothers. My father was a historian of sorts, and even he couldn't tell me much about the blade or many of the other artifacts that my Giants shaped and infused with the Talent millennia ago."

Mikel snorted. "So what you're saying is that I'm on my own. There's not a lot of guidance you can give me other than the fact that the blade is designed to connect with the Bearer and form a partnership of some type. And because you're not sure how it's supposed to work or what the results might be if I try to do as you suggest, you brought me out here where I couldn't hurt anyone and I could cause the least amount of damage if I made a mistake while you put me to the test."

Cadmus smiled broadly. "Exactly."

"Not really a recipe for building my confidence. You do realize that, don't you?"

Cadmus shrugged. "I've never known you as one who has lacked confidence."

"I'll take that as a compliment."

"If you must," Cadmus allowed. Then the Frost Lord became serious. "I didn't bring you out here to play games. I don't know all there is to know about the Blade of Light, but I know enough. The artifact has selected you. Why? I don't know. But when a weapon crafted with the Light and the Talent chooses you, it is not something to discount or ignore. Until you learn how to work with the Blade of Light, you're a threat to yourself and anyone around you."

Several pointed comments immediately came to mind. Mikel kept them to himself. Cadmus was trying to help him. At least he thought he was. "Not very comforting."

"It wasn't meant to be, Steelheart." Cadmus clapped his friend on the back, though not so hard as to knock him to the ground. "We still have a few hours before we need to head back. Let's begin. Let's see what you can do with that ancient blade that doesn't involve you swatting me with it."

2. NASTY SURPRISE

It was quiet. Dawn still a few hours away when Lucius Hanover stepped toward the back of the small shop, only a couple of lamps lighting his way. It had once been an apothecary. One of the few serving the people of the Crux living on the First Ring. The streets often flooded when the Churn surged over the seawall.

That explained the damage to the shop. Much of the wood had rotted with mold growing along the walls and the ceiling. Sandbags that offered little protection sat piled along the outside of the shop.

The owner had closed after the last flood. Little thought was given to reopening because of the expense of restocking all the herbs, salves, and other items destroyed when the Churn flowed almost to the Third Ring.

Hanover had bought the space on the cheap recently. Quietly as well, through one of his many holding companies, so that it would be that much harder to follow the change in ownership.

He smiled thinking about that. Hanover did like coming out ahead. He couldn't think of anything in life more pleasurable than that. And that was saying quite a lot considering his many less than savory proclivities.

Yet his pleasure did little to assuage his anger.

Even after the passage of more than a month he was having a hard time keeping his temper under control. And with good reason he believed. His grievances legitimate.

He had been so close.

So close!

Yet that harpy had ripped his greatest dream right from his grasp just moments before it became a reality.

He still couldn't believe that his perfect plan hadn't been so perfect after all. Even more, he still couldn't believe that he wasn't sitting on the Crux throne.

Hanover growled softly, making a visible effort to focus on the present. Understanding that no matter how much fun it might be, wallowing in the past did him little good.

It certainly didn't help him deal with the complications that arose after he failed to seize the throne.

The crushing debts were bad enough.

Hanover had spent a large part of his family's fortune to place himself in the position that he lusted after. Yet now the First Families had turned a deaf ear to his plight, having forgotten all that he had done for them along with the promises that they had made to him as a result of his largesse ... and the pressure that he applied. Subtly at times, and not so subtly when a more direct approach was called for.

Yet none of that mattered now.

He was overdrawn.

He had obligations to meet.

He didn't have the means to pay what he owed.

And since his silent ally had offered little material support, making his disappointment in Hanover's failure plain, the Lord of the Crux needed to expand his business operations in certain directions at a much faster pace to recoup his losses and pay his debts.

Directions that he wouldn't have considered if he didn't face such dire straits.

Decisions made with such alacrity.

Desperate times and all that.

"It's all here?"

Marek nodded, the commander of Hanover's Guard stepping up next to him. He had worked for the Hanovers since he was a child. Beginning before Lucius was born. Doing whatever was required of him. His loyalty unassailable. "Yes, it arrived last night. Right on time, in fact."

"You checked the shipment?"

Marek nodded. "The highest quality. Just as you were promised."

"All of it?"

"All of it. You have nothing to fear in that regard."

Lucius nodded. Good. He had sunk a good part of what little of his wealth he had left into this deal. Understanding the risk. Willing to take it because the potential reward was too much for him to resist.

If it played out as he believed it would, from this one contract he would have the capacity to rebuild much of what he lost from his family's treasury. Although it would require more of his time and effort than he usually desired to devote to his business dealings, he was willing to do the work.

Because just a handful of these deals could put him back in a position where Celindria Dengannon would have no choice but to consider him as a consort, placing him right next to the throne. And then, after a few years passed ...

Well, he didn't want to get ahead of himself.

Regardless, what was required of him now was a small price to pay for the riches promised to him. Milk of the poppy was difficult to acquire on the Crux. Primarily because it was illegal in the Kingdom, its use restricted to the handful of physicks who worked in the capital city.

Nevertheless, there was a small market that went beyond the medicinal demand, and Hanover planned to grow that market.

He didn't believe that it would take much to do so.

The high cost of his product played to his advantage. As did the fact that he already had an in with the market.

Many of his friends in the First Families, along with the sons and daughters of the wealthier merchants and traders who had aspirations to live just below the Royal Ring, would be interested. In fact, if Hanover played his cards right, milk of the poppy would become a status symbol, an item exclusive to the rich, and that guaranteed that he would make a fortune. Because he would be the one to control the market.

"Let's see it," Hanover ordered.

Marek nodded then stepped past Hanover, stopping in front of the small fireplace behind the counter. He traced his fingers along the mantle until he felt the slight indentation. Pushing in, a segment of the paneled wall next to the fireplace swung open to reveal a storage space lit by several lamps.

Wary of thieves, the previous owner kept his more expensive products hidden before the last flood destroyed his inventory.

Hanover's milk of the poppy had been placed there when it was delivered only a few hours before.

There was a slight problem, however.

Hanover's eyes widened first in disbelief and then concern as he stared into the hidden room. "Did you move it?" Based on the quantity Hanover had purchased, the hideaway should have been packed to the rafters. Several thousand pounds of milk of the poppy should have been stacked in neat bundles one on top of the other.

But it wasn't there.

Nothing was there.

The room was empty.

"This isn't possible," Marek gasped. "No one has been here since last night. We locked up the shop. No one could have gotten in."

"How can you be sure?" Hanover demanded as he stepped into the storeroom. He didn't see anything to suggest how his product could have been moved without any of his men knowing. Even so, he had been cleaned out.

"We had watchers on the outside just as you ordered. And we had men in the main part of the shop. Right there." Marek motioned back toward the way they had come. "There is no way anyone could have gotten in here without my knowledge."

Lucius didn't know what to say. What to do. His blood was boiling. Tempered only by his shock.

All of it stolen.

The last of his money in the form of a high-priced drug vanishing with not a hint as to where it had gone or who had taken it.

How?

It just didn't make ...

Then he knew, the realization making his entire body shake with anger and the desire for revenge.

Only one person could have done this to him.

Only one person had the means.

Only one person would dare.

That one person had been cutting at the edges of his business and his wealth ever since Celindria stole the throne from him.

Lucius growled in rage. That one person needed to die.

"Only a few more bundles," Samuel said, watching as Benji and Harold shoved a large crate over the sea wall. "Once we've finished making our offering to the gods of the Churn, we've been invited to a good meal and all the ale we can drink at The Fox's Lair."

Jensen and Micah handed their comrades another crate filled with sealed packages, ignoring the occasional splash of whitewater that surged up over the breakwater. A common occurrence along the rim of the Crux where four powerful rivers met, the resulting roil and boil often rising higher than the rogue waves that could be found in the Silent Sea. As a result, the small island only was accessible via gondolas connected by Giant-crafted chains that reached from the four harbors of the Crux to the small towns on the mainland.

"It seems like such a waste," grumbled Jensen.

"Like we're throwing away money," added Micah. Still, that didn't stop the pair from handing over the crate to Benji and Harold and then picking up one of the few remaining that were lined up neatly by Samuel's feet.

"You know the law," Samuel said. "Milk of the poppy is an illegal substance in the Crux."

"I'm not worried about the Queen and her soldiers," Jensen said.

"Neither am I," Samuel replied. "But I am worried about the King of the Underworld. Remember, boys, his laws supersede all others. He's stated in no uncertain terms that there's no place for the drug on the Crux. And I can tell you from experience that you definitely don't want to get on his bad side."

The end of the chapter.

To keep reading *Sacrificing the Queen*, visit my author website at PeterWachtBooks.com or Amazon.

WHAT TO READ NEXT

THE REALMS OF THE TALENT AND THE CURSE

LEGEND OF THE DRAGON LORD

A Painful Truth (short story)*

Stealing the Light

Sacrificing the Queen (Forthcoming 2025)

Roar of the Broken Bear (Forthcoming 2025)

Rise of the Dragon Lord (Forthcoming 2026)

THE TALES OF CALEDONIA

(Complete 7-Book Series)

Blood on the White Sand (short story)*

The Diamond Thief (short story)*

The Protector

The Protector's Quest

The Protector's Vengeance

The Protector's Sacrifice

The Protector's Reckoning

The Protector's Resolve

The Protector's Victory

THE TALES OF THE TERRITORIES

(Complete 8-Book Series)

Stalking the Blood Ruby (short story)*

A Fate Worse Than Death (short story)*

Death on the Burnt Ocean

Monsters in the Mist

The Dance of the Daggers

Bloody Hunt for Freedom

A Spark of Rebellion

Shadows Made Real

Shadow's Reach

Storm in the Darkness

THE SYLVAN CHRONICLES

(Complete 9-Book Series)

The Legend of the Kestrel

The Call of the Sylvana

The Raptor of the Highlands

The Makings of a Warrior

The Lord of the Highlands

The Lost Kestrel Found

The Claiming of the Highlands

The Fight Against the Dark

The Defender of the Light

THE RISE OF THE SYLVAN WARRIORS

*Through the Knife's Edge (short story)**

THE FALLEN KNIGHT SERIES

*The Death of the Dragon (short story)**

The Dragon Awakens

Duel With a Dragon (Forthcoming 2025)

Beware the Dragon (Forthcoming 2025)

The Dragon Returns (Forthcoming 2025)

* Free stories can be downloaded from my author website at PeterWachtBooks.com. My books are also available on Amazon and other online retailers.